CAPTIVE IN TIME
By Sarah Dreher

Other books by author:
Stoner McTavish
Something Shady
Gray Magic
Lesbian Stages

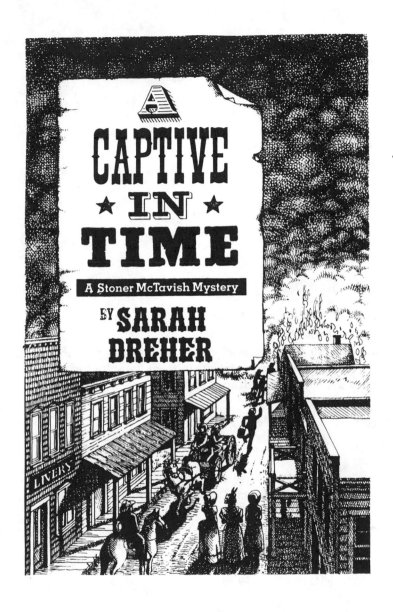

A CAPTIVE IN TIME

★ IN ★

A Stoner McTavish Mystery

BY SARAH DREHER

New Victoria Publishers, Inc.
Norwich, Vermont

Cover design by Ginger Brown

Library of Congress Cataloguing-in-Publication Data

Dreher, Sarah.
    Captive in Time /by Sarah Dreher.
        p.   cm.
    ISBN 0934678-22-7: $9.95
    I. Title.
    PS3554.R36C37   1990
    813' .54--dc20
                                                    90-31304
                                                    CIP

For Audie
with thanks to Lis and The Cowboy

Chapter 1

Half-awake, Stoner dropped her hand onto the alarm button and silenced it. Her body felt like a waterbed, every cell firm and supple and a little bit alive. A familiar feeling, the aftermath of love-making. She opened her eyes.

Gwen lay beside her, hair jumbled on the pillow. "What?" she mumbled through her sleep.

"Go back to sleep," Stoner said softly.

"American History," Gwen muttered.

Stoner smiled. "It's Saturday. You don't have to teach."

"Travel."

"That's right." She touched Gwen's face, gently moving her hair to the side with one finger. "Kesselbaum and McTavish, Purveyors of Travel Arrangements to the Citizens of Boston since 1981 is open for business. I have to go."

"Yuppies," Gwen grunted.

"Uh-huh. Saturday is Yuppie-Day."

Gwen rolled over onto her back and rubbed her eyes. "What would you do," she asked drowsily, "if I quit teaching?"

"Make love to you twenty-four hours a day."

"No good."

"Why not?"

"Have to stop for coffee."

Stoner grinned. "I can take a hint." She shoved back the covers and sat up. The cold floor against her bare feet jolted her awake. "Any particular kind?"

"Jamaica Blue Mountain."

"Whoa!" Stoner said. "You must need some heavy-duty nerves."

"Mid-terms to grade. I think I hate teen-agers." Gwen pushed herself up on one elbow and tried to bring order to her hair. "Why does my hair al-

1

ways look as if squirrels have been nesting in it?"

Stoner rammed her feet into her slippers. "It doesn't."

"It does in the morning."

"I like it."

"You have no standards."

"Do so." She leaned down and kissed Gwen softly on the forehead. "I'll bring your coffee before I leave."

"You spoil me." Her eyelids fluttered shut. The skin on her face went smooth with lethargy. "I love you, Stoner McTavish."

"I love you."

Stoner watched her for a moment, then forced herself to face the day.

Saturday. The rest of the world would be celebrating another weekend, while she and Marylou, McTavish and Kesselbaum, the Dynamic Duo, fought shoulder to shoulder against the forces of fouled reservations, lost luggage, and cruise bookings.

She hated cruise bookings. Given a choice, she'd do all the charters, European Tours, FITs and DITs, even spring break at Disney World if it would get her out of cruise bookings. But cruise bookings were, after all, what made the Travel world go 'round, and Marylou couldn't do them all.

Especially not this year.

This year, thanks to Hurricane Hugo, they had to do them twice.

It was because they'd named it after a man, she thought as she slipped into the shower and let cool water-needles bring her fully awake. Nature had taken offense, and expressed Her outrage in the way She knew best— by ripping the roofs off everything in sight.

All of the Caribbean cruises they had happily booked back in May and June were up for grabs. To make matters worse, calls to popular island resorts resulted in answers that were suspect at best. No one was willing to admit they were kissing off the tourist season for this year. Which was understandable but frustrating. Because, when Mr. and Mrs. U. S. Tourist arrived at their anticipated island vacation to find their hotel was a roofless pile of rubble, who were they going to blame?

You guessed 'er, Chester. Kesselbaum and McTavish, that's who.

Then there were the cancellations and changes. Which left lots of room for mistakes, working as they were under extreme pressure. She could bear it once a year, but twice? And there were consequences to messing up. You can mess up a person's work schedule, or bank account, even an occasional medical diagnosis. But Heaven help you if you mess up a vacation. Travellers who want to sail to Rio on Royal Viking expect to sail to Rio on Royal Viking, not end up headed for Mexico on the Cunard Princess. And when unhappy travellers get home, their first stop is ...

Right again.

2

Marylou seemed to take it all in stride, happily chatting away on the phone, exchanging tickets as easily as shuffling cards, soothing ruffled feathers, dropping the word—on the q.t., of course—that this particular undeveloped bit of Mexican jungle would, within the year, be the vacation spot of the Western Hemisphere, and wouldn't you feel smug, knowing you had found it first? All the while on the lookout for new and exotic restaurants, recipes, and men. And still finding time to lecture Stoner on Safe Sex.

But for Stoner herself, Cruise Season, the Sequel was a nightmare. She was in a constant state of panic, convinced she'd screw everything up. Sleepless with worry. Cranky and irritable and good for nothing but watching old "Cagney and Lacey" tapes on the VCR.

St. Croix was the worst. St. Croix was, post-Hugo, gone. They were going to have to deal with a lot of wealthy, disappointed people. And disappointment on a Yuppie has about the same effect as gasoline on a brush fire. Certainly Marylou wouldn't trust her to handle St. Croix.

Stoner wrapped a towel around her wet hair and glared into her closet. The day called for something practical, something no-nonsense. Clothes to Get Things Done In.

She decided on the pale denim Liz Claiborne jump suit Gwen had picked out for her at the Outlet Mall in Kittery. If you're going to deal with Yuppies, she told herself, you might as well come armed with designer labels. She wished she'd paid more attention to that video she'd seen at J.C. Penney, the one that showed you thirty ways to tie a Liberty scarf. She and Gwen had tried it when they got home, but the best she'd managed was some kind of cowboy-like arrangement that would do for robbing banks and not much else. Which caused them to break out in the giggles, and one thing led to another until they were prostrate on the living room floor, after which Gwen announced it was the first time she had ever made love under a card table.

Stoner tried to appear cool, and claimed she had made love under card tables before, which Gwen declared a crock. She knew a card-table virgin when she saw one. So they decided to make love on, over, under, or in every piece of furniture in Gwen's apartment. Stoner wondered if it was really appropriate behavior for two women in their thirties, but Gwen said she had missed out on all the fun in her twenties because she thought she was straight, and she was damned if she'd be deprived for an entire lifetime.

She decided not to try the scarf today.

Downstairs, Aunt Hermione was already puttering around the kitchen. Aunt Hermione worked on Saturdays, too, to accomodate those clients whose schedules didn't allow them to take time off for frivolous pursuits

3

like consulting clairvoyants and finding meaning in their lives.

She ran a comb through her damp hair and trotted down to breakfast.

Her aunt was standing by the stove in her nightclothes, scrambling eggs.

Stoner went up behind her and gave her a hug. "Good morning."

"My goodness," Aunt Hermione said. "The sex must have been fabulous last night."

"For Heaven's sake!" She felt herself go red and turned quickly to search the refrigerator shelves.

"What's wrong, dear? You're a pink as a boiled lobster. Are you having a hot flash?"

She found the coffee in its neatly-labelled, air-tight container. "I am not having a hot flash. I'm at least ten years too young for hot flashes." She brought the jar out and struggled with the lid. "It's your language."

Her aunt pursed her lips and frowned thoughtfully. It made her look like a snowy owl. "I don't know why you find it offensive, Stoner. Grace says it turns her on. I believe that's the expression she uses— 'frank language turns me on'. Yes, that's an exact quote."

"Well, you and Grace are ..." She tapped the jar lid against the sink. "...older."

"Considerably. And more liberated. It comes with being witches, I suppose. One knows how to enjoy." Aunt Hermione scooped the eggs onto a plate already festooned with bacon, home fries, and buttered grits. She offered it to Stoner. "Would you like this? I can make another."

"No, thanks." She pressed down on the jar lid with the palm of her hand and twisted. The friction scraped her skin. "Damn."

"If you don't mind a personal comment ..."

"Why should I mind a personal comment? I've lived with you for sixteen years ..."

"Seventeen."

"... and it's been seventeen years of non-stop personal comments." She glared at the jar. "What's one more personal comment?"

"If you could develop a more free-wheeling attitude toward the Material Plane, I'm sure it wouldn't give you so much trouble."

She took a deep breath and twisted. The lid gave, popped off. Coffee beans spewed in all directions. "That's right," Stoner said as she knelt to scoop them up. "Blame the victim."

"I do hope I'm not doing that." Aunt Hermione nibbled on a slice of bacon. "I only mean you so often seem at odds with the Things of this world. As a Capricorn, of course, you do have an attraction for objects and a love of order. But I wish you'd try to enjoy it a little more."

Stoner tossed the handful of beans into the garbage can. "I try. Really, I

4

do. But Gwen wants Jamaica Blue Mountain and ..."

"The last time Gwyneth wanted that," Aunt Hermione said, "I just made regular and tossed in an extra half teaspoon of instant. She didn't know the difference."

Stoner had to laugh. "You really did that?"

Her aunt nodded.

"No wonder she doesn't want to move in here."

"She doesn't want to move in here because she doesn't want you to have to put up with her bad moods. She told me."

Stoner measured the coffee beans into the grinder and gritted her teeth in anticipation of the noise. "I thought it was my bad moods she was afraid of."

"Well," said Aunt Hermione as she stirred her tea, "when the time is right, you'll be together."

She pushed the button on the grinder. It sounded like gravel being chewed. "God, I hate that noise."

"You always have. Even as a child, you hated loud or unpleasant noises." The older woman smiled. "Any time your mother ran the garbage disposal, you clapped your hands over your ears and scurried from the room."

"I was afraid she was going to put me in it," Stoner said as she filled the coffee pot and plugged it in.

"Why was that?"

"She used to threaten to." She glanced at her aunt, who looked ready to commit mayhem. "She was just teasing."

"What adults find amusing is seldom funny to a child. Children know things. They bring the wisdom of Spirit to the world, until we humiliate them into forgetting. I've often felt it would be a much more liveable world if children were in charge."

Stoner felt a sudden upsurge of affection for her aunt. She put her arms around her. "I love you, Aunt Hermione. If it hadn't been for you, I'd probably have killed myself before I was twenty."

Aunt Hermione squeezed her hand. "When I took you in, I thought I was only saving you from my wretched sister and her useless huband. You'll never know what unexpected joy you've brought into my life."

They held one another for a moment. "Stoner," her aunt said at last, "something's going to happen to you in the next few days. I'm not sure what it is. I only have an impression. Please, promise me you'll be careful."

Stoner drew back and looked at her. "Careful of what?"

"I wish I knew. But I sense danger around you. An odd kind of danger. It's very confusing."

She felt a tingle of apprehension, and tried to brush it off. "I'll be care-

5

ful." She forced a laugh. "I'll bet I know what it is. Cruise bookings."

Marylou was up to her shoulders in the dreaded cruise bookings by the time Stoner pushed her way through the travel agency door.

"Thank Goddess the Cavalry has arrived," Marylou sighed. She reached for a bagel with cream cheese and lox from the Deli down the street.

"I'm sorry I'm late." Stoner hung her coat in the closet and checked her reflection in the mirror for wind damage. "Gwen slept over."

"Ah! The delectable Widow Owens. Tell me everything."

"Yes, we made love. Yes, it was great."

Marylou left her desk and cornered Stoner in the closet. "Details!"

"No."

"Please?"

"No."

"You're with her nearly every night. You never tell me anything."

"There's hardly anything to tell. Most of the time she falls asleep."

"While you're making love?" Marylou was horrified.

"While we're watching television. She even falls asleep during 'China Beach'."

Marylou "tsked" sympathetically.

"It's the teaching. The September-to-Thanksgiving Hell Marathon at Watertown Junior High."

"No problems between you, then?"

Stoner smiled, remembering the morning, remembering last night. "No problems."

"Hot night, huh?" Marylou licked cream cheese from her fingertips.

"You could call it that."

"Will you tell me if I do all the cruise changes?"

Stoner was tempted. "No."

"Stay in the closet, then," Marylou said with a pout, closing the door and leaving Stoner in darkness.

Stoner opened the door and followed her to her desk. "You know I can't talk about that personal stuff, Marylou."

"Don't give it another thought." She rummaged through the brown paper sack until she found a poppy seed bagel and handed it to Stoner. "You had a chance to brighten my drab, miserable day with a little spice. But never mind. I'll just have to suffer."

Stoner tore off a chunk of bagel and spread it with cheese. "What's wrong? The cruises?"

"The cruises are under control. It's my mother."

Stoner looked up. "Is she all right?"

6

"She's fine. The eminent psychoanalyst Dr. Edith Kesselbaum is fine. The eminent psychoanalyst Dr. Edith Kesselbaum is just ducky. The eminent psychoanalyst Dr. Edith Kesselbaum is in her glory. The rest of us are in pain, but not Dr. Edith Kesselbaum."

"Marylou ..."

"My mother," Marylou announced to the jangling of silver bracelets and imitation tearing of hair, "has decided to start cooking."

"You're kidding."

"My mother, the Queen of fast-food, the darling of Pizza Hut, Burger King's Poster Child, has decreed that the 90's will mark the Return to Traditional Values ..."

"That was the 80's," Stoner interrupted.

"You know my mother. She marches to a different drummer. Anyway, to commemorate R.T.V. ... as Max and I call it ... we're supposed to have no fewer than three family meals a week, which she will prepare."

"I don't know," Stoner said. "She doesn't strike me as the June Cleaver type."

Marylou rolled her eyes.

Stoner chewed on another chunk of bagel. "I give it a week. Ten days at the most. What about Max?"

"So far he's as appalled as I am. But I think he's starting to get ideas about backyard barbecues. Stoner, do you realize what this means?"

Stoner shook her head.

"The Kesselbaums," Marylou said in a slightly hysterical tone. "The Kesselbaums are, at this moment, poised on the brink of the 1950's."

"Sounds good to me," Stoner said. "You'd be a knockout in a poodle skirt and saddle shoes."

Marylou scowled. "Get to work."

She went to the brochure shelves and moved Trans-Canada Railroad Tours from Europe, where someone had left it, to North American where it belonged. "Uh, Marylou ..."

"No, you don't have to help with the cruises today."

"Other stuff is piling up, you know," she said guiltily, and tossed "Visit Charming, Historic Charleston" into the waste basket.

"I know."

"FITs and DITs particularly ..."

"Yes," said Marylou. "In fact, as I was coming through the door this morning, I said to myself, 'Today would be the perfect day for Stoner to take care of the Foreign and Domestic Independent Tours.' Those were my exact words to myself."

"I'm good at it. I like to look things up."

"Precisely."

7

"I like sitting down with people and finding out what they like and making it happen."

"That's why you're so good at it," Marylou said.

"It's probably why I went into the travel business, to do FITs and DITs."

"I've always thought so."

"So maybe I should ..."

"Stoner McTavish!" Marylou shrieked. "Have you heard a single word I've said?"

"Huh?"

"The FITs and DITs are on your desk!"

"Oh." Stoner glanced up and grimaced sheepishly. "Thank you."

"You're welcome. You owe me."

She picked up the Martinson folder and her file on Baja California.

"Last night," Marylou said gloomily, "she went to the library and checked out the Campbell Soup cookbook. I may have to leave home."

Marylou went to lunch early, declaring that—now that it was the only decent meal left in the day—she had to make the most of it.

Stoner waved her off and settled down to try to put together an Individualized Tour for the Middle East that combined scenery, history, economy, and safety.

The agency rep from COTAL called to say the packet of information on Latin American tours they had requested was in the mail.

Mike Szabo, one of their favorite clients, called. He and his wife had been on a driving trip to the West Coast, but his wife's cousin had died suddenly and they had to fly home. Did either she or Marylou know anyone who'd be willing to go out to Denver and bring their new car back? He'd pay for their time and expenses. Stoner promised to wrack their collective brains as soon as Marylou got back from lunch.

The Czechoslovak Travel Bureau called to report that things were a little unsettled, but they were doing everything they could to make sure tourists didn't miss connecting flights. He added that, despite "administrative changes", they would continue to welcome American business.

Trump Shuttle called to invite them to be their guests on a Boston-Atlantic City inaugural. Stoner said she'd get back to them on it, and hung up wondering if she dared trust herself on the slot machines, or if she'd gamble away years of savings trying to strike it rich so she wouldn't have to spend another winter in the city.

She was about to call Aunt Hermione and ask her to try to pick up some psychic vibrations on the subject when the Carharts waltzed in.

Glenn Carhart was high tech all the way. Charcoal gray suits and vests, with matching overcoat. Steel gray eyes with a metallic glint. Black hair slicked back "Wall Street" style—which always looked to Stoner as if the wearer were an aging greaser fresh from a pool hall (complete with a pack of Lucky Strikes tucked into rolled-up T-shirt sleeve), or had just fallen overboard in Boston Harbor.

Ellen Carhart gave new meaning to the word "beige". She was tall and blonde, wore amorphous dresses of varying shades of tan, and topped it all off with pale make-up. Her skin beneath thick powder was dry and stretched. Every bone in her body was visible. Stoner wanted to feel sorry for Ellen Carhart, who really didn't look as if she was having a very good time with life, but the woman so obviously considered herself superior to the general populace that sympathy was hard to come by.

The Carharts drove a black BMW convertible with CD player and stereo speakers. They ate only in restaurants with French names, hanging plants, and dress codes, and usually drank white wine or Perrier with a twist. They went to St. Croix every year and stayed for two weeks at the Pirate's Cove. The Pirate's Cove was classified "very expensive" in Birnbaum's. In fact, the Pirate's Cove was one of those "if you have to ask, you can't afford it" playgrounds. Stoner figured she and Aunt Hermione could probably live very nicely for at least a year on what the Carharts spent on their two week vacation at the Pirate's Cove. Surrounded by sparkling sands and rain forest, native villages and old sugar plantations dripping with the history of slave exploitation, they preferred to pass their days shuttling between the Pirate's Cove's three beaches and the golf course, with mad, impetuous side trips to the health spa. They had never gone anywhere else, as far as Stoner knew. Nor had they expressed any interest in going anywhere else.

Stoner often wondered why they did business with Kesselbaum and McTavish. Maybe they liked the personal approach. Maybe it was their Yuppie idea of Safe Slumming. Maybe they sat around with their friends sipping white wine and Perrier with a twist and told delightful stories about "those two travel agency women—really, you must meet them—straight out of a Steinbeck novel, quaint and folksy"...

She forced herself to smile in a borderline-charming manner and said, "Yes?"

"Your partner," Glenn Carhart said. "The other one ..."

"Marylou. Yes."

"... insisted we come in."

Ellen Carhart piped up. "We're having a little difficulty about St. Croix."

Stoner nodded sympathetically. "Yes, St. Croix is difficult these days."

"That other one," Glenn took over. "... Marylou? ...seems to think we should change our plans."

9

"It would probably be a good idea."

"We can't possibly do that," Ellen Carhart said with finality, checking out Stoner's jump suit. She was momentarily thrown off balance, but quickly recognized it as last year's model and resumed her position of superiority.

"You can't?"

"We always go to the Pirate's Cove."

"I understand," Stoner said. "But ...well, things are kind of a mess in St. Croix right now."

"We called the Pirate's Cove," Glenn announced. "They will be open for business in November."

Stoner nodded. " 'Open for business' is one thing. I mean, some of the rooms may be intact, but that doesn't mean they're necessarily back to normal. And from what we can tell the vegetation was pretty torn up all over the island ..."

Ellen Carhart flashed her a smile. It made her uncomfortable. It was one of those "I'm running things here and I'll get my way no matter what you think" smiles. The kind of smile that oily insurance agent had flashed her when he sold Aunt Hermione a useless homeowner's policy over Stoner's apparent objections—the kind of smile he didn't flash when he found out Aunt Hermione and Stoner were working as decoys for the Consumer Protection Agency.

Stoner reached for the phone. "I can try to reach them ..."

"It's a gimmick, right?" Carhart asked.

"A gimmick?"

"So they can up the rates. They have 'expenses', serious losses ..." He shrugged affably. "Hey, business is business. I can understand that."

"They had a hurricane," Stoner said.

"We know that," Ellen Carhart said impatiently. "We saw it on the television."

"Then you know what things are like there."

"We know," Ellen said. "Those people ran completely amok. Looting. Stealing. No self-discipline." She flipped her jewelled wrist. "Well, it's only what I'd expect."

"Expect?" Stoner repeated, not quite willing to believe she was hearing what she was obviously hearing.

"Those native people." Ellen Carhart shuddered.

Stoner tried to get a grip on her temper. "Native people."

"At least at the Pirate's Cove we're not at the mercy of their upturned palms."

Stoner glanced up at Glenn, hoping for a glimmer of embarrassment. He was nodding in a self-satisfied way.

10

"It is their island," Stoner said with the last of her self-control.

"They do all right," Glenn Carhart announced, "with the good old Yankee dollar."

"They certainly did all right with the hurricane," Ellen put in. "Those that weren't too lazy to walk into a store and steal what they wanted."

"Excuse me," Stoner exploded. "But has it occurred to you that maybe—just maybe—people living in poverty, whose livelihoods depend on the good graces of tourists with white faces and fat wallets, might harbor a little resentment? And has it occurred to you that maybe, when the roofs blew off their houses, the roofs blew off their resentment, too?" She leaned forward. "In fact, Mr. and Mrs. White Yankee Carhart, if I were you I'd be a little uneasy about going to St. Croix just now. Or St. Thomas. Or Puerto Rico. Or anywhere in the Caribbean. Because, Mr. and Mrs. White Yankee Carhart, everyone has their breaking point. And, frankly, I don't think 'those people' need rich bigots like you cluttering up their beaches."

They left in a huff. Climbed into their illegally parked black BMW with CD player and stereo speakers and shot out of there, spraying the car parked behind them with gravel.

Stoner closed her eyes. "Oh, shit."

"What's up, love?" Marylou breezed through the door and picked up the phone messages. "Was that the Carharts?"

"Yes."

"Did you settle the St. Croix thing?"

"Yeah, I settled it."

Marylou glanced at her. "I don't like the way that sounds."

Stoner told her what had happened.

Marylou shook her head. "You have got to stop watching 'Designing Women'. What Julia Sugarbaker can get away with in Atlanta is not necessarily appropriate for Stoner McTavish in Boston."

Stoner offered to call them. To try to fix it.

Marylou held out the Szabos' message instead. "I'll take care of the Carharts. The Szabos need their new car. Go to Denver."

≈ ≈ ≈

The Rockies lay behind, far to the west. To the east, the last of Colorado hugged the ground beneath a pewter November sky. Miles of wheat and prairie grass, cut to silver-gray stubble for the coming of winter, stretched on either side of the highway. A sharp breeze caught dusty shreds of chaff and set them whirling.

Stoner steadied the car against the sudden gust of wind and glanced at the sky. A flock of geese, no more than dots, plunged southward in a ragged V. She picked up the road map that lay open on the seat and

11

propped it against the steering wheel, telling herself this was foolish and life-threatening behavior but doing it anyway because she could see for 10 miles in any direction and she was alone on the road. Boy, was she alone on the road. Had been alone on the road for the past three hours, since lunch. Come to think of it, lunch hadn't been exactly a mob scene, either. A nearly empty restaurant that smelled of chlorine and rest room air freshener—a combination guaranteed to make her gag. A limp Double Cheeseburger, small Coke and soggy fries served up by a fourteen-year-old working for Republican below-minimum wages, who should have been in school but was probably a single parent from an anti-choice family living in a town where social services had gone under with Gramm-Rudman budget cuts.

She brushed dust from the map and tracked down her current position. She seemed to be somewhere in the vicinity of one of four towns where the combined population totalled fewer than 1,000 souls. Not that she planned on dropping in for a visit, thank you very much. But she was beginning to suffer from Interstate-itis, that sneaking feeling that she had died and gone to Hell, where she was doomed to drive I-70 through eternity as punishment for sins too numerous and awful to mention.

Try to look on the bright side, she told herself as the highway passed over what professed to be a farm road but resembled a dried creek-bed just waiting to flash-flood as soon as it found a likely victim. Ahead lies Kansas, home of John Brown (whose body lies a'molderin' in the grave), and the Menninger Foundation (in case sanity takes wing), and Topeka. Especially Topeka. Topeka has, in addition to the aforementioned Menninger Foundation, motels. Motels and restaurants. Motels, restaurants, and telephones. And telephones mean I can call Gwen.

She pressed harder on the accelerator. Or, as the boys-of-all-ages said, "put the pedal to the metal"—which was a pretty frivolous way to describe behavior that was not only illegal but dangerous, thoughtless, reckless, and irresponsible.

She eased up on the gas.

The scenery went on with deadly sameness.

Stoner turned on the radio and punched the "seek" button. Combine the wonders of modern technology, the awesome power of the micro chip, and all she could come up with were a country-western station, a hate-talk show, and a radio minister whose stock in trade seemed to be telling people in pain they deserved to suffer because they were trash.

The radio had a tape deck. She wished she'd brought the latest Melissa Etheridge. Or at least some early Dory Previn.

So here we are, me and nobody, in the middle of November in the middle of Nowhere. On my way to Where.

≈ ≈ ≈

Something moved across the road ahead, unidentifiable in silhouette, interrupting her thoughts. She eased her foot from the accelerator and let the car lose speed. She squinted. A piece of paper scurrying in the wind, probably. Or maybe a field mouse, or prairie dog, or even a chipmunk—if they have chipmunks out here in the flats. Do chipmunks live where there are no trees? If so, do they like it? Is their consciousness different from that of forest chipmunks and woodpile chipmunks and corn-crib chipmunks? If they met, would they run out of conversation after five minutes?

The black figure stopped, dead-on in the middle of her lane, and seemed to look directly at her.

She hit the brakes.

The motor, predictably, died.

The little creature, which revealed itself to be a snake, lowered its head and slithered nonchalantly off the road. It disappeared into a mass of whiskered grain.

Well, that act of mercy ought to take a few lifetimes off my Karmic sentence.

She turned the key in the ignition and was greeted with silence.

She turned it all the way off, and on again.

Nothing.

Darn.

She flipped on the hazard lights—at least the electrical system was still working—and stepped out to have a look under the hood.

The motor, like the car, was new and smelled of oil and burned paint. It didn't smell of leaking gasoline.

Stoner checked the oil—A-okay, as they say—and was reaching for the radiator cap when her guardian angel tapped her on the shoulder and reminded her that unscrewing the radiator cap on a hot car was not a good idea. Not a good idea at all.

She let the hood drop and climbed back into the driver's seat. The fuel gauge read half-full. The temperature was no higher than it should be. Everything else seemed normal.

Great. There's nothing wrong with the car except that it won't start.

But there might get to be a great deal wrong with it if I go on sitting in the middle of I-70 at the edge of Colorado with cold dusk coming on.

She put the car in neutral, opened the door, got out, and pushed it to the side of the road.

Now what?

Well, we can wait for it to heal itself. Cars are famous for spontaneous remissions.

13

Except that spontaneous remissions usually happen with three young mechanics standing by while you try to demonstrate "that funny noise" that's been driving you nuts.

We can flag down a Good Samaritan. Who will probably turn out to be an axe murderer in search of his next victim.

Or we can wait a polite twenty minutes and start hoofing it.

She picked up the road map and scowled at it. She wished she knew how far she was from civilization. Even backward civilization. At least she was in farm country, where—if she could just find a town, however small—she was certain to find a mechanic.

The last landmark she remembered had been the South Fork of the Republican River (not a good omen). But that had been nearly an hour ago.

Which meant that the light would be going before long.

It was already cold. Too cold for her down vest. A down vest was fine for fall protest marches, taking the T to the Cambridge Women's Center, or trotting over to Indigo for a drink and a quick game of pool or a little dance-and-cuddle with Gwen, but clearly inadequate for the Great Colorado November Out-of-Doors.

She decided to go into the trunk of the car, into her suitcase, and find her parka. That would pass some time.

It passed about five minutes.

She thought about turning on the radio, despite its dismal offerings, then decided against it. It could be a long night. She might need the electricity.

She hummed to herself and tapped the steering wheel. It used up about ninety seconds.

She dug a pad of paper from her knapsack, but couldn't find a pencil. That used up two minutes, max.

Stoner sighed and got back out of the car. She walked up and down the gravel shoulder for a while, counting crushed beer bottles and cans and mashed cigarette packs.

The sky began to darken.

Anxiety time.

Night would come down fast and hard out here. No long, lingering twilights that gave you time to cut one last patch of grass, or find the tools you had left in the back yard, or toss another hot dog on the barbecue.

Just night, sudden and awful.

The temperature dropped for no good reason.

Damn.

She went back to the car and tried again. Nothing. She checked all the gauges, dials, buttons, LED readouts, perused the owner's manual and trouble-shooter's guide.

Nothing.

Damn, damn, damn.

The sky to the east was rapidly going achromatic. To the west the setting sun sucked pink-edged clouds toward the horizon. Inky purple seeped through a slatey wash. In another hour she wouldn't be able to see.

The sensible thing would be to sit and wait for a car or truck or even the Highway Patrol. But it could be hours, days before anyone showed up. From what she had seen of traffic so far today, it could be spring before help showed up. From what she had seen of traffic so far today, Armageddon had arrived, and she was the last person left on earth. Besides, she had to do something. She couldn't just sit here passively and hope to be rescued. Some people, she knew, considered sitting sensibly in one place hoping to be rescued a perfectly legitimate Something to be Doing. If What to Do in This Situation were a topic on *Family Feud*, sitting and waiting would be answer number one.

She also knew that if she sat and did nothing—even though most people considered it Doing Something—she was going to go stark, raving mad. Because it had never been her experience in life that help just arrived. Help arrived for other people. Some people were deluged with Arriving Help. Some people had nervous breakdowns just trying to find things for all that Arriving Help to do.

It wasn't a problem she had ever had.

She tried the car again.

Nope.

Time to start walking.

She checked the contents of her knapsack. Decided her wallet, comb, a change of clothing (including two T-shirts, underwear, and socks), tooth brush, quartz crystal, backpacker's first aid kit with snake bite accessory and needle and thread would be adequate. Added the down vest. Checked her jeans pockets—Milky Way wrapper (leave that behind), lucky Susan B. Anthony dollar (keep it, you never know when you'll need luck), pack of Clove gum (intact—present for Marylou, who was addicted), old shopping list she couldn't find last time she went to the store. Checked her parka pockets—lint and crumbs, just back from the cleaner.

Okay. We go.

As she looked up from locking the car she noticed, on a slight rise of ground, an object she hadn't been aware of before.

It looked like a sign. An old, weather-beaten, decaying sign.

Hey, what's to be particular? A sign is a sign. Signs generally mean there is something around. Something to put up a sign about. Information. Information is the essence of signs. And, at this moment, information is just what we need.

15

As is dinner, preferably with a good Manhattan beforehand. But, things being how they are, information will do.

She waded through the grain stubble and tried not to think too explicitly about what else might be wading, scurrying, or slithering unseen beside her at that very moment.

Colorado played its cute western trick of telescoping distance so that things were farther away than they were perceived to be. She should have brought the car's side-view mirror, in which objects were closer and larger than they appeared to be. Maybe that would compensate for ...

It really was terribly cold.

By the time she reached the sign, it was almost too dark to read.

TABOR

Well, that was a friendly thing. Tabor. A town called Tabor? People named Tabor? A wild beast, perhaps, indigenous to the area and called a Tabor?

Whatever it was, it was four miles away and down a dirt track. She glanced back toward the car. Already darkness had puddled up on the road. She knew the car was there, but couldn't see it. Nor could she see the friendly little lights of other cars barrelling down the Interstate. Not even an axe murderer.

At the end of the dirt track, a deceptive distance away, no doubt—four deceptive western miles as opposed to sensible, predictable eastern miles— she thought she could make out a light. Maybe a building. Maybe two buildings. If she were closer, she might even find hundreds of buildings. Cafes, neon lights, video arcades, shopping malls, telephones.

If she started walking now, by the time it got completely dark she would be able to see the street lights, which would give her some hint as to the size and nature of the place.

She didn't know what else to do.

Chapter 2

The wagon appeared out of nowhere, pulled by an aging mule and driven by a young boy. In the fading light, he looked about fifteen. He stopped the wagon beside her and waited.

"Hi," Stoner said. "Nice evening."

The boy nodded.

"I've had some car trouble, out on the Interstate. Do you know where I can find a garage?"

He stared at her, not seeming to understand.

"A garage," she said again, patiently. "I need to find a garage."

The boy just went on staring.

"Do you speak English?" she asked.

"Sure," he said in a voice that hadn't begun to change yet. "I ain't ignorant."

"Then can you tell me how to find a garage? For my car?"

The boy only shrugged. "Don't know about that."

She was beginning to grow impatient. "Well, is that a town down there?"

He looked where she was pointing. "Tabor."

"Yes, Tabor. That's what I'm looking for. Is it a large town?"

"Biggest around. You the Marshall?"

"What Marshall?"

"U.S. Marshall. The one they sent for on account of the fires."

"Sorry. No."

He seemed pleased about that. "Then you must be the one Blue Mary wants picked up."

Stoner shook her head. "I don't know anyone named Blue Mary."

The boy stood up in the wagon and studied the rolling prairie. He looked back at her. "Nobody else around."

"Not that I've seen," Stoner agreed.

"You must be it, then. Name's Billy. Git in."

Stoner climbed up onto the rough seat. "I appreciate the ride, but I'm afraid I'm not the person you want."

"Blue Mary don't make mistakes," the boy muttered. "Said you'd be here. You ain't the Marshall, and you're here."

≈ ≈ ≈

From far out, topping a slight rise, she could see the town. Yellow-gold lights glowing in windows, like candles or kerosene lamps. Stars were winking on overhead in a cobalt sky.

The wagon rattled past a burned-down house. "Is that the fire you mentioned?" she asked.

Billy nodded. "One of 'em."

"Have there been a lot?"

"Some."

She could see too well. Even in the near-dark she could make out shadows and the edges of things. Could see them by moonlight, even though the moon was past full.

She realized what it was. Tabor didn't have street lights. No oily, orange-yellow, sick-looking smear hovering over the town, making the sky look like something out of a futuristic Doomsday movie.

Budget crunch, no doubt.

What Tabor did have was a single, deeply rutted dirt street lined with unpainted rough wood structures. Warped plank sidewalks. Tree branches nailed to rotting wooden posts for hitching rails. A livery stable at one end, the town well at the other, and between them on the east a saloon named "Dot's Gulch" (conjuring up images of dry river beds, bleached bones, and hulking buzzards), a Saddler's—separated by an alley that wandered off into the prairie and got lost—a Land Office, stage depot,and several broken-looking buildings of unknown function. About a quarter mile away, on slightly higher ground than the rest, stood a whitewashed church.

On the west side of the street lay an "Emporium", a Chinese laundry and tailor, post office and bank, barber shop, one-room jail, and what seemed to be warehouses or storage sheds. Oil lamps burned in the second floor window above the Emporium. She could just make out, hand-painted on the glass, "J. Gustafson, M.D. Folks and livestock. Painless dentist. Haircuts and loans." Tabor's version of a medical arts building. Light poured through the doors of the saloon. There was a disturbing absence of people.

It looked like a movie set, or a ghost town after the tourist season.

She glanced over at the boy beside her. Boy he might be, but he was male, and here she was, accepting a ride from a stranger. Even if she escaped without being raped or robbed, she'd never be able to show her face again in her Post-Feminist Feminism rap (formerly CR) group at the Cambridge Women's Center.

"This is fine," she said in a cheerful and (she hoped) forceful voice. "I'll get down here."

"You don't wanta go to Blue Mary's?"

She decided to pretend she knew what she was doing. "There are some things I have to do in town first."

He hesitated, then shrugged.

Stoner jumped down from the wagon onto the dusty street. "Thanks for the ride."

Without answering, the boy clucked to the mule and disappeared into the shadows.

She looked around. Every building needed paint. Some looked as if inertia alone were holding them up. There was glass in a few of the windows, mostly those of the few active businesses. The rest were boarded up. A pitiful place. Even the dirt seemed poverty-stricken.

Again she found herself missing Gwen, who would probably love this town, and quote a few lines of Shirley Jackson in honor of the occasion, something pithy like "I have often thought that with any luck at all I could have been born a werewolf..." Or even, "I wonder if I could eat a child."

Not that there was a child around to eat. Or an adult, or a dog or cat or any living thing.

Particularly unsettling was the lack of telephone poles, or wires of any kind. Nor was there any evidence of a mechanic, not even a car dealer, not even—and this made her even more anxious—a railroad track or grain silo.

What do people do in this town?

What people?

A gust of cold wind blew dust into her face and rattled off down the street.

She thought of calling, shouting. But calling and shouting always made her feel foolish. Gwen thought nothing of shouting. Especially in grocery and discount stores. On more than one occasion, Stoner had been humiliated to hear her name soaring above the aisles of canned tomatoes or Glad Wrap. Once, in an Ames in—she couldn't remember where, not that it mattered, they were all alike, anyway, and they were on a trip and stopped to stretch their legs and Stoner had gotten side-tracked by a rack of bottom-of-the-line, dirt-cheap irregular plaid flannel shirts while Gwen checked out the ladies' room—she had actually had her paged. Paged! Along with this week's special, price-checks, and security codes.

19

"Stoner McTavish, please report to the Customer Courtesy booth."

She'd ducked behind a display of plastic beach toys until all the other shoppers stopped looking around, then skulked to the front of the store.

"Why did you do that?" she asked Gwen later, back on the road, after a less-than-indifferent dinner at Papa Gino's.

"I couldn't find you," Gwen said, as if it were the most natural thing in the world.

Stoner slouched down in the seat. "I was so embarrassed."

"My goodness," Gwen said, glancing over. "People do that all the time."

"When they lose their children."

"Well, as far as anyone knew, you could have been my child. They weren't watching you."

"I suppose," Stoner mumbled. She made a point of never getting side-tracked in a discount store again.

No, shouting wouldn't do. Not here in Tabor. Tabor didn't strike her as a shouting kind of town. The logical move was to go and look for some-one—Dot's Gulch offered possibilities, being better lighted and more friendly-looking than the average Tabor offering.

She started toward it, then hesitated.

If there's nobody there, I won't shout. But I will scream.

Which, out here in the middle of the Great Lonesome Uninhabited, would be an exercise in futility.

She caught movement out of the corner of her eye. Her heart leapt to her throat.

She looked more closely. A torn sheet of newspaper, brittle and rained-on-looking.

Stoner forced herself to laugh. If this keeps up, she thought as, out of habit, she grabbed the litter and stuffed it in her pocket, I'll spook myself before anyone lays a hand on me.

She took a deep breath and pressed on Gulchward.

Deep shadows lay across the street, hard-lined and impenetrable. What had looked like alleys from a distance, now resembled black, mysterious tunnels. If she peered deep into one, she thought, she would probably see the Gates of Hell.

She stuffed her hands into her jeans pockets and made a mental note to tell Gwen they had to stop watching late-night horror shows.

She paused outside the saloon. It was a two-story building. Heavy bur-lap drapes covered the downstairs windows. The windows on the second floor were outlined in lace and led out onto wooden balconies. The build-ing itself was weathered planking that looked as if it had never been paint-ed. No sounds from within, only the odor of spilled bourbon and old to-

20

bacco. But the light was bright, and welcoming. She pushed through the swinging doors.

It was an old-fashioned western bar, with green-felt-covered poker tables and wagon wheel chandeliers holding oil lamps. A stairway led to upstairs rooms, and rows of dusty liquor bottles flanked an old, silvery, gilt-edged mirror. A closed door, probably to another room or outside, was nestled under the balcony. Behind the bar stood a tall, husky, broad-shouldered, middle-aged woman in a low-cut, floor-length, frilly green dress of dusty velveteen. Her graying hair was piled high on top of her head, a few unruly wisps escaping at the nape of her long neck. She was drying glasses with a cotton rag.

The woman stopped drying and stared.

Stoner strode to the bar. "Hi."

The woman turned, put her glass down, placed her hands on her hips, and slowly looked her up and down. "Jee-sus!" she said under her breath.

"Hi, my name's Stoner McTavish and I've had car trouble out on the Interstate. I wonder if..."

She realized she was looking down the barrel of a shiny, pearl-handled pistol. "Excuse me?" she stammered.

"What say we slow things down a bit?" the woman said. "And put your hands where I can see them."

"Yeah. Sure." She rested her hands on top of the bar. "I didn't mean ... I mean..."

The woman gestured for her knapsack. Stoner slipped it off and handed it over. Without looking, the woman tossed it under the bar.

"All right, let's begin at the beginning. What's your name again?"

"Stoner McTavish."

The woman seemed to be running that through a mental file. Her brown eyes were alert, the skin on her hands and forearms weathered.

"You certain about that?"

"I think so," Stoner said, bewildered.

The woman's eyes narrowed. "You wouldn't try and put one over on me, would you, Belle?"

Stoner looked at her blankly. "Belle?"

The woman nodded slowly.

"I don't know anyone named Belle," Stoner said, "but if I look like her..." She tilted her head toward the pistol. "Hey, you're the boss."

"Around here I am," the woman said evenly.

"Yes," Stoner said. "Is ... uh ... Belle a personal friend?"

"Friend?"

"Uh-huh."

"Not damn likely."

A long and silent minute passed.

"Well," the woman said at last, "I know you aren't Martha Jane Cannaray, despite your peculiar manner of dress. Not unless you've put on a few extra years since we last met."

"No." Stoner's attention was torn between the nasty-looking silver pistol and the woman's kindly eyes. "Definitely not any Martha Jane."

"You're a long way from Texas."

"I've never been to Texas."

"That a fact?"

Stoner nodded eagerly. "Do I sound as if I were from Texas?"

That one really made the woman think. "Nope. But you could be real clever."

"I'm not," Stoner said. "Honest. Ask anyone."

"No one around to ask, far as I can see."

Stoner sighed. "Isn't that how it always is?"

"That's the God-given truth." The woman seemed to relax a little. "Guess you can't be Miss Belle, then. Too bad. I'm hoping to meet up with her one day, if the law doesn't catch her first."

"You mean Belle Starr?" Stoner asked.

"That's the one. You know her?"

"I'm afraid not." She smiled in a friendly kind of way.

The woman smiled back, a little. "Where from?"

"Boston. Massachusetts." She wished the woman would put the gun away. "This is a movie set, right?"

"Nope."

"Tourist town?"

"Nope."

Conversation ground to a halt. Now what? "Well," she said hesitantly, "you have a nice little place here."

"It'll do. Boston, you say? Long way from home, aren't you?"

"It seems like it," Stoner admitted. "I flew out to Denver yesterday, and I've been driving all day today..."

The woman cocked the gun with a sharp click. "Let's take that one over, friend."

Stoner laughed. "You have a great routine. I'll bet kids love it."

The bullet shot past her ear and embedded itself in the opposite wall. "Don't make me do that again," the woman said. "Pine boards aren't easy to come by."

Whoa! Looney-Tunes Time. "Right. Sorry."

"Wanted?" the woman asked.

"Wanted?"

"Just 'cause you're not Belle Starr, that don't make you honest. You wanted by the law?"

Stoner shook her head. "I don't think so." The situation was turning kind of anxiety-producing, in a mildly terrifying sort of way. "Look, if you need identification or something, check my knapsack. My driver's license is in there."

"Licenses for this, licenses for that," the woman snorted as she managed to dump the contents of Stoner's knapsack onto the bar without once breaking her hold on Stoner's eyes, "That's the trouble with you city types, too much law'n order."

"Agreed," Stoner said. "But what are you going to do? As long as Congress is afraid to stand up to the NRA, every nut in the country can buy a gun."

She looked at the pistol in the woman's hand and was immediately sorry she had brought up the subject. "Assault rifle. I meant assault rifle. Nothing against guns. Fine in their place. Collecting. Nice, harmless hobby. History. Constitutional Rights and all. Self-defense. Hey, what with the gangs and drug dealings swarming through the streets, a woman needs all the protection she can get. I mean, 'just say no' is one thing for Nancy Reagan. She has lifetime Secret Service protection. But the rest of us ..."

"Gal, you don't make any sense at all," the woman said. "You just bust out of somewhere?"

"No. Really. I mean, look..." Carefully, moving in what she hoped was a non-threatening way, she reached for her wallet and flipped it open to her driver's license. "There's my license. That's me. It's not a very good picture, but they never are."

The woman peered down at the license. "Yep, that is one God-awful picture. Should have gotten your money back."

"Yes," Stoner said. "I'll tell them that next time."

"Mr. Brady offered to do my portrait once," the woman said. She laughed. "Least, he said he was Mr. Brady. Naturally I had to go and fall for it. Story was as phony as pyrite." She shrugged. "What the heck? I was young and innocent. No harm done." She pulled out Stoner's Bank of New England ATM card. "What's this stuff?"

"A kind of credit card."

"What's it do?"

"When you need money, you put it in the Automatic Teller slot, and punch in your code and the amount you need, and the machine gives it to you."

"You don't say. Around here we call that a hold-up."

"It comes in handy after hours and on weekends, you know, when you've forgotten to go to the bank. I never remember to go to the bank—Marylou says it's because I'm basically hostile toward banks as symbols of the patri-

23

archy, she's probably right. Anyway, it's saved me a lot of embarrassment."

The woman replaced the card and picked through the rest of the items in her wallet—credit cards, blank check, three receipts from Stop and Shop, a season pass to Crane Beach, a transaction slip containing her account balance (two months old), five coupons she had won at Skee-Ball Alley in Old Orchard Beach, Amtrak ticket stubs, and her library card. She held up the knapsack, shook it upside down, poked around at the spilled contents, and peered inside. "No gun," she said in a disapproving tone.

"I don't carry a gun," Stoner said. "I think it's ... dangerous if you don't know what you're doing."

"Dangerous even if you do know," the woman said, and put her pistol on the bar. "But you're thumbing your nose at the Devil, going around unarmed in these territories."

Territories? Stoner was beginning to be impressed with the woman's ability to stay in character. If she was, in fact, in character. There was the possibility, terrifying to contemplate, that Calamity Jane, here, actually believed herself to be living in the Old West, guns and all. In which case, a great deal of caution and agreeableness were called for. She cleared her throat. "What should I call you, Ms., Mrs., Miss...?"

The woman laughed. A rich, throaty, sexy, whisky-husky, seen-it-all laugh. One of those generic middle-aged-woman laughs that always made her knees go a little weak with excitement.

"Call me Dot, everyone else does. Well, mostly they call me Big Dot— on account of I'm so formidable—but you needn't."

"Then you're not married?"

"Was. Law man name of Paul Gillette, back in Kansas City. But he was a lazy sort, so I cut out. How 'bout you?"

Oops. "Well, I'm...uh...well, not married but in a relationship, if you know what I mean."

Dot shook her head. "Can't say's I do."

Now what? Do I look this armed, probably-crazy woman in the eye and tell her I'm a lesbian? "I have a friend," she said ambiguously.

"Well, good for you. It's a cold world without friends."

"I mean, a...well, a close friend."

Dot studied her pistol for a moment for inspiration. "Close gal friend?"

"Sort of," Stoner said.

"You might not want that to get around," Dot said in a low voice. "Folks hereabouts sometimes get a little strange about things like that."

"Yes," Stoner said. "I can imagine."

"See, you got no gun on your person, and no man backing you up. Leaves you in a vulnerable position."

"I'll remember that."

24

"We have some terrible people out here."

"Well," Stoner said, trying to be polite, "there are terrible people everywhere."

Dot nodded. "Look like you've been riding hard."

Stoner brushed specks of Colorado from her jeans. "Yeah, it's been a long day. And the wagon trip was sort of dusty."

"What wagon trip?"

"A boy picked me up about 5 miles out of town."

"What boy?"

"He said his name was Billy."

"Found you out on the prairie?"

"That's right."

The woman's eyes narrowed suspiciously. "Just standing out there, were you?"

"There wasn't much else to do, with the car broken down."

"Axle?"

"I don't think so. Maybe something in the computer...

"If it wasn't the axle," Dot said, "it was probably the engine, not the car."

Stoner nodded. "Could be the engine. That's why I need a mechanic."

"You got your own engine?" Dot said tightly.

"It's not really mine. I borrowed it."

The woman stared at her in amazement. "You stole an entire car and engine?"

"They gave it to me. Well, they didn't give it to me, they asked me to drive it for them." She could tell she wasn't getting through. "Look, I'd show you the registration, but it's locked in the glove compartment."

"I have a little trouble with your story, stranger."

"If you had a phone, we could call the State Police and straighten the whole thing out."

Dot crunched her eyebrows together in an agony of thinking. "This is getting worse by the minute. Let's go back to the point where Billy found you."

"Fine," Stoner said. "You ask questions, and I'll try to answer them."

"You were just standing there. On the prairie."

"Yes."

"The stage went through day before yesterday, and you were standing out there all that time."

"Stage?" Stoner asked.

"No other way to get here," Dot said.

"The car..."

"Look, you and I both know you didn't get here in any car."

25

"We do?"

"The Kansas Pacific tracks are a good twenty miles north of here."

"What does that have to do with...?"

"You might have walked," Dot went on, "but your boots look too new for that. Or maybe you sprouted wings and flew."

"I flew," Stoner said. "But I didn't sprout..."

Dot's hand inched toward the gun. "Care to hear what I think?"

"I certainly would."

"I think you made up that story about being from Boston. And I don't believe you ever owned any old railroad car in your life, much less an engine to go with it. It's coming to me with increasing clarity that you're running from the law."

"What makes you say that?" Stoner asked, genuinely curious. "The Stop and Shop receipts?"

"On the other hand, you don't look very tough, so whatever you did, it can't be worth a hill of beans. Am I right?"

Stoner didn't know what to say.

"Well, never mind." The woman seemed to have talked it through to some sort of decision. She put the gun out of sight under the counter. "I apologize for being nosy. Whatever trouble you're in, it's your business, just so you don't bring it in here. It was your clothes that put me off."

"I'm sorry," Stoner said.

"Funny clothes," the woman said. "Kind of foreign-like." She examined the car keys, opened the first aid kit and moved the contents around a little. " 'Course the junk you have in that sack makes the rest of it look like yesterday's news."

Stoner decided she was already in enough trouble. No point in making things worse by taking offense or trying to explain, or any of the things a rational human being would do in the current situation. "Listen," she said, "about the boy, Billy. I probably shouldn't have taken that ride. He said there was someone he was supposed to meet and take to someone named Blue Mary. He obviously mistook me for someone else, but I was desperate..."

The woman looked at her with renewed interest. "You a friend of Blue Mary's?"

"I never met her."

"Too bad," Dot said. "It would account for you being so peculiar."

"Do you think I did the wrong thing? I mean, do you think there's someone out there expecting a ride? I tried to tell the boy I wasn't the one he was looking for, but he seemed so sure..."

"You certainly are bent on getting into trouble."

Stoner shrugged. "I have a way of doing that."

26

"Blue Mary...you might say she's a controversial sort of individual..."
She caught herself and gave Stoner a sheepish kind of smile. "There I go
again, sticking my nose in where it doesn't belong."

"Nonsense," Stoner said. "I'd appreciate any light you could shed on
the situation."

Dot laughed. "If you're on Blue Mary's business, you'll find out what
you need to know, when you need to know it." She tossed Stoner's knapsack across the bar. "Let me give you some advice. I don't know what
goes on back east, but half the stuff in that sack won't do you a damn bit
of good out here. Fresh socks, a decent knife, and a nice little gun, maybe
a few trinkets you can hand out if you run into hostile Indians. Makes you
look friendly and well-meaning..." She held the crystal up to the light.
"This might be good for trade, but once it's gone, where are you?"

Good question.

"Handsome thing." Big Dot used the nearest kerosine lamp to make
rainbows on the wall. "Looks like some of Blue Mary's paraphernalia.
You sure you don't know her?"

"I'm sure," Stoner said. "Look, is there a public phone in town?"

"Phone?"

"Phone. You know." She made a telephoning gesture. Dot looked totally blank. "I need to...to communicate with my friend back in Boston."

Dot shook her head. "Sorry, we don't even have the Western Union."
She reached for a glass. "Pour you something?"

It struck her as a brilliant idea. "I wouldn't mind a Manhattan."

Dot raised an eyebrow. "Come again?"

"A Manhattan. Bourbon and bitters."

The woman threw back her head and howled. "You must keep some
pretty fancy company, girl. Where'd you pick up that receipt, Paree?"

"Receipt?"

"For the drink."

Right. Receipt. As in "recipe". As in 19th Century American receipt/
recipe...

Stoner was beginning to feel tired, cranky, and no longer in the mood
for Dot's fantasy world. "Just bourbon, then. Straight, a little ice."

"Ice? Only time we have ice in this establishment is when the water in
the rain barrel freezes. And that's just when we don't need it."

"Forget it. Bourbon. Neat."

"Nobody ever asked for bourbon sloppy, far as I know," Dot said as she
turned toward the shelf of liquor. "Don't shoot me in the back, now, 'less
you absolutely have to."

She decided to try to make an end run around Big Dot's craziness.
"Look, I really need to get a message back east. How do I...?"

Dot scratched her head for a second. "I don't recall anyone wanting to do that for quite some time. Maybe never."

"But if they did?"

"Well, just write her up and I'll hand her over next time someone comes by going that way."

"That isn't good enough," Stoner said, beginning to feel hysterical. "My car's broken down, and there are people expecting me to call them, and they'll be worried sick …I'm worried sick…"

Dot leaned across the bar and patted the back of Stoner's hand. "Now, you just relax. Everything's going to be all right."

"How can everything be all right? I don't even know where I am!"

"You're in Tabor, Colorado Territory. Not the best spot in the world, but far and away not the worst." Dot looked at her in a worried kind of way. "Is there something troubling you, honey?"

Stoner felt a stinging behind her eyes. I am not going to cry, she told herself firmly. I'm a thirty-two year old adult, and I refuse to cry.

Dot pushed the glass across the bar to her. "On the house. Drink up."

She took a small swallow. The liquor cut a path down her throat like hot lava. "Good God!"

"You think that's bad," Dot said, "you oughta try the cheap stuff."

The initial shock wore off. She felt her muscles relax a little. "I probably shouldn't drink this on an empty stomach."

"Can't hurt you." Dot poured herself a drink and put the bottle back on the shelf. "Not unless you make a habit of it." She tipped her glass toward Stoner in a salute and tossed it off. "Wish I knew what to do about your problem, kid, but personally I can't make head nor tail of it. "

Stoner rubbed her face and unzipped her parka. "That's okay. It's Marylou's fault, anyway."

"That's your galfriend, this Marylou?"

Stoner shook her head. "Gwen's my girlfriend. Marylou and I work together. See, Marylou's straight—sort of—and so was Gwen… I mean, she was married, but her husband was a kind of a scoundrel so we killed him… "

The older woman nodded. "Familiar story out here, know just how you feel. So that's why you're on the run?"

"I'm not on the run. We didn't really kill him. It was self-defense."

"Sure it was," said Dot, and poured them each another drink.

Stoner raked her hand through her hair. She knew she was babbling, but couldn't seem to stop. "Anyway, I live back in Boston with Aunt Hermione. Gwen used to live with her grandmother but her grandmother's homophobic, so she moved out and got her own apartment."

"Homophobic?" Dot asked. "That some kind of disease?"

28

"In a way."

"Wasn't there anything your friend could do to help that? Being kin and all."

"If there is, she doesn't know what it is. Every time she tries, her grandmother ends up quoting the Bible at her."

"Good thing she got out, then. Once that Bible-thumping urge takes hold, it's Godawful to shake." Dot leaned toward her across the bar, casually, confidentially. "We had a spell of the cholera out here a few years back, caused some folks the Screaming Jesus. Folks who hadn't exactly been living exemplary lives up to that point, if you get what I mean. Came as quite a surprise to the rest of us. This Raving sickness you're talking about contagious?"

"Yes," Stoner said. "It is." She swallowed half of her second drink, which didn't feel the least bit hot now that she had burnt all the feeling out of the nerve endings in her throat. She shrugged out of her parka. "Anyway, we have these clients at the travel agency, a married couple, who had to cut short a trip to Denver because of an illness in the family So they flew home, only they left their car behind, and they didn't want to go back for it. They have more money than time, you see. And they asked us to pick it up, but Marylou couldn't do it because she's afraid to travel—she says she doesn't approve of travel, but we all know she's afraid—and Gwen couldn't come along because she's teaching…"

"Yep," said Dot, "teaching's a big responsibility. I did a little of that myself, in my younger days. Didn't take to it, though. This line of work suits me better."

"Anyway," Stoner pressed on, beginning to feel a little light-headed and in danger of losing her train of thought, "I flew out alone—well, Marylou insisted I do it because of St. Croix and the Carharts. I think she's planning to tell them she fired me. But she can't fire me, can she? I'm a full partner. So I was driving the car back when it just stopped, and I went looking for a garage, and ran into that boy, and here I am. And I'm supposed to stay in Topeka tonight, and call Gwen, and she's going to be frantic."

Dot's eyes broke into little crinkles at the corners. "Aw, honey, you just have yourself all mixed up. You couldn't get to Topeka from here by sunrise tomorrow if you rode all night. And if you're thinking of hauling along a wagon, you'd be lucky to make twenty-five miles a day. Want my advice? Travel light."

"I don't have to get to Topeka," Stoner said. "If I can just find a telephone…"

"I'm afraid you won't find one of those things in Tabor. Might be someone over at the Army post could help you out, though."

Her spirits lifted. "There's an Army base here?"

"Fort Morgan to the north. Not much of a place, really, and too far to walk. Couple days on a good horse. They haven't been much help to us with our problems, though. Of course, all they really care about's killin' Indians, and we haven't had Indian trouble like some folks. When things start gettin' crowded, that's when the trouble begins."

She could feel herself begin to come over maudlin. "I don't know what I'm going to do."

"Not much until morning," Dot said, gesturing toward the blackness of the street. "But don't you worry, honey. We won't let anything happen to you."

"Something already has happened to me."

Dot crossed her arms in front of her chest and leaned against the mirror. "We should get you something to eat. Probably half starved, I expect that counts for your funny ideas. Lack of food can do strange things to you. I once knew an old man, didn't eat properly—you know, like they don't when there's no woman to cook for them, pathetic, helpless creatures. Anyhoo, this old coot, he lived on nothing but dried beans and sow belly. Year after year. Had the gas so bad you could smell him coming if you happened to be downwind. One day got the notion he was some kind of star gunslinger. Got himself a Colt .44 and went up and down the street shootin' out windows. Much as I hated to, I finally had to take him down. Too bad to lose the old guy, but he was worth a lot less than window glass." She shook her head regretfully. "All on account of those dried beans and sow belly."

"I'm not crazy," Stoner said wildly. "And I haven't been eating dried beans and sow belly, whatever that is. I just want to go home."

"Well, I can't blame you for that. Home's where the heart is."

In this case, Stoner thought, home might also be where the mind is.

"When I first moved out here from Kansas City, I thought I'd die from nostalgia," Dot went on. "But now that I've put down roots, I don't think you could pry me out of Tabor with a crowbar."

Maybe if she put the conversation on a normal level... Sort of pretended to go along ..."You stay here all winter, then?"

"Sure do."

"Don't you get lonely?"

"A little bored, sometimes," Dot said. "Looking at the same old faces day after day. But before you know it spring's here and business picks up considerably."

"Yes," Stoner said. "I can imagine it would."

"Some years are better than others, of course. Sometimes the Doc spends two, three whole weeks at a time sober and we get some halfway

30

decent poker played. And two winters back we had a bunch of those Government people got caught in a blizzard just to the north of here. They made things pretty lively for the girls."

"The girls?"

"Lolly and Cherry, my girls."

"You have daughters? Here?"

Dot glared at her with flared nostrils. "I'm not ashamed of what I do, Missy. And I'm not ashamed of my girls. So I'll thank you to keep your eastern opinions to yourself."

"Excuse me?"

"They're nice, clean girls. No diseases, and they don't have anything to do with buffalo skinners."

Oh! That kind of girls! Naturally. What was a gen-yew-ine Wild West Frontier Town without its trove of hopeful young musical comedy actors trying to pick up a few bucks playing Dance Hall girls and telling themselves a Big Time Producer would drop in any day now? "I didn't mean anything," she said apologetically. "I misunderstood."

"Well, all right."

"I don't have a thing against... I mean... It's legal in Nevada, you know."

"I'm sure that's a fine thing," Dot sniffed. "But my girls do very nicely here. They don't have any need to run off to foreign countries."

"Nevada's not a... " It was hopeless. "Never mind," she said with a sigh.

"Honey," Dot poured out a glass of water and pushed it across the bar, "if you don't mind my saying so, you don't look real well."

"I don't feel real well."

The woman reached over to touch her forehead. "Chills?"

Stoner shook her head. She stuffed her hands into her pocket and came up with the scrap of paper she'd picked up outside. She glanced down at it.

It was part of a page of newspaper. The banner read Tabor Gazette. The headline announced:

Last of the Buffalo?

Migration season passes with no reported sightings

She glanced at the date. November, 1871.

"See you have the local paper," Dot said. "Or what's left of it."

Stoner nodded and handed it to her. "Is it current?"

"This month's. Probably be the last one for a while, though. They were puttin' it out in an old shed out toward the Wilsons', but it burnt."

"Billy mentioned something about fires," Stoner said. "You've had a lot?"

"Enough to make folks nervous. Preacher sent for the U.S. Marshall.

31

Hope I don't have to hang 'til he gets here."

Buffalo, 1871, dance hall girls, Marshalls. Stoner began to get an uneasy feeling.

"This name of yours," Dot said. "McTavish. That Scottish?"

"On my father's side, and half my mother's."

"Well, I don't know how things are where you hail from, but out here some folks aren't real friendly toward Scotsmen."

"Really?"

"It's the English, mostly. Kind of a prim bunch. You might want to keep your eyes open. And you dressing funny, to boot, and having business with Blue Mary ... well, kid, I can come up with about sixteen kinds of trouble you might be in already."

"But I haven't done anything except get lost."

"You're a stranger, stranger. And this is a nervous town."

"Not half as nervous as I am," Stoner said.

"Know what I bet?" Dot asked.

"What?"

"I bet a good hot meal'd fix you up."

"Probably, but I didn't see any..." She started to say "Burger King" and stopped herself in time. "...restaurants."

Dot laughed. "Tabor's not fancy enough for restaurants, honey. The closest you'll come to that is right here." She looked over Stoner's shoulder. "Billy, run get this lady something to eat."

Stoner turned. The boy had slipped in sometime during their conversation and was slouched in a chair, boots propped on top of one of the tables and hat pulled low over his eyes. He looked like the posters of James Dean in "Giant". But she wasn't about to mention that, because of course no one in Tabor had heard of James Dean or movies, because everyone in Tabor was either nonexistent or living in a different century.

Billy swung his feet down, letting the chair legs hit the floor with a bang. He shuffled through the door under the stairs.

"Kids," Dot said with a shake of her head. "He's a good worker, but sullen. Poor little devil just showed up here in town one day about six months ago. Claims his Ma died of the ague, and his Pa was killed in the war."

"Vietnam?"

"Antietam. Virginia. Fought with Hood, or so Billy claims. Anyhoo, I gave him a job, on account of he looked so pitiful. And he's done all right. Works hard, keeps his mouth shut and his hands off the girls. They're grateful for that, let me tell you."

"I'm sure they are," Stoner said.

"He seems satisfied enough, cleaning up around here, running errands for Blue Mary." She gazed thoughtfully at the door the boy had gone through. "But sometimes I wish he'd take an interest in something besides that darned six-shooter of his. You know, every minute he has free he's out back there practicing. I'm just afraid he's got it in his head to be a gun-fighter."

"Like Billy The Kid," Stoner suggested.

"Who?"

"Billy the Kid. A famous gunfighter."

"Never heard of him," Dot said. "Must be new in the Territory."

Stoner sighed. "Must be."

"You want another drink?"

"I don't think so, thanks. I really should try to find a mechanic."

"Then there's the other trouble," Dot went on, ignoring her. "Some folks'd like to pin that on Billy, but I don't think you can blame a person for everything just 'cause they're new in town, do you?"

"Not at all. Look ..."

"If that we're the case, we'd be blaming all our troubles on you, wouldn't we?"

"I suppose we ..."

"Shucks, we've all been new in town one time or other. Some town. Somewhere."

Stoner felt like screaming. "I HAVE TO FIND A MECHANIC." she said as urgently as she could.

The woman shook her head. "Kid, I know you're upset, but I honestly don't know where you're going to find a..."

"In a garage! A garage!"

Dot leaned across the bar, a look of concern on her face. "Now, honey, just go easy..."

"This is a nightmare," Stoner muttered, rubbing her eyes with the heels of her hands. "Some kind of horrible nightmare!!"

Dot reached up and grasped Stoner's wrists. "Something pretty awful must have happened to you out there on the prairie," she said in a gentle tone. "How about telling Big Dot about it?"

"Nothing happened. My car stopped, that's all."

Dot shook her head sadly. "Just when we seem to be getting along, you go and start talking crazy again."

"I do?"

"Garages, telephones...You have to admit, kid, that's kinda strange stuff."

"You want to hear strange stuff?" Stoner said desperately. "I'll give you strange stuff. Super-sonic transport. Television. VCR. Word proces-sor. Vistavision. World War II. Stealth bombers. MX missiles. Drive-up

33

windows. Video games. Hydrogen bombs..."

"Easy, kid," Dot said with some alarm. She came from behind the bar and took her by the shoulders and eased her into the nearest chair. "Billy'll be here with your dinner in a minute. Just try to hang on, and don't start quoting Scripture."

It occurred to Stoner that this woman—crazy or not—was being extremely kind to a stranger who, in Dot's mind, wandered in from the prairie in the dark babbling like a maniac. "Thank you," she said guiltily. "You're very nice."

"One thing I've learned in my years—the number of which is none of your business—is, being mean wears you out a lot quicker than being nice. Of course, now and then you have to make an exception to that rule." She ruffled Stoner's hair and laughed. "Not talking about you, mind you. Anybody could tell you couldn't hurt a fly."

"I've hurt a few flies in my day," Stoner said defensively. "I killed Gwen's husband, remember?"

"That doesn't count," Dot said. She kicked a chair out of the way and perched on the table and looked at Stoner. "I'm a good judge of character. Have to be, in my business."

Stoner glanced up at her and felt her stomach tighten, as if someone had punched her. For just a moment there...

"What's the matter?" Dot asked.

"What you said reminded me of someone."

"Is that so?"

"Have you ever met a woman named Stell Perkins? She runs a lodge. In Wyoming."

Dot frowned and turned inward for a moment. "That's mighty big territory. Whereabouts is her place?"

"Near Jackson. In the National Park."

"The National Who?"

Stoner decided to ask the question she maybe didn't want the answer to. "Dot, that newspaper ... was it ... I mean, do you know the date?"

"Approximately. Monday." She frowned, figuring. "Somewhere around November thirteen, I'd guess. I can look it up if it's important to you."

"I mean the..." She swallowed hard. "The year."

"Seventy-one. What year'd you think it was?"

Stoner picked at the felt table cover, dislodging a bit of cigar ash. "Nineteen seventy-one, or eighteen seventy-one?"

"1871, of course."

She winced. "Well, that accounts for our language difficulties."

"Beg pardon?"

She realized that she was—at least for now—dependent on Dot's good

34

will. And Big Dot (don't forget, they call her 'Big' because she's formidable) was already a little suspicious. It might be best not to let her think Stoner'd gone completely off her rocker.

"Nothing. I think I'm a little disoriented."

"Probably the wind," Dot said. "Been known to drive some folks crazy." She reached over and rested the back of her hand against the side of Stoner's face. "You sure you don't have a fever?"

She felt tears welling up again. "I don't know. Maybe."

"Tell you what, soon as you finish your dinner, I'll have Billy take you straight out to Blue Mary's. She's got a way with problems."

Not another one. I can't take another one. "I don't think I want to see Blue Mary. She's probably as crazy as I feel."

Dot rested one foot on a chair seat and leaned her arms on her knee. "There are those who think she's out of her chimney. In my opinion, it's just because she's different." She frowned and thought. "Of course, she's real different."

Great, Stoner thought. You want to foist me off on this Blue person who's so different even you think she's different. We're talking different beyond our wildest dreams.

"I don't want to see Blue Mary," she insisted.

Dot smiled at her. "Honey, you have a friend in this town, and that's me. But there's three things you don't have: a gun, a man, and a choice."

Chapter 3

The stew was hot and rich, thick with potatoes and carrots and gigantic chunks of meat. "This is terrific," she said.

"Billy made it," Dot said, nodding toward the boy, who had resumed his James Dean pose against the wall opposite and seemed to be studying her from under his hat.

Stoner smiled at him. "You cook very well. And the dumplings are fantastic."

The boy shrugged. "Guess so. Flour was kinda weevily."

Stoner accomplished the impossible feat of stopping a swallow that was already underway.

Dot laughed and tossed her napkin at him. "Don't pay any attention to him," she told Stoner. "He's only trying to get your goat. It means he likes you."

"Do not!" Billy slammed the chair legs against the floor again (it seemed to be one of his favorite things to do) and stalked out of the room in an adolescent huff.

She had to admit the stew, weevily or not, made her feel better. Tabor might exist on the fringes of lunacy, but these two people were friendly, and with cold darkness well settled in, there was no way she was going to get a mechanic to fix her car tonight even if she could find a phone—which she doubted. So she might as well make the best of it. Dot was harmless enough (as long as the pearl-handled pistol stayed behind the counter). It might be interesting to find out how life was lived in this particular version of 1871 Colorado.

For one night.

First thing in the morning she'd find a telephone, even if it meant walking all the way to Topeka. Or go out on the highway and flag down a passing axe murderer. There were lots of ways out of this mess. But not at this hour of night.

36

She leaned back in her chair. "How many people live in Tabor?"

"Well," Dot said, "it's hard to say. Counting the folks on the ranches, the dirt-scratchers, sod-busters, dream chasers, cattle drovers, assorted souls like yourself running from the law, and those just passing through ... hundred, maybe. In town, we got the Doc, Peter Kwan the Chinaman that runs the laundry—such as it is—, his wife, the Hayes' at the Emporium, the saddler, land officer, and a couple dozen others."

"Blue Mary doesn't live in town, then?"

Dot laughed. "That'd be the day. Personally, I'd like having her around, she's good company. But other folks find her disturbing." She shook her head. "Nope, that wouldn't be a good idea."

"Why not?"

"Well," Dot said uncomfortably, as if she didn't feel right about talking about this, "you see, Blue Mary's kind of a ..." She stopped herself abruptly. "Shucks, you'll find out. You're going to be staying with her."

"I don't know," Stoner said. "I mean ..."

"Blue Mary says you're staying with her, it means you're staying with her." Dot leaned down close to her. "Take some advice," she said in a whisper. "Don't try and go against what Blue Mary wants."

Oh, great. Now I have to spend the night with this woman who's so peculiar she's considered peculiar in this most peculiar of all possible towns.

So peculiar that Big Formidable Dot doesn't even have the courage to say the word for what she is. So peculiar that nobody has the nerve to cross her. So peculiar...

Doors slammed beyond the upstairs balcony. Women's voices and the scuffle of bedroom slippers drifted down.

Dot glanced up. "There's my girls now. Hey!" she shouted. "You kids wanta come down and meet company?"

"What kind of company?" one of the voices asked suspiciously.

"Female company. You don't have to dress."

"Better not have to," the other voice said. "It's my day off."

"I know it's your damn day off," Dot called back. She glanced at Stoner. "The way they gripe, you'd think I was running a sweatshop. Though if this territory fills up any faster I'm going to have to take on some more help."

It struck her full force that Big Formidable Dot, in addition to being Big and Formidable, might really be a madam. And that this saloon, this quaint copy of the Long Branch or whatever Miss Kitty on "Gunsmoke" called her friendly little place, could be a real, honest-to-God brothel.

This whole incident was going to make for real interesting telling when she got home.

If she ever got home.

She looked up to see, floating down the stairs, two women of indecipherable age, dressed in identical pink, frilled, silk kimonos and worn fuzzy mules.

The first, whom Dot introduced as Cherry Calhoun, was a tall, thin Mulatto with carrot-orange hair and bright red lips. The other, Lolly La France (which Stoner suspected was her professional, not her real name), was short, voluptuous, and white. Rings of various sizes, shapes, and colors dotted her hands like dandelions on an April lawn. Both arms were nearly buried beneath silver bracelets that clanked and jingled in time to her endless nervous hair patting and arranging.

"This is Stoner McTavish," Dot said.

Arms akimbo, her kimono falling open to the waist to reveal a considerable expanse of the most beautiful, satin-smooth, coffee-with-cream skin Stoner had ever seen, Cherry looked her up and down for a long few minutes, and pronounced her "underdressed but sweet".

"And taken," Dot said to Cherry. "Mind your manners."

Cherry laughed, a high, perfectly-tuned, round note of joy. It reminded Stoner of wind chimes.

"Are you from around here?" Stoner asked.

"New Orleans." Cherry whirled in a circle, revealing more perfect skin. "How about yourself?"

"Boston," she said.

"Boston." Cherry mulled it over. "Do they like Cajun women in Boston?"

"I guess so," Stoner said.

"Have many?"

"I don't know. Probably. I mean, I don't know much about .... you know, your line of work."

"You listen to me, child," Dot said firmly to Cherry. "In Tabor, you're a novelty. In a city, nothing." She turned to Stoner. "Cherry's a restless sort, always wanting to move on. I keep telling her you can't get any better than this."

Stoner said a silent prayer that Dot wouldn't ask her to confirm that.

"Listen," Cherry was saying to Dot, "I've only been free for six years. There's a lot of living I still have to do."

"Oh," Stoner said. "Have you been in ... uh ... jail?"

"Honey..." Cherry leaned over and touched the underside of Stoner's chin with her perfect index finger. "I've been in slavery."

Stoner smiled into the woman's perfect eyes. "Married?"

Cherry threw back her head and laughed up the scale two octaves and back down. "That's a good one, Honey. I have to remember that."

"She means real slavery," Dot explained. "Her parents, grandparents,

38

all of them."

"Slaves every minute we've been this side of the Atlantic," Cherry said. "I'm the first Freewoman in my family."

Lolly had jingled and jangled and sidled her way around the table until she stood between Stoner and Big Dot. She looked down into Stoner's dinner plate. "Stew again?" she whined. "Honest to God, Dot."

"There's nothing wrong with that stew," Dot said.

"Really," Stoner agreed eagerly. "It was delicious."

"Yeah," Lolly said. "It was delicious last night, and the night before, and the night before ..."

"Now you know you have no call to complain about Billy's cooking," Dot said.

"It's so boring. If we don't have something besides stew pretty soon, I'm gonna follow the Army."

"You do that, Missy," said Cherry. "See how you like horse meat."

Lolly picked up Stoner's plate and wrinkled her nose with disgust. "This might as well be horse meat."

Dot swatted her a good one across the rear end.

Lolly howled.

"Watch that mouth of yours around company. You want to ruin Stoner's dinner?"

"That's all right," Stoner said. "I was finished, anyway."

Lolly leaned over Dot's shoulder. "Come on, Dot," she wheedled, twisting a lock of Dot's hair around one finger. "Can't we have something good?"

Big Dot grabbed Lolly's nose and shook it affectionately. "How about we turn Cherry loose in the kitchen tomorrow night?"

"No, Ma'am." Cherry said huffily. "I'm not going to sweat over a hot stove for any white whore, no more."

"I'll do the work," Lolly said. "You tell me what to do, like you always do."

Cherry made her face hard and doubtful. It looked like an act. "Maybe," she said. "Depends on how nice you are to me 'til then."

Lolly pouted at her.

Big Dot caught Stoner's attention and rolled her eyes Heavenward. "When you get back to Boston," she said, "ask around if any girls want to skittle on out here. I'll take them on, no questions asked." She gave Lolly a little push. "You two go get some warm clothes on if you're going to loaf around."

"I will not," said Cherry. "It's my day off."

"Shucks," Dot said. "I plumb forgot. You oughta remind me from time to time. But it's colder than a chicken coop out, and I don't know what'll

39

become of me if you get sick."

The women grumbled and obeyed.

Dot sighed a heavy sigh. "I don't know, Stoner. Sometimes I think being in business for yourself is just too darn much responsibility."

"I know what you mean," Stoner said.

"Every now and then I get so worn out, I think about going back to my husband."

"Don't do that," Stoner said in alarm. "Get a partner."

Dot thought that one over. "Not a bad idea. You interested? All you gotta be's a good worker and handy with a gun."

Stoner felt her eyes double in size. "Thanks, but I don't think I have the expertise ..."

"Hell," Dot said, "you don't need to know all that much. I'll teach you to shoot."

"Really, I ... uh ... "

"I know," Dot said with a laugh. "You want to get back to that whoop-de-doo big city life."

"Maybe Cherry or Lolly ..."

"Good God, girl," Dot said. "Do you know what you're saying? Those kids have no head for business."

"Yes," Stoner said. "I can see that."

"But they're good girls." She chuckled. "'Course, you have to know to stay out of the way of Cherry's pride, not that I blame her. And Lolly—well, I guess she must be part kitten. She'll crawl up on anything warm."

Stoner could remember feeling that way herself at times. As a matter of fact, what with the cold and the confusion and the lostness and—she had to admit it—fear, she wouldn't mind nestling against that woman's soft, motherly bosom herself.

"You want any more to eat?"

Stoner shook her head. "Thanks, I've had enough to last me a week."

"Sure," Dot said. "Bet you'll be hungry again in an hour."

"I doubt it." Stoner patted her stomach. "This wasn't exactly Chinese."

Dot stared at her. "Chinese? You eat Chinese cooking?"

"It's really good," Stoner said. "I mean, there are bad Chinese restaurants, just as there are bad Mexican restaurants, and American, and Thai ..."

"I swear," Dot said. "You folks back east have lost all sense of proportion." She got up. "Guess we better get you and your pitiful belongings out to Blue Mary's."

"Look, Dot, I ..."

The woman cut her off with a gesture. "We've already been all through this."

"Yes, but..."

"No 'buts'. You're going to Blue Mary's."

That sounded like an order to her. And orders brought the adolescent in her crashing to the forefront. "You heard what Cherry said," she snapped. "Lincoln freed the slaves."

Dot slammed her fists onto her hips. "Look here, I'm damned if I'm going to spend the rest of the night arguing with you. You can let Billy take you out to Mary's, or you can go back out there on the prairie and freeze yourself to death, or maybe you can find some doorway to huddle in. But as far as I'm concerned, Milady, this discussion has officially ended."

"Fine," Stoner snapped. She grabbed her knapsack from the bar. "How much do I owe you?"

Dot folded her arms across her chest. "Two bucks'll do it."

The woman was charging 1871 prices, for God's sake. Stoner rummaged through her wallet until she found a five dollar bill. She slapped it down on the counter. "Keep the change."

Dot didn't go near the money. "Good luck," she said, and abruptly turned her back.

Stoner stomped across the room and out the door.

The night was moonless now. The wind had dropped, leaving behind a hard, dry, numbing cold. Overhead, stars hung like pin-prick holes in black ice. Every window in every building along the street was dark. The yellow light that poured through the saloon door behind her was mighty alluring.

No, she told herself roughly. You are not spending one more minute in this crazy place.

She shivered a little, and hunched her shoulders against the cold.

Come on, a little chill won't hurt you. Meditate. Think warm.

She tried to visualize a roaring bonfire, but couldn't hold the image. The tips of her fingers and earlobes were beginning to go numb.

Well, don't just stand there, walk.

She forced herself to step beyond the saloon's pool of light.

The temperature seemed to drop fifteen degrees. By the time she had reached the end of the street—walking as briskly as she could and swinging her arms to get her heart pumping—she realized that this made no sense at all. There was nothing out there but sky and night and prairie.

Maybe nothing else. There could be anything out there, and most of it probably not friendly.

Something moved in the shadows of the livery stable. She froze. A rustling sound. Horses, shifting in the hay-lined stalls?

It seemed too close for that.

She shrank into a corner between a wooden barrel and a wagon, where the darkness was solid and maybe she wouldn't be seen.

41

The sound came again. Not the casual, natural movement of horses in hay, but the sound of stealth, of someone or something ... creeping.

Stoner felt the hairs on the back of her neck prickle.

The rustling stopped abruptly, as if the creature had noticed she was there.

Dot was right. I should have brought less plastic and more metal. A knife, a gun, anything for self-defense.

Minutes passed.

She thought she could hear breathing from just inside the livery stable door. She held her breath, and realized in the stillness it was her own breathing she had heard.

Or was it?

She exhaled softly and drew in another lung full of cold air. She waited. There it was again, low and quick.

She wished she had worn something besides a white sweatshirt under her khaki parka. White had a tendency to be obvious, even in pitch dark. And if whoever or whatever was prowling around was a local, they weren't going to be fooled into thinking she was a native. Not in these inauthentic, 20th Century tourist clothes.

The prowler breathed deeply, seemed to move forward, closer to where she stood. It paused. There was silence, then a series of low clicks, like small sticks shaken together in a box. Another pause. A faint sandy rasp.

Familiar.

Associate. Summer, evenings, heat, charcoal, barbecue ...

Matches.

Someone had tried to strike a match. It hadn't worked. Now they were waiting, unsure ...

Listening.

Stoner clenched her teeth, fighting cold and fear.

The silence lengthened.

Maybe I imagined it. Maybe I'm just spooked. Maybe it's only horse noises after all. Or mouse noises, or rat noises, or ...

She started to move out of her corner.

A sudden scurrying in the dust. A sharp click. She recognized that click. It was the sound of a pistol being cocked.

Adrenalin spurted through her. Her heart pounded in her throat. She steeled herself.

More minutes crawled by.

It could be completely innocent, you know. A townsperson out taking in the evening air.

But innocent townspersons don't skulk, and whoever this was, was definitely skulking.

42

On the other hand, the skulker may have heard her coming along (skulking? Did she sound like skulking?) and was startled into a defensive, counter-skulking posture. In which case, the sensible thing to do would be to step forward in a lively manner, identify herself, apologize for startling Whoever, and go on her way.

For some reason, her body rejected that alternative. It refused to move.

She decided to trust her instincts.

Another light click as the gun was uncocked. A whisper of clothing. Then light footsteps, backing slowly, cautiously into the barn.

It was several long seconds before she dared to breathe again.

She looked back toward the saloon. "All right, Big Dot," she muttered to herself. "You win."

She ran back to the light.

"Well," said Dot, who hadn't moved from where she'd been when Stoner left. "Took you long enough, I'll grant you that."

"I'm sorry I yelled at you."

Dot dismissed her apology with a flick of her wrist. "Forget it. Good thing I like you, or you'd be pressing that cute little nose of yours against a locked door right this minute."

Stoner rubbed her arms. "Cold out there."

"Yep," Dot said. "Want some coffee?"

"I'd better get wherever it is I'm going before it gets any later." She hesitated. "Dot, I thought I heard someone down by the livery stable."

The big woman frowned. "Heck of a night to be out for a stroll."

"That's what I thought, too." She shrugged. "It was probably my imagination."

"Maybe it was, maybe it wasn't," Dot said. "We've had enough trouble around here of late. What all'd you hear?"

Stoner told her as much as she could. "You mean the fires?"

"I'm not sure if it has anything to do with anything. A couple of funny accidents. Barkers' cow dying. Morgans' chicken coop turned over and set on fire. Couple of house burnings. Some talk of arson, a little finger-pointing. Been going on over a year's time. Hard to tell if it means something, or if it's just something that happens. Life out here's full of accidents."

"But you reported it."

"Reported it?"

"Billy said the preacer had sent for the Marshall."

Dot barked a laugh. "We got no sheriff in this town. Never did. Fort Morgan's too far away for help. U.S. Marshall passed through once before, on his way to Abilene. Stayed about a week. I'm not real optimistic about help from that quarter." She leaned over the bar and took out her

43

pistol. "Wouldn't hurt to have a look."

"I don't think you should," Stoner said quickly. "It's dark. Besides, if it was someone, I think they left."

Dot put the pistol back. "You happen to see Billy out there?"

"No," Stoner said. "Do you think it was Billy?"

"Well," said Dot, "that'd be a shock and a surprise." She went to the door beneath the stairs and called him.

He came into the room at a run, panting a little. His cheeks were pink, as if he'd been outside in the cold.

"Stoner thought she saw someone down by the livery stable," Dot said. "You been lurking around out there?"

The boy looked hard at the floor. "No, Ma'am."

Stoner had the feeling he was lying.

"You know how I feel about you walking the streets after dark."

"Yes, Ma'am."

"You know how I feel about falsehoods."

"Yes, Ma'am."

"So if that was you down there, I want you to tell me the truth."

"No, Ma'am." Billy's face was scarlet with mortification.

Stoner felt sorry for him. Maybe the boy had been out, playing cops and robbers with shadows. That wasn't a sin, not even a crime. She wasn't beyond a bit of fantasy play herself, and she was twice his age. "It wasn't him," she said.

"You sure about that?" Dot asked sternly.

"Positive. Whoever it was didn't sound like him."

Dot looked sharply at her, then at the boy. "I've known this little demon nearly six months, and I couldn't tell you what he sounds like."

"He sounds like ... like a kid. The person I heard sounded like an adult."

Keep your mouth shut before you make it worse, she told herself, you don't even know what you're talking about.

Dot seemed to know she was being double-teamed. "All right," she said with a heavy sigh. "Billy, get that wagon hitched up."

"I already done that," he mumbled. "That's what I was doin'."

"You go with him, then," Dot said to Stoner. "Give Blue Mary my regards."

≈ ≈ ≈

Maybe he knows how crazy this all is, Stoner thought as the wagon creaked through the night and cold. He's not from Tabor.

"So," she said casually and cheerfully, "Dot says you're new in town."

The boy hunched his shoulders up around his ears.

"Where did you come from originally?"

44

"Where?" he squeaked.

"What town or state or whatever."

"Illinois." He pronounced it Ill-a-noise.

"Where in Illinois?"

"Around."

She waited for him to elaborate. The silence grew longer, punctuated by the crunch of the wagon wheels on hard-packed, pebbly earth. The horse huffed and puffed smoke signals of vapor into the night.

It occurred to her that Billy might be on the run. "I didn't mean to pry," she said, trying to rub the chill from her knees.

"Okay." He glanced over at her. "You cold?"

Stoner laughed. "It's not exactly skinny-dipping weather."

Now, that was a stupid thing to say. One does not use sexual language, however oblique the reference, with embarrassment-prone adolescents.

The boy was holding the reins in his teeth and struggling out of his sheepskin-lined denim jacket.

"Don't give me your jacket," Stoner said quickly. "I'll be fine."

"It don't stink," the boy said as he shook the sleeve from one arm. "Not too bad, anyhow."

"I didn't mean ..."

He passed her the coat. It smelled familiar, but not unpleasant. She sniffed it surreptitiously. Witch hazel. She smiled. Billy probably doused himself regularly with witch hazel so people would think he shaved.

It was also soft, and warm with his body heat. "You're sure?"

"Yeah, I ain't cold."

Ah, the metabolism of the young. She draped the coat across her lap and buried her hands beneath its warmth. "How much farther is it?"

"About a mile."

It occurred to her that there could be anything at the end of that mile. White slave traders. Gangs of thieves and cutthroats. Drug-crazed High School dropouts hopped up on MTV and eager to rape and pillage. On a stupidity scale of one to ten, leaving her car had been a five. Letting an unknown boy drive her across the Great Empty Nowhere in the middle of the night was an eleven.

She cleared her throat. "So, what do you do in Tabor?"

"Not much."

"Well, yes, I certainly understand that. Tabor isn't the Video Arcade capital of the world, is it?"

His silence suggested he thought she was completely batty.

"Do you go to school? Have a girl friend?"

"School?"

"School. You know, reading, writing, 'rithmetic."

45

"Nope."

"Tabor doesn't have a school?"

"I don't go to no school."

"You must have a regional school or something."

Billy glanced over at her, then looked back at the road without speaking.

"Football? Proms? Current events?"

"I don't like school," he said morosely.

"Well, nobody likes school. I have a friend back home who teaches school, and she doesn't even like it."

"What's she do it for, then?"

"She hasn't found anything she likes better. And she has to make a living."

"Can't get a man?" the boy asked with typical male arrogance.

"She doesn't want a man."

"Sure." The word was brushed with sarcasm. "Real ugly, huh?"

No, Stoner thought, Gwen is most definitely not real ugly. Not even by conventional standards. Looked at through the eyes, Gwen was attractive. Looked at with the heart, she was breath-taking.

She thought of taking a few moments to raise the little punk's consciousness. But Ignorance is the domain of the young. Let life educate him. Right now she needed his wagon and his coat. And his good will.

"I'm sorry," the boy mumbled. "I shouldn'a said that."

"You shouldn't have thought it," Stoner said in spite of herself.

"Yes, Ma'am. I'm sorry." The horse puffed and plodded for a few minutes. "Folks just talk like that. Honest, I didn't mean it." His voiced cracked, either from emotion or hormones. He twisted the reins tighter around his hands. "Shit."

Stoner felt sorry for him, touched his arm. "It's okay, Billy."

"I'm always saying the wrong damn thing."

"It's okay."

"Sometimes I think maybe I just oughta go back to Illinois."

Stoner smiled. "Seems like drastic punishment for a slip of the tongue."

She had forgotten what it was like to be fifteen. Trying to convince yourself you could handle your own life, and all the while feeling like a scared little kid inside. Playing it cool and together in front of your friends, and afraid any second the façade would crack and show you up to be a baby and a fool. She never wanted to be fifteen again, in this life or any other.

They crested a slight rise and saw, where the blackness of the night sky met the blacker blackness of the night earth, a single light burning in the window of a house.

"Ah," Stoner said. "Civilization."

"Naw," Billy said. "Blue Mary's. Least they ain't burnt her out yet. Some day I'm gonna come over this hill and find nothin' but a pile of ashes."

"Do you think someone's setting the fires?"

The boy nodded. "Can't prove it, though."

"Why would someone do that?"

"That's what don't make sense. I been places where folks git burned out for a reason—like they's Indians or Chinese or talk different from others. Immigrants. But what's goin' on here just don't fit."

"People must be a little nervous, then."

"Yeah. Preacher keeps 'em from gettin' too spooked, I reckon."

He fell silent.

"Is something wrong?" Stoner asked after a while.

Billy shook his head. He seemed to have shrunk a little.

"What's troubling you, Billy?"

"Nothin'," he said sharply, and lapsed back into stubborn, adolescent silence.

The night seemed huge, a monstrous arch of empty darkness. She felt as if it might suck her into itself, dissolve her skin and let her soul dissipate like campfire smoke into Nothingness.

"Tell me about the people here," she said.

"Whata you wanta know?"

"Well, what brings them here?"

Billy thought for a moment. "Some of 'em was looking for the California gold fields," he said. "Just couldn't go no further. Some runnin' from back east. Some gettin' away from the war, I reckon. The Kwans come out here workin' on the railroad—it went through north of here—and settled down. Probably run away's my guess."

"Aren't they afraid of being found?"

Billy laughed sharply. "Railroad's not gonna spend money trackin' down a couple Coolies. Probably figure wolves or rattlesnakes got 'em."

She tried to look around through the darkness, but even the hosizon was lost. Only the light from Blue Mary's cottage shone through the night, like a fallen star. She hoped the mule knew what it was doing. "What kind of work do people do? Ranching?"

"No ranches around Tabor. Cattle drives come through now and then, but it's too late in the year for that. "

"Farming?"

"Some. Mostly kitchen gardens. Blue Mary has a nice one. Flowers, even. But it's frost-killed now. Maybe she'll show you."

He pulled up in front of a small, compact cottage. Smoke and the odor of burning wood rose briefly, then drifted down to hover near the ground.

The air smelled faintly of mint and basil.

"Well," Stoner said. She draped Billy's jacket over his shoulders. The boy shuddered at the maternal gesture. "Are you coming in?"

He shook his head. "Gotta get back."

"I guess I'll see you around, then," Stoner said, feeling as if she wanted to say more but not certain what it would be.

"Guess so."

"Thanks for the ride."

"Welcome." He hesitated a moment. "Listen, that weren't me at the livery stable. I followed you, but it weren't me that scared you." He slapped the reins against the mule's rump and drove off.

Stoner watched until the darkness had swallowed him up.

She turned to the house and raised her hand to knock.

"Come in, Stoner," said a woman's bright, welcoming voice. "I've been waiting for you."

Chapter 4

She drew back.

The door opened a crack. A blade of gold light sliced the darkness. "Stoner?"

The voice was familiar.

But it couldn't ...

The crack widened. Lantern light silhouetted the woman's short, soft body and made a halo of her fine silver hair.

"Aunt Hermione!" She threw herself into the woman's arms. "I'm so glad to see you."

"Stoner ..."

She pulled back. "I ought to be angry with you," she said. "What kind of a practical joke is this?"

"Stoner, dear, I'm not ... well, I am and I'm not ..." The woman pushed the door wide. "You'd better come in."

It was a one-room cottage with a loft for sleeping. Rough wood panels glowed apple russet. Raw stripped tree trunks served as rafters and held bunches of drying herbs. The hard lines of the stark windows were softened by gingham curtains. Home-spun cloth rugs in bright colors lay on the floor. Waves of heat and the scents of cinnamon and coffee drifted from a wood-burning stove. A table had been set with mugs for two and an arrangement of dried flowers. Bentwood chairs and a sleeping cot of lashed logs and rope springs completed the furniture. Despite its rustic look and uncharacteristic neatness, it was warm and homey, exactly like Aunt Hermione.

"I don't know what this is all about." Stoner hung her knapsack over the back of a chair and went to the stove. "I sure hope you can explain it." The coffee was hot and smelled freshly-made. She picked up the pot. "Is this the real thing? Or fake Jamaica Blue Mountain?" She laughed from relief. "Want some?"

49

The woman had turned away to hang Stoner's knapsack on a wall peg. "No, thank you, dear. But you help yourself."

She filled her cup and returned the pot to the stove. "I can't tell you how glad I am to see you," she said, straddling a chair. "That town's so full of crazy people ..."

"Stoner," the woman said, and turned toward her, "look at me."

It wasn't Aunt Hermione.

She looked enough like her to be her sister, but it wasn't Aunt Hermione.

"Oh, God," Stoner said, embarrassment driving her to her feet. "I'm sorry. I mean ..." She gestured weakly toward the coffee pot, the stove, her cup. "I didn't mean to be rude. I'd never just ..."

The woman smiled. "It's all right. I know you've had a very disturbing day."

"It's remarkable," Stoner said. "You look almost exactly like her."

"Please," the woman said. "Sit down."

She did. "Are you related?"

The woman thought it over. "You might say that. Distantly related." She came and sat across the table. "They call me Blue Mary."

"I heard a little about you," Stoner said.

"None of it too flattering, I imagine," Blue Mary said. "The local folks call me a witch. I suppose I am, in the technical sense of the word. But what they mean isn't quite so flattering." She laughed, a cheery, life-loving laugh, just like Aunt Hermione's. "The people out here have faced droughts, blizzards, starvation, flood, unfriendly Indians, and wild animals. And do you know the one thing that terrifies them? Herbal healing."

"Big Dot doesn't seem ..."

"Ah, yes." She nodded. "Well, Dorothy's an exceptional person."

"Look, I really am sorry."

Blue Mary held up a hand. "Please. Once you start apologizing, you never stop."

"How do you know that?"

"I know a great deal about you," Blue Mary said. "Not everything, of course." She sighed. "No matter how hard I try, the memory is still spotty."

"Yeah," Stoner said. "I know what you mean. Sometimes I get so frustrated."

The older woman smiled. "And you only try to remember one lifetime."

So Blue Mary, like Aunt Hermione, believed in multiple lives. "One's as much as I can handle."

"Nonsense," Blue Mary said. "One's all you want to believe in."

50

"Aunt Hermione and I have plowed this field a million times."

"It's ridiculous to try to hurry another's spiritual evolution, isn't it? But the temptation ..." Mary rolled her eyes, eyes that were the brightest blue Stoner had ever seen, eyes that seemed, even in the dim light, to shift from royal to turquoise and back in rhythmic waves.

Stoner felt held by the eyes, mesmerized. "You have beautiful eyes,"

"Thank you, dear. I'd forgotten how sweet you are."

Right. Stoner sipped her coffee. It was hot and strong, and tasted faintly of spices. "I've had car trouble," she said at last.

"Yes, I know."

"How do you know that?"

Blue Mary looked at her innocently and enigmatically. "It's my business to know."

The Tabor equivalent of a Chamber of Commerce Information Booth. "Then you know where I can find a mechanic?"

"I'm afraid we won't have a mechanic in Tabor for at least another forty years. Assuming Tabor makes it into the next century."

"Okay, then, a telephone."

"Twenty years. They'll try Western Union in the next year or two, but it won't last. Not enough people to make it worth while, don't you know?"

She was beginning to feel uneasy again. "I suppose Triple-A is out of the question."

The woman shook her head slowly, sadly. "It's a shame. Such a nice place. But entirely too remote. They made some serious errors when they put the town here." She smiled a little. "But how could they know? Like all the rest, they put it where they happened to be."

"There seems to be a lot of wheat around," Stoner said, sipping her coffee, making small talk.

"Not wheat, prairie grass. It won't last, either. It'll go the way of the buffalo. And the town itself—bypassed by the railroad, bypassed by the major trails ..."

Bypassed by time.

"I'm afraid Tabor is doomed."

"Aren't we all?" Stoner muttered. Blue Mary wasn't going to help. Blue Mary was as whacked-out as Big Dot. Maybe, if she could get Cherry or Lolly alone, one of them would admit they were living in the Twentieth Century.

She doubted it.

"I know you're discouraged, Stoner," Blue Mary said. "But you will get out of here. I promise."

Stoner looked up. "How?"

"By doing what you came to do."

51

"I came to find a mechanic," Stoner said firmly.

"No, dear. You came for an entirely different reason."

Humor her. "What did I come for?"

Blue Mary cogitated. "I'm not sure. Spirit says you answered a call. They're reluctant to amplify. None of my business, I suppose."

"I suppose."

"Not that we're lacking for problems, understand. There's always some sort of need in a town like this, cut off from civilization as we are."

"Yeah," Stoner said with a nod. "Dot mentioned the fires."

"Yes, the fires. Very mysterious. No discernible pattern, you see."

Stoner took a swallow of her coffee. "Billy seems to think you're in danger."

"That's what's so strange about it. Ordinarily, in a situation like this, I'd be one of the first victims. In times of anxiety, the first victims are always the women with special healing powers—the witches, as they call us. Or the foreigners. But so far no one has bothered the Kwans. If there is a motive behind this, it isn't simple prejudice."

Blue Mary was smiling at her, as if she sensed and understood her frustration. "I believe I'll have some of that coffee, after all. I never could resist the smell of good coffee." The woman got up to get it. "They say it keeps you awake, but one sleepless night seems like so little when you've slept through as many as I have. I made up a bed for you in the loft, by the way. Not what you're accustomed to, I'm afraid. But you've slept in worse."

Stoner looked around the little cottage. It was friendly and comforting. And if there was one thing she needed at this particular moment, it was comforting.

She was tired.

Face it, there wasn't anything she could do tonight.

First thing in the morning, she promised herself, she'd start walking. And she wouldn't stop until she got out of this mess.

That made her feel a little better. What the heck, Blue Mary seemed harmless enough. Probably related to Aunt Hermione. And at least she hadn't pulled a gun. Yet.

Blue Mary looked at her with a smile that crinkled the corners of her eyes. "You find this all quite bewildering, don't you, dear?"

"A little."

"You've always been such a linear thinker. B has to follow A and come before C. You're not accustomed to time's eddies and currents."

This is true. "Time's eddies and currents" sounded suspiciously like Gwen's "The Universe is an M & M" theory. Charming, in an abstract way. But common sense rejected the notion of a Universe folding back on itself. Common sense required the "Universe With a Snow Fence Around It" theory. She hadn't quite worked out the details of what lay beyond the snow fence, but Gwen didn't have any good answers to "What lies outside the candy shell of the M & M", either. Personally, the idea of a Universe that melts in your mouth, not in your hand ...

"I guess ..." She chose her words carefully. "I guess, as far as you're concerned, it's ... uh ... 1871?"

"November 13, 1871. I think you'll find we're all agreed on that."

Stoner sighed. "I figured." She took a sip of her coffee. "It's all very strange."

"I suppose it is," said Blue Mary gently. "I do wish it didn't disturb you so."

"All I know," she said, "is that I was driving down I-70 when the car died, and now I'm here and everyone seems to think it's 1871."

"Yes," said Blue Mary, "that's an accurate way of putting it. Sparse and rather dry, if you don't mind my saying so, but accurate."

"Sorry," Stoner said. "I don't feel very poetic."

Blue Mary reached for a dainty leather draw-string pouch in the middle of the table. She pulled out a stack of small papers and a palm-full of dried and shredded leaves. "Lobelia," she said, rolling herself a cigarette and offering the pouch to Stoner. "Indian tobacco. Rather calming and harmless."

Stoner shook her head. "No, thank you. I don't smoke."

"I forgot, you never did." The woman went to the stove, lit a splinter from the dying fire, and touched it to the tip of her cigarette. "Imagine," she said as the fragrant smoke drifted about her head, "you're walking down the street, on your way somewhere— not somewhere terribly important but somewhere you had to be sooner or later." She took a puff on her cigarette. "Now, across the road, you see something going on, or an object in a store window. Something that attracts your attention. You want to take a closer look, so you leave your side of the street and drift over, drawn by this curious thing. You plan to continue on as soon as your curiosity is satisfied. You haven't really interrupted your journey, just taken a little side trip along the way. Do you understand?"

"I understand," Stoner said, "but what has that to do with ..."

"That's what you've done here. Except that you haven't been travelling on an actual physical street, but a street of Time."

"But nothing attracted my attention, and I didn't cross this street voluntarily."

"Of course you did," said Blue Mary. "You just don't remember it."

Well, that certainly made her feel better, knowing she had merely Stepped-out-of-Time-for-a-minute-back-soon. Made everything perfectly all right. Just normal, mundane stuff going on here, yes siree.

She wanted to scream.

"It's just, assuming you're right and I've been whisked back in time ... Well, it's a little hard to see the point."

"Point?" Blue Mary considered. "I suppose there's a point, if there's a point to life. Flowers unfolding in the sun have a point, which is to unfold in the sun. It's how they express their flowerness."

Right. And ending up in towns full of lunatics in the middle of the night in the middle of the prairie is how I express my Stonerness.

Which, come to think of it, was probably the truth.

Well, first thing in the morning she'd express her Stonerness by making a bee-line for her car. Assuming she could find the car. But surely she could find the Interstate. If she could get to the town of Tabor, she could find the dirt track Billy had driven her down, and that should lead her to the hill with the sign, and from the hill the road was visible ...

"Of course, there's something you came to do, no doubt. Something you have to set right." Blue Mary was looking at her with an amused smile. "It's really quite ordinary, Stoner. And quite wonderful."

Stoner nodded politely. "I'm sure it is."

"People from your time don't accept it, of course. Except for a few of the more brilliant physicists. But by—oh, say the middle of the 21st Century—time hopping will seem almost mundane."

She could ask Blue Mary the way to town, claiming she wanted to talk with Dot or buy something at the Emporium. Some small non-Twentieth Century item, of course. Nothing like batteries or mouth wash or Band Aids or detergent or sugarless gum, or ... Tooth paste. She was willing to bet they sold tooth paste at the Emporium. Or did they? Maybe tooth paste was a later invention.

She wished Gwen were here. Among other things, Gwen would know about the little details of Nineteenth Century American life. That's what history teachers were paid to do. Know these things. Travel agents were not paid to know about Nineteenth Century American life. Travel agents were paid to know about Now and about Next Season. Period.

A gun! She could claim she needed a gun. Maybe she really would need a gun, if they tried to stop her from leaving.

And who would she be willing to kill?

Billy? Blue Mary? Cherry or Lolly? Big Formidable Dot, whose accuracy is Legend?

No way.

Anyway, guns were expensive. She didn't have much cash, she probably couldn't use her VISA card, and she doubted the Emporium would take Traveler's Checks.

So it had to be something small and inexpensive. Also something Blue Mary wouldn't have on hand. Which probably ruled out such useful things as buttons and shoe laces.

"You don't need an excuse, dear," Blue Mary said sweetly. "You can leave any time you really want."

Stoner looked up, her face flushing with guilt. "It's not nice to read people's minds. Aunt Hermione says it's rude, and an invasion of privacy, and probably unethical and will do things to your karma."

"I wasn't reading your mind, Stoner. We've done so many, many things together through the ages, we know one another as a glove knows the hand it enfolds. Our souls must love each other very deeply." She puffed on her cigarette. "I do wish you could accept that."

"Yes," Stoner said politely. "So do I."

"But I have to be patient, don't I? I suppose that's my lesson for this lifetime." She chuckled a little. "Though why I would want to go on and on, learning patience lifetime after lifetime, is beyond me. Whatever we keep doing together, Stoner, we must be missing some essential element. Or maybe we just enjoy it."

Dot had called Blue Mary "peculiar". Dot would probably call the Hydrogen Bomb a firecracker.

And yet she had had this same conversation with Aunt Hermione. On more than one occasion.

That didn't make her feel any better.

Nor was it particularly germane to her problem, which was to bust out of this insanity, get her car fixed, and hit the trail for Kansas City. And the sooner she hit the sack, the earlier she could hit the trail.

She yawned.

"Sleepy?" Blue Mary asked.

Stoner nodded. "Too much excitement, I guess."

"Well, you go on up. I have a few things I must do down here, but let me know if I disturb you."

Disturb me? You already disturb me. Everything that has happened in the past six hours disturbs me. "I'll be fine," she said.

"Would you like one of my nighties?"

Stoner cringed at the thought. Once, when she had forgotten to do her laundry, she had worn one of Aunt Hermione's nightgowns. It barely covered her knees, caught her under the armpits, rode up in the night, and made her feel as if she were in the hospital. But it had cured her of forgetting to do her laundry.

"No, thanks," she said. "It's only for one night."

Blue Mary patted her hand. "Of course, dear." Her voice was sweet ... but definitely humoring.

Morning arrived soft and gentle as mist. The air felt warm, one of those strange spells of warm weather that sometimes happen in November.

Stoner lay in bed, luxuriating in the silkiness of half-sleep. Even the swish of traffic around Boston Common was muted to silence. She tried to remember if there had been a demonstration planned at the State House for this morning. The police appeared to have roped off the streets. She should probably check it out, see if it was something she wanted to lie down in front of a police cruiser over.

She could hear Aunt Hermione downstairs puttering with breakfast. She really ought to get up. She wanted to tell her about her odd dream, see what she made of it.

In a few minutes. Right now, the impulse to be lazy was irresistible. She wondered why her alarm hadn't gone off.

It must be Sunday. She tried to remember if she and Gwen had planned anything for today. Probably not. Maybe they'd go to the Aquarium, or to the Science Museum to see the latest film at the Omni. Or maybe take a drive to the North Shore and absorb the eerie off-season atmosphere of Salisbury Beach.

Or maybe they'd just stay home and continue their love-making tour through Gwen's apartment.

The odor of coffee and corn bread drifted up to her. She stretched.

Corn bread? Aunt Hermione making corn bread? Aunt Hermione never made corn bread.

She opened her eyes.

The peaked roof pressed close over her head. The mattress beneath her rustled with the crunch of straw and corn husks. The handmade quilt was smooth beneath her fingers.

She remembered.

Her mouth tasted of sleep and anxiety. She crawled from the bed and pulled on her jeans and sweat shirt. Stuffing her socks in her pocket, carrying her boots, she eased her way down the ladder.

"Good morning," said Blue Mary brightly. "You seem to have slept well."

She put her shoes down and tried to force her hair into a semblance of order. "Thank you. I did."

"If you're going to the outhouse, be careful. There's a porcupine that seems to think it's the place to spend the winter."

"Yeah, okay."

Blue Mary held out a wooden bucket of water. "Take this out with you. You'll find a basin for washing up in the shed. Just look around, you can't miss it. I'm afraid I have to ask you to be parsimonious with the water.

56

The fall rains are late this year, and we have to save as much as we can."

"No problem," Stoner said as she laced up her boots. "We ran into the same trouble last summer in Boston. We had a short dry spring, and the pipes from the Quabbin are leaking something fierce. They're talking about diverting the Connecticut River but the Watershed Council ..." She realized she was probably making no sense whatsoever. "I'm sorry. I don't usually chatter like a magpie before breakfast."

Blue Mary smiled. "It's all right, dear. I expect you're a little nervous." She settled herself at the table and looked at Stoner expectantly. "Are you going to try to get away right after breakfast, or wait until later in the day?"

She didn't know what to say. Blue Mary looked at her with a non-blaming smile. "I would like to get home," she admitted.

The older woman nodded sympathetically. "I'm sure you miss your friends. Especially your business partner and that 'certain someone'. And I'll bet she misses you."

"Probably," Stoner agreed. Blue Mary and Aunt Hermione must spend hours every week talking on the phone, the woman was so well informed.

On the phone. The phone. Where did Blue Mary hide the phone?

"But think how entertained she'll be, hearing of your adventures."

"Entertained. Yes."

"And envious, in her way. Imagine what it would mean to a history teacher to take little field trips like this." Blue Mary sighed in a very Aunt Hermione-like fashion. "Living history."

"Yeah," Stoner said, shuffling her feet nervously. "I'll be sure to tell her all about it." She edged toward the door. "I'd better ... you know ... I won't be a minute."

"You take your time, dear," said Blue Mary. "Neither of us really has anywhere to go this morning."

The cold water from the tin wash basin woke her senses with a shock but didn't change much else. She stood in the doorway to the shed and looked around, at the brilliant blue sky, the waves of dried prairie grass rolling away to the horizon on all sides. In the distance, to the west, she thought she could make out a thin column of smoke. She squinted and stared, but there didn't seem to be any house attached to it.

Like everything else out here, it was probably an illusion.

She rubbed her face with a coarse linen towel, and searched until she found a potted plant to feed with the wash water. A small, grayish-green shrub with tightly-rolled leaves. She didn't know much about herbs, only what she had learned trying (unsuccessfully) to help Aunt Hermione remember what was what and what it did. But she made a guess that this was a dormant rosemary.

If Blue Mary knew so much about her, she wondered as she ran a comb through her hair, using her reflection in a pane of glass as a mirror, why hadn't she heard about this distant relative from Aunt Hermione? She had to admit she felt a little hurt. Her aunt talked to her about everything, openly and in great detail. Except for her clients, of course, the people for whom she read palms, Tarot cards, personal objects, auras, and sometimes just the air. She'd never talk about a client. Not in any identifiable way. That was unethical, and would come back on her three-fold.

She draped the towel over a peg and wandered back to the front door. Why would Aunt Hermione keep Blue Mary a secret, then? Because she was "peculiar"? Hardly. On any random day, Stoner could count on walking through the door of their shared Beacon Hill Brownstone to find Aunt Hermione serving tea to a collection of street people, punk rockers, and deprogrammed Jesus freaks. Blue Mary was right up her alley.

Breakfast was on the table. Steaming corn bread, home churned butter in a little terra cotta bowl, coffee—this time smelling of vanilla bean—and a platter of eggs. Blue Mary gestured to her to help herself, and dug in.

"Tell me," Stoner said as she tore off a chunk of corn bread. "You know so much about me. Do you know Aunt Hermione well?"

Blue Mary seemed to find that amusing. "Oh, yes. Very well."

"I see. Did you ever meet her sister? My mother?"

"Not really," said Blue Mary. "We're not contemporaries, you see."

She didn't see. "I've often wondered," she said idly and for no good reason except to try to extend the parameters of the conversation and maybe snare some useful information, "how she and Aunt Hermione can come from the same family, and be so different."

Blue Mary chuckled kindly. "Oh, my dear, it has nothing to do with family. When we get ready to manifest, we simply hop on board the next available bus, so to speak. We take our chances on our fellow passengers. Unless, of course, we have things to do together."

"Of course."

"Look at yourself," Blue Mary went on. "Do you really believe it served any purpose, earthly or Divine, for you to be born to your parents?"

"Not much," Stoner admitted. "But I did get to meet Aunt Hermione."

"Which you would have done anyway."

"Do you really believe that?"

"Of course," Blue Mary said in a tone that implied she found it amazing that it wasn't an everyday truth like sunrise. "Your souls would have searched high and low for one another, while your ego would have been extremely restless and wondered what was wrong with you. That worry— since you worry so much about being normal, Heaven knows why—would have brought you, sooner or later, to Dr. Edith Kesselbaum, who would

58

have recalled Hermione from the Boston Horticultural Society and found some excuse to bring you together."

"I'm relieved to hear my soul's working so hard," Stoner said with a wryness she hoped fell short of rudeness. This woman apparently knew everything that had passed between her and Aunt Hermione from Day One. It really was disturbing. It made her feel cut off, like a stranger, like crying.

"How are the Blue Runners, by the way?" Blue Mary asked.

"What?"

"The McTavish Blue Runner Stringless Hybrid Snap Beans," the older woman said.

"They're fine," Stoner said. "You even know about the Blue Runners?"

"Of course."

The existence of the Blue Runners wasn't exactly common knowledge, except among urban organic gardeners. The Blue Runners had first been bred by Stoner's grandfather on her father's side, whose hobby in his retirement years was vegetable genetic engineering. He had created the Blue Runners as a container-grown plant that thrived on automobile exhaust and was ideal for city gardens. In his will he had left the beans to Aunt Hermione, who had caught his fancy at a family reunion. She had continued the strain, experimenting from time to time (sometimes with terrifying results, like the year she produced beans the size of cucumbers which smelled like catnip and attracted every cat in downtown Boston until their pocket garden resembled a feline version of Cujo). She also kept a list of selected gardeners to whom she sold the seeds under the table, thereby ensuring herself a comfortable unreported income. By and large, the whole enterprise was a well-kept secret.

"That surprises you," Blue Mary said with a little sigh. "I suppose not much of what I've been telling you has gotten through."

"I'm sorry," Stoner said. "I have a hard time with things like that."

Blue Mary nodded and said, "Capricorn," in exactly the same tone of voice Aunt Hermione would have used.

"It's uncanny," Stoner said, "how much you resemble her."

Blue Mary shrugged, hands open and palms upward in an Oh-God-give-me-strength gesture. She picked off a crumb of corn bread. "Have you decided what method to use to try to get out of here?"

Stoner glanced at the woman, to see if she were offended or angry. But Blue Mary appeared quite calm, as though Stoner were doing exactly what she'd expect any reasonably sane person to do. "Not really. I thought I'd go into town and play it by ear."

"Probably your best bet," Blue Mary said with a thoughtful nod. "But remember, a part of you believes the right thing would be to stay here. It won't be easy to leave." She pulled a scrap of paper from her apron pocket. "I've drawn up a small list of items you might bring me from the store." She gave Stoner a friendly wink. "If you decide to come back, of course."

≈ ≈ ≈

Getting into Tabor was difficult in itself. She hadn't realized Blue Mary's cottage was so far from town. By the time the one dirt street came into view, she had walked away a sizeable chunk of the morning. She stood on a hill overlooking the town and took off her parka and stuffed it through the straps of her knapsack.

She took a deep breath. The sky went on forever today, thin and clear and warm. The sun was like a white spotlight. Grass stubble and yellow clay earth glowed in crystalline light. Farms, barns and rough houses and windmills, were scattered across the prairie in a hap-hazard way. Beneath the little rise she stood on, Tabor lay spread out like the setting for a toy train. Someone was unloading a wagon behind the Emporium. A lone male figure sauntered up to the door of the Saloon, pushed, waited, pushed again, then ambled on toward the Livery stable. Apparently, the day began and ended late at Dot's.

The town seemed nearly deserted. Windows, shades drawn, reflected the sun in silver sheets. Somewhere in the distance a horse whinnied and stamped its feet, the sound travelling easily on the thin air.

She still had a long way to go. If, somehow, the road and car weren't there (impossible!), it would be dark by the time she got back to town. Too dark to trek all the way back to Blue Mary's. Well, that would be inconvenient, but not a tragedy. Maybe she could find a bed for the night at Dot's. Assuming Dot was open for a little hotel business.

Despite the warmth of the day, the ground was frozen as hard as concrete beneath a layer of mud thin as cake icing. Grass stubble cracked underfoot. She descended into the shadow of the first building on the edge of town. Despite the faded "Jail" painted over the door, it looked like a deserted storage barn of some kind. Through a dusty, cobweb-etched window she could see a jumble of old barrels, crates spilling excelsior onto the hard dirt floor, a broken pitchfork. Mouse droppings covered the windowsill. She shuddered. If these people had to stay in Tabor through the winter, if they were being paid (a small fortune, she hoped) to maintain authenticity or keep vandals out or whatever, no wonder they slipped over the fine line between sanity and delusion. One way to bear the cold and isolation and inconvenience would be to pretend you didn't have a choice. Maybe the only way.

Whatever, she reminded herself, it wasn't her place to judge. They were only trying to survive, like everyone else. The way they went about it might be a little odd, but that was their business. She probably did things they thought were odd. If she walked a mile in their moccasins, she might be convinced it really was 1871, too.

She felt better.

Talking to herself always made her feel better.

Is that odd, or what?

She glanced over at the Emporium. The light behind the window was dim, but she could see there were people moving around.

It might be nice to have something to nibble on, for the road. Probably not a candy bar, though. These folks had most likely never heard of Snickers or Whoppers or Necco Wafers. But she bet they had some kind of portable food. Especially in 1871.

Come on, she told herself with a little laugh. You could be half-way to Chicago in the time you waste rationalizing. You're curious. So just scurry on over there and check the place out.

She pushed open the door, and set a leather strip of sleigh bells to jingling. The sudden dimness after the white sunlight left her momentarily blind. As she waited for her eyesight to clear, she let the smells of the place speak to her. Dust. Wood. Kerosene. Coffee. Cinnamon. And, weaving through it all, an earthy, musky odor like stale swamp water and rotting leaves.

Objects began to take shape. There was a long wooden counter, tables containing articles for sale, shelves ringing the walls. On the counter stood jars of candies—licorice whips and peppermint sticks, mostly. Crockery jars of butter—Grade A at fifteen cents the pound, Grade B at thirteen cents. Bricks of maple sugar lay in a glass case. Barrels of soda crackers and pickles in brine. Rolls of dry goods. Kegs of nails. A pot-bellied stove pumping out heat. Axes and shovels and picks and hoes. Harnesses hanging from wooden pegs. Pots and pans and lanterns and heavy white dishes. A box of assorted cutlery. Ropes in a variety of sizes. Wooden tubs. Tobacco, loose and in chewing plugs. Plump, colorful cotton bags containing grain. More barrels—flour, graded "high white" and "middling", and buckwheat meal as coarse as fieldstone gravel. There were seasonal vegetables—potatoes, turnips, cabbage, pumpkins, just like at home. Fish hung from the rafters by their tails and were labelled "salted cod", next to cured hams and slabs of bacon. Behind the counter on a shelf were crocks of honey and boxes of soda crackers. Tins of tea—black and Japan—and coffee called Mocha and green Rio. And eggs in wire baskets, three dozen for thirty-five cents.

If you overlooked the appalling absence of video tapes for rent, Hayes' Emporium of Tabor, Colorado, seemed equipped for Nuclear Winter.

A group of three middle-aged women, in long cotton dresses, knitted shawls, gloves, and dusty hats clustered together near the sewing supplies. They stared at her and set to gossiping shamelessly, their whispered voices rustling like the sound of mice behind a plaster wall.

"How do, stranger," said a man's voice from the shadows. "Something I can do for you?" He came into the light, a skinny, oily-looking weasel of a man.

"Maybe. I'm not sure."

"Well, you just take your time, young man. Look around. Give a hollar if you need help. Hayes is the name, Joseph Hayes."

Stoner felt herself bristle, and had to stifle an impulse to whip open her shirt and flash him a breast. She didn't need trouble, just food. "Thank you," she said tightly. "McTavish here. Stoner McTavish."

Something like recognition crawled across the man's face. He looked closer, looked her up and down, evaluated her hair and clothes, then zeroed in on her chest. "Say," he said, a little too heartily, "you're a gal!"

"That's right."

"Well, hell, don't that beat the devil? You must be one of them Bloomer girls."

Bloomer girls? As in Amelia Bloomer? As in Suffragist?

"No," she said. "This is how I dress."

"Well," said Hayes again, and went behind the counter where he could keep his eye on his cash box.

She wandered past the shelves, trying to decide what would be light enough to be portable but substantial enough to stave off hunger if she couldn't get a ride and had to walk to the next town down the line. There were jars of tomatoes, with labels she didn't recognize—no Sweet Life or Libby's or Contadina for the good citizens of Tabor, no ma'am. Wouldn't be authentic.

Dried apricots and apples were promising. And nuts. If they'd take a Traveler's check, she could maybe get a canteen. There was bottled soda, but she didn't relish lugging glass bottles across the prairie, although, from the looks of them, they'd bring a fortune in a flea market back home.

She examined a collection of disgusting-looking strips of something that must be meat but really resembled left-over special effects from a slice-and-dice movie. They hung on strings from a sisal rope, swaying in the air currents, collecting dust and (in season) flies.

She was gradually working her way toward the Tabor Biddies' Society. Their disapproval hung in the air like storm clouds.

"Morning," she said pleasantly, with a nod and a smile.

The ladies found something fascinating to examine on the counter, much too fascinating to pass the time of day with her.

It made her angry. She wondered what offended them most: her cloth-

62

ing? Haircut? Lifestyle? Presence?

She was about to challenge them when she imagined what Gwen would say. "Dearest, there really are some battles you don't have to fight."

"Nice day," she said instead.

They ignored her.

"Nice town."

Silence.

"Friendly place."

One of the women glanced at her. Her face was pale and stiff, nose thin and hooked, her mouth turned downward in an inverted moon. She looked as if she might have digestive problems.

Stoner held out her hand. "Name's Stoner McTavish. From Boston."

The woman looked down at her hand with dread and loathing.

Stoner held her ground.

Slowly, good manners fighting disgust all the way, the woman extended her own hand. She touched her fingertips briefly to Stoner's and withdrew like a shot. "I," she said loftily, "am Mrs. Caroline Parnell. My husband is the Reverend Mr. Henry Parnell."

"Well, I certainly am thrilled and delighted to meet you," Stoner said, hoping her enthusiasm sounded as forced as it felt.

"McTavish," Mrs. Caroline Parnell said. "A Scottish name?"

"On my father's side, yes."

"I am English," said Caroline Parnell, as if that explained something and deserved some sort of respect.

"Hey," Stoner said. "And the rest of you ladies are ...?"

Biddie number two stepped forward as though called to the guillotine. "Mrs. Emma Underwood."

"Emma Underwood," Stoner said. "And your husband is ...?"

"Mr. Underwood," said Emma Underwood, and turned abruptly away.

Cool.

She turned her attention to Biddie number three.

The woman blushed and studied the tips of Stoner's boots.

"Hannah Reinhardt," said Mrs. Caroline Parnell. "An immigrant."

Silence descended. Immigrant status was apparently Hannah's only claim to fame.

"I can't tell you," Stoner said, "what a very great pleasure it's been to visit in your fair city "

The ladies cut her off by turning away.

She decided to make her selections and get out.

The Biddies returned to their whispery, papery gossiping.

Another middle-aged woman entered the store from a back room. Her face was round and angry-looking. She nodded to the Biddies.

63

The Biddies nodded in return.

Mrs. Caroline Parnell said, "Arabella" in a curt kind of way.

"They'll be here on Saturday," Arabella said, her voice defiant.

"That's your business, Arabella, and I want nothing to do with it," said Mrs. Emma Underwood.

"Here," Arabella repeated. "In the store." She went to join Joseph, who was apparently her husband, behind the counter. He flashed her a quizzical glance and turned his attention to his account books.

Stoner longed to transport the Four Queens of Tabor onto the streets of New York—Forty-second Street, preferably, with the sleaze traps and porn houses open for business—at ten o'clock on a Saturday night.

The sleigh bells jingled. A gust of air raced across the floor and wrapped around her ankles.

Billy walked in.

Stoner tossed him a smile.

Conversation stopped.

Arabella Hayes whispered something to her husband.

He stepped forward. "What do you think you're doing in here?" he asked.

The boy looked up, apprehension and determination tightening the muscles around his jaw. "Lookin' for ..."

"There's nothing for you in this store," Joseph Hayes corrected.

"Yeah, I ..."

Stoner saw Hayes' hand move toward a riding crop that lay just out of sight on the counter, and called out, "Billy!"

The boy ignored her. "Look," he said defiantly to Joseph Hayes, "I ain't done nothin' to you."

"Ain't you, now?" the man mocked. His hand closed over the handle of the whip and brought it to his side.

The other women in the store looked on approvingly. Their eyes shone with tiny silvery, hungry lights. Stoner could have sworn one of them licked her lips.

"I could buy stuff here if I wanted." Billy said. "I got money. Just as good as anyone's."

"Is that a fact?" Hayes said with a grin. "And just where'd you get all this wonderful money?"

"Workin'."

"Aaaaah!" the man crooned. "The little bastard works." He glanced around at his approving audience.

Billy bristled. "You know durn well I work. And I ain't a bastard! My Pa died in the War."

"His Pa died in the War," said Joseph Hayes in a phony-sad voice.

64

"Now, ain't that just a cryin' shame." He narrowed his eyes and focused hard on the boy. "You get your bastard ass out of my store."

"I ain't ..." The boy began.

Hayes' arm shot out faster than a diamondback rattlesnake. The leather hit the boy's cheek with a wet "pop".

Stunned, Billy stared at him.

The man started his backswing.

Stoner managed to cross the distance between them in two strides. She planted herself between the boy and Hayes, and grabbed the man's wrist. "Hold it right there," she said.

Hayes tried to shake her off. "This ain't none of your business."

"The word is 'isn't', and I'm making it my business," Stoner said, while the lightning and critical part of her mind wondered how many mediocre TV shows she had gotten that line from. "Billy, get out of here," she said over her shoulder.

Hayes yanked his wrist from her grip.

"Get out," she ordered the boy. "Before you get us both killed."

The door bells jangled as he ran.

Hayes glared at her.

"Congratulations," Stoner said to him. "You've just bought yourself a few years in the slammer."

"What the hell's your problem?" He tipped a bow toward the Biddies. "Excuse me, ladies." He turned back to Stoner. "It's a free country, and it seems like this here's my store."

"Child abuse is against the law, even in this arm-pit of a town. I'll be back with the police." She turned to the other women. "You're all witnesses to what went on here. I suggest you make yourselves available, Mrs. Reinhardt, Mrs. Underwood, Mrs. Reverend Henry Parnell. And especially you, Mrs. Hayes." She stomped out of the store and slammed the door hard enough to crack the glass.

She caught up with Billy halfway down the street. "Hey," she said, and placed a hand gently on his shoulder, "are you okay?"

He pulled away, but not before she could see the angry red welt on his cheek, the tears that streamed down his face.

"Come on, Billy, talk to me."

"I ain't no baby," he said in a broken voice. "And I ain't no bastard."

"It doesn't matter." She pulled him to her and wrapped her arms around him.

He was stiff as a log for a moment, then everything seemed to let go at once. His body went soft. He buried his face in her shoulder and wrapped his arms around her waist and hung on.

She stroked the back of his neck. "What's his problem?"

65

He snuffled a little. "Folks don't like me 'cause I ain't got no Pa."

"That's ridiculous." But she knew it wasn't ridiculous. People could be this bad back home, though they got a little more subtle as they got older. "I'll bet, if Dot heard about this, she'd go somewhere else to shop."

"Ain't nowhere else to shop."

"But if Hayes feels that way about you simply because you don't have a father, how can he justify doing business with Dot?"

The minute she had asked the question, she knew the answer. Dot's Gulch probably brought in more business than all the other Tabor establishments combined. Stoner sighed. "This is no place for you, Billy."

He reached up and straightened his hat, knocking her hand away. "No worse than any other," he said.

"It is worse. If you don't have anywhere to go, come back to Boston with me. We'll find a way to ..."

He pushed her away roughly, almost angrily. "I don't need no pity."

"Billy."

"An' I don't need you. I don't even think I like you."

Stoner sighed, exasperated. "Honest to God," she said. "There's nothing more frustrating than trying to talk to an adolescent boy."

That settled him down. He stared at the ground and traced a crooked circle with the toe of his boot. "Sorry."

"Let me see your face." She took the boy's chin in her hand and tilted his head back. He closed his eyes. His cheek looked sore, but there was no blood. "I guess you'll live."

"Guess so." He opened his eyes in a squint and looked at her. "You fixin' to stay in Tabor?"

Stoner laughed. "No, I am definitely not fixin' to stay in Tabor. What I am fixin' to do is go out and find that place where you picked me up last night. Then I will find my car. Then I will find the State Police or the nearest civilized—and when I say 'civilized' I definitely do not include Tabor—town. Then I will get my car repaired, at the end of which time I will bust out of this puke hole known as eastern Colorado. If I've offended your sense of civic pride, I apologize, but if your civic pride is offended, your civic pride is seriously misplaced."

"You know what?" Billy said.

"No, what?"

"You talk funny."

Stoner took him by the shoulders and shook him affectionately. His hat fell off, revealing a head of full, straight brown hair. It looked as if he had cut it himself, with a hedge trimmer.

He made a dive for his hat and slammed it on his head, then glanced up shyly at her. "I'm peculiar about my hat," he said.

Stoner smiled at him. "Adolescent boys are like that."

"I can give you a ride," he said. "I got the wagon."

"Don't you have to get something for Dot?"

"Nah," he said. "I only went in that old place 'cause I seen you through the window." He planted his hands on his hips. "You want a ride, or not?"

Without food, or water, with the sun already on the down side of day? Yes, she wanted a ride. "Sure, if it's no trouble."

Billy snorted. "Trouble. Hell, I was born to trouble."

"Well, all right, then." Forget about provisions for the trip. She wanted to get out of Tabor, and get out fast.

The boy hesitated. "There's somethin' I want ya' to know, though, 'fore you go."

"What's that?"

He shuffled around in the dust uncomfortably. "I didn't do it. Some folks think I did, but I didn't."

"Did what?"

"Set the fires." He risked a glance up at her. "Do you believe me?"

"Of course."

"Hurts my feelin's when they think that."

She touched his shoulder. "I know. People will believe what they want to believe, Billy. You can only do your best."

Hesitantly, he reached out and took her hand and squeezed it. "Thanks. You're a good lady."

She squeezed back. "So can we get out of here?"

He trotted off toward the alley that led behind Dot's Gulch.

Stoner followed.

Now she really wanted to leave. Before she started caring about him more than she already did.

Chapter 5

The Sanctified Man straightened his tie and examined his reflection in the livery stable window.

So. That was the one they'd been talking about down at the saloon. And consorting with the Bastard.

The Bastard. He smiled to himself. That was what he called It, anyway, in his talks with Hayes. Someday, maybe even someday soon, he'd tell Hayes who the Bastard really was. But not yet. Not until Hayes had proved his understanding.

Now the Stranger was here. The one he'd been waiting for. The woman in man's clothes. The one the Witch's Book told about. The one the Witch's Book called "The Fool."

"The Fool." The Sanctified Man chuckled to himself. The Witch thought she was clever, wrapping her Book in silk to hide its nature, placing it deep in the box by her bed. But he'd seen. He'd seen, peeking through her window in the darkest of night. And when she was away gathering her putrid herbs under the full moon, he'd crept in and taken it from its hiding place and stolen it away. It told him all he needed to know.

He wanted to act now. To strike at the Beast and its lackey and tear them apart, there, in the sunlight, the whole town gathering to watch. They'd know who he was then, the gawkers and gigglers, the children who ran behind him on the streets and mimicked his jerky, scarecrow stride. The women who pretended respect to his face, and made nasty gossip when they were alone. The whore Lolly who had laughed at his impotence—too stupid to understand that it was her own filth that had left his member weak and unmoved. All of them. They'd all know, and praise and fear him as they should.

He spat in the dust.

Once he had destroyed the Beast and the Stranger, the Witch would be simple. Without her Master, her Power would be nothing compared to his.

Even a fool could see what they were up to, the Witch and all her sister Witches, with all their talk of Equality and Voting Rights for Women. Get themselves into the Government, then use their Magic to overthrow the Christ and install their Satan-God. Turn decent, Christian men and women into cattle. Beasts of burden. Animals fit only to crawl and grovel and beg for scraps while the Witches feasted on the fat of the land.

His own wife knew the Truth. Soon all the rest would know.

Soon.

The Sanctified Man slipped his hand into his pocket and fingered his knife. He could slip up behind It and thrust the icy blade between Its ribs, into the kidney area where the pain would be greatest. Just to hear It scream. To see the look of terror as It realized It had been found out at last.

Then, before It could gather up Its Unholy strength, a second blow with the knife, deep into Its heart. And again, again, again. Until It was finished.

Once the Beast was dead, the Stranger would melt like butter under summer sun.

The Sanctified Man swallowed and licked his lips. He would hang the Thing on a high pole, stripped of Its Earthly disguise, in all Its hideous nakedness for all the world to see.

He was ready. Yes, he was ready. Ready to begin the fasting and the purification Ceremonies. Just the way God had told him.

He'd been smart to set those random fires. Now, when he began the Holy Burnings, the ignorant townspeople wouldn't guess these fires were sacred. He couldn't take the chance of others becoming curious, wanting to join him. Too many people, and something might go wrong.

When they realized how he'd saved them, they'd know his Power. He was certain of that. Not only Tabor, but all those fools back there in Kansas.

Kansas. He spat into the dust.

He'd made a couple of mistakes back in Kansas. Used the knife before he was sure. No one was more surprised than he when the Thing didn't transform. Honest mistakes. But they'd called him a murderer, called him crazy, even. Imagine that. He'd talked himself into forgiving them, because they hadn't read The Word and didn't know any better.

They'd been all ready to hang him. But he'd gotten away. Burned down the jail with a match they'd been too excited to find, tucked away in the toe of his boot, and even had time to grab his Jesus-knife before he faded off into the night.

Oh, yes, it would be sweet to do it now. But the Word was very specific on the Rituals.

Better to wait until the time was right.

The Sanctified Man pouted a little. He didn't like waiting. It made his forehead ache.

Something spoke in his heart. "Welcome the Pain. Let it be a constant reminder that Thou art My Servant."

Humbled, he turned to the street. He'd found a good life here in Tabor. A wife. A position in the community. God had rewarded him well. Better to do as Jesus said. He couldn't risk a repeat of Kansas.

Last week he'd been tempted to take the Witch. But he'd waited, and now the Witch had delivered the Stranger into his hands.

He thanked Jesus for teaching him the lesson of patience.

The Sanctified Man slipped the knife back into his pocket, pasted a smile across his face and stepped forward into the sunlight.

≈ ≈ ≈

The sky was clear. A few wisps of cloud brushed across the perfect blue, feathers strung out behind like mares' tails. There one second, the next swept away by the upper air winds.

"We should report him," Stoner said.

"Who?"

"Hayes." She touched the flaming welt on Billy's cheek. "What he did to you is child abuse."

Billy frowned and pulled away. "I ain't no child."

"How old are you?"

"Fifteen."

"Legally, you're a child."

The boy snorted. "Who you gonna report him to?"

"The police. Or sheriff. Whatever passes for the law in Tabor."

"Nothin' passes for the law in Tabor."

She looked at him. "You don't even have a police department?"

"Nope." He glanced over. "Look, this ain't one of your back East fancy towns, with everything divided up into neat parcels and people with titles and occupations and all. This here's Tabor. Tabor. And Tabor and civilization ain't the same thing."

"Yes," Stoner muttered. "I'd noticed."

They rode on in silence. "Anyway," Billy said after a while, "what if we did have all them law folks just dying to protect innocent widows and children? Whata you think they'd do to him? Haul him off to jail?"

"Probably not," Stoner said, remembering the reality of how things worked in the world. "But he'd be arrested. It might make him think twice."

Billy gave a short laugh, like a pistol shot. "Ain't nobody about to think

70

twice about what they do to me."

"You know, Billy, you have a terrible self-concept."

He swallowed hard and slapped the reins against the mule's rump. "Well, don't worry. Probably ain't contagious."

She sensed it would be foolish, and probably provocative, to try to press the issue. He was surly enough as it was.

Still, there was something about the boy that she liked. Liked very much, in fact. Something that told her he was a scared kid underneath, putting on a big act because life had knocked him around.

Stoner laughed to herself. Life. Two days in beautiful, psychotic Tabor was enough to make you feel thoroughly knocked around by life.

"If you could be anything you wanted," she asked, "what would that be?"

He started to speak, then stopped himself. "Nope," he said roughly. "I ain't gonna tell."

"Why not?"

"You'd just laugh at me."

"I wouldn't. I swear it."

He shot a look at her from beneath his hat. "Yeah, you would."

"Billy, you're armed and driving the wagon. If I laughed at you, you could put me out right here and let the wolves get me."

"You'd want to, though," he said petulantly.

"Dreams aren't funny," Stoner said firmly. "I never laugh at dreams. It's bad for your Karma."

The corner of his mouth twitched in a smile. "You sound like Blue Mary. She talks about funny stuff like that."

"We're both strange. Are you going to tell me?"

"I'm thinking on it." He chewed his lower lip for a second. He cleared his throat. "I want to be a school teacher," he burst out, his voice cracking under the strain.

"I thought you didn't like school."

"I lied about that," he said. "Your friend, the teacher, what's she teach?"

"History."

"No kidding? That's what I'd like to teach." His eyes actually glistened with excitement. "It must be great."

Stoner smiled. "It has its good points, and bad points, like anything else. You could do it."

Billy hooted. "Lady, I can't even read and write."

She was beginning to feel a little annoyed with his self-deprecation. "So learn to read and write, and then go to school, and teach history."

"Yeah," Billy said. "The entire town of Tabor's lined up just bustin' to

71

teach me."

"Get out of Tabor. Nothing's keeping you there."

"Where'd I go?"

"Denver. Topeka. Anywhere." Oh, God, she thought suddenly, don't let him tell me he'll disappear into air if he leaves. Don't let me find out this is the Twilight Zone.

"Can't."

"Why not?"

He was silent. The wagon wheel creaked and cracked with the sound of old wood and leather. The mule stumbled along, hooves pounding the earth like a drum, grunting and sending up little puffs of mist from its nostrils into the still air.

"I'm wanted," he said in a voice so low it was almost a whisper. "Tell you the truth, first time I saw you I thought maybe you was after me, way you just showed up there. That was before I realized you was a girl."

She decided to let the obvious sexism pass. Adolescents were notoriously immune to consciousness-raising. "Wanted?" she asked.

Billy nodded. "Killed a man. "

"Really? So did I !"

"Cold blood?"

"Self defense."

"Yeah, me too. Only it was my Ma that was in danger."

"It was my—friend."

"Ain't you afraid they'll string you up?"

Stoner laughed. "Of course not. They didn't even charge me. There was a coroner's inquest, and I told my story, and that was that."

"Yeah?" He glanced at her skeptically. "Where'd all this happen?"

"Wyoming."

"Well, that figures. You can do anything in Wyoming. That's rough territory."

"It was rough for Bryan Oxnard, all right. The man you killed, was he your father?"

"Guess so. Ma said so, he said no. Nobody else's ridin' out to claim me, so it must be true."

"What did he do to your mother?"

Billy started to take off his hat, seemed to think better of it, and mashed it down harder on his head. His ears stuck out beneath little wisps of hair. Stoner thought it was adorable.

"He was drunk," Billy said. "Wasn't the first time. He'd get liquored up and turn mean. For a while he'd just hit out at anything that crossed his path. Lately he'd come lookin' for us."

"Did he beat you?"

72

"Couple of times. Mostly he went for my Ma."

Stoner decided it would be futile to ask why the authorities hadn't been informed.

"I couldn't let him do that any more, see, on account of she ain't well. I mean, it always made me feel bad, but I was just so scared of him ...Anyway, one night he came for her, and I guess something in me finally got up the nerve to go for him back."

"Good," Stoner said. "What did you do?"

"Picked up a jug and busted his head open." He smiled a little. "His own damn liquor jug. Busted it right over his damn head. 'Scuse my language. Booze and blood and stuff all over the place. Smelled like Big Dot's on Saturday night."

"And you took off?"

"You bet I did. Jeez."

"Are you sure he was dead?"

"Sure looked dead."

They had reached the crest of the hill.

"There she is," said Billy. He pulled the mule to a stop in front of the Tabor sign and stood up. Wind tugged at his hat. He held it on with one hand and pointed to the horizon with the other. "I don't see no machine, d'you?"

Stoner shook her head. She was disappointed, but somehow not surprised. Somehow, the closer they came to the point where she had last seen the car, the more she doubted she'd find it.

"Wanta go down the hill and get a closer look?" the boy asked, a touch of sympathy softening his usual brusqueness.

"Might as well."

The wagon lurched and rattled down the slope of matted prairie grass. Stoner felt each bump like a blow to her spine. Her shoulders ached as she was tossed from side to side. She was going to be a mass of bruises and lacerations before this was over. Not that it mattered. Not that anything mattered but getting out of here.

The front wheel hit a rock and sent her flying across the seat into Billy. He threw an arm in front of her to steady her. "Thanks," she said, and grasped his hand. "I don't know how you can ride in this thing."

"Ain't hard," the boy said. "You get used to it."

She was silent for a moment. This boy was too young for this, to spend the rest of his life—a long time—living out a fantasy. After all, it was one thing for a bunch of adults to decide to live in Disneyland, but Billy was only a kid. There was still time for him, time to get his problems straightened out and go to school. Time to be what he wanted to be. It wasn't fair.

"Whose idea was it," she asked, "for you to live here?"

73

He glanced at her. "In Tabor?"

Stoner nodded.

"Mine."

"Why?"

"Huh?"

"Why here?" She gestured, taking in the barren countryside. "Couldn't you have found a better place?"

"Suits me," he said gruffly.

"But don't you ever want to ... be like other kids? You know, hang out in malls, ride around in cars, pick up girls, whatever kids do?"

"Nope."

She found it hard to believe. "Why not?"

"'Cause I never been in a car, except for a box car once between St. Louis and Kansas City and it weren't much for ridin' in. Never heard of nothin' called 'malls', don't much like girls—not young silly ones, anyway—and I ain't like other kids."

"Of course you are. I mean, you might not have had all the opportunities other kids have, and there are a few things you might want to clear up, but ..."

"I ain't gonna talk about this," he snapped.

"I'm sorry. I didn't mean to step on your toes."

He kept his eyes glued to the horizon, his jaw set in a rigid pose.

"Really," Stoner said. "I didn't mean any harm."

"Yeah? Them people back there in Tabor, they don't mean no harm, neither. But they manage to do it, don't they?"

"Yes, they do."

The wagon curved around the side of a slight hill. In the distance lay what looked like a pile of coal. A burned-out farm. "Why don't they like you, Billy? Why are they so quick to blame you for everything?"

"You heard what Hayes said. I got no family."

"But that's not a crime. Lots of people don't have families."

He snorted. "I never met none."

"Big Dot doesn't have a family, does she? And Lolly and Cherry?"

"Guess not," he groused.

"But you all look like a family to me."

The boy glanced at her. "A family?"

"Sure. You love each other, don't you?"

Billy blushed from his fingertips to his hairline. "Them women, they's whores."

"And what difference does that make? You do love them, don't you? Like family."

"So what if I do?" he said loudly. "Nothin' wrong with that, is there?"

74

"Nothing at all," Stoner said.

"Jes' 'cause them old clucks back there got everything all figured out, that don't make it so, does it?"

Ah, yes, the old Biddies. Keepers of the sacred flame of Civilization. Defenders of Respectability. Mistresses of Morality. "Certainly not."

Billy gave a self-satisfied nod. "That's what I figured."

They had reached the bottom of the hill, where the car should have been, where Interstate 70 should have been. And, of course, there was no car, and no Interstate. Only a dusty wagon track coming from nowhere and leading nowhere. Stoner pointed to it. "What's that?" she asked.

"Wagon trail. Topeka to Denver."

"Wagon trail."

"You know. For folks going west."

She sat for a while, helplessly, looking at the track. She got out of the wagon and walked around with her hands in her pockets.

Now what?

It was possible, of course, that Billy had taken her someplace totally unrelated to where she was trying to go. Possible that her car, and escape, lay just over a different hill. Possible that, just beyond the range of her hearing and sight, perfectly normal people were busily going about their perfectly normal business in their perfectly normal ways.

But why would the boy do that?

Let's think about what this could all mean:

1) I have unknowingly fallen into a nest of drug dealers and smugglers, who, under the cover of being an innocent ghost town (out of season), and sponsored by the National Security Council, are covertly supplying guns to the Nicaraguan Contras. In which case I will never get out of here alive.

2) Tabor is a town made up entirely of persons experiencing a mass psychosis, a folie á multitude , who believe they are actually doing what they're doing. But they wouldn't care whether I left or not, would they? They wouldn't be shifting the scenery to try to keep me here.

3) Like something out of a Shirley Jackson novel, the town is a vampire, the large-scale equivalent of Hill House. And I'm the latest victim, to be sacrificed to feed its endless hunger.

4) The residents of Tabor make up a religious sect whose most cherished belief is that everything that has happened since 1871 is a sin and an abomination—which may be right—and who have forsaken evil worldly ways. Kind of like the Amish. But even the Amish stop short of publishing 19th Century newspapers. Nevertheless ... These good souls also don't believe in sex, and the only way to add to their numbers is to kidnap helpless travelers on the Interstate and force them to remain forever in Tabor.

But then there's Blue Mary, who is an intimate friend and relative of

Aunt Hermione—even though Aunt Hermione has never mentioned her—
who would certainly have known about this place and warned me away
from it.

Which left her with

5) Blue Mary is right.

She couldn't decide if that was the most comforting, or most disturbing
explanation of all. Disturbing? That she had taken a detour in time and
ended up in a backwater? Why would that be disturbing?

Because she might not get back?

Or because the mere fact of it turned everything she took for granted
upside down?

But that had already happened to her, many times. Look at Shady
Acres. Look at Siyamtiwa. Look at Gwen, for heaven's sake. Gwen, who
was the one person in the entire world she most wanted to love her. The
last person in the world she ever expected to love her. Gwen, who loved
her.

As long as we're talking about miracles, there's a real miracle. To be
loved by the woman you love is the greatest miracle of all.

A wave of homesickness hit her and made her feel as if all her insides
were being pulled into the ground.

She looked around, hoping for distraction. The wagon was empty. The
mule pressed its nose into the dust, trying to make a meal of dead grass
and stubble. A hill away Billy stood, hat in hand, making conversation
with a small group of Native American women.

Stoner hesitated to approach them. They seemed to be laughing, having
a good time. She shouldn't interrupt. On the other hand ...

The women looked up curiously as she approached.

"Hi," she said.

One of the women stepped forward, crossed her arms across her chest,
pulled a down-turned mouth, and said, "Hi."

Stoner had to laugh. "Do I look that bad?"

"Bad."

Billy clamped his hat on his head and pulled it low. "I was askin' them
about your wagon."

"Any luck?"

"Nope." He turned back to the women, said a few words in a language
she didn't understand.

The women nodded solemnly, and began drifting away.

"Maybe I should explain to them ..." Stoner began.

"You speak Arapahoe?"

"No."

He shrugged. "Forget it. They wouldn't understand you."

"That woman did."

"She didn't understand you," Billy said gently. "She mocked you."

"Oh." She felt very foolish, and very alone.

Billy glanced at her, then at the sky. "I wish you'd trust me," he said in a low voice.

"I do trust you. It's just that I find myself in a very peculiar situation."

"Yeah, it's peculiar, all right. Big Dot filled me in, kinda." He laughed. " 'Course, she thinks you're stone cold nuts. But probably not dangerous."

"I must remember to thank her for the compliment," Stoner said wryly.

"You gotta admit, it looks suspicious."

"Suspicious !!" Her anger flared out of control. "I'll tell you what looks suspicious. A town full of people in costumes acting like 1871, that's what looks suspicious." She kicked at the ground. "And do you want to know the worst of it? When I get out of here, I'll never be able to explain it to anyone, because it's so crazy no one would ever believe me." She felt her voice rise to shrillness, out of control. She didn't care. "But it's irrelevant, isn't it? Because you people are never going to let me out of this fruitcake place."

"Boy," Billy said, "you sure are short-tempered."

"You'd be angry, too, if you suddenly found yourself in a strange town, in a different century, and you didn't know how you got there, or what you were doing there, or how to get away, or if you'd even see your home again ..."

Fear and loneliness made a huge ball in her chest that swelled and swelled—she found herself crying.

"Hey," Billy said, slipping an arm around her shoulders awkwardly, "I'm real sorry. Honest. I didn't mean to hurt your feelings." He stroked her arm gently. "Come on. Don't cry any more, okay? I'll help you get home. I promise. Just don't cry, okay?"

She pulled herself together. "Okay." Her nose was running. "Do you have a Kleenex?"

"Huh?"

"Kleenex. Tissue. Something to blow my nose on."

"Sure." He reached in his pocket and brought out a large handkerchief. "This all right? It's clean. I didn't use it yet or anything."

"Thank you." She took it, wiped her eyes and nose. "I'll wash it for you."

"You don't hafta do that."

"Really, it's no ..."

"Stoner, I can do it."

Something about his voice made her look up. Something soft, velvety.

Billy put one palm gently along the side of her cheek. "I can do it," he

77

said again, and kissed her.

It wasn't at all what she would have expected from an adolescent boy. From an adolescent boy she would have expected roughness, fumbling, coarseness to hide teen insecurity. But Billy's kiss was soft, warm, tentative and yet sure and asking—like a woman's kiss.

She felt her body respond, and pulled back roughly.

"Oh, Jeez," the boy said. His face was scarlet. "I'm sorry. Jeez, I never woulda done that ... I'm sorry."

She didn't know what to say.

"I never done anything that bad before. Honest."

"Well," Stoner said shakily, "you killed your father. That's pretty bad."

"Not as bad as this. Jeez, I swear, I won't do it again."

Stoner nodded. "That sounds like a good idea."

"I didn't mean to ..."

"All right." Right now she had to get away from him. To think—not about what he had done—she had to think about her own reaction. The way her body had gone warm from head to toe. The tingling ...

Shit, she thought. I'm stuck in the Nowhere of the Nineteenth Century, I've lost my clients' car, and I'm getting turned on by a boy.

The Lesbian Nation had been taking some strange turns in recent years. Hard-core radical dykes calling themselves "hetero-dykes" and sleeping with men. Long-term couples breaking up because one of them was determined to have babies. Former lesbian separatists demanding space for their male infants at Lesbian Gatherings. And now this.

Maybe the Government was putting something in the whole wheat flour.

≈ ≈ ≈

Cullum Johnson shifted his aging bones in the saddle and looked off to the horizon. He had a sneaking suspicion he'd been nodding off just now, the dream of falling from a high place not a dream at all but just his mind putting together the impressions his body took in. Falling. Falling off his horse. The not-dream waking him before he really fell.

He'd caught himself nodding off a lot in recent months. And slipping from the saddle. Once or twice he'd bruised himself real bad. Once he'd had to lie on the ground until the dizziness passed and he could drag himself back onto his horse. He figured there weren't too many falls like that left in him.

He pulled Toby to a stop and got down, stretching each joint and muscle until it worked right. The horse nudged him between the shoulder blades. "I know, Tobe," Cullum said. "You wanta see what's over the next hill, and so do I. But you got to be a little patient. You have the misfortune to have an ancient gentleman for a boss." He scratched behind Toby's ears

78

and breathed into his nostrils, the way the horse liked. "You're a good horse, Tobe. Damn near killed me breaking you, and I reckon these days I'd have given up and gone looking for something with a little less piss in 'er. But I sure would have missed four exciting years, for which I thank you with all my heart."

Sometimes Cullum felt guilty about Toby. He'd been a frisky colt, you could tell just looking at him he was born to high adventure. But Cullum's adventuring days were about over, as he was reminded each year when the geese flew south and he felt his strength fly with them. Oh, he'd ridden the horse far, and hard. But not on a regular basis. Some days, he just saddled up and rode through the Tennessee woods kind of leisurely. And one summer, just a couple years back, he came on the horse unexpectedly one day—musing over something or other, he was, couldn't recall now what was so darn important—and found himself muttering, "Looka that horse, running to fat. Body shouldn't have a horse if they ain't gonna keep it fit." And then his mind cleared and he realized it was Tobe, and when he thought back he remembered a lot of days when it just seemed too hot or too damp or too some-damn-excuse to leave the comfort of his cabin.

After that he'd done better, making sure the horse was exercised every day. He knew it was good for them both. But if it had been just him, he wouldn't have bothered.

So he reckoned Toby had kept him alive, after a fashion. Not that that was a blessing necessarily. To tell the truth, he hadn't much cared what happened to him after he lost the red-haired gal. She was some beauty, she was, and he'd courted her like she was a queen. Bringing her presents, playing the gent at all times. Got so she'd confide in him, place her heartaches in his hands, and he'd just spread his love over them until the hurt didn't hurt so much. Once she'd even let him see her cry, pressed her pretty forehead against his big ugly shoulder and let her tears fall on his shirt. Telling him about the shoemaker who'd promised to take her west, and she'd believed him until that morning she went running down to his place of business and found he'd left in the night, bag and baggage.

"I should have known," she'd said in her pretty voice. "A fine man like him, with an honest trade—he wouldn't want a used woman like me."

He'd patted her silky hair in a comforting way, and wished he hadn't been wearing that scratchy old plaid wool. If he'd known she was going to put her sweet skin against him, he'd have spent his last dollar on a shirt of pure satin.

Yeah, he'd loved that little red-haired gal. Didn't care that she was an unchaste lady. Shucks, most gals were unchaste ladies these days—if they weren't married or teaching school or making dresses. Maybe even if they were. Didn't seem right, though. Man could go off with never a look back, leaving the woman behind to make the best of it in a town that treated her with scorn.

That little red-haired gal hadn't done a durn thing wrong, not a durn thing every other woman in town hadn't done. Trouble was, she'd gotten herself carried away with passion and sweet talk, and done it without benefit of clergy.

He wanted to help her. Didn't have much money, but he shared what he could. And listened to her troubles and wiped her tears. And then he made his only mistake.

He asked her to marry him.

She'd looked at him kind of perplexed, and then got real quiet for a long time, staring down into her lap. When she looked up again, she had the most sorrowful look on her face, it nearly broke his heart. "Cull ..." She was the only one who called him Cull. It made a special feeling in him. "Cull, you're my dearest friend in all the world. But I never ..."

That was when he remembered he was old.

He tried to laugh it off, real fast, before it could hurt what they had between them. But he knew it was too late. They both knew it. He took her out walking a couple of times after that, but the old easiness was gone. After a while he quit stopping around for her. He knew it made them both too sad.

A couple months later, he'd come out to the barn one winter morning and found his old mare, Foxfire, dead in her sleep.

It took him a long time to care about anything again. He let the cabin go unpainted that spring. The only crops in his garden were the ones that came up on their own.

But he needed a horse. At least until he made up his mind for certain to die. Seen too many folks kind of waste away, neither here nor there on the issue of living or dying, letting nature take its course so as to avoid personal responsibility. And personal responsibility was one thing Cullum Johnson never avoided. Lot of folks didn't think much of bounty hunting as a way of life, but by God that was his calling and he was damned if he'd apologize for it.

So, as long as he was going to go on taking up space on this planet, he might as well do it with a little dignity. And dignity required eating and wearing decent clothes and working a little from time to time when the need arose. And that required a horse.

He buried Foxfire and went looking, and there, just three farms over, was Toby. Like he'd been waiting for him.

Cullum gave the gelding's neck an affectionate squeeze and swung back into the saddle. "Let's move along, boy. Days ain't gettin' longer, and I ain't getting younger."

≈ ≈ ≈

The next day it began to snow. Hardly noticeable at first, the day as warm and sunny as the last. A few thin little clouds hung in the robin's egg sky. Then a few more. By mid afternoon, snow was falling intermittently in misty flakes.

Stoner tossed the last of the split logs onto the wood pile and set the axe in the chopping block. She wiped the perspiration from her face with her shirt sleeve.

Darn. She'd hoped Billy would come by with the wagon, so they could go have a look at that burned farm. As long as she was stuck here, she might as well try to shed a little light on the mystery. Maybe she should have told him what she had in mind. He'd promised to try to get away in the early afternoon, but Dot must have needed him.

A little band of Indian woman stopped by to do business with Blue Mary, trading for the things they needed but were refused at the Emporium.

Maybe they were setting the fires, to drive away the settlers. That's how it went in Hollywood's version of the story. But Blue Mary had said they hadn't had trouble with the Indians. And, anyway, if they did do it, they wouldn't just set the fires and slink away into the night. They'd have made sure the settlers knew who had done it. That's how it worked with political statements.

What she needed to do was take a walk and try to think this through and maybe come up with some brilliant ideas about getting back to 1989. Impossible to think in the cabin, where Blue Mary and the Arapahoe women were chattering and laughing and generally raising a ruckus."

"I'll be back in a while," she said, as she slipped into her parka.

One of the Indian women detached herself from the group and came toward her. She said something in Arapahoe.

Stoner looked to Blue Mary for translation.

"Your coat," Blue Mary said. "She's curious."

She took off the parka, held it out.

The woman drew back.

"It's okay," Stoner said, and smiled.

The woman fingered the material gently, turned back the bottom flap, ran her hands along the hem. She lifted the coat in one hand, bounced it up and down for a moment, then turned and looked at Blue Mary with raised eyebrows.

"She doesn't understand how it can be so light," Blue Mary explained.

"It's the material," Stoner said. "Rayon and Thinsulate."

The Indian woman looked at her. "Ray-on? Thin-su-late?"

Oh, boy. How do I explain synthetics? "It's ... it's ... well, it's not real.

81

Someone invented it, made it. Probably for the Space Program. You know, for the Astronauts … on the moon."

Blue Mary gave a little giggle. "Without being rude, dear, might I suggest you not say things like that? You sound quite mad."

"Sorry." She turned to the Indian woman, raised her hands palms-upward, and shrugged. The universal symbol for "Go figure".

The Indian woman grinned and said something to her.

"She says it's warm," Blue Mary translated.

Stoner nodded. "Very warm."

The woman spoke again.

"She says you'll need it," Blue Mary said. "There's going to be a blizzard."

"You must be mistaken," Stoner said to the Indian woman. "It's a beautiful day."

Blue Mary translated.

The woman stared into her eyes as if trying to warn her of serious danger, and spoke rapidly.

"She says November sun is like a man. Warm on the outside but with a heart of ice."

"I'll keep that in mind," Stoner said.

"She's right, you know," Blue Mary said. "The weather out here can be treacherous."

Stoner looked at the Indian woman, at her thin cotton dress, the threadbare shawl around her shoulders. "Here," she said, holding out her parka. "You take this."

The woman dropped her eyes to the floor and shook her head.

"Please," Stoner said. "I want you to have it."

Blue Mary hurried around the table and drew her aside. "They won't take charity," she said softly. "You're shaming her."

"I'm sorry." She caught the woman's eye. "I'm sorry." She pointed to herself. "Foreigner. Ignorant."

Blue Mary translated.

The Indian woman smiled and patted Stoner's hand reassuringly.

"I do wish she'd take it," Stoner said to Blue Mary. "Her clothes are so …so inadequate."

"If you really mean it," Blue Mary said, "go out for your walk. Leave the coat on the ground. Then it will seem as if she found it."

"Will they know it's for her?"

"They'll know."

Stoner slipped into the parka, looked around the room, and cleared her throat. "Guess I'll go on out to the outhouse," she said loudly and casually.

The Indian women conferred among themselves.

82

Blue Mary told them what she'd said.

"Ah," said one. "Pee-pee."

"That's right," Stoner said. "Pee-pee."

Another round of buzzing and whispering.

"They wonder what's wrong with you," Blue Mary said.

"Wrong with me?"

"They think you must be deformed."

"Why?"

"Because you're afraid for anyone to see your private parts."

That did it. Blushing down to her toes, she turned and stormed out of the house.

She took off the parka, dropped it by the side of the dirt track, and strode off across the prairie.

≈ ≈ ≈

The messenger picked his way through the fog-choked alleys. One hand clutched the collar of his meager cloth coat tight around his throat. Some day the fog would kill him, he thought. But he was still glad to be back in San Francisco.

He found the door he was looking for and knocked. Waited, shivering, until it opened a crack and the old Chinese woman looked out.

"Chang," he said.

The old woman opened the door a little wider and he slipped inside. It was warm there.

He looked around. These people had money. Not a lot of money, but more than most Chinese in America. Their furnishings were old, but cared for. Rugs lay on the floor, and thick drapes hung by the windows. A lacquered chest stood in one corner of the room.

Merchant class.

The old woman brought him tea, fragrant and warm. He sipped it gratefully. As he looked up over the rim of his cup, he saw the young one standing in an inner doorway.

He had heard about her. Her cousins who worked on the railroad had spoken of her beauty often. She was destined to marry well, they said. Her beauty was legendary among the San Francisco Chinese.

The messenger had to smile. Her cousins were fools. Their most enthusiastic descriptions didn't begin to touch her radiance. Eyes as dark and rich as the cone flowers that dotted the slopes of Mount Shasta. Hair so shining black he could almost feel its silkiness with his eyes. Graceful, delicate hands that hovered like hummingbirds over the tiny cakes and lifted the translucent china teacup to her carmine lips. Although she wore the American style dress, full skirt and ruffled bodice, her posture and manners were as Oriental as those of the Empress. Such a woman was a treasure, and would bring Honor to her family.

He finished his tea and delivered his message.

The old woman gave him money as May Chang turned and went to her room.

Before the door was closed, she had taken down the carpet bag she used as a suitcase and begun to pack.

≈ ≈ ≈

The creek bed was dry as dust, but still showed the channels, smooth as flowing hair, where the water had run during the September rains. The banks were high, the ground below flood level scoured clean of all but a few large round rocks. When the stream was full, it must be quick and treacherous. But it ambled down from one of the burned farms. Burned in the summer, Blue Mary had said.

Stoner strolled along the bottom, running a little from time to time. She might not make it all the way, but she could see if anything had washed down. She wasn't sure what she was looking for, exactly. But it was better than doing nothing. Beneath the soft dust that rose around her ankles, she could feel the hard-frozen, clayey ground. Stopping for breath, she leaned against the bank and watched the sky.

It was nice out here. Quiet. Solitary. She could feel her mind relax.

The clouds were gathering together into a few large clouds, fluffy and pristine as whipped cream.

A hawk flew overhead, slowly, searching the ground.

She supposed pickings were pretty slim this time of year.

She wondered what day it was. Counted. She'd arrived on Monday, the 13th. Had spent the 14th trying, unsuccessfully, to get out of here. Had spent another day prowling around town hoping to pick up clues or gossip and chalking up the world's most complete collection of dirty looks for her trouble. Today must be Thursday, the 16th.

Three days overdue in Topeka. They'd all be frantic now, back home. Marylou knew her itinerary. They'd probably call the State Police, wouldn't they?

Of course they would. And if the police wouldn't help, Gwen and Marylou and Aunt Hermione would come themselves. Any time now, someone would show up looking for her. They'd find her car, wherever she'd parked the car. And from there Tabor would be the natural place to look.

That made her feel better. If she couldn't get away from this end, at least somebody would be taking action on the other. She sort of hoped they wouldn't come until she could get to the bottom of the fires.

Great! Two days ago you were frantic to leave. Now you want to hang around and solve mysteries.

Must have read too many Nancy Drews as a kid.

Humming, she started back up the creek bed.

She almost missed the dugout. Cut into the side of the bank above the high water level, it was no more than a single room, the only light coming from a narrow doorway covered by a torn and ragged blanket, so thick with dust it blended with the ground.

Stoner peered inside. A bundle of blankets lay on the dirt floor near a rusting wood stove. The table and single chair were old and worn and cracked. She lifted the chair. It was light as a feather, all the life long ago drawn out of the wood. A tin plate, spoon, and cup lay neatly on the table, looking as if the owner had left suddenly, or expected to return.

She wondered who had taken refuge here. It must have been a long time ago, whoever it was. A trapper, maybe, using the dugout as a shelter from the weather as he made the rounds of his traps. Or an outlaw, hiding from the posse. Or just a loner, a wanderer. A college dropout, hiking across the country to "find himself".

No, they probably didn't have college dropouts back then.

Maybe a gold miner stopping over on his way to Colorado.

A cowboy looking for lost calves.

Or an arsonist, hiding the tools of his or her trade.

She put the plate down.

Dropping to her knees, she crawled across the floor, looking for signs of an underground cache.

Nothing.

She examined the walls, and the seams where the walls met the floor.

If the dirt had been moved, it had been replaced with considerable skill. The same was true outside. She walked up and down the creek bed, peering behind rocks and boulders and under water-scoured driftwood.

No luck. The place was clean.

The sky was beginning to go gray. An occasional snowflake touched her hair. Better get back to Blue Mary's, just in case the Indian women were right.

She scrambled to the top of the creek bank and squinted into the distance. She could barely make out Blue Mary's house, a pebble in the midst of the prairie. Smoke rose from the chimney.

She started toward it at a trot.

By the time she got back to the cabin, the snow had begun falling in earnest.

Stoner caught herself smiling. Nobody could come looking for her now. They'd have to wait until the storm let up.

It shocked her to realize she was a little bit glad.

Chapter 6

The snow came from everywhere and nowhere. A white glare that swirled and drifted and blew blinding curtains across the countryside. The landscape was transformed. Where valleys used to be, there were hills of white. Fence posts buried in snow became outbuildings, outbuildings turned into barns as the drifting pellets of ice widened the edges and obliterated the shapes of things.

The wind raged, cutting through heavy wool clothing like an icy knife. Farm animals turned their tails against the blasts, heads down, waiting out the storm in misery. To walk through the snow was to walk through a tunnel where north and south, east and west, even up and down were lost in the polarized light and shifting wind.

As night wore on, the wind rose, the volume of snow increased. Furious, it attacked the cottage. Like a ghost bent on revenge, it pounded against the walls and roof, and searched between the boards with hungry, endlessly-patting fingers.

Stoner tossed another slab of wood into the stove, and turned back to help Blue Mary stuff chinks and cracks with torn rags.

"Are you sure you're warm enough, dear?" Blue Mary asked.

"I'm fine," Stoner said, and hoped Blue Mary wouldn't notice how her teeth chattered. She could use another blanket, but there were no more in evidence, and she didn't want to run the risk of depriving the older woman of needed warmth.

"Don't be coy with me, Stoner. I know you're not as accustomed to the cold as we are out here. Generations of central heating have taken their toll."

"Really, I'll be fine."

"You probably should have kept your coat."

Stoner shook her head. "She needed it more than I do." She tried to imagine what it was like, out there on the prairie, with no shelter but banks

86

and brush piles and drafty tepees.

"At least drink some more of that tea. If you catch your death of pneumonia, Hermione will never forgive me."

"She'll never forgive me for not calling, and driving her crazy with worry," Stoner said as she poured the tea.

Blue Mary wedged a bit of red flannel into the window frame and looked over her handiwork with a satisfied expression. "I'm sure she'd understand. Besides, time isn't passing the same there as it is here."

"That's nice," Stoner muttered, and hoped that wasn't true. Because if it was, no one would be looking for her. And if no one was looking for her ...

Blue Mary took the cup of tea Stoner had poured for her and sat at the table. "When you get back to your own time, you'll pick up right where you were when you became side-tracked."

"Good thing I'd pulled off the road. I'd sure hate to be dropped back into a car going seventy-five miles an hour."

"You know, dear," said Blue Mary, "I think it's very healthy, the adjustment you're making."

"Adjustment?"

"To being here."

Stoner raked her hand through her hair. Adjustment? Maybe. She still believed the whole thing was crazy. But, under the circumstances—the circumstances being that she couldn't for the life of her imagine how to get out ..."I didn't have a choice."

"Now, Stoner, we've plowed this field before." Blue Mary went to the warming oven above the stove and pulled out a cast iron pan of corn muffins. She slipped them onto a plate and passed the plate across the table. "I'm sorry these are so dull. We're dependent on fresh fruits, you know. And this time of year the choices are limited."

Stoner broke open a muffin and inhaled its firm sweetness. "Does it always snow so early here?"

"Never. In all my years here, this is the first time. It's usually December, at least. Most often Christmas."

The wind had worked itself into a state over being denied access to the house. It hurled rock-like snow pellets at the window. It ripped the smoke from the chimney, making the fire leap up in angry red flares.

Stoner pulled herself closer to the table and huddled over her tea cup. "How long have you lived here?"

The older woman thought about it. "More than thirty years. I came out here from New York State in—it must have been the mid-forties. Goodness, how time flies."

"I suppose you've seen a lot of changes."

"Around Tabor, yes. Of course there was no such thing as Tabor when I

87

first arrived. Just a bend in the river, Indians, buffalo, and cattle herds passing through."

Stoner sipped her tea. "What made you decide to stay?"

"It just felt right. As if I belonged here." She smiled. "You must know the feeling. You go somewhere you've never gone before, as far as you know, and something about it just says 'home'."

"Yes," Stoner said. "I felt that in the Tetons."

"Did you, dear?" Blue Mary looked at her sympathetically. "How sad you don't feel you can just go there and live."

"Yes, it is."

Blue Mary broke a muffin in two. "Well, perhaps someday you will. If not in this lifetime, than in another."

"Yeah," Stoner said noncommittally. "You never know." She finished off one muffin and reached for another. "What do you do? For a living?"

"Whatever seems to be needed. My small garden produces some vegetables and herbs. There's always a call for a good midwife, and ... forgive my pride, but I do believe I'm among the most capable. Some fortune telling. A bit of healing. A little teaching. Not in the conventional sense, of course. But, if someone shows an interest in things beyond the obvious, well, I do take pleasure in passing along what I know." She laughed in a delighted way. "I suppose that's what's earned me my reputation as a witch."

"That and the fortune telling, I'd guess. Do you read palms?"

"A little. I'm most comfortable with the Tarot, but I seldom get an opportunity to use it. People are very superstitious, you know. It frightens them."

"I see."

"So I try to make it look as if I'm picking up impressions from the things they say, or out of the air. They're more comfortable with that. Most of the townsfolk wouldn't admit it publicly, but I believe I've been consulted by someone from every family in Tabor." She blushed. "Not that I'm trying to brag, mind you. But I must confess I'm proud of that. It shows a certain ... acceptance, don't you know?"

Stoner smiled. "Yes, I know."

"Well, not every family, to be perfectly honest. Speak the truth and shame the Devil, as they say. But most."

"I'll bet the Reverend Henry Parnells give you a wide berth."

Blue Mary cocked her head on one side. "No, I have had my dealings with the Parnells. Caroline had some female trouble a while ago ..." She caught herself. "Oh, dear, it's probably unethical of me to talk like this."

"I don't know." Stoner sipped her tea. "Who am I going to gossip to?

I'm not even from this time."

Blue Mary laughed. "Astute, as always. Still, I suppose it matters in a Karmic sense."

"Everything," said Stoner, "matters in a Karmic sense."

"Actually, I've known Caroline since she was a child. She was always very high-strung. And righteous. The most righteous child I've ever seen. Not at all like the rest of her family." She sighed. "I suppose she had some terribly upsetting experiences in a past life, don't you imagine?"

"I ..." Stoner began.

"I forget," Blue Mary cut in. "You don't believe in past lives."

"Yeah, I do. A little. I think."

Blue Mary smiled. "Hardly enough faith to found a church on, dear." She stirred her tea aimlessly. "I'd rather hoped being married to the Reverend would ease her soul. Give her a nice outlet for all that righteousness. But it hasn't seemed to help. I'm afraid righteousness just feeds on righteousness." She thought for a moment. "To tell you the truth, she seems like a very unhappy person since the Reverend came into her life. But perhaps I'm judging too quickly. They've only been married just short of a year."

"None of those women struck me as a barrel of fun," Stoner said.

"No," Blue Mary said thoughtfully, "I don't suppose they are. It's a difficult life for a woman, out here. Nothing but hard work and not much respect." She took a sip of tea. "Still and all, I sometimes wonder why adversity softens some people, but makes others hard as nails."

"I sometimes wonder that myself."

"There was gossip at first, that it was her money that attracted him." The woman smiled. "Not a fortune by your Twentieth Century standards, of course, but she does own the property they live on, and there is some income. If it weren't for Carolyn's inheritance, Tabor wouldn't be able to afford a preacher."

"A mixed blessing," Stoner muttered.

Blue Mary howled with laughter. "It certainly is."

Something landed on the roof in a short series of thumps. It sounded like falling tree branches. But there were no trees near the house. Except for the few that grew near the creek there were none for sixty miles.

She looked questioningly at Blue Mary.

"Wolves," the older woman said.

"Wolves?"

They seemed to be chasing each other from one end of the house to the other.

"The storm drives them close. Looking for shelter, I suppose. Or food." She smiled reassuringly at the look of disbelief and apprehension on Stoner's face. "They're quite harmless. They'll find the shed in a minute. And as soon as the storm ends, they'll move along."

Snow was sticking to the windows now, packing against the house, obliterating even the view of the dark and angry sky. Stoner glanced around uneasily. "This is some storm."

Blue Mary nodded. "Our weather is always violent. Heat, cold, drought, floods. Never a dull moment."

"Boston weather's dull."

"Is it?"

"Damp and miserable all winter. In summer the humidity chokes you. Things tend to rot in Boston."

"You don't care much for cities, do you?" Blue Mary asked.

"Not much. They always seem like somewhere to be until you find a place to live."

"Ah."

"Of course, I don't know if I'd be comfortable out here, either."

"I'm sure you wouldn't," Blue Mary said. "And after what you did to Joseph Hayes the other day, I don't think you'd be exactly welcome."

Stoner grinned sheepishly.

"Dorothy and the girls stopped by while you were out walking. They were going for a little drive." She saw the look of eagerness in Stoner's face and placed a calming hand on her wrist. "In their wagon, Stoner. They don't have an automobile."

"Oh."

"You know, dear, I try very hard not to tell others what to do. After all, we're each on our own path, aren't we? But, if you don't mind a teeny bit of advice ..."

"Sure."

"I'd be careful of how I dealt with Mr.Hayes. He's been known to be very nasty. And you're a stranger in town, after all."

Stoner smiled. "No problem. If he gets rough with me, I'll threaten to die, which will mean I won't be around in 1989 to come back here so he can rough me up. Then everything that's going to happen in his lifetime won't be able to happen. That ought to put the fear of God into him."

Blue Mary threw back her head and laughed. "Very good. But I think it's a little more complicated than that."

"Rats."

"But, seriously, Stoner. Do handle Joseph with kid gloves."

Stoner frowned. "He's a thoroughly unpleasant individual. I don't know how he stays in business."

"Maybe you didn't notice," said Blue Mary. "His is the only business of its kind in town."

She wasn't about to let that go. "Then shop out of town."

"There's not a town within fifty miles of Tabor."

"What about Fort Morgan?"

"That's an Army Fort, not a store. They wouldn't have what we needed."

"Well, the railroad, then."

"Merely a track, Stoner." Blue Mary smiled. "It must be difficult, with your life experiences, to understand the complete isolation of this time and place."

"But what Hayes did to Billy ... Why do people put up with that? How can he get away with it?"

"I'm afraid there are all too many who share his viewpoint," Blue Mary said sadly. "As for the rest ...Well, you see, out here everyone serves a function. Joseph's is to supply what's needed—in a material sense. If he decided to pick up and leave, what would the rest of them do?"

"I know what I'd do," Stoner said heatedly. "I'd start a delivery service. Once a week I'd take my wagon to the next town—no matter how far it is—and bring back whatever supplies are wanted. Put him out of business."

"The round trip would take you a week," Blue Mary pointed out.

"I don't care."

The older woman smiled. "There's that Stoner stubbornness again." She leaned across the table and squeezed Stoner's hand affectionately. "I can't tell you how happy I am to see you. "

"Thank you."

Blue Mary got up and poured them another cup of tea.

"Do you think this is such a good idea?" Stoner asked. "There's a blizzard between us and the outhouse." She glanced up at the roof. "Not to mention the wolves."

"Just use the thunder mug," Blue Mary said. "It's in the corner of the loft."

Goody! A new addition to the list of horrors. She groaned.

Blue Mary patted her hand. "I'm sorry, dear. If I'd known how difficult this would be for you, I'd have tried to talk you out of it."

Stoner ran her hand through her hair. "Mary, what am I doing here?"

"Doing what you do best," Blue Mary said. "It's so like you, Stoner, to go where you're needed."

"Why am I needed here?"

"I don't know," Blue Mary said. "I should know, of course. But sometimes I have trouble remembering the future."

"Yeah," Stoner muttered, "I have the same problem. Should have written myself a note."

"It has to do with Tabor. More than the fires. The fires are only the sur-

91

face." The older woman frowned. "Something's not right in Tabor." She seemed to listen to an inner voice. "I can feel it. Smell it. Have you ever smelled evil, dear?"

Stoner shook her head.

"Most people think it would smell like some noxious substance. Fire and brimstone, I suppose, from their Sunday School training. Or excrement. But it's actually quite an innocuous odor. Rather like tin."

"That's nice," Stoner said.

"Tin," Blue Mary mused. "That's what I've been smelling for a few weeks now. Definitely tin."

Stoner hoped the woman wasn't having a brain tumor-related olfactory hallucination.

No, she recalled, brain tumors make you hallucinate the odor of burning rags.

She wondered how she happened to know that.

Edith Kesselbaum. She'd told her, one day in therapy, back when Stoner was a teenager and had run away from home to live with Aunt Hermione. She'd had headaches. Terrible headaches, for about two weeks. They'd terrified her. She was convinced something horrible was happening to her, something neurological and irreversible that would leave her mindless and drooling. Finally she got up the nerve to tell Edith.

"Nonsense," Edith had said, and explained about the oily rags. "Your headaches, Stoner, are caused by repressed hostility. Go back to Hermione's, call your mother, and tell her to go fuck herself. That should take care of any headaches."

Well, she hadn't quite had the nerve to do that, but just thinking about it had cured the headaches.

≈ ≈ ≈

The Sanctified Man sat close by the fire and read the Word by candlelight, pinching the bridge of his nose between thumb and forefinger to ease the strain in his eyes. He sometimes missed the reading glasses he used to wear. But that was before he realized that using them was a slap in God's face, a criticism of the way He had created His servant. So he had sacrificed the glasses to God's Greater Glory, and offered up his discomfort as a prayer.

Over the howling wind and clatter of sleet on the window, he heard a timid knock. The damnable woman again. "Come," he grunted.

The door opened a crack. His gray, mousey wife peeked in.

"Well?" he snarled. "What is it now?"

She cleared her throat. "It's turned so cold. I thought you might like ..." She hesitated.

"What? What?" he snapped.

She seemed to shrink before his very eyes. "A warm drink? A blanket?"

"Did I ask for warm drinks? Did I request blankets?"

"I only thought ..."

Her timidity sickened him. "You thought," he mocked. "You thought? Is it a miracle? Are you thinking?"

His wife looked at the floor.

He gestured her forward. The way she sidled up to the fire, greedily but cautiously, her pale skin touched with bluish goose bumps, pleased him. She was cold. He could let her stay here, in the only room he allowed her to keep heated, or banish her back into the cold upstairs. She knew it, too. As far as she was concerned, he was God.

God in Heaven, God on Earth. God appointing a series of lesser Gods. A Pyramid of Gods, each level having dominion over the levels beneath.

For a moment he wondered what his place was in the pyramid. Then he laughed. God had given him The Word. God wouldn't give the Word to the ones on the bottom. He would only give the Word to the ones who understood its truth.

He wondered if there were many others like him, chosen. He hoped not.

He remembered when the Word had come to him.

Winter, it had been. A long, chilly weekend in San Francisco. The ship he was crewing on had been at sea for months—the Silk Clipper out of Canton. His throat was dry for the taste of liquor. His bones cried out for rest. The smell of opium in the misty air clawed his mind with desire.

He had dug deep into his pockets and came up with a few pathetic coins, barely enough for a meal and a one-night room. For an instant he thought he'd been robbed. Then he remembered the damn ship's captain with his supercilious smile, handing him a quarter of the wages he was due, holding back the rest, telling him he wasn't worth even that, wasn't worth what an eighth of a man was worth. Calling him shiftless, calling him a drunk, calling him ...

Even now, the poisonous words stung in his chest.

He had gone directly from the ship to the nearest saloon. Within an hour, his wages were gone, the thirst unsatisfied, like rats in his belly. He begged the barkeep for more, then threatened, drew his knife. One of his own shipmates—his own shipmate!—had tossed him from the bar like a sack of garbage. He had cursed them all and stumbled away, cold and alone and miserable. Drawing the opium-tainted fog deep into his lungs as if he could satisfy his hunger that way. It only made it worse.

The night grew deeper, the fog thicker, the cold unbearable.

He had failed again, just like the old man back in Ohio said he would.

93

The old man. His own father. His FATHER who threw him out, calling him names...

... They were always calling him names. God, when would they stop calling him names?

The horse had thrown him. It deserved to die. Why couldn't his father see that?

All the things he had done—the animals he had killed, strangling the small ones with his bare hands, the big ones clubbed or stabbed—why couldn't they see it wasn't his fault? The animals had offended him. Every one of them. The dogs that ran at him, sniffing and jumping. The cats that watched him through their evil green and yellow eyes. The cow that had kicked him when he tried to milk her. And the horse.

He wished the horse were here now, so he could punish it again.

Failed. Couldn't even do a rat's job on a rat's ship.

In the light of a street lamp he saw a familiar figure. Stocky, bandy-legged, swaggering ...

He caught his breath.

It wasn't possible.

His father. Here. Alone. Drunk.

His father, lurching along the street like a common seaman.

Pressing close to the sides of buildings, he followed.

The man stepped into the darkness between the gaslights.

He thought he'd lost him.

No, there he was again. In the next light.

He followed him for a while. Dark—lost, light—found, dark—lost, light—found.

Slowly, he crept closer, an idea coalescing out of the mist in his mind.

Dark—light, dark—light.

The man stepped once more into darkness.

Now!

His hands were around his father's throat. The old man tried to turn, but he clung to him like a grasshopper to a sprig of fresh spring wheat.

The old man clawed at his hands.

Years of brooding hatred gave him strength. He held on.

Like dancers they whirled and spun, now in darkness, now in light. Locked together, father and son, knowing when the dance was done only one of them would be alive.

He didn't plan on it being the old man.

His father was growing weaker. He could feel it. There was a sound like drowning.

His hands tightened.

Tiny bones cracked beneath his fingers.

The old man fell, was silent.

He waited. Reached out. Touched the body.

It was already cooling.

Safe now. Safe to drag him forward, into the light, and spit his victory into the old man's face.

He tugged.

The body was heavier in death. His arms shook with fatigue.

Inch by inch, they moved forward until he could see ...

There was something wrong with his father's face. The features were different, the eyes tilted at an angle, the lips thinner ...

It wasn't his father.

He stood there for a moment, gulping air, stunned. Not his father?

It had to be his father.

But ...

As if a hand had reached down and brushed the confusion from his mind, he understood.

It was his father, all right.

But his father had changed his face.

His father was a devil. A vampire.

His father had called him those names to destroy his soul. His father was ... AFRAID!

Afraid of HIM!

His father knew what he himself had been too young to know.

He was one of God's chosen!

Christ's Avenger!

The Sanctified Man began to laugh. His laughter filled the alleyways and poured out over the water. Flew between the creaking ships that rode at anchor in San Francisco Bay.

Christ's Avenger!

Shhh! They'll hear you! The stupid ones, with their sheep-like brains and their hollow eyes. They'll hear you, and come and find you. Throw you into their stinking jail. Call you murderer ...

... more names ...

try to hang you.

He chuckled, clamped his hand across his mouth to stop the sound.

Hang me. Hang me?

The laugh tickled his throat.

In the distance he heard footsteps.

Running.

Coming toward him.

Moving quickly, he went through the Demon's pockets.

Money!

More money than the rat-brained ship's captain had stolen from him. More money than he had ever before held in his own hands. So it was true. The money—a sign from God that it was true.

The Sanctified Man faded into the darkness. God led him down alleys, led him to the door of the Garden of Forgetfulness.

He gave the skinny man his money. The skinny man gave him the pipe. He sucked at it as an infant sucks its mother's breast.

Toward dawn, God gave him the Word.

≈ ≈ ≈

It must have been the dropping of the wind that awakened her. The silence was deep, like an indrawn breath.

She listened for the wolves, but it was quiet on the roof.

In the room below, Blue Mary snored lightly in her bed.

Daylight filtered through the windows, gray as the light from a television screen glimpsed from the street.

Moving carefully, she slipped from her bed and came down the ladder. The fire had died sometime during the night. The air, the ladder's rungs were like ice.

She crossed the room, hopping from braided rug to braided rug, avoiding the hard, cold floor. There were a few small embers left in the stove. Touching a splinter of wood to a glowing coal, she blew until a flame appeared, then added twigs and sticks, and finally logs.

No paper, no matches. Not bad. A few more days and I'll be as comfortable in the 19th Century as if I'd been born here.

Now, there was a chilling thought.

She froze, realizing ...

... she had begun to accept it. To believe she had stepped out of her own time into this one.

It gave her the willies. And excited her.

Colorado. 1871.

She wished she'd taken more of an interest in history. She didn't even know who was President.

What was it Edith Kesselbaum had told her they always looked for in Mental Hospitals?

"Oriented as to time, place, and person." The Sanity Triad.

Well, she might have a hard time passing that one at the moment.

She glanced through the kitchen window. Everywhere she looked, snow lay deep and thick. If rolling hills had served as landmarks before— and they hadn't, really, not in any truly helpful way—they were useless now. The snow had drifted, reshaping the landscape, making hills where yesterday there had been valleys, ravines of yesterday's hills. And, from

96

the looks of the sky, the storm wasn't over. The calm that had wakened her wasn't the blizzard's ending at all, merely a lull in the fury.

Even as she watched it, the wind came up again. It pushed hard, round snow pellets across the drifts, leaving behind little trails like the trails of crabs in the sand when a wave goes back to sea. New snow began to fall, drawing a curtain across the horizon.

"Good morning," said Blue Mary behind her. "If it is morning."

"It's hard to tell, isn't it?"

"These storms," said Blue Mary with a little sigh. "The light seems to come from everywhere at once. And there's no dawn or dusk. One minute it's day, the next it's black as pitch."

Stoner shuddered. "Looks as if I'm stuck here no matter how I feel about it."

"I'm afraid so, dear." Blue Mary patted her shoulder sympathetically. "I just wish you wouldn't take it so hard. You really could enjoy it, you know."

Enjoy it? Enjoy being lifted out of her life and routines and plopped down in the middle of another life? "Nobody," she said, "is this hard up for adventure."

Blue Mary shrugged on her coat and reached for her boots. "I think we'd better visit the out house while there's still a chance. From the looks of it, things are going to get worse."

"My sentiments exactly." She pulled on her vest and wrapped a blanket around her. "I don't suppose you have snowplows out here."

"I'm afraid not." Blue Mary pulled open the door and plunged into the drifted snow. Stoner followed. "But you'll find we can get around, in our own primitive way. Sleds, you know."

Stoner floundered in a waist-deep drift and struggled to her feet. "You mean horses can get through this stuff?"

Blue Mary glanced back at her. "Goodness sake, Stoner. Can you find something to worry about in everything?"

"Just about."

They reached the back of the house. Blue Mary brushed the snow from a bench and climbed up onto it, shading her eyes with her hand as she peered toward the rapidly-disappearing horizon. "That looks like a thread of smoke from Billy's chimney. I hope everything's all right."

Stoner climbed up beside her to look. "I thought he lived in town, at Dot's."

"Dorothy wouldn't have minded." Mary squinted against the white-silver glare. "But Billy's stubborn. Rather like you. Wants to be independent, don't you know?"

She couldn't see a cabin. Not even a shack. Not even the suggestion of

97

a dwelling under the snow. "Where does he live?"

Blue Mary pointed. "Over there."

She looked, realized the carved-out room in the creek bank lay over there. "In that hole?"

"The dugout. Yes. It's not all that unusual. Many folks who come out here start out with a dugout, then move up to a soddy. The people who made that particular one were washed away three—maybe four years ago."

Stoner looked at her. "That child lives in a hole in a riverbank where people were washed away?" Her voice rose. "What's wrong with people around here?"

Blue Mary touched her arm. "Now, Stoner, you have to understand, it's just how things are."

"I do not have to understand," Stoner said angrily. "And as far as 'how things are' goes, that is ... is unacceptable."

"Stoner ..."

Stoner brushed her off. "Unacceptable." She pulled her blanket tight around her and plunged into the snow.

"Where are you going, dear?"

"To get Billy. The poor kid's probably half frozen and scared to death."

"Don't be silly. Billy can take care of ..."

"I don't care if he can take care of himself. It isn't right." She turned to look back. The sudden motion threw her off balance. She fell flailing in the snow. "I don't care if he's been on his own for the past fifteen years." She thrashed about, trying to get up, spewing billows of snow into the air. "That kid has had a rough life, and it's high time someone made it their business."

Blue Mary trotted over to her, seeming to drift across the snow, and held out her hand. "It's a fine sentiment, Stoner, and certainly no more than I'd expect of you." She hauled her to her feet. "But, if you don't mind a suggestion ..."

Stoner brushed at the snow in her hair and eyelashes. "What?"

"If you must go over there, at least wear the snowshoes."

≈ ≈ ≈

The storm had taken it upon itself to do some genuinely serious, sincere snowing and blowing.

By the time she had gone two hundred yards, she realized she was probably deranged. At the very least an idiot.

Sometimes the wind blew at her back, pushing her forward at a pace that was much too fast for balance and control. Then it whipped around to the front and threw sleet in her eyes. Between times it punched her from the left, then the right, then both at once, and went back to sleet-throwing and back-pushing.

She trudged on, keeping her eyes on the horizon—or what had been the horizon until recently. Every once in a while she glanced behind, to be sure her snowshoe tracks were going on in a straight line.

As far as she could tell, from the four or five prints she could see before the wind whisked them away, she was still headed toward Billy's.

This is easy, she told herself. Remember what Aunt Hermione taught you about going out-of-body. Send your mind to your destination and follow where it tugs you.

Of course, it would help if she had ever actually managed to do it.

She tried to visualize the dugout, clearly and in detail. Aunt Hermione was definite on that point—the more concretely you can visualize what you're looking for, the better your chances of finding it.

The most she'd ever achieved was a feeling of drifting to one side.

Aunt Hermione had been pretty excited about that. Had said she had real talent.

Right.

Well, look, you're not trying to go out-of-body now. Just to Billy's.

Certainly you can visualize Billy.

She tried, but what came to her most clearly wasn't his face, or even his clothes or voice or gestures, but the way it had felt to hold him, back there in town.

It made her stomach feel warm and tingly.

Great. Out on the prairie, probably going to get lost and freeze to death, and all you can think of is titillation.

She tried to make her thoughts wide and flat, to pick up some pull in some direction.

The wind decided to direct a lengthy attack on her face.

"Listen," she said aloud, "I'm trying to do a little good here, so if it's not too much trouble, how about you give me a break?"

The storm paid absolutely no attention to her. Just went on blowing snow into her eyes.

She realized she was taking the weather personally, and that it wasn't such a mentally healthy thing to do.

Cold. Cold like she hadn't felt before.

She was used to New England cold. New England cold was damp and nasty and felt kind of gray. It came on slowly, starting with a few chilly fogs in early November—the advance party, creeping into your bones and setting up camp. Then the Thanksgiving time-out, seeming warm because the troops had been moving in a degree at a time. A truce over Christmas—just so there wouldn't be any danger of snow, so there wouldn't be a

Christmas-card look to things. Then, finally, when everyone's resistance was low and this year's flu fad had become well established, the full January Invasion.

She dug an ice crystal out of the corner of her eye and rammed her hand back into her vest pocket. Her finger tips ached from the cold.

Keep on truckin'.

The January Invasion. January in Boston was ugly. The temperature could be below freezing for weeks at a time, but the snow would find a way to turn to dirt. Trash-laden slush with an invisible sheen of ice, making a trip down the sidewalk a Journey into Terror. Rivulets of scummy water, deeper than they looked. City soot everywhere. In the snow banks. On your clothes. On your skin. In your mouth.

The Armies of Winter in January had one goal in life — to turn everything and everybody in Boston the identical shade of gray.

Winter, the great equalizer.

God, we've got to get out of Boston.

Well, you're out of Boston now. Smell that fresh country air.

She took a deep breath. Cold wind rushed in and turned her lungs to leather and tied a band of iron around her chest.

Not a good idea.

She stopped. The snow was so thick now she could see about as far as you could from the inside of a closet.

You know, McTavish, this was a pretty stupid thing you got yourself into.

Yeah, that's beginning to occur to me.

You don't know beans about winter survival, and you don't know the territory.

You read it here first, folks.

So what are you going to do?

Well, I think maybe I'll stand here and think.

And freeze to death.

It's not a bad way to go, you know. You kind of fall asleep.

Not going at all's better.

True, but it's beginning to occur to me ...

Yes?

OH, SHIT, I'M LOST!!

Wait a minute, wait a minute, let's not panic.

LET'S.

No, she told herself firmly. This is not the way you do things. You do not run wildly off into the night screaming like a banshee. You're Stoner McTavish, named for Lucy B. Stone. You ran away from home at the age of sixteen. You have a useless degree in Journalism. You move hundreds

100

of people from place to place every year. You're the world's authority on lost luggage. You're reputed to have minor psychic powers. You're not afraid to love ...

...well, not very afraid ...

...just a little afraid.

You, Stoner McTavish, are a WARRIOR!

I want to go home.

The sky had turned from silver to slate. Darkness coming on, and coming on fast.

The wind raged, howled, roared.

It reminded her that there were wolves out here.

Wolves. Wolves are nothing more than unevolved dogs.

I like dogs.

Dogs like me.

Therefore, wolves will like me.

Wolves will like me very much.

Wolves will like me very much FOR DINNER.

She spun in a circle, completely lost now.

I'm going to die here. I'm really going to die. I don't know where I am. I don't know when I am.

I'm going to die in the wrong century and nobody will know what happened to me.

I'm going to die with my eyes frozen shut and my hair turned to ice, and the last thing I'll know will be the sound of the wind and the clawing cold and the smell of wood smoke ...

The smell of wood smoke?

THE SMELL OF WOOD SMOKE!!

She sniffed the air, found the direction, and lurched forward.

≈ ≈ ≈

The stove pipe was nearly hidden in the snow, but it was easy to see the great dark crack where the creek cut through the prairie. Stoner took the slope sideways, bumping her way to the bottom. She pushed aside the moth-eaten blanket and threw herself into the room.

Billy sat in a corner, wrapped in a pathetic Indian robe, huddled close to the stove. A faint glow showed through holes in the rusted and pitted iron. His hat was pulled low over his eyes. A single candle, stuck into the dirt in the center of the room, was the only light. The furniture was gone.

The boy looked up, his eyes startled, frightened, red-rimmed. "Jeez," he said. "What're you doin' here?"

"I came to save you," she panted.

He stared at her, at her frozen hair, at the rim of frost bite along her ear-

101

lobes, at her shaking knees and trembling hands. "Gosh," he said, "good thing you showed up when you did. I was just about a goner." He burst into laughter.

"Very funny." She came as close to the stove as her snowshoes would allow.

"I'd offer you a chair," the boy said, "but I just burnt it."

She held her hands out to the pitiful fire. The air was sharp with cold. "Billy, this fire wouldn't even melt ice."

He shrugged.

"You can't stay here."

He turned his face away from her. "Nowhere else to go."

"What about Dot's? Why didn't you stay in town?"

"This here's my home," he said stubbornly.

"This isn't a home."

"Only home I got."

She realized he was right. She was being small-minded. Just because this place was a mud room cut into the side of a creek bank was no reason to put it down.

She squatted to get closer to his level. "I know how you feel, and I didn't mean to be rude. But you could freeze here."

"Might," the boy said petulantly. "Least I'd be somewhere that was mine."

Okay. Here we are, faced once more with adolescent stubbornness. What works with adolescent stubbornness?

Reason?

No way.

Peer pressure?

What peer pressure? To exert peer pressure, you have to be a peer.

Common sense?

Forget it.

Guilt? Look what I've done for you?

Hah.

Inspiration! Appeal to his macho pride!

"Look," she said, "you can stay until Hell freezes over if you want, but it's much too cold for me. I probably wouldn't make it through the night. If I interfered with your privacy, I apologize. But I'm here, and if I try to go back to Blue Mary's alone, I'll get lost. You know your way around out here. Will you help me?"

Billy got to his feet slowly. He looked as if he hurt. His shoulders beneath the denim jacket were thin. His lips were blue. "Might as well," he said, hitching up his pants and feeling for his gun. "Jeez, girls."

Stoner pulled the blanket from the doorway. Wind and snow slammed

102

into the room. The fire blazed for an instant and died. The candle went out. She groped for him in the dark, handed him the blanket. He led the way outside.

"Don't suppose it's occurred to you," the boy muttered as they trudged up the bank, "it ain't gonna be real easy for me to walk in that snow."

He pulled himself up a few strides. She could tell from his ragged breathing he was weak. She followed.

"Billy, when did you eat last?"

"Dunno. When did you?"

"This morning."

"Sometime 'fore that."

She wished she had brought something. Even a chunk of corn bread. Well, at least he wouldn't be heavy if she had to carry him.

They had reached the top. "Over this way," Billy said, and started off into the dark and snow.

Stoner grabbed him. "Whoa. Let's be sensible about this, okay?"

"Sensible?" He laughed sharply. "You come all the way out here in this dog turd of a night, and you're talkin' about sensible?"

"We can't just go plunging off. This snow's deep in spots. You don't have snowshoes, do you?"

"I did. Burned 'em."

"Well, then, we have to have a plan."

He stood and looked out over the expanse of snow. "So what're we gonna do?" he asked, typically male helpless.

Stoner made an effort to control her temper. "I think we should walk together where we can. And when it's too deep, I'll carry you."

She waited for his indignant explosion. It didn't come.

"Think you can?" he asked after a moment. There was something in his voice. Fear?

"If I can't, I guess we'll freeze to death, won't we?"

"We could go back to my place."

"Where there's no food and no heat. It could be days before this lets up." She reached out to touch him. "Nobody's going to come looking for us, Billy. We're all we have."

They set out, Billy following in her snowshoe tracks.

It was rough going. She was already tired, and the wind had picked up. Light flakes swirled around them in a vortex, erasing any sense of distance or direction. Billy seemed to know where they were going, would tug at her blanket from time to time to correct her.

She hoped he really did know.

Maybe he was right in the first place. Maybe they should go back to the dugout.

103

No, it was certain death back there.

Trust his knowledge of this place.

She trudged on.

If my Higher Spirit brought me all this way through time and space just to freeze to death on the Colorado prairie, my Spirit and I are coming to a parting of the ways.

I mean, Colorado isn't even a State yet, for God's sake.

Billy corrected her direction of travel.

I don't believe it. I'm crawling across the frozen wastes and complaining because Colorado isn't a State?

All right, she had accepted it. She had, indeed, somehow traveled back in time, just casually crossed the street on an errand of mercy or whatever. To do what? This?

She nodded to herself. Yep, that made sense.

Made sense?

Apparently, freezing to death has a serious impact on one's mental capacities.

If she was going to warp out of time whenever someone needed a traveling companion in a blizzard, she was going to be doing a lot of warping.

It had to be more than this.

They came to a place where the snow was deep, high as Billy's hips. He tried to push through it, and fell. She gave him a hand up and could tell, by the feebleness of his grip, that he was weakening.

"This is it, kid," she said. "Piggy-back time. Hang around my neck and wrap the blankets around us. It'll keep us both warm."

He surprised her by doing it without argument. She felt his arms go around her, felt his body press against her back. He was warmer than she'd expected. Very warm. Unnaturally warm. Feverish.

"Don't you feel well?" she asked over her shoulder.

"I'm okay."

"Tell me the truth, Billy."

"Not so great, I guess."

"What's wrong?"

"I dunno."

Oh, God, let him hang in there until we get to Blue Mary's.

It should be soon. They'd been walking for—well, to tell the truth, she hadn't the slightest idea how long they'd been walking. On a normal, sunny day like yesterday—was it only yesterday? ... it shouldn't take more than half an hour to get from Blue Mary's to Billy's. But in the dark, in the snow, with her sense of time and direction completely scrambled ...

The boy seemed to get heavier.

"Billy?"

104

"Huh?" he said, startled and sleepy.

"Don't you pass out on me now, Buddy. I need you."

"Yeah. Okay."

She walked a few more steps, felt him go limp again. "Billy!"

He didn't answer.

She shook her shoulders. "Damn it, Billy!"

He started to slip.

"Oh, shit."

He fell away from her and crumpled in the snow.

Stoner stood looking down at him. The wind swirled curtains of white around them. The darkness was solid.

She tried to lift him, and realized how weak she had become. Couldn't even raise him enough to get a good grip. She slipped out of her snow shoes and sat on them. Clumsily, she pulled the boy close to her, arranged one blanket beneath them, covered them both with the other. It seemed to take her forever, and exhausted the last of her strength. His breathing was shallow. She felt for his pulse, but it was hard to read with the wind shrieking and tearing at her.

As soon as it's light, she thought, I'll be stronger. We'll get up and go on. I'll feel better after a little rest. I know I will.

"Don't you die on me, boy," she whispered. "Don't you dare die."

His hat was beyond her reach. It didn't seem right, to make him lie here in the snow and wind without his hat. He'd hate to die without his hat.

But to get it she'd have to move out from under him, crawl through the snow, crawl back, lift him, cover them ...

She couldn't do it.

Tears of weakness and frustration and impotence leaked from her eyes. They froze in her eyelashes.

"I'm sorry," she whispered.

Chapter 7

She wasn't sure when she first became aware of the white wolf watching them.

The wind had dropped a little. She must have dozed off. Snow lay nearly half an inch deep over her arms and hands. In a flash of panic, she brushed it away as if it were radioactive.

Billy was very still in her arms. She pressed her face to his chest. It rose and fell gently. His lungs bubbled like a spring.

Oh, God.

She looked back toward the wolf.

The wolf smiled.

She remembered reading that wolves smile at their prey just before they kill it.

She hoped the present situation was the exception to the rule.

They stared at each other.

Billy stirred, opened his eyes. "What?" he murmured.

"Nothing." She stroked his hair. "Only a wolf. It seems to be just watching."

The boy grunted. "Always hang around when someone's dying." His eyelids fluttered and closed.

No!

Fear made her angry. She turned on the wolf."Get out of here, you mangy, overgrown mongrel. You can't have this boy."

The wolf looked around, as if wondering who she was talking to.

"Look," she said, "we made an agreement. Thousands of years ago. You hunt, we cook. You find the game, we let you sleep by the fire. Remember? You keep the bad guys away, we invite you into the cave. But we don't eat each other, right? Friends, right? Friends are friendly, right?"

She hoped word hadn't filtered back from the future regarding what men had done to Wolf's descendents. She had the feeling it would render all treaties null and void.

She reached down, surreptitiously, and grasped the butt of Billy's gun. She didn't want to shoot it. Of all the forms of killing she knew of, she hated the senseless hunting down of animals for sport the most. But if it came down to whose life it was ...

Please, she begged the wolf silently, don't make me do it.

The wolf edged closer. She could almost touch it. It was a beautiful creature, nearly as white as the snow. Its fur was clean and seemed to glow in the near-darkness. A small wolf, not much bigger than a large German Shepherd—which, under the circumstances, was quite large enough, thank you. Its eyes were yellow-brown. The nose was coal black. It smiled again, showing black lips and gums.

The teeth were formidable.

She tried to read its attitude, but couldn't.

I really should brush up on my Wolf-as-a-second-language.

"Well, Mr. or Ms. Wolf, one of us has to make the first move."

As if it had understood her, the wolf lowered itself to its belly, rested its head on its paws, and studied her.

Stoner studied it back.

The wolf cocked its head, then stretched its front legs and eased itself a few feet closer. The ridges above its eyes formed comical bumps. It gave a huge sigh and lowered its head again.

She ought to try to chase it away.

She picked up a handful of snow and tossed it in the wolf's general direction and said "Git" the way one might if one were in control of the situation and fearless.

Which one weren't.

Wolf merely lowered its head in a hurt kind of way and gazed into her eyes.

It was trying to put thoughts in her mind. The way dogs are always trying to put thoughts in your mind. Thoughts like DINNER and WALK and GO-FOR-A-RIDE and LOVE.

What were Wolf's thoughts?

Probably not GO-FOR-A-RIDE.

Probably not LOVE. We haven't even been introduced.

Wolf crawled a little closer.

"Listen," Stoner said, "I'm not going to hurt you. You don't have to demean yourself."

Wolf got to its feet and trotted boldly over to her.

Which was a terribly unsettling thing for Wolf to do under the circumstances.

The animal pushed its nose close to her hand.

She decided not to move.

Slowly, it maneuvered its snout beneath her wrist and shoved upward. The motion placed her hand on its neck.

"Okay," she said, and buried her fingers in its fur. It was warm and soft. "Okay, I get it. This is a friendly encounter, right?"

Wolf put its forehead close to hers and panted. It had terrible breath.

"Good grief," Stoner said, "don't you floss?"

Come on, if you lived on dead and rotten things, you'd have bad breath, too.

Come to think of it, she did live on dead things. Rotten things, too, if you counted little delights like Brie cheese and mushrooms. Fermented things like beer and wine. Things plucked from the ground, things that grew in dirt, things ...

"Listen," she said to Wolf, "human beings are disgusting. Don't get involved."

Wolf smiled.

It lowered its head and took a corner of the blanket in its mouth and looked up at her and moved its eyebrow bumps around.

What does a wolf do with your clothes in the middle of a blizzard?

Anything it wants.

It began to tug at the blanket, pulling Billy away from her.

That was going too far. Stoner gripped the boy tightly and got to her feet. The blankets fell to the ground.

"Leave him alone!"

Wolf snatched a blanket and trotted off into the storm.

"Fine. Good riddance. You're nothing but a thief. THIEF!"

The animal trotted back to her and worked its eyebrows again. It began backing up, trailing the blanket in front of her.

"Go on, get out of here."

It growled in an insistent kind of way and backed up a little more.

"I mean it. We have serious problems here."

Wolf sat in the snow and wagged its tail and appeared to think. Suddenly it leapt to its feet and disappeared into the night, leaving the blanket behind.

The boy's body was steaming with fever. She had to do something. She retrieved the blanket and shook him.

"Billy. Wake up."

His eyelids fluttered open, then closed.

He lapsed back into unconsciousness.

Twisting her body, she managed to maneuver him onto her back again. His arms hung lifeless over her shoulders.

The wind screamed in her ears.

Walk. It doesn't matter what direction. Just pick one at random and walk.

Her snow shoes felt like lead as she shuffled forward. Every step took all her strength.

Step.

You can do it.

Step.

You can do it.

Step.

I can't do it.

Maybe fire the gun. Maybe someone would hear ...

The wind screamed. No one could hear anything over that. And there was no one to hear it, even if they could. Miles of snow and shrieking wind between her and the nearest house.

Except Blue Mary's.

Wherever it was.

A sharp, insistent bark behind her.

She turned.

Wolf was back, had dropped an object in the snow at her feet.

She wiped frozen tears from her eyes with an aching hand and peered at it. Snow blew into her face. Fatigue and wind blurred her vision. She shook her head.

The wolf picked up the object and moved closer.

Stoner bent down.

It was the pot of rosemary from Blue Mary's back porch.

She began to laugh. "Good Wolf. Beautiful Wolf."

The wolf went into a conniption fit of barking and wagging and eyebrow rolling.

"World's Greatest Wolf."

It jumped up, nearly knocking her over, and licked her face.

"I swear, I'll never make fun of Lassie again."

Wolf sat down and gave her a quizzical look.

"That was after your time. Well, let's go home." She started in the direction from which the wolf had come. "And don't forget the flower pot. Blue Mary'd kill us."

≈ ≈ ≈

He'd pushed Toby as hard as he could, fighting the blizzard, hoping to come to a town, or a farm, or even a band of friendly Indians. His eyebrows had filled with caked sleet. His two week beard was white. The bandanna he'd tied around his mouth and nose to try to block the cold was so hard he could have carved buffalo meat with the edge of it.

Tobe's strength was about gone. Cullum could hear the horse's wheez-

109

ing, gasping breath, like human sobs. Could almost hear the crackle of ice crystals forming on his lungs.

They had to stop.

He grunted a gentle "whoa", and slid from Toby's back.

Might as well die here as anywhere.

But he surely did hate to have it end this way, on the border between Kansas and Colorado, where nobody knew him. Where there'd be no one to grieve.

He supposed they'd just plant him where they found him, when they found him. Maybe say a few words over his bones. He'd done that often enough for other fellas, and felt as much sadness as he could for them, his unknown brothers in loneliness. But it wasn't like having someone remember you a little—some funny way you had of standing while you were thinking hard, or a bawdy story you'd told once. Even something mean or shameful you'd done. At least it'd be personal.

Cullum looked around. Christ, he didn't want to die out here.

Nearby he could just make out a slanting bit of ground. It might give them a little shelter. The way the snow was piling up against it, maybe they could find a drift, hollow out a tight cave, and keep each other warm.

He held on tight to Toby's reins and struggled forward. They'd be separated in an instant in this blindness. And, live or die, he wanted to be close to his old friend.

It helped a little, the hole he dug in the snow. At least they were out of the wind, even though the entrance drifted shut almost before they were inside.

He left the saddle outside, coaxed the horse to lie down, pushed himself tight against Toby's side, and covered the two of them with the saddle blanket.

Cullum felt warm sleep come close. He guessed he ought to pray, though he'd never been much of a praying man, and wasn't sure how to go about it. Shucks, he wasn't even sure who to pray to, or what to ask for. "Well, old fellow," he said at last, "you've been one heck of a pal. I hope we wake up in the same place."

He reckoned that'd have to do for praying.

≈ ≈ ≈

It didn't take more than half an hour to reach the cabin, but she was nearly done in. Billy hadn't regained consciousness. She could tell he was still alive by the way the heat percolated off of his body, but it looked serious. And, considering that they were without medical facilities—except for the legendary alcoholic Dr. Kreuger ...

He should be in a hospital. Definitely a nine-one-one situation.

Come to think of it, she wasn't feeling too great herself. Her eyes were dry. Her joints ached in a minor but anxiety-producing way. Time and space stretched oddly. She'd start a thought—nothing terribly profound, something like "I wonder what's on TV tonight"—and by the time it had finished unwinding, it would seem as if hours had passed.

Sort of like being stoned, without the profundity.

She hoped she wasn't catching whatever Billy had. Some kind of flu. That's what it felt like. Last winter's flu.

She wondered if immunity went backward through time.

She wondered if they had different viruses a hundred years ago.

She wondered about all those headstones she had seen in the Pioneer's Graveyard in that town not far from Denver, where she'd stopped to stretch her legs. Young people, the dates of death clumped in years. Cholera, she had assumed. Or typhoid. Some relatively rare and nearly extinct disease.

But what if it had been flu?

What kinds of flu did they have back then? Back now. Back whatever.

Hong Kong?

Spanish?

Singapore?

Thinking made her head hurt. At least, she thought it was thinking that made her head hurt. She hoped it was thinking ...

Wolf was still with her, trotting on ahead, looking over its shoulder from time to time in a worried kind of way.

Lights. Cabin lights.

The wolf shot forward, bounced against the front door.

The door opened. Light spilled like honey across the snow. The wolf threw itself against Blue Mary.

Mary laughed and pulled its ears. "Stop that, you silly thing. And give me my rosemary."

She took the pot and inspected it for damage.

Wolf sat and wagged its tail.

Satisfied, she placed the pot in the snow. "Now, Miss, what have you done with our friends?"

"Mary!" Stoner called.

Blue Mary peered out into the storm. "Stoner? Thank the Goddess! I was afraid this old wolf had taken it into her head to make a meal of you."

Wolf gave a disgusted snort and flounced off into the darkness.

"I think you insulted her," Stoner said. She slipped out of her snowshoes and stepped through the door into warmth and light.

"She'll forgive me," said Blue Mary. "Animals seldom hold a grudge. Probably more highly evolved than we are. Did she annoy you in any way?"

111

"She was a perfect lady." She let Billy slip from her shoulders. Blue Mary caught him.

"He's awfully sick," Stoner said. "I thought we wouldn't make it."

"Oh, the poor child." Blue Mary brushed the snow from Billy's back and struggled to unwind the blankets.

Stoner helped her.

Together, they managed to get the boy to the bed, pulled off his shoes, and covered him with a deep quilt.

Blue Mary felt his forehead, examined his eyes and fingernails. She took a strand of his hair and rolled it thoughtfully between her fingers. She nodded, then bent down, forced his mouth open, and sniffed his breath. "Influenza," she said authoritatively. "Could be a lot worse."

"Really?" Stoner went to stand by the stove. She could feel the blood returning to her fingertips. It was painful. "He seemed nearly dead to me."

"Influenza can be fatal, of course, if you don't catch it in time. But not as bad as meningitis, or typhoid, or ..."

"Thank you," Stoner said wryly. "It's always a treat to look on the bright side."

Blue Mary glanced toward her. She came forward and peered into Stoner's eyes. "You don't look well, yourself. Your eyes are glassy."

"To tell you the truth, I don't feel great."

The older woman took her hands. Stoner winced. Her ear lobes and nose began to burn.

"Frostbite, too." She shook her head. "You young people are so impulsive."

"It's a good thing we are," Stoner said testily. "Or he'd be dead."

Blue Mary smiled. "Of course, dear. But I can't help wishing you'd gone over there a little better prepared. At the very least, that knapsack of yours could have carried something hot to drink."

"You're right. I'm sorry."

"Well, now," Blue Mary said, and patted her cheek gently. "Let's get you out of those wet things and I'll concoct something for your frostbite."

She stripped out of her shirt and jeans, wrapped herself in a blanket, and stood shivering in front of the fire. Blue Mary brought her a flowered night gown of soft flannel. She slipped it on, too grateful for the warmth and dryness to be self-conscious. Her head felt like a chunk of cement. Her vision was fuzzy, as if there were something in her eyes. She brushed at them, but it didn't help.

Billy lay across the room on the bed, unmoving. As soon as she could get up the energy, she thought, she'd go see how he was. As soon as she got up the energy.

Blue Mary stirred boiling water into a baked earthenware pot contain-

112

ing dried herbs. She wrinkled her nose. "A vile concoction, but it's the best we can do."

Stoner brushed her hair out with her fingers, letting the hot, dry air from the stove eat up the dampness. "I guess you don't have stuff like penicillin and antibiotics, huh?"

"No," said Blue Mary. "And, to be perfectly honest, I'm not looking forward to that time. We've managed to accomplish quite a lot, you know, with Nature, intuition, and old-fashioned kindness." She tasted the contents of the pot, frowned, and added a pinch of something from a corked clay jar. "Not that I'm against progress—though I suppose I am, a little. But it seems so easy to lose our sense of values."

"Yeah," Stoner said. It took a lot of effort to say that much. It took a lot of effort even to listen, and made her dizzy.

Blue Mary checked the pot again and judged it satisfactory. She poured the brew into two large mugs and passed one to Stoner. "Drink all of this if you can. It'll help." She took the other mug and went to where Billy lay.

"Do you need help?" Stoner asked.

"We all need help," Blue Mary said with a little laugh. "But in the sense you mean it, no, I think I can manage."

Stoner took a sip of the hot liquid and grimaced. It was bitter, and smelled of small, damp places that haven't been opened in years.

"That's the valerian," Blue Mary explained, reading her thoughts. "It'll relax you. And it masks odors that are even worse. Frightful, isn't it?"

Stoner drank again. "Anything this bad must be good for you."

"A useful plant, valerian." She slipped her arm under Billy's head, propping him against her chest. "Very helpful against insomnia and menstrual cramps. And it will absolutely rid a house of fleas." She tilted the mug against Billy's lips. Stoner couldn't tell if he was drinking. "Of course, rodents are obsessively attracted to it. There are those who believe the Pied Piper of Hamlin actually carried valerian in his pockets."

She forced down another swallow and tried not to imagine the stuff coming out through her pores and drawing every rat, mouse, squirrel, woodchuck, and muskrat in a twenty-mile radius to lick her skin.

At least opossums didn't qualify as rodents.

God is Good.

She managed to shuffle over to the armchair and sit down. The mug felt as heavy as a bucket of sand. She thought her neck would break from trying to support her head.

I'm sick, she thought.

It felt as if the force of gravity had increased ten-fold. Every movement, even blinking her eyes, took as much strength as she could muster.

This really isn't good. I could get stuck here. What if the chance comes to get back home and I miss it? What if I'm too sick to take it? What if ...?

"Dear," said Blue Mary gently, "you're spilling your drink."

Stoner opened her eyes.

"Finish up, now."

She felt the mug taken from her and pressed to her lips. She was too weak to resist. She let the warm liquid flow into her mouth.

"Swallow, dear."

It hurt. Like burning claws drawn down her throat.

She swallowed again, and the burning spread up into the back of her nose and ears. She wondered vaguely if Mary had given her acid to drink. Or maybe something in the herbs had a funny reaction to something in the clay mug, like orange juice and that Mexican pottery some years back. Or maybe ...

"That's good," said Blue Mary, and took away the mug. "Now your hands."

She tried to hold them out, but couldn't move. She felt Blue Mary take them, one at a time, smoothing something onto her fingertips and ears, touching her nose. The burning in her skin faded to a distant echo.

"I'm sorry, Mary," she said weakly. "I didn't mean to ..."

She fell into unconsciousness.

≈ ≈ ≈

It was nearly dawn. The Sanctified Man watched as the eastern sky shaded to gray, then steely blue. The snow had stopped. The day would be clear.

He cracked his knuckles nervously. He should accomplish great things today. There was much to do. The storm would keep the Stranger inside the Witch's house, no doubt. But that was all right. He needed time to prepare. He must purify himself of the scum of his worldly incarnation. A bath. The suit of clothes he had stolen in San Francisco lay untouched in a trunk in the attic. He considered ordering his mousey wife to wash and press them, but if she were unclean ...

No, he couldn't take chances. He had to do it himself. And sharpen the Jesus knife, and pray.

So much to do.

Something troubled him. Held him back.

The Word spoke of a Gathering of Witches. If he destroyed the Beast now, the Gathering would never happen.

That might be good.

On the other hand ...

If he waited until the Beast had called them all together ...

He could kill them ALL.

114

He frowned, wondering how many there'd be, and if they'd be too much for him. But with God's help ...

He leafed quickly through the rough ledger in which he'd copied down the words God dictated to him. Searching for instructions, a suggestion.

Nothing.

Would God leave him in this predicament, abandon him at the moment of his greatest need?

God, Who had brought him to this particular place at this particular time to do His work?

Nonsense.

He grinned. There'd be a way. GOD would show him how. When the time came, he only had to be where they were, and GOD would step in and destroy them. He only had to open the door.

The Sanctified Man thought about the carnage, the spilled blood and broken bones, the torn flesh. Thought about it and licked his lips.

He wanted to look at the Beast's picture again. To imagine how It would look, too see what the townspeople would see when the bastard was unmasked.

He went to the fireplace and pried the loose stone from its bed. The Witch's Book, still wrapped in silk, lay deep in the darkness. He drew it out and leafed through the unbound pages that the witch called her Tarot.

There It was. The horned, taloned, bearded, winged Beast. Red-eyed and terrible. And beneath the true image, Its human disguise. The naked man/woman, the sexes portrayed separately but linked by chains that showed they were one, and one with the Beast...

Just the way the Bastard had appeared to him that day. The day he hid by the creek and watched the Bastard wash itself...

And above them all, the reversed sign of the Witch.

And the Devil's number, XV. Fifteen, the Bastard's age.

Glorious, glorious, glorious.

≈ ≈ ≈

Dreams.

Fever dreams.

She ran through a field of wildflowers, the sun warm and yellow on her body. Queen Anne's lace, purple cone flower, blue gentian, wild geranium and Columbine danced and swayed beneath a high blue sky. There was a smell of peaches and wild raspberry in the air.

A cloud passed over, and suddenly it changed. The flowers transformed to thorny brush that tore at her legs and ankles. The breeze brought the reek of rotting vegetation. It stung her nose and made the bile rise in her throat.

She looked around, realized she was lost.

115

The tangled brush was growing. Twisting itself into a fence of thorns. Blocking her way. Spiny tendrils worked their way between and around one another. They grew higher, and shut out the light.

Now she was in a tunnel of thorns, the sky far away and gray with storm clouds. The wind rose. The rotten smell grew stronger, more than vegetation, overlaid with the sickly sweet odor of decaying flesh. She tried to climb. Razor-sharp spines tore her hands to ribbons.

Too late, she realized the thorns oozed a cloudy yellowish substance. Her hands were covered with it. It seeped into her open wounds. Acid. She felt it burn through the skin, the layers of muscle and tendon and nerve, down to and through the bones themselves.

She screamed.

"It's just a dream, Stoner," a gentle voice said. "You'll be all right."

Strong arms lifted her and pressed a cup of water to her dry, cracked lips. Strong hands cradled her head against a large, soft bosom.

She tried to open her eyes. They were stuck. "Aunt Hermione?"

"Don't try to talk," Aunt Hermione said. "You need your strength."

Her aunt smelled of clove and nutmeg. "Did you quit smoking?" she murmured.

"Shhh."

A soft, cool cloth touched her face, wiping the stickiness from her eyes. It felt fresh and clean.

She drifted back to sleep.

Someone pursued her through an unknown city. The streets were dark. Lighted windows glowed flatly, self-contained rectangles of white that cast no radiance to the sidewalks below.

She tried to appear casual. To get to safety before the shadowy figure behind her knew she was aware of his presence.

The trouble was, she didn't know where safety was.

City. Should be a police station. Should be people hanging out on steps and fire escapes, drinking cheap wine. Going through trash barrels. Homeless people everywhere.

Everywhere but here.

The footsteps behind her were sharp and steady.

She noticed she had begun to pick up her pace, and slowed herself deliberately.

She passed an alley and stole a quick peek. Nobody.

Come on, come on. You have to be here.

She knew they'd help her. At least hide her.

The footsteps sounded nearer. Rhythmic tap of hard leather on cement.

116

Moving faster.

She tried to lengthen her stride without increasing her speed.

The footsteps came on faster.

She started to run.

Don't look back. Keep moving.

The footsteps were closer, just behind her.

She stopped. Got ready to fight. Turned.

No one was there.

Bewildered, she peered into the darkness. Nothing. Silence.

She looked around.

Looked up.

The thing fell on her from the sky.

Gwen touched her face with satin hands. Smoothed her hair. Stoner groped for her.

Gwen held her.

≈ ≈ ≈

He could feel the rumble through his sleep, like an earthquake coming, or a boulder rolling down a mountain the way they did back in Tennessee. But he wasn't in Tennessee, he reminded himself. He was in Kansas Territory, right on the verge of Colorado, and that was a terrible place to be. Bad enough to live in. Ghastly for dying.

The ground trembled, beating like a giant heart. Cullum opened his eyes.

Everything around him was white. Brilliant white light that stabbed his eyes.

They were having some kind of earthquake, that was certain. But it looked as if day had come.

He couldn't hear Toby breathing.

Anxiety sent his blood racing. He got up, pressed his face against the horse's side.

It was there, beneath the pounding from above he could just make out the thump-THUMP of the horse's heart.

Cullum tugged at the bridle. "C'mon, old boy. I think we better get ourselves out of here."

The pounding went on and on. Come to think on it, that didn't sound like any earthquake he'd ever heard of.

He tugged again. Toby raised his head, looked at him, lay back down.

The horse was weak, needed food. He had to find food for him.

But where? Even if they could get out of here, and weren't mowed down by that monster pounding out there, every bit of grass for a hundred miles would be covered with snow.

117

Damn that thing, huffing away up there. What the hell was ...?

His mind cleared in an instant.

It was a locomotive.

He scrambled around to Toby's head. Jerked roughly on the reins. "Git up, you old bag of bones, you doggoned useless creature." He was laughing and crying at the same time. "We're gonna make it."

Toby seemed to understand. His head shot up. He rolled over, tucked his feet under his chest, and with one mighty push launched himself upward.

His head broke through the snow above. Cullum, still clutching the reins, flew clear of the snow cave.

The sky was clear and blue. The air was frigid. Sunlight blinded him. He closed his eyes for a second against the light, then opened them slowly, carefully.

There was the locomotive, stalled in a snowdrift, but still chugging and snorting. And the passenger cars, folks leaning out the windows, wiping clear spots through the frost to stare at him.

The engineer came running toward him, shovel in hand. The fireman and brakeman glanced up and went back to clearing the tracks.

"Jesus Christ, man," the engineer yelled. "You scared us all half to death. Where the hell did you come from?"

Cullum didn't reply. He was already wading through the snow, Tobe at his side, headed toward the next-to-last car. The one where the horses stood in warm, hay-lined stalls and buried their noses in buckets of oats.

≈ ≈ ≈

There was day, and night, and day again.

Someone changed her nightgown and wiped her face. Someone helped her to the bathroom.

No, not the bathroom. It wasn't a toilet. It felt like ...a potty?

Had she only dreamed growing up?

She thought hard, tried to understand. She counted to a hundred. She couldn't be a child. If she were a child, she wouldn't be able to count to a hundred.

A bedpan. She was in a hospital.

But the air was icy, too cold for a hospital.

They took her back to her bed. It was warm. Warm and hard, and made a funny crackling sound as she lay back down.

Terrible facilities for a hospital. It must be the Medicaid cuts. Someone should report it.

She drifted off to sleep again.

118

Water was rushing past her head. A river of water. Pouring. Falling in cascades on rock and hard-packed ground.

Stoner opened her eyes. The light was gray. Just above her head, so close she could touch them if she had the strength, were the rough plank boards of the roof of Blue Mary's cottage.

It was raining. Raining as if the heavens had split. As if someone threw buckets of water at the house. As if someone had turned a fire hose on the roof.

Maybe the house was burning.

She tried to get up, but she was too weak.

She lay back in sleep.

Voices.

She listened. The rain had stopped. People were talking, somewhere below her. She couldn't make out their words. But she recognized the voices. Blue Mary and ...

She couldn't believe it, but there was no mistaking that velvet tone and southern lilt.

Gwen.

Gwen here? Now?

Then she remembered ...how long ago? Days? Weeks? Gwen touching her. Holding her.

She felt a great, aching yearning. "Gwen," she said. Her voice was little more than a whisper. "Gwen."

They couldn't hear her. Their voices went on.

She gathered all her strength. "Gwen."

The rhythm of their conversation didn't break.

"Please. I need you." Tears gathered in her eyes, blurring her vision.

The voices fell silent. They were listening.

She couldn't stop crying, couldn't talk through her tears.

She heard the creak of the ladder. She was coming. Gwen was coming.

Gwen came close to her. Touched her face, felt her forehead. Gwen's hands, soft and strong, took Stoner's hand.

Oh, God, she loved those hands.

She opened her eyes.

Billy smiled down at her. "How ya' doin'?"

"Billy?"

"You surely did scare us."

Stoner frowned, confused. "Billy?"

The boy gave an embarrassed little laugh. "I thought I was sick, but oh, boy. You were really in a bad way."

She shook her head. It looked like Billy. But it didn't talk like Billy.

119

"Who are you?" she asked at last.

"Well," Billy said, "that's something Mary says we have to talk about. Soon as you're up to it."

"She's conscious," Blue Mary called from the bottom of the ladder. "She's up to it."

"I wish someone would explain something," Stoner said irritably. The sensation of Gwen was fading into memory, leaving her empty and alone.

Billy ran his fingers across Stoner's knuckles. Exactly the way Gwen would. She closed her eyes.

The boy's hand tightened on hers. "You faint again?"

"No, I haven't fainted." She withdrew her hand from his. "Please don't do that."

"I'm sorry."

There was no need to be hard on him. "It reminds me of someone I miss very much, that's all."

"Gwen?"

She looked at him. "How do you know about Gwen?"

He shrugged. "You talked a lot about someone named Gwen. When you were in the fever."

"Are you going to tell her?" Blue Mary called. "Or am I?"

"Okay, okay," Billy said. He hesitated, fingering the edge of the quilt. "Look, I didn't mean any harm, but I've been lying to you."

Her heart skipped a beat. "You have?"

"See, I couldn't let you know, because ...well, it's kind of complicated."

"You can tell her the complicated part later," Blue Mary prompted. "Say what you have to say and have done with it."

"Jeez," Billy said, "she certainly can be rough at times."

"Runs in the family." She looked at him expectantly.

"Well, what I got to tell you is ...well, I'm not fifteen years old." He sat in silence.

"That's it?"

"Mostly."

"But everything else you told me, about killing your father and not being able to read and write, and wanting to be a teacher? That was all true?"

"Pretty much."

Blue Mary shook the ladder. "Darn you, Billy. Don't make me come up there."

"And-I'm-not-a-boy. There."

Stoner stared. "You're not a boy."

Billy blushed deeply. "That's right. I'm a girl. Okay?"

A girl? "Okay."

"I'm twenty-five, not fifteen. Okay?"

She felt the grin spread over her face. "Okay."

"But you can't tell anyone. They'll send me back if they find out."

"Back where?"

"Tennessee."

"I thought you said you were from Illinois."

"Well, for cryin' out loud," Billy said loudly. "Tennessee, Illinois, they're both back east." She shook her head. "Do you have to be so precise?"

Stoner touched the woman's hand. "I didn't mean to upset you."

Billy pulled her legs up and wrapped her arms around them and rested her head on her knees. Without the hat to distract her, she could see how delicate Billy's features were. Especially her eyes. Her eyes were dark blue shading to lavender, the color of a twilight sky reflected in a mountain lake. Her hair was light brown, with strands of red and blonde. It was chopped off shoulder-length, the way the few men she had seen in Tabor wore theirs. "See, if they find me, and they think I'm a boy, maybe they'll just shoot me dead. But if they find out I'm a girl ..."

"Woman," Stoner corrected.

Billy looked at her. "What's the difference?"

"Where I come from, we call females your age 'women'. It's a sign of respect."

"Kinda weird," Billy said. "But interesting."

"If they find out you're a woman, what will they do?"

"Put me in an insane asylum. See, girls ...women don't go around killing men unless they're insane."

Stoner stared at her. "Do you really believe that?"

"Of course I don't," Billy said huffily. "I think you're insane if you don't kill them. Their skin's too rough, and they smell bad."

"I see."

"But they'd call me crazy, anyway." She glared at Stoner in a way that Stoner found absolutely charming. "And I'd rather be dead than in an insane asylum."

"I suppose you're right," Stoner said. "Though it does seem to me you'd meet some pretty interesting women."

Billy snorted. "Think I want to be treated like that? Have you seen what they do to you in those places?"

"Actually, no. I'm not from ...around here."

"Yeah," Billy said. "Mary says you're from the future or something."

Stoner nodded. "That seems to be the general consensus."

Billy leaned close to her and dropped her voice. "Listen, does Mary ever strike you as kind of strange?"

121

Her hair touched Stoner's face. It was soft and silky and cool. Without thinking, she reached up and ran her hand through it. So much like Gwen's hair.

Billy smiled at her.

Stoner pulled her hand away quickly. "Yes," she stammered. "A little strange, but I guess you get used to it ... her."

"I hear you up there," Blue Mary shouted from below. "Watch what you say."

Billy turned and looked down the ladder. "I said you're strange," she called to Mary.

"And lucky for you I am," Blue Mary said. "Now, don't wear her out."

Billy looked at Stoner with a sweet worried look. "How are you feeling?"

"Just tired," Stoner said. "I'll be all right."

"When you get well, maybe I could take you out for a drive." She blushed. "You know, show you the scenery. It's real pretty down by the river."

"That would be nice," Stoner said. "I didn't get a chance to appreciate it last time."

Billy laughed. She had a warm, easy laugh. Stoner tried to push herself up on one elbow. Her strength gave out and she fell back. "How long have I been like this?"

"Four or five days. We were getting a little nervous. Well, I was. I thought you might be done for."

She remembered snatches of dreams. Remembered someone changing her nightgown. Remembered ..."Was it you that ... I mean, did you ... you know." She fingered the nightgown. "This."

"I helped."

Oh, shit.

Stoner groaned.

"What's the matter?" Billy asked.

"I'm a little self-conscious about ... about strangers seeing me undressed."

"I don't know why," Billy said. "You have a beautiful body."

Stoner pulled the quilt over her face.

"Besides," Billy went on, a laugh in her voice, "I'd hardly consider us strangers, would you?"

"I don't know. Would you?"

"You don't remember?"

"Remember what?"

Billy tugged the quilt from her head and peeked at her. "Guess I'll have to tell you sometime. When you're up to it."

122

She couldn't bear it. "Mary!!"

Blue Mary's face appeared at the top of the ladder. "Now, you stop tormenting that child," she said to Billy. "She needs her strength."

"What's she talking about?" Stoner begged.

"She gave you a bath," Blue Mary said. She shook her head. "I really don't know what all the fuss is about."

"You gave me a bath?!"

"Yeah," Billy said, and grinned. "I did everything for you that needed doing."

Stoner ducked back under the covers.

"Hey," Billy said.

"Let me die."

She tugged at the covers. "Come on, Stoner."

"No."

"I didn't mean any harm."

"No!"

"I told you not to tell her," Blue Mary said. "I told you she'd be embarrassed. Now leave her alone and help me with dinner."

Stoner kept her eyes closed until she was certain they'd gone. She saw me naked. She gave me a bath.

Oh, don't be silly. There's nothing wrong with that. Lots of people have seen me naked.

Yeah? Name five.

Gwen, and Aunt Hermione, and ...

And?

... my parents.

They don't count.

And my first lover, and my lover before Gwen ...

So what's the big deal?

She's a stranger and she saw me naked.

From the room below she could hear Blue Mary's voice. "Honest to Goddess, Billy. You're as silly as an adolescent in love."

≈ ≈ ≈

The next day she was able to come downstairs, even though it took all her strength. Her knees and arms felt like wet Kleenex.

Billy watched her, grinning as if Stoner's recovery were her own personal achievement.

"God," Stoner said as she dropped onto the hard seat at the table. "I can't believe how weak I am."

"You've had a bad time of it," Blue Mary said. "No defenses against our brand of influenza, I suppose."

She glanced out the window. The plains beyond were snowless, gray. The sky hung like a thin slatey curtain over the landscape.

Billy brought her a mug of coffee and sat down opposite and watched eagerly as she drank.

After a while it began to make her uncomfortable. "You don't seem as if you were sick at all," she said.

Billy shrugged. "I get down low, but come back fast."

Blue Mary brought her a plate of fried bacon and beans. The odor awakened a ravenous hunger. "Now, you can eat as much of this as you like, but try to go slow. Your stomach's probably sensitive."

She felt herself turn crimson. "I didn't throw up, did I? Along with everything else?"

"Only a little," Billy said.

Stoner wanted to sink through the floor. She picked at the beans and bacon. "Big Dot warned me against food like this."

Blue Mary smiled. "Told you that story, did she? Did she tell you how she shot the old coot?"

Stoner nodded.

"Did she bother to tell you he'd fired on her first?"

"No, she didn't."

"Well, that's just like her," Blue Mary said. "Modest to a fault."

Billy was shifting around in an excited kind of way. "Dot shot someone? In cold blood?"

"Not really," Blue Mary said. "Her blood was running hot at the time."

"Yeah, but he'd fired on her, and she still managed to shoot him? She wasn't scared?"

"I'm sure she was scared," Blue Mary said patiently. "But it didn't make her inaccurate."

"Think she'd teach me how to shoot like that?"

Blue Mary shook her head. "I really doubt it. You know how she feels about that."

Billy pouted and kicked a chair.

"You know, Billy," Blue Mary said with a laugh, "you're beginning to act like a boy."

Billy looked up sharply. "I am?"

"Furniture kicking?" Blue Mary prodded.

"Aw, heck," Billy said with a shrug and a grin, "I've always been a furniture-kicker."

Stoner realized she was grinning, herself. Staring at Billy as if she couldn't get enough of her. And grinning.

"What happened to the snow?" she asked quickly.

"Didn't you hear the rain?"

124

She could remember, but it got all mixed up with her dreams. "I guess I did."

"It usually happens that way with the first snow," Blue Mary explained. "Warm rain comes along and just washes it away."

Stoner stirred her beans, and noticed that Billy was watching her, too. "I guess it was foolish of us to go out in the storm like that."

"Not in the least," Blue Mary said. "If you'd left Billy there another twenty-four hours, she wouldn't have pulled through. She was a very sick young lady."

"You saved my life," Billy said.

"In more ways than one," said Blue Mary. "In fact, you seem to have given her a whole new reason to live. I don't think I've seen her looking so well since I've known her."

Billy jumped up from the table and made a dive for her denim sheepskin lined jacket. "I better go in town," she said abruptly. "Promised Dot I'd do some work for her." She picked up her hat, shoved her hair behind her ears, clamped the hat on her head, and strapped on her gun belt. She was a teen-aged boy again. "You want anything?"

Blue Mary reached into a crockery jar and drew out a small leather purse. "There's a list in there for Dot," she said. "And money. If Dot lets you take the wagon, you can drop those things off. And mind you don't overdo yourself. You may feel fine now, but you don't want to relapse."

"Sure thing." The door slammed and Billy was gone.

Blue Mary looked after her with a cogitative smile. "I can't tell you how gratifying it is to see Billy so animated. She came here— oh, a little over six months ago, I suppose. She always seemed terribly tense and troubled."

"She's very nice," Stoner said.

"And very fond of you, you know."

"I like her, too. I even liked her when she was a boy." She ate a forkful of beans. They were sweet and rich with molasses. "Mary, what's she going to do?"

Blue Mary shook her head. "I have no idea."

"I mean, it's fine for her to go around pretending to be a boy now. But sooner or later people are going to wonder why she isn't growing up."

The woman poured herself a cup of coffee and joined Stoner at the table. "I expect they will."

"Did she really kill her father?"

"Oh, yes." She added some sugar to her coffee. "I've seen the 'Wanted' posters."

Stoner looked up, alarmed. "You mean there's a price on her head?"

"Not a large one, but enough that someone will take the trouble to track her down one of these days."

"What will happen if they catch her?"

"Probably just what she says—they'll put her in an asylum." She sighed. "I don't know what asylums are like where you come from, but they're quite dreadful here. The patients are chained to the walls, and starved and beaten. Raped, of course. The guards are neither gentlemen nor bright. If a woman isn't insane when she goes in, she is within a few months."

Stoner put her fork down. "Mary, we can't let that happen to Billy."

"We certainly can't."

"Isn't there anything we can do?"

Blue Mary shook her head. "I've wracked my brains, Stoner. She's safe enough for now. Nobody in Tabor has suspected anything out of the ordinary. It's not unusual for young men to drift about out here, you know. And they often stay in one place through the winter. But usually they move along come spring. I'm afraid, once the weather warms up, folks are going to begin asking questions." She sipped her coffee, then looked up brightly. "But perhaps you'll think of something."

"Sometimes, when we can't think of what to do, Aunt Hermione reads the cards."

"Goodness," Blue Mary said. "I'd completely forgotten." She got up and went to a box beside her bed. "That's odd."

Stoner went to stand by her. "What's odd?"

"They seem to be missing."

"Are you sure?"

The older woman dumped the contents of the box onto the bed and searched through the pile. "Gone."

"Maybe you put them somewhere else."

"Oh, I wouldn't do that." She stared at her belongings for a moment, puzzled. "Maybe it was the Indians," she said at last. "They often borrow things—they know they're welcome to, though it wouldn't stop them if they weren't. They always bring them back."

"What would Indians want with Tarot cards?"

"I really don't know," Blue Mary said.

≈ ≈ ≈

The stage coach ground to a stop, mired in mud. May Chang stepped down, holding her skirts high with one hand. It wasn't dignified, but she was tired of washing the hems of her dress and petticoat every night before she went to sleep. Maybe, if she was careful, she'd have the luxury of merely hanging up her clothes and falling into bed. If she had a bed. She wondered where they'd let her sleep tonight. Denver had been luxurious,

126

the hotel clerk assigning her to a room with barely a glance. But there had been other towns—towns like Rocky Creek, Utah.

In Rocky Creek, they wouldn't even let her sleep in the stable, and she'd walked the streets all night, fighting back tears of exhaustion and shame, enduring the lewd whispers, the sneers and taunts of "Chink" and "Slant-eye" and "Yella skin". Trying not to show her fear, because she knew once they sensed her fear she was lost.

She'd seen more than one example of what white men could do to a yellow-skinned woman. And to red and brown-skinned women as well. Rape, robbery. Women beaten to death. Women maimed and driven to madness. Women of colored skin brutalized by colorless men.

She supposed the colorless men also did these things to their colorless women. Sometimes, as she passed a white woman on the street, she noticed the tight skin, the turned-down mouth, the flatness of misery and despair in her eyes. She wanted to stop the woman and ask her—not rudely but with concern, sympathetically, as if they were sisters—ask her if it was her man who made her so unhappy. Ask her if there was any way she could help. Ask her what they might do together to bring a little justice into this unjust world.

May Chang glanced over at her fellow passengers. They stood in a tight little group, closing her out. She had tried to smile at the skinny, frightened-looking blonde girl who got on board with her new husband just outside Wheatland. May's heart had gone out to her right from the start. She wanted to offer her companionship and comfort. But the girl had shot her a look of such animosity it had made her heart shrivel. She didn't try again.

When would they learn, these white women? Couldn't they see it was gender, not color, that defined the enemy?

The horses strained against their harnesses, sweating and grunting, eyes rolling white and bloodshot with panic and fatigue. The driver lashed them brutally. They only reared in place. The coach rocked from side to side.

The driver swore and cracked his whip, working himself into a fury.

He's going to kill the poor things, May thought. She ran to the coach. "Please, sir, let me help."

The driver peered down and spat over the side, the spittle dotting her foot. "Git outa here, Goddamn Slant-eye."

She forced herself to ignore the insult. "They're only frightened. I know horses. Back in San Francisco ..."

"You don't know bullshit," the driver snarled. He slapped the reins.

"Sir. They're not being disobedient. They're afraid. Let me lead them ..."

He wheeled and struck out at her with the whip, barely missing her shoulder. "I tole ya' to git outa here." He brought the whip down across the horses' backs.

127

The horses screamed.

"Excuse me, sir," May Chang said quietly. She reached into her cotton string bag and brought out the tiny, pearl-handled gun.

The driver looked down. His mouth fell open.

She pointed the gun at his face. "I will lead the horses. It'll be so much better, don't you think?"

He took off his hat, ran his hand through his greasy hair. His hand trembled.

Like all bullies, May thought, he is a coward.

"Yeah. Yeah, it might work."

Keeping him in her sight, her pistol in his sight, she moved to the horses' heads and stroked their sweaty necks. When they had calmed, she stepped backward, holding their bridles in one hand, talking softly, using the gentlest tones she knew. The wagon creaked forward a few inches. Then a few inches more. And a few inches more. And then they were on solid ground.

May climbed up into the driver's seat. "I think our trip will be more pleasant if I ride here with you, don't you?"

He couldn't take his eyes from the gun. "Yeah."

"Would you like to call the others to board now?"

"Sure. Good idea." The driver turned to the little knot of passengers. "Let's load up, folks." He looked back at May. "I don't think they seen what happened," he said in a pleading voice.

"That's good," May said. "Now we have a secret between us. It will make us respect one another, isn't that right?"

"That's right," the man said eagerly. "You got it dead right."

She stole a glance at her skirts. They were caked with mud. May sighed.

The driver signalled the horses forward. "Lady," he said as they picked up speed, "they ain't gonna know what to make of you in Tabor."

128

Chapter 8

The sheet of paper blew across the street and came to rest around the Sanctified Man's ankle. He tore it from his foot and crumpled it in his fist. Filth. The town was knee-deep in filth.

He started to toss it away, but something caught his eye. Scuttling close to the side of a building, out of the wind, he smoothed it out. He frowned as he picked his way through the words. The frown turned to surprise, then laughter as comprehension kicked in.

All Tabor ladies are invited, it said, *to meet with representatives of the American Woman Suffrage Association. Mrs. Lucy Stone will speak, followed by an informal reception and tea. Sunday, November twenty six at Hayes' Emporium.* The witches were gathering.

God had sent him a message, disguised as trash. Glorious! It was time to set the trap.

≈ ≈ ≈

Billy came back from town with the wagon, groceries, and a surprise. They could hear the singing long before they reached the house. Blue Mary heard it first. She had been rolling a ball of yarn from a skein Stoner was holding, and jumped up with a little "yip" of delight.

"It's Dorothy and the girls!"

Stoner put the yarn aside and got to her feet. The sudden movement made the room tilt.

"Mary," she said, putting out a hand to steady herself. "Do they know Billy's a ...?" But by the time she had reached the door the older woman was flying down the path.

Okay, she told herself, when in doubt, shut up.

Lolly burst into the cabin in an explosion of laughter and jangling bracelets and chilly air. She carried a wicker basket with a hinged top, which she waved under Stoner's nose in a careless and potentially life-threatening way. "Wait 'til you see what we've brought," she bubbled. She

129

whipped off a linen napkin that covered the contents of the basket. "Turkey! Dried apple pie! Pastries! Cherry's been in the kitchen all day. It's as good as Christmas. Where do you want me to put this?"

"Uh ..." Stoner said, feeling a little overwhelmed. "I guess on the table."

Lolly began setting things out. "I know you need a decent meal. All you get in this house is healthy stuff. Honestly, Blue Mary's a doll, but her taste in food ..." She grimaced. "I don't know how you've stood it even this long."

The odors of the food mingled and swirled around her. The turkey was especially pungent. Strong. Gamey. It made her feel a little sick. "I really didn't notice," she said. "I haven't been too well ..."

"I know. I know." Lolly broke off a chunk of vicious-looking pastry and pushed it at her. "Try this. It'll have you up and dancing in no time."

Stoner took it in her hand and studied it. It looked like part of a croissant stuffed with chocolate. An odor of cherry liqueur hovered over it. "I don't know, Lolly. It might be kind of rich."

"Of course it's rich," Lolly said, popping the rest of the pastry into her own mouth. "That's why it's good for you."

"I ..."

"It's being measly with yourself that makes you sick. Trust me."

The others had reached the house. "Lolly!" Dot said sharply. "Don't force things on her. Do you want her to throw up right here and now?" She turned to Stoner and draped an arm around her shoulders. "How ya' doing, kid?"

"Better, thanks."

Cherry swept into the room with more dignity than Stoner had ever seen anyone manifest. She placed her basket carefully on the table and touched Stoner's hand. "I'm so glad to see you up and about," she said formally. She turned back in time to see Lolly begin to raid the basket. "Keep your greedy hands out of that, Miss," she said, and gave Lolly a gentle slap on the arm.

"Come on," Lolly whined. "You told me I could have some."

"When everyone has been served." Cherry rolled her eyes at Stoner. "She has the worst manners of any white woman I've ever met. And, believe me, I've met white women with terrible manners."

"Privilege," Stoner murmured. "It makes us arrogant."

"Yes," said Cherry. She turned back to the table and began setting out the food. A small turkey and a smaller boiled ham. An assortment of relishes. Grape pie with whole wheat crust. Hazel and hickory nuts.

"Billy's giving the horse a little water," Blue Mary said as she pushed the door shut. "He'll ..." She stressed the 'he'. "... be right in."

130

"I must admit," Dot said as she cast a critical eye over the table setting, "I missed the little devil the past week. Still doesn't look too well, does he?"

Blue Mary settled herself at the head of the table. "He'll be out back working with that gun before you know it. He has youth on his side."

Lolly was scanning the layout of food, obviously in Heaven. "Just look at this," she squealed, enraptured.

"It was very kind of you, Dorothy," Blue Mary said. "I hardly know what to say."

Big Dot shrugged in a half-embarrassed way. "Shucks, we needed an excuse to get out of there. And I know this gal ...," She sat and pulled Stoner down next to her, "can't get her strength back on the things you subsist on."

"I suppose you have a point," Blue Mary said.

"Of course she has a point," Lolly exclaimed as she piled her plate high with ham and sweet potatoes and a deadly looking slice of mince meat pie. "Nobody can live decently on weeds and seeds. It's bad enough we have to eat Dot's cooking."

"It's hardly been weeds and seeds," Stoner said. "Last night it was beans and bacon."

Dot raised an eyebrow. "Thought I warned you about that stuff."

"I didn't have a choice."

Cherry looked at Lolly's plate with distaste. "You go on eating like that, you'll get so fat you'll have to take up a new line of work."

"Well I just might do that," Lolly said, reaching for another turkey leg.

"And what else could an old whore like you possibly do?" Cherry asked. "Teach school? Take in washing? You lack the education for the first, and the stamina for the second."

"There must be other things a woman can do out here," Stoner said, feeling a little sorry for Lolly.

"Get married," Dot said. "That's about it."

"I could always go bad," Lolly said stubbornly. "Like Belle Starr and Sally Skull and Calamity Jane."

Dot glared at her. "You watch what you say about Miss Mary Jane Cannaray. She happens to be a personal friend, and she's not 'bad', just different."

Lolly turned to Stoner. "Have you ever noticed how all of Dot's friends are 'different'?"

"As a matter of fact," Stoner said. "I have."

"She happens to be more tolerant than most, that's all," Cherry said. She peered at Stoner's plate. "I worked my fingers to the bone over this food. Aren't you even going to taste it?"

Stoner picked up a turkey wing and tried a tentative nibble. It was delicious.

"Are you married?" Lolly asked her between bites of dried apple pie.

"No, I'm not."

"What kind of work do you do?"

"I'm a travel agent."

They all looked at her. From the expressions on their faces, she might as well have said she was an astronaut.

"A travel agent," she explained. "When people want to go somewhere—like on business or on a vacation or something—I help them get there."

Cherry leaned forward and touched her napkin to her mouth. "How do you do that?"

"We ... my partner Marylou and I ... we make hotel and motel reservations, get plane tickets ..."

The others looked at each other. "Motel reservations? Plane tickets?" Dot asked.

"That's right, you don't know about planes, do you?"

"Of course we know about plains," Dot said. "We're sitting right in the middle of some of the biggest plains in the country."

"No, I mean airplanes." She searched her brain for an analogy. "They're like train cars, sort of. Metal. Carry lots of people. Only they go through the air. On wings." She realized how crazy that sounded. "You have to see it to believe it."

"I expect that would help," Dot said politely.

Stoner caught Blue Mary's eye. Help me!

"Things are very modern back in Boston," Blue Mary said. "Would anyone like tea?"

"Water's fine," Lolly said, reaching for the pitcher and refilling her glass.

"I'll bet you don't have an acid rain problem out here," Stoner said.

"Not sure what it is," Dot said around a mouthful of cake, "but I never heard of us having it."

"It's caused by pollution. From factories. See, the smoke from fossil fuels goes up into the atmosphere and gets trapped in clouds, and when it rains what falls is kind of acid."

"What sort of acid?" Cherry asked.

"Sulfuric, I think. I'm not sure."

"And you're telling me that back in Boston it rains sulfuric acid."

"Well," Stoner said uncertainly, "it's not very strong, but technically, I guess ... Well, it's ruining our lakes."

"Are you really from Boston?" Cherry asked, "Or from Hell?"

132

Stoner laughed. "Sometimes it's hard to tell the difference."

"At least they have decent food," Lolly declared.

Cherry snorted. "Food, food, food. That's all you care about."

"My friend Marylou's like that," Stoner said to Lolly. "You'd be crazy about each other. She could take you to every exotic restaurant in the city. I go with her sometimes, but I'm not very knowledgeable. I'll bet, within a week, the two of you would be comparing notes like professionals. "

Lolly beamed from ear to ear. "When you go home, take me with you."

"I wish I could," Stoner said. She realized she was becoming very fond of Lolly. "Marylou's more particular about food than anyone I ever met." She laughed. "The irony of it is, her mother only eats junk food."

They all looked at her again. "Junk food?" Lolly asked.

"Junk food is ...well, it's what you get at a take-out restaurant. You know, when you're too busy to cook. We have hundreds of them. Burger King. Kentucky Fried. Pizza Hut."

The blank stares made her a little hysterical. "Taco Bell? Arby's? Roy Rogers? McDonald's? You never heard of McDonald's? They're all over the world. They have them in Japan."

"Gosh," Lolly said, "you've been everywhere."

"Excuse me?"

"You've been to Japan?"

Stoner raked her hand through her hair in a frantic way. "No, I haven't been to Japan. But I could go if I wanted. If I could afford it."

"Know what you mean," Dot said. "It'd cost a fortune, a trip that long. But I don't think I could stand looking at the ocean for weeks at a time, even if I could scrape together the money."

"Hours," Stoner said. "From L.A., twelve hours max."

"Mary," Dot said to Blue Mary in an undertone, "I don't think she's as recovered as she thinks she is."

"Japan is nothing," Stoner insisted. "Some people have been to the moon."

Dot shook her head. "Delirious."

"I saw it on television."

Blue Mary came around the table and touched her shoulder. "Stoner, dear, it's time to calm down. We don't want to frighten our guests."

"Sorry."

There was an awkward silence.

"Well," Cherry said at last, "it's not my place to say what's possible and what isn't. My goodness, the things I've seen in New Orleans."

"The French Quarter?" Stoner asked.

Cherry turned to her. "Have you been there?"

"No, but it's very popular with our clients. Especially the Soniat Hotel.

On Chartres."

Cherry's eyes lit up. "I know the place. It's a little rough on Saturday nights, but fairly decent. Near the river."

Stoner felt as if she'd made contact with alien life forms. "That's right. Have you ever been to the Quadroon Ballroom?"

Cherry threw back her head and laughed. "And in what capacity would I have been in that place, may I ask? My Mama wasn't exactly in a position to show me off to fancy gentlemen."

Stoner had the sudden panicky feeling she'd committed some horrible social gaffe. "I didn't know about that," she said quickly.

Cherry turned to the others. "The Quadroon Ballroom," she explained, "is where high-born Mulattos make their debuts into New Orleans society."

Dot cut herself a slice of pie and raised one eyebrow. "That so?"

"The local wealthy young white men are generally in attendance," Cherry went on. "They look the girls over and select a mistress."

"Really," Stoner said, "I wasn't implying ... I mean, I didn't even ... I mean, I thought the Quadroon was just someplace people went to dance."

"It's all right," Cherry said, and touched her arm lightly. "I'm flattered you'd include me in such company."

"But I wouldn't," Stoner prattled. "I mean, I'd never imply you were a kept woman."

"There are worse ways to live. The woman is financially established for life. Her children are educated at the man's expense. She never wants for anything."

"Well," said Lolly, making a face, "I'll bet she has to be on the look-out for the wife."

"Not at all. These things are usually done with the wife's blessing." Cherry turned to Stoner. "But, you see, one has to have attained a certain level in Mulatto society to even get into the Quadroon. And with my background ... "

Stoner took another piece of turkey. "Have things been very different for you since Emancipation?"

"Yes and no," Cherry said thoughtfully. "For many of the Negro race, yes. But I had already emancipated myself, you might say." She glanced at her. "But you don't want to hear that dreary story. Not on your first day back from the brink of death."

"I do," Stoner insisted. "Very much."

Cherry looked around at the rest. "Do you think you could bear to hear it again."

"It's my favorite story," Lolly said. "It makes me cry"

"My great grandmother was brought here from Africa in the early days,

134

to a plantation in Mississippi, down toward Natchez. Her daughter, my grandmother, who was half white, was sold to another plantation in Alabama, where she married one of the other slaves. Not married in the legal sense, of course. We weren't permitted that. My mother was bought by a lawyer in Georgia named Calhoun—no relation to the South Carolina Calhouns—who became my father, though he wouldn't admit it. Nor would his wife, but I'm certain she knew."

She broke off a crumb of cake and ate it, touching a napkin to her mouth. "My mother worked her way up to become the Calhouns' cook, and I was allowed to play in the kitchen. But what really attracted me was the library. I had a fascination with words and reading, and I promised myself if I didn't do anything else in my life, I would learn to read."

"Negroes weren't supposed to read in the Confederacy," Blue Mary explained. "Education of any kind for Negroes was against the law."

"The Calhouns had a son," Cherry went on. "A repulsive child, actually, and a bully. He was several years younger than me, but he could read and write, and I managed to manipulate him into teaching me. He had his price, of course, and I'm sure I don't need to tell you what it was."

"No," Stoner said. "You don't."

"I'd get books anywhere I could. Going through people's trash. Trading sexual favors, all I had to offer. I even borrowed from the Calhouns' library without their knowledge. I returned them, of course. But one time I got caught and they beat my mother. That was the end of my borrowing."

"How old were you?" Stoner asked.

Cherry frowned thoughtfully. "I'm not exactly certain. We didn't keep track of such things. But I know I hadn't reached womanhood."

She sighed. "When that finally happened, the Calhouns—father and son—were after me day and night as if I were a bitch in perpetual season. I found it distasteful. It's one thing to tolerate discomfort when one has something to gain from it. But quite another if there's no personal benefit, don't you agree?"

"Absolutely," Stoner said.

"I couldn't hide how I felt about them, so they sold me to a drover from Mississippi. A thoroughly wretched human being. Sadistic. Fortunately, he was also rather stupid, and a drunk. I spent about a year with him, and slipped away one night when he had drunk himself into unconsciousness—which he did with increasing frequency. As we were in New Orleans at the time it was easy to lose myself among the Mulatto ladies of the night. He never found me." She gave a sharp laugh. "To tell you the truth, I don't think that man had ever looked at my face. He wouldn't know what he was looking for. Then the War broke out, and afterward I decided to come out here. The Yankees, for all their high-mindedness, were really no better than our owners had been. Men are men, aren't they?"

"Yes," Stoner said. "They certainly are."

Cherry leaned forward and tapped the table with her perfect finger. "They were so proud of themselves for 'freeing' us—and there's no denying it's better to be free than slave—but I wonder what their reaction will be when they realize they'll have to pay us for our work, and educate us. I wonder what they'll do when we decide we want to be not just free, but equal."

I could tell you, Stoner thought. About another century of poverty and lynchings and prejudice. About slow, painful progress through the law. About Martin Luther King, Jr. And Malcolm X and H. Rap Brown and the Black Panthers. About the Civil Rights Movement and marches and sit-ins and boycotts and raised hopes. About assassinations and riots, and "Burn, baby, burn." Black pride and black culture, and new respect for your African heritage. School desegregation and affirmative action. And the 1980s, the Decade of the White Male, and the piece-by-piece erosion of what you've gained.

"I suspect," she said carefully, "there are difficult times ahead."

Cherry laughed and reached for a biscuit. "Difficult times behind, difficult times ahead. Life goes on."

Lolly had been unusually quiet. Stoner glanced over her. Tears trembled in the corners of her eyes. "Lolly?" she said.

"It's so sad," Lolly burst out. "I wish I could kill those people."

Cherry reached across the table and stroked Lolly's hand. "We do what we can, honey," she said. "And what we have to do. And we have a good life, now don't we?"

Lolly nodded. A tear escaped and cut a channel through her face powder. Then another. And another. She blew her nose on a rumpled handkerchief. "See what I mean? I just adore that story."

"Suppose you got yourself a gun," Cherry said. "Suppose you went after that old Calhoun and his upstart son? Suppose you hunted them down and shot them dead? You know you'd be caught, and what would Cherry do without you?"

"You'd do all right," Lolly murmured. "You got along before."

"But who'd I have to tease? Who'd pester me to cook fancy tarts for her? Who'd mend my clothes and gossip with me around the stove all winter?" She threw a wink in Dot's direction. "Not the boss-lady. The boss-lady's got her business to see to, and you and I, we have each other to see to, now, don't we?"

If they don't stop all this sweetness, Stoner thought, I'm going to start crying, too.

"Just look at you," Cherry said with pretend sternness. She stood up. "I'm going to have to take you in the other room and fix your make-up before Stoner gets the idea Western whores are careless about their appearance. We have to set an example."

"Well," said Dot as Cherry and Lolly left the table, "I suppose the boss-lady'd better clean up after the working girls." She gathered up a pile of plates and went to the sink.

"Isn't Billy coming in?" Stoner asked as she followed her with mugs and silver.

Dot glanced out the window. "We'd best save something out for him. Looks like he's talking to a cowboy out there."

"A cowboy?" Blue Mary came to the sink. "It's late in the year for cowboys. Must be a drifter."

"Don't you have cowboys around in the winter?" Stoner asked.

"During the spring and summer months, mostly," Dot explained. "Driving cattle to the markets over in Kansas City and St. Louis. But by fall they're pretty well settled in on the ranches. Doesn't make much sense, driving cattle when they might freeze to death as easily as not."

Stoner looked out. The sunlight was cold and hard, the gentle hills like mounds of cement. Billy was talking with a dusty-looking man on a dusty black horse.

"I wouldn't want to be a drifter in Tabor these days," Dot mused. "Folks are ready to hang any strange face." She turned to Blue Mary. "You probably didn't hear. There was another one last night."

"Oh, dear," Blue Mary said. "What was it this time?"

"The Allens, out on the Ridge. The whole family was killed. Did you know them?"

"Not really," Blue Mary said. "I'd run into Jenny Allen now and then in town, but she never warmed up to me. Introverted kind of person. But I suspect she'd have opened up a little in time." She shook her head. "What a shame."

"Sounds to me like the same kind of thing as back in August when the DeSantis' barn burned." She turned to Stoner. "They'd been struggling along for some time, just had to pack up and move back to Mexico." She scrubbed roughly at a dish. "Too bad, too. They were good folks."

Blue Mary shook her head slowly. "It seems to be intensifying. This is the first time there's been loss of life."

"Well, I wish they'd find out who's responsible," Lolly said as she and Cherry came back into the room. "It's getting to be bad for business."

"It is?" Stoner asked.

"Everybody's jumpy," Cherry explained. "Can't keep their minds on what they're doing."

"There's been talk," Dot said with apparent reluctance.

Blue Mary looked at her expectantly.

"Cherry overheard some of the ladies after church ..."

"Honest to God," Lolly sputtered, "are you hanging around that place again?"

"Can't do any harm," Cherry said.

"Can't do any good, either. What do you want to go listening to that old Booger for?"

"I'm not listening to the old Booger. I'm listening to the gossip."

"If he catches you inside the church, he'll run you all the way to the saloon, like he did last time."

"Excuse me ..." Stoner said.

"And wasn't that a picture?" Cherry laughed.

Stoner cleared her throat and said, "Uh ..."

They all looked at her.

"Who's the old Booger?"

"The parson," Dot snorted as she poured more hot water from the kettle into the sink.

Blue Mary picked up the piece of worn flannel she used as a dish towel. "Now, Dorothy, you know that's just your prejudice against the clergy."

"Is not," said Dot. "I've known one or two good ones in my time. Though, to be honest, I think it's a shameful way to live, going around telling folks what you disapprove of about them, and expecting them to pay for the privilege."

"I don't know about that," Lolly said. "I had a customer a while back who paid me extra to do it to him."

"Hush, now." Cherry gave Lolly a poke in the ribs. "You'll shock our company."

Stoner laughed. "Don't worry. I've heard of such things."

"Well, you shouldn't have," Dot said. "A nice girl like you."

"Woman," said Blue Mary. "She wants to be called a woman."

"Oh?" Dot raised one eyebrow. "What's that about?"

Stoner tried to think of how she could explain the Women's Movement in twenty-five words or less. Maybe, if she left out the part about equal pay ...

"Where she comes from," said Blue Mary, "it's a sign of respect."

"Well," said Dot, "that certainly gives me something to think about."

Outside, the cowboy turned his horse and rode off. Billy started for the house.

Blue Mary placed a dried plate in the cupboard. "What's the talk?"

"You know how people are," Cherry said. "They get suspicious of anyone they don't know."

"Me?" Stoner asked.

"They could," Dot said. "You might recall I was. But the burnings started several months ago. You weren't in the area, were you?"

Heck, no. I wasn't even in this century.

She waved at Billy. Billy waved back.

"I think you should know, Mary, there's talk of taking action against our boy."

Blue Mary turned to look at Dot. "What kind of talk?"

"It's still at the idle chatter point, but if things keep going the way they are ..."

"Billy wouldn't do a thing like that," Stoner said.

Dot shrugged. "You know it, and I know it. All the town knows is, he arrived wearing a gun, no horse, no family, and he's pretty tight-lipped about what went before."

"But Billy's a ..."

"Child," Blue Mary cut her off. "Just a child."

"It's our friend Hayes who's behind the talk, mostly. You know how he is."

Blue Mary nodded. "Did you know his wife's become a Suffragist?"

Cherry and Lolly broke into peals of laughter. "Glory be," said Dot. "There's a God after all."

Blue Mary turned sober. "Dorothy, how long can you protect Billy?"

"I don't know. I'm doing the best I can."

"No one doubts that," Blue Mary said. "Stoner might be able to help, too."

Dot brushed a damp curl from her forehead with the back of her hand and looked over at Stoner. "You think so?"

"If I could find out who really did it ..."

"Well," said Dot, "not meaning to doubt your abilities, but—for once in my life— I'll welcome the U.S. Marshall. If he ever gets here." She plunged her hands back into the dish water. "Trouble is, you know durn well the first thing he'll do is arrest Billy."

"But ..."

"Now, don't worry," Blue Mary said. "By the time he arrives, you'll probably have the whole thing taken care of."

Dot glanced over at Stoner. "Thing I'm worried about ... what if folks decide to take matters into their own hands first?"

Billy kicked the door open and strode into the room. She swung one leg over the bench, straddling it, and began to gnaw on a turkey leg.

It was one of the cutest things Stoner had ever seen.

"Cowboy says they're bringin' a herd through Tabor," Billy said. "Campin' by the West Fork. Be in town Saturday night."

Dot sighed. "Well, if that doesn't beat the devil. Hope I have enough rot-gut whisky to bring us through the crisis."

"Shoot," said Cherry. "I was getting used to having my evenings to myself."

Lolly grimaced. "I guess it's better than buffalo skinners, but ..."

"Buffalo skinners!" Cherry rolled her eyes skyward. "Don't even talk to me about buffalo skinners."

"Hey, Dot," Billy said gruffly. "Gonna need me over the next couple days?"

"Not particularly. You have important business elsewhere?"

Billy pulled her hat down over her eyebrows, not quite hiding the blush that spread across her face. "Thought I might show Stoner around."

Lolly giggled.

"In that case," Dot said, and shot Lolly a withering glance, "you might as well borrow the wagon." She looked hard in Billy's direction, then turned to Stoner. "I feel the need of some air. Come with me."

"Sure." She got up and took Dot's shawl from the peg beside the door and slid it around the woman's shoulders.

"Thank you," Dot said. "Where's that thing of yours?"

Stoner retrieved her vest and pulled it on.

Dot fingered the edge. "That is the damnedest stuff. What'd you say it was?"

"Rayon and thinsulate, I think."

Dot shook her head slowly, as if at a loss in a world that had moved too fast for her to keep up. "Long as it does what it's supposed to, I guess." She stepped out into the sunshine.

Stoner followed.

"Trouble with having your own little house," Dot said, slipping her arm through Stoner's, "is there's no privacy. Now, if we were at the saloon, we wouldn't have to come out in the cold to talk."

"That's okay." Stoner drew in a deep breath of cold, dry, fresh air. As she exhaled, she felt as if she were blowing her sickness away. "You have wonderful air out here."

Dot gave a sharp laugh. "You wouldn't say that come spring. Smell of manure hangs mighty heavy."

They walked for a little while in silence, listening to the crack of dried and frozen weeds underfoot.

"Are you feeling a little more settled?" Dot asked.

"I suppose so."

"Guess our ways are hard to get used to."

"Well," Stoner said, "it's ... I don't know ... disturbing. Not being able to get home and all."

Dot gave her arm a sympathetic squeeze. "Homesick?"

140

Stoner nodded.

"I used to get homesick something fierce when I was a kid," Dot said. "Probably still would if I let myself." She thought for a moment. "Well, not exactly homesick, considering this is my home and a durn sight better than the one I left. Sometimes I try and put it all together, wondering how I could be nostalgic for a place I distinctly recall not even liking very much. I suspect it has to do with memory prettying things up, like some kind of cheap, sentimental artist. Suppose?"

"I suppose."

"Sometimes it comes to me that this homesick business is just another kind of loneliness." She glanced over at Stoner. "The kind of loneliness that's like a wind blowing through the chimney of your heart. Know what I mean?"

Stoner nodded. "I never found a cure for that."

"Neither did I," Dot said. "Maybe there isn't one."

"Maybe."

"If there's any such thing as Heaven, it must be where you don't feel lonely." Dot laughed. "Hard to imagine, though."

They walked for a while. The ground beneath her feet was hard, but not like the dead hardness of sidewalks. This ground had a feeling of sleeping life to it. Slow and old, but life. When earth is made into concrete, she thought, something goes out of it—the way a bluejay's feathers lose their vibrancy when it dies.

"What are you pondering so hard?" Dot asked.

"Life and death."

"A lot of both out here."

"Yes. Dot, is it always so violent? I mean, all the talk of killing, people carrying guns ..."

Dot nodded. "You could say so. You have killings back in Boston, don't you?"

She had to admit they did.

"The only difference is," Dot said, "out here we generally don't kill anyone we don't know. 'Cept those of us who are paid to."

They walked a while longer.

"There's something I have to tell you," Dot said at last. "I hope you'll keep it in mind that you're a stranger to me. I wouldn't want you to be insulted."

"I won't be."

"It's about Billy."

"Okay."

"Ordinarily I don't have much good to say about men. Wouldn't spit on the best part of 'em. Far as I'm concerned, they're a necessary evil, and

141

sometimes I'm not sure just how necessary. But now and then you meet one who's different—one that thinks about what they're doing and how the world's going, one that sees beyond drinking himself into oblivion and how much blood he can spill and who he's gonna poke his bell-clapper into next."

"I know," Stoner said. "I've met a few."

"Well, something tells me Billy could be that kind of man. Oh, I know he tries to act tough, and God help you if you try and separate him from that six-shooter. But he's been through hard times, and he's still young. If he's treated right he might grow up decent."

Stoner tried to think of something of an inconsequential and non-committal nature to say. She couldn't.

"Anyhoo," Dot went on, "it's easy to see he's got an infatuation with you, and how you handle him could have a lot to do with the kind of man he becomes. Do you understand?"

"Of course I do." Billy? Infatuated? With me?

"You don't mind me talking to you straight like this?"

"Not at all." Billy?

"And I can count on you to handle that young heart with care?"

"Yes, you can." Infatuated?

Dot squeezed her arm. "I knew you were a good sort first time I met you."

Stoner looked at her. "Dot, the first time you met me, you pulled out a gun and shot at me."

"Doesn't mean I didn't like you."

"All I can say is, " Stoner said with a laugh, "I'm glad you didn't like me a lot."

Dot laughed along with her. Then she turned serious. "I expect you'll be moving along one of these days."

"I expect I will."

"If I know the boy, he'll want to go with you."

"I'm sorry," Stoner said, and she really was sorry. "I don't think I can take him."

Dot gave a huge sigh. "I figured not."

"If you're right ..."

"I'm right. I know men and women."

Excuse me, Stoner thought, but sometimes you don't exactly know the difference. " ... I don't know how to leave him behind without hurting him."

"Lordy," Dot said sadly as she watched a hawk circle overhead, "neither do I."

≈ ≈ ≈

142

It bothered Cullum, that close brush with death. Not the chance of dying. He'd been prepared for that from the minute he took up bounty hunting in a serious way. No, what really bothered him was the way that train bogged down right where he needed it.

A thousand miles of track and it stopped right there. Right over his head.

It spooked him.

If he'd been a religious man, he might have figured the Good Lord had saved him for something special. But he wasn't religious, just due for some good luck after a run of bad.

Still, it made him uneasy, nearly dying like that, and then being saved—well, it felt kind of like a warning. Like maybe he should rethink this job he was doing.

≈ ≈ ≈

The day had barely gotten underway when Billy arrived to pick her up. It looked as if she'd scrubbed the wagon seats. There was new hay in the back, and a picnic basket, and a bucket of oats for the mule.

"Hey!" Billy said brightly.

"Hey, yourself." Stoner climbed up into the wagon. "Nice day."

"Truly is." She tapped the reins against the mule. "Any place in particular you want to go, or should we just ride?"

"Riding sounds nice. Though I wouldn't mind taking a look at that place that burned the other day."

Billy swept her hat off in a mock bow. "I'm at your service, Ma'am."

She looked her up and down rather openly. "I'm glad Blue Mary hasn't teased you into one of those gol-durned skirts of hers. Wouldn't look right."

"Wouldn't feel right, either." Stoner laughed. "It's a good thing I was born in the Twentieth Century. I'd never get used to the dress codes."

The wagon juggled and jiggled over low frost heaves, tossing her from side to side.

"You okay?" Billy asked.

"Sure. But they should put seat belts on these things."

"Seat belts?"

"Something to tie you in."

Billy laughed. "Sounds like a great idea to me. Though it'd be a little awkward if you had to get out in a hurry."

"Yes," Stoner said. "They haven't really solved that one yet."

The wind was blowing down from the Rockies, picking up speed and strength when it hit the flatlands. It smelled of melted snow and prairie grass dust. But the air and sun felt good against her skin. Being cooped up, no matter how quaint and charming Blue Mary's cabin, had made her feel all pulled into herself.

"Things are kind of funny, where you come from, aren't they?" Billy asked.

"Kind of. I guess it depends on your point of view." She studied the woman's profile, so much like Gwen's in its softness and strength.

I have to stop this, she told herself sharply. Billy is Billy, no matter how much she reminds me of Gwen, and it's not fair to compare them.

Billy glanced over at her. "I guess this wasn't such a good idea. Too much wind and not enough scenery."

"It's fine," Stoner said, and meant it. She was glad to be here. Not just to get out of the house, but glad to be with Billy.

"Where's your coat?"

"I didn't think I'd need it. I gave it away."

"That was kind of foolish," Billy said.

"I guess so."

"You've been pretty sick, you know."

"I know. So have you."

"I'm used to it." She was silent for a few turns of the wagon wheels. "Maybe you should get that blanket out of the back."

Stoner had to laugh. "I'll be fine, Billy. Don't be such a Mother Hen."

"Well, I worry about you."

"Don't."

"Someone has to," Billy said. "You don't worry half enough about yourself."

"What about you?" Stoner said. "You have a lot more to worry about than I do."

The woman sighed. "I wanted to worry about someone else for a change."

Billy pulled the mule to a stop. They looked out over an expanse of prairie. "Doesn't look like much right now, does it?" she asked.

"Nothing does in November."

"It's pretty in the spring and summer, with the paint brush and larkspur and buttercups. Blue Mary says you can find all kinds of things out here even now—things like burrowing owls and prairie dogs, roots and seeds and stuff you can eat. But I never have. Guess I lack her touch." She smiled. "Saw an eagle once, though. Just flying around and around over a patch of bluestem grass. And all of a sudden it dove right at the ground, like it wanted to crack its head open or something. But it came back up with a snake in its claws." She laughed with delight. "Boy, that was something to see."

So was Billy, Stoner thought. With her face silhouetted against the pale blue sky, the wind pushing her hair around, the collar of her denim jacket brushing her cheek, the reins resting in her strong and gentle hands. She might have come from Tennessee, but she belonged here, among the grasses and the endless sky.

"Do you like it here?" Stoner asked.

Billy nodded.

"Do you want to stay? In Tabor?"

"Not much point in talking about that, is there? I have to move along come spring." She hesitated. "Maybe sooner than that."

"Why?"

"Someone set fire to the livery stable last night."

"Did it burn down?"

Billy shook her head. "They caught it in time. There's an old stray dog hangs around there at night. Must have seen it or smelled it and started barking."

"The night I got here," Stoner said, "I thought I heard someone striking a match down there. Remember? You were there, weren't you?"

Billy fell silent.

Stoner wondered what she was thinking.

"I didn't do it, Stoner," she said in a low voice. "I didn't set any of those fires. Honest."

"I didn't mean that. I never thought you did."

"Lots of folks do."

"Lots of folks think lots of things. That doesn't make them true." She took Billy's hand. "If you could stay in Tabor, what would you do?"

"Learn to read and write. Maybe start up a ranch. Maybe farm a little. I might even be able to teach school, once we had enough kids to start a school. Tabor might be a big city some day."

"I doubt it," Stoner said, remembering what Blue Mary had told her. "But you could still do the things you want."

Billy played with her fingers. "That's sweet of you to say. But there's no point in dreaming. If I don't get hung for murder, I'll probably get hung for burning."

"In the first place," Stoner said firmly, "it was self-defense, not murder. And if we could find out who started the fires ..."

"Sure," Billy said ironically. "There's a real good chance of that."

"There might be."

Billy looked dubious.

"I mean it," Stoner said. "I've done this kind of thing before."

"No kidding?" Billy gave a low whistle. "This travel agent business is more complicated than I thought."

≈ ≈ ≈

Part of a stone fireplace still stood where the house used to be, and the windmill turned lazily, uselessly in the breeze. Other than that, the remains of the house and barn were little more than heaps of charred wood.

Stoner looked the place over.

She walked a circle around the cinders, starting at the outside and working her way in.

Billy leaned against the wagon and watched her. "Wish you'd let me help," she said.

Stoner looked up. The wind blew a wisp of hair into her eyes. "You can, soon. I want to get a general overview first." She studied the ground. "Did anyone say which burned first, the house or the barn?"

"Does that make a difference."

"Maybe. If the house went first, it could have been an accident. A spark from the fireplace or stove or something. But if it started in the barn ..." She thought for a second. "Of course, it could have been an animal knocking over a lamp, like Mrs. O'Leary's cow."

"Whose cow?"

Stoner brushed the hair out of her eyes. "Never mind." She turned her attention to the barn. "Would there be anything inflammable stored in there?"

"Not unless you were a damn fool."

"The people who lived here, were they damn fools?"

"Not that I heard," Billy said. "Dot would've said."

"I'm sure she would have." She really didn't have the slightest idea what she was looking for. Mostly, she wanted to give Billy hope—hope that she might change her life if she took charge of it, hope that there were people who cared about her. And if, along the way, they happened to find out who was burning Tabor—well, that would be a bonus.

She picked up a handful of ashes and sniffed. The kerosene odor was unmistakable. She signalled Billy to her side. "What does this smell like?"

Billy bent over the charred wood. "Coal oil."

It was a start. She looked around. The blackened remains of what looked like a tin watering can lay at the edge of the burn area. Stoner picked it up. "What's this used for?"

Billy took it. "When they store the coal oil out back in drums ..." She pointed to a metal container some distance from the house. "They carry it in this. To fill the lamps and stove, if they have that kind of stove."

"Is it usual to keep these in a barn?"

"Nobody in their right mind would do that," Billy said.

"So," Stoner said. She set the can to one side. "We know this was arson."

"Excuse me," Billy said, "but we already knew that."

"But the arsonist was careless. Chances are he or she left other clues." She began picking through the rubble.

146

"Stoner," Billy said. "Do we know what we're looking for?"

"Not really," she admitted.

Billy shrugged. "Well, whatever you say. But it seems like a funny way to spend your time."

"What we need to understand," Stoner said as she turned over a half-charred board and searched the ground beneath, "is the motive. Why would someone want to burn these people out?"

"I don't know." Billy squatted down and scowled at the ground. "Most folks liked them. Far as I know, they didn't owe any money, and they went to church regularly."

"No enemies?"

"Not that I've heard."

"What about the others?" She saw something—a bit of hard material, she thought—sticking out from under a rock, and wiggled it gently.

"Some were liked, some not."

"No pattern?" The piece of material came free in her hand. She turned it over. It looked like part of a bridle.

"I haven't thought about it much, but ..." Billy shook her head. "Those folks didn't have much in common other than they lived here."

"Do you know of anyone who might be trying to destroy Tabor?" She tossed the bridle back into the ashes and went on searching.

Billy stirred the dirt. "Seems to me, if you didn't like it here, you'd just move away."

"You're being blamed for some of these fires. Is there anyone who'd want to get rid of you?"

"It'd be easy enough to chase me off. You wouldn't have to burn down the town." Billy took out her gun and checked the cylinder.

"Dot thinks you have an unhealthy attachment to that thing," Stoner said.

"I know."

"Do you really need it?"

"Feels like I do." She gave the cylinder a twirl. "I keep thinking something terrible's going to happen any day, and I want to be ready."

"With a gun?"

Billy looked up at her. Her eyes were deep with fear. "What if they do decide I set these fires? What if the law comes after me? I have to protect myself."

Stoner felt a huge, warm rush of sympathy for her. Billy wasn't a runner. She could sense that. And she wanted to belong, so much so she stayed around Tabor despite the danger, despite the way she was treated. Maybe, if they really could solve these burnings—if Billy could solve them, maybe she'd be accepted. Maybe the town would rally around her

147

and protect her. Maybe ...

It seemed like a pretty far-fetched wish.

But Aunt Hermione believed in the powers of will and visualization.

She promised herself she'd hop up to the Causal Plane and try to make it happen. Every chance she got.

And meanwhile try to accomplish something on this Plane.

For now, she wanted to take Billy in her arms and hold her. Just hold her.

Billy bent down and came up with something that sparkled in the sunlight. "What do you make of this?"

It was a knife. A regular, bone-handled knife, but rather small and delicate. Almost like a fillet knife.

Stoner took it, ran her thumb carefully along the blade. Sharp as a razor. She held it up. "How common are knives like this?"

"I don't think I've ever seen one."

"Aha."

"Aha?"

"We'd better keep it. It could be important."

Billy tossed the knife into the wagon.

"Careful!" Stoner said. "Don't smudge the fingerprints."

"Why not?"

"They can be useful. If the arsonist has a record, his or her prints will be on file with the FBI. If we can lift one off the knife and match it ..." She broke off, remembering where she was, feeling foolish.

"What's the FBI?"

"A Federal law enforcement agency."

Billy went back to studying the ground. "Really? What do they do?"

"Probably nothing, yet."

"That's another one of those things, huh?"

"What things?"

"Things from wherever you're from."

"Right." She went back to poking in the soil, but her heart wasn't in it.

"Listen," Billy said, "there's something I have to tell you."

Stoner looked up.

Billy sat back on her heels. "That day, when we went looking for your machine, remember?"

"Yes, I do."

"Remember how I kissed you that day?"

Stoner nodded.

"I guess it was okay with you because you didn't slap my face or anything."

"It was okay."

148

Billy stared at her boldly. "I know you thought I was a boy, and that made it okay. So now you know I'm not and maybe it's not all right any more, but ..."

"It's ..."

Billy cut her off. "Please, let me say what I have to say. It's not easy, but I've been working on it for a long time and I have to say it." She took a deep breath. "A lot of folks would think what I did was a nasty thing on account of we're both females. And if you think it's nasty, I'm sorry. But I'm not ashamed, because I meant it and the feeling behind it was a good feeling. I loved you a little that day, and I love you a lot now. There's nothing nasty about loving someone, and I won't let you or anybody else tell me there is." She dared her with her eyes. "And that's all."

Stoner went to her and touched her face. "I don't think it's nasty. I think it's one of the loveliest things I've ever heard."

Billy shrugged. "I'm not real good with words."

"Yes, you are." She took Billy's hand, knowing she had to say something but not knowing what to say. How to explain. About Time, and Gwen. "It's so complicated."

Billy extricated her hand from Stoners' and turned to the wagon. "Let's go to Dot's," she said lightly and quickly. "We can eat on the way."

"If you want to."

"Well, I don't want to stand around here feeling all awkward and funny."

The sun had passed noon. Already the breeze was turning colder.

"Don't you want to talk ..."

"No. I said what I had to say, and that's all there is to say about it." She picked up the reins. "For cryin' out loud, do you want to freeze to death, or what?"

Stoner took one last look around. They weren't going to find anything else here. She climbed into the wagon.

Love, she thought.

Here she was, lost in time and space, which was enough to cause anyone serious First-Run nightmares. And now this woman was in love with her. And, to tell the truth, she was a little bit in love with this woman.

If I let myself, I could love her greatly.

But if I let myself love her and I get whisked back to the Twentieth Century the way I got whisked into this one ...

Or wake up in a hospital bed and find out this was all caused by a cerebral hemorrhage or mental illness or something ...

... my heart will break.

And what about Gwen? I love Gwen. Part of what I love about Billy is the way she reminds me of Gwen.

149

Which isn't fair to Billy.

But, if Blue Mary and Aunt Hermione are right, if we really do keep going around, lifetime after lifetime with the same spirits in different bodies, then Aunt Hermione is Blue Mary, and Blue Mary is Aunt Hermione, and Billy is Gwen, and Gwen is Billy, and a rose is a rose is ...

So if I let myself love Billy, I'm really loving Gwen.

As the I Ching says, no blame.

But it's my 1989 self loving her 1871 self. What are the ethics in that?

Not that there's anything wrong with loving Billy. Love is a blessing, and there's plenty to go around.

It's acting on that love that could be problematic.

The complications were multiplying geometrically.

Chapter 9

"If what I told you is going to make you so quiet," Billy said as the town came into sight, "I'm going to regret having said it."

"I'm sorry."

Billy shot her a tentative smile. "What is, is, and what isn't, isn't."

Stoner returned her smile. "Well, that's profound."

"I don't want to lose your friendship. That's what matters the most."

Recognizing the truth in that, she felt herself relax. "Yes, it does."

But she wondered if it was really that easy?

They rode in silence for a little while. "You're a hard woman, Stoner," Billy said at last.

"What do you mean?"

"I offer to take you for a drive. We spend half the day picking around in old burnt-up fire ashes, and now you won't let us eat."

Stoner laughed and reached for the picnic basket. "Did you put this up?"

"Me? Shoot, I wouldn't do that to you."

"I've had your stew. It was fine."

"Yeah, but that's all I can make—stew."

She peeked under the napkin, praying it wasn't one of Lolly's lunches. Yesterday's treats had met her rich-food needs for a month.

Cheese and bread, a bottle of water, and a hunk of summer sausage. "Oh, thank God," she said.

"Dot did it." She glanced over. "Worried?"

"A little."

"I thought about asking Cherry to make us a picnic, but I didn't want to spend all winter getting teased."

"It seemed to me," Stoner said, "Lolly was putting the pressure on Cherry pretty hard."

"Yeah, she gets her to come through about once a month."

151

"She might have used me as an excuse today."

Billy chuckled. "Honey," she said in a perfect imitation of Cherry's voice, "it worked once, but you are not all that exciting."

"Thanks for the compliment." She took the bread from the basket, rummaged until she found a carving knife, and made Billy a sandwich and one for herself.

"It's nice, their friendship."

Billy nodded, chewing thoughtfully on her sandwich.

"It reminds me of me and Marylou, kind of."

"Marylou?"

"My business partner. She bullies me, just the way they do each other." She took a sip of water. "Come to think of it, it's her fault I'm here."

Billy looked at her. "It is?"

"I was making a mess of things back at the Agency. Sometimes I think I'm not cut out for that kind of work."

"Don't look to me for advice," Billy said. "I don't even understand that kind of work."

They were going downhill now, coming close to town. Billy pulled back lightly on the brake. "This old mule's so doggone lazy," she said, "the wagon'd catch up with him and run him down if we weren't careful." She laughed. "Any mule's lazy, but when you get yourself a lazy one ..."

Just looking at her, strong against the sky, made Stoner's skin hum. She wanted to ride like this all day.

"Billy."

"Um?"

"Take your hat off, would you?"

She stuffed it under the wagon seat and ran her hands through her hair, loosening it.

Stoner reached over. "You really have lovely hair."

"Thanks," Billy said gruffly, and blushed a little. "Looks kinda choppy since I cut it."

"I don't think so. Back home, you'd probably start a trend."

"Goodness," Billy said. She was silent for a moment. "You know the worst thing about these plains?"

Stoner shook her head.

"There's nowhere to go that you can't be seen for a hundred miles."

"I know."

"I'd like to just hold you. Nothing to scare you or make you go all funny, nothing like that. I just want to remember what it's like to hold you. I haven't done that since you were sick."

"And I missed it." She remembered something Gwen had once called them, before they were lovers. Romantic friends. She liked that. "I want to

152

hold you, too."

A few more moments went by.

"Folks out here wouldn't take kindly to that," Billy said.

"Well," Stoner said, "that hasn't changed much in a hundred years."

Her mind was racing. They could go to Blue Mary's, but Blue Mary was probably there. There was no privacy at Dot's Gulch. Billy's dugout was impossible—the rains that had melted the freak snow had pretty much done it in. Billy had been staying in the storeroom at Dot's ever since, and the traffic in and out of there was endless, especially at this time of day. And out here, the sky so wide, where you could be seen for miles ... it felt too exposed, too raw.

"What are you thinking?" Billy asked.

"Not much."

A wave of sadness swept over her. They wanted to hold each other, that was all. Just hold each other. And they couldn't even do that. That simple, tender gesture that wouldn't hurt anyone. Not even that.

Just like at home.

Billy took her hand. "It's an ungiving world, Stoner."

Stoner nodded and let herself feel Billy's hand tucked around hers.

It would have to do.

≈ ≈ ≈

"Son!"

She glanced over to her right. The crudely-built, whitewashed, pine-slab church building stood like a fort on a hilltop. Its spire stabbed the water-color sky. The doors were open. A middle-aged man in black wool pants, rolled-up shirt-sleeves, and a faded paisley vest ran down the path toward them.

"Rats," Billy muttered under her breath. "It's the Old Booger." She rammed her hat on her head and lifted the reins to give the mule a hurry-up nudge.

Stoner put a hand on her arm. "Hold it."

"What?"

"You don't want to alienate everyone in this town, do you? Not without provocation."

"I have provocation. I've been provoked on and off ever since I set foot in Tabor."

"Well, just in case things work out so you can settle down here—though God knows why you want to—try to keep a lid on your temper, okay?"

Billy sighed heavily.

The preacher reached the wagon just as Billy brought it to a halt. "Afternoon, son," he said. "My good wife told me what happened to you at the Emporium last week. I'm so terribly sorry."

Willing enough to pass it along, but she didn't do anything to stop it, Stoner thought. She forced herself to hold her tongue.

Billy slouched down in the seat and eyed the preacher warily.

"I've had a talk with Mr. Hayes. It won't happen again."

"Well," Billy said awkwardly, "thanks."

"It's a hard life we have here," the preacher explained, and smiled in Stoner's direction. "Sometimes people forget the niceties."

Niceties? Simple human decency is a "nicety"? "I see," she said.

The man turned back to Billy. "Son, I haven't met your friend."

Billy pulled her hat lower. "Stoner McTavish," she mumbled. "From back east."

"Scotsman?"

"Mostly."

"Welcome to Tabor." He made a little bow. "Henry Parnell, at your service."

"Pleased to meet you." Stoner reached down to shake hands, and realized too late that ladies probably didn't do that sort of thing out here.

Parnell hesitated, shot her the "what's-a-woman-doing-in-men's-clothes?" look she was rapidly becoming accustomed to, then grasped her fingertips and gave them a brief waggle. It was sort of like picking up an earthworm.

She reminded herself that this man had intervened on Billy's behalf on more than one occasion, and tried to choke down her feeling of distaste.

"I hope you're enjoying your stay with us," he said.

No, I am not enjoying my stay. I don't want to be here, I don't know how I got here, I want to go home, and I think your town is a thoroughly unpleasant place that I don't care if I never see again in this life or any other. "Yes," she said. "Very much."

Billy snorted through her nose. Stoner surreptitiously stepped on her foot.

"It would give us the greatest pleasure," Parnell said, "if you would join us for Sunday services."

"Thank you," Stoner said, having no intention of taking him up on it. "I may do that."

"I notice you've been out the Allens' direction." He shook his head sadly. "Terrible situation. Just terrible."

"It looked pretty bad," Stoner said.

The preacher straightened his vest. "I sent for the Marshall quite a while ago. I wonder if they even plan to send one."

"Surely they would," Stoner said.

He sighed. "This is a big territory, and U.S. Marshalls are few and far between." Parnell smiled, showing his teeth. "Forgive me. It's much too nice a day to be gloomy. But I do worry about my flock."

Billy uttered a grunt of impatience.

"William," Parnell said, "I need a small favor from you."

Billy glanced up.

"There's a stack of lumber out behind the church. Could you take it out to my good wife?"

"Dunno," Billy said. "This ain't my wagon."

"We'd be glad to," Stoner cut in.

Parnell expressed an oily smile. "Bless you both." He backed away from the wagon and turned to go. "We'll be looking forward to seeing you Sunday, Miss McTavish."

≈ ≈ ≈

The red-haired girl hadn't minded that Cullum was a bounty hunter. Most folks looked down on that way of life, though they were willing enough to pay him to do their dirty work. Hell, way he figured, he was like the buzzards and vultures and carrion crows. Ugly as sin, but the world surely would be a stinking place if they didn't do what they were made to do.

Still, there were times when he wasn't comfortable with it. Like now.

Cullum squinted against the sun, trying to catch a glimpse of a town, a cabin, any place he could walk around for a while, chat with the folks, ask a few questions

The girl he was after was a runaway. At least that's what he'd been told. Some kind of argument over the girl's work. Cullum spat in the dust. Over the father's drinking, more likely. More than an argument, too, from the looks of it. It'd been a long time since he'd seen a goose egg the size that buckeroo was sporting on his head. Bottle injury. Or maybe a frying pan.

The fellow hadn't been one of Cullum's favorite people, either. Hostile sort. Kind that was accustomed to getting his way. Wife looked like a starved, kicked hound. He was tempted to tell the fellow to go do his own dirty work.

But, hell's bells and gingerbread, family business was family business and none of his own. Besides, it looked like the daughter could handle herself.

Johnson chuckled to himself. He was looking forward to meeting this gal, but he'd best keep alert.

≈ ≈ ≈

"Durn it," Billy grumbled as she tugged a slab of rough-cut wood into position. "Why'd you get us into this?"

Stoner brushed her hair off her forehead and ended up with a speck of

155

sawdust in her eye. She blinked rapidly. "I'm not sure. I just had a hunch."

Billy heaved the wood onto the wagon bed. "Well, next time you have a hunch, leave me out of it."

"I'm sorry." She dug at the corner of her eye with the tip of her little finger. It seemed to push the sawdust deeper. "It seemed like a nice thing to do, and it wouldn't hurt you to store up good deeds."

"Huh," Billy grunted, and heaved another board onto the wagon.

Stoner pulled her upper eyelid down over her lower eyelid the way Aunt Hermione was always telling her to.

Billy kicked at the pile of lumber and sent it clattering to the ground. "We were having a perfectly nice time, weren't we?" She pulled a long board from the scattered heap. "Weren't we?"

"Yes," Stoner said, "but ..."

"So what'd you want to go and ruin it for?"

The sawdust felt like a chunk of jagged metal in her eye. "I didn't mean to ruin it. It seemed ..."

"Now we're stuck with this stupid job " Billy rammed her fists onto her hip bones and glared at Stoner. "Are you planning on helping me with this, or do you just want to watch?"

Stoner felt a wave of warm tingles rise from her feet to her face, the way she sometimes felt when Gwen yelled at her—not in an angry way, but ... well, taking command. She swallowed. "I do plan to help. But there's something ..."

"Jeez." Billy left the pile of boards and trotted over to her. "I didn't mean to make you cry."

"I'm not crying. I got something in my eye."

"Let me see." Billy thumbed back her eyelid and peered into her eye. "Look down."

She did.

"There it is, the little devil." Billy pulled a handkerchief from her pocket and made a sharp corner in the cloth. She took Stoner's chin in her hand. "Don't move, now. I don't want to blind you."

"Billy," Stoner said, standing very still and feeling as if she were melting into the ground. "Did Mary tell you anything about ... well, about why I'm here?"

"Some." She drew back. "Got it." She held out the handkerchief for Stoner to see.

"I believe you." Her eye still felt irritated. She rubbed at it.

"Stop that," Billy said, and shoved her hand away from her face. "Honest to God." She dampened her handkerchief with water from their picnic and bathed the hurt from Stoner's eye.

The melting feeling became more compelling. Quickly, she bent to pick up an end of the long board. "What did Mary tell you?"

"Some cock-and-bull story about time travelling." She hefted the other end. Together they tossed it into the wagon and bent for the next.

"Did it make any sense to you?"

"Sure." Billy lifted a smaller board by herself and slammed it onto the pile. "Damn convenient, if you ask me."

It was obvious that Billy was angry.

"Convenient?"

Billy grabbed a handful of wood blocks and launched them at the buck-board. The mule shifted anxiously.

"You're scaring the mule," Stoner said.

"If you ask me," Billy went on, turning her back and gathering up slivers of wood from the ground, "it's real handy if you don't like the way things are going. 'Excuse me, it's been swell knowing you, but I have to go back to my own time.' " She tossed the slivers onto the pile.

Stoner hoisted some short boards and added them to the stack. "I know it sounds crazy. It sounds crazy to me, too. But it's the truth …at least as far as I can understand it."

"Good," Billy said. "Your understanding surpasses mine."

Stoner stopped working. "Billy, have I offended you in some way?"

The woman glanced at her, then away. "Course not."

"I don't believe you."

Billy shrugged. "Don't believe me, then." She lifted an armload of boards and tossed them into the wagon.

"Please," Stoner said. "Talk to me."

The woman turned her back. Stoner went to her. "Billy …"

Billy was crying.

"Hey," Stoner said, and turned her and took her in her arms. "I have hurt you. I didn't mean to."

Billy wrapped her arms around Stoner's waist and held on tight. "It's nothing," she said, the anger gone from her voice. "I'm just being silly."

"I doubt that." Stoner kissed her temple gently. She didn't care if they were standing out in broad daylight, behind the church, visible for miles around.

"It's not fair," Billy said after a moment.

"What's not fair?"

"For this to feel so good."

Stoner smiled, aware of the woman's firm, soft body against hers, aware of her every breath. She tried to still her own breathing. Feelings of power surged through her. She could destroy the world, she thought, with the sheer strength of her will. "I know," she said.

"I love you," Billy said.

157

Stoner took a deep breath. "I think I love you, too." She started to laugh, knowing it was inappropriate but unable to help herself because she was nervous, and happy, all at the same time. "Back home they write songs about situations like this."

"Out here," Billy said, "they mostly write songs about cows." She backed away and slipped her hands into her pockets and frowned. Suddenly the cloud of puzzlement lifted from her face. "You have someone. Back home."

"Yes. But back home isn't back home in the usual sense. I mean, if I went back to Boston now, she wouldn't be there. Yet." She shook her head. "I can't make any sense of this."

Billy picked up one end of a board and motioned for Stoner to pick up the other. "Know what your trouble is?" she asked as they heaved it into the wagon. "You think too much."

"You're absolutely right," Stoner said.

"I don't want to come between you and ...?"

"Gwen."

Billy shoved the planks around a little. "You mentioned her, when you were in the fever."

"I thought you were her."

"Pretty name."

"It's Welsh," Stoner said irrelevantly.

"Bet she's a pretty girl."

"Woman."

"Pretty woman."

"She is to me," Stoner said.

"I wish I were pretty."

Stoner looked at her. "Billy, you're beautiful."

"Sure." She pulled a rope from under the driver's seat and began tying down the boards.

Stoner watched her. "You're upset," she said at last.

"A little. I never told anyone I loved them before."

"I'm sorry. Not that you told me, but that things are ... well, the way they are."

Billy made a vicious knot and yanked it tight. "I know."

"Billy ..."

The woman swung up onto the seat and lifted the reins. "I don't want to discuss it, okay? Let's just get this job done."

≈ ≈ ≈

It was the Anti-Christ, all right. And the Stranger was part of it.

He peeked out from his hiding place below ground.

158

The Bastard and the Stranger, embracing.

It was no more or less than he would expect.

And pretending to do favors for the Preacher. No one in town would suspect them once word got around they did favors for the Preacher.

No one except him.

They'd been out to the burned place. Must have been. There was nothing else to see out that way.

He was willing to bet they'd found the knife.

≈ ≈ ≈

Stoner watched as Billy hobbled the mule and set about untying the ropes that held the lumber on the wagon. There was such grace and sureness to her movements. The way she concentrated on each knot, patiently working it out. The way she tossed the rope over the load, then pulled it through the bottom and wound it into a skein and fastened it with a loop of rope around the sheaf and tossed it again. No wasted motion, taking her time. It was mesmerizing.

She thought of what it felt like, being touched by those hands, stroked by those fingers, held by those arms. She imagined resting her head against Billy's shoulder, feeling safe and loved, telling her ...

Billy turned toward her. "Is something wrong?"

"No." Stoner shook her head. "I was just thinking."

"Want to talk?"

She tilted her head toward the house, where Caroline (Mrs. the Reverend Henry) Parnell stood peeking at them through the curtains. "Not here."

She lifted one end of an eight foot four by six. Billy lifted the other. They carried it to the cleared ground beside the ashes of a burned outbuilding where Billy had laid out three short pieces of lumber to form a low platform that would keep the clean, new wood off the ground.

"I've never seen lumber this thick," Stoner said as they went back for another board. "What do you think he's building?"

Billy ran a glance over the wood. "Pig house, I'd guess."

"A pig house?"

"From the thickness of the wood. Pigs can knock down just about anything. Hefty devils."

"Stronger than horses?"

"More determined. Probably smarter. " Billy lifted an end of board and signaled for Stoner to lift the other. "You don't want to mess with pigs."

"Absolutely not," Stoner said. "Messing with pigs isn't one of my favorite pastimes." They tossed the board on the pile with an earsplitting clatter. "Did you live on a farm?"

159

"Not really. We kept pigs, though. For eating."

Right. No running out at 1 am to your local Super Stop and Shop for a pound of sugar-cured, preservative-loaded, nitrite-infested bacon. Not in this century. "Do you miss your home?"

"Some." Billy paused and leaned against the wagon to pull a splinter out of her hand. "I miss my animals. And my couple of friends." She looked out over the unbroken horizon. "And I surely do miss trees."

"I know what you mean." Stoner shoved the sleeves of her sweat shirt up to her elbows. "What about your mother? Do you miss her?"

Billy thought hard about that. "Sometimes I get lonely for her. But when I think about it, it's not her I'm lonely for. She's all right, but she couldn't be much of a mother, always worrying about what he might do next."

Stoner wanted to put an arm around her but held back. Caroline Parnell was still watching.

"So I guess what I really get lonely for," Billy went on, "is someone to love me. Take care of me. Not all the time, but every now and then."

"Yeah," Stoner said.

"My mother needed me to take care of her." Billy scuffed at the dust with her foot. "You know, there are times I'm glad I'm on the run, so I don't have to do that." She glanced up. "Do you think I'm terrible to feel that way?"

"Not at all. As Dr. Kesselbaum says, 'Emotions are information and therefore outside moral consideration.' " She grinned. "Dr. Kesselbaum is a gold mine of profundity. Some of the things she says even make sense."

Billy laughed and went to pick up another board. "Who's Dr. Kesselbaum?"

"My partner Marylou's mother." She hefted her end of the board. "She used to be my therapist."

"Your what?"

"Psychotherapist."

"What's that?"

Stoner pondered how to explain that to a pre-Freudian mind. "A psychotherapist is someone you tell your problems to and they help you understand them and figure out what to do."

"That's good," Billy said. "It's nice to have close friends like that."

"Well, a therapist isn't exactly a close friend. Sometimes you don't even know the person when you start." Sometimes you don't know the person when you finish, either, she thought, but decided that was too complicated.

Billy raised one eyebrow. "You tell your problems to someone you don't know? Funny custom."

160

"I'll bet all kinds of people tell Dot their problems."

"Sure. But they're drunk." She smiled like sunshine. "On the other hand, I've been telling you my innermost thoughts, and I don't really know you."

"True," Stoner said, returning her smile. "But I came highly recommended."

Billy laughed. "You mean Blue Mary? She didn't know you, either."

"Maybe she did and maybe she didn't," Stoner said. "It's hard to tell."

They dumped their board and went back for another.

"What do you mean?" Billy asked.

"Sometimes I get the funniest feeling she's my Aunt Hermione."

"Jeez," Billy said. "Seems to me you ought to know if a person's a relative or not."

"It would seem that way, wouldn't it?" Stoner hesitated. "Billy, do you believe in reincarnation?"

"I dunno," Billy said. "We had some Spiritualists back in Tennessee that used to talk about it." She shrugged. "Shoot, I have enough trouble with this life right in front of me. I don't need to go worrying backward and forward. Do you believe in it?"

"I'm beginning to."

"Well, I hope you enjoy it."

She heard a window bang open behind them.

"Billy Devon!" Caroline (Mrs. the Reverend Henry) Parnell's voice came at them like a crowing rooster. "Stop that lollygagging and finish your work!"

The window banged shut.

"Lovely individual," Stoner said as she gathered up an arm load of carryable wood. "Is that your name? Devon?"

"Not my real name. I'd be crazy to use my real name out here." Billy picked up a load of wood twice the size of Stoner's. "But, yeah, it's what I go by."

"Would you tell me?"

Billy hesitated. "It kind of scares me, not knowing you all that well. I mean, I think you're okay, but what if you turn out to be a bounty hunter or something."

"That's all right," Stoner said quickly. "I understand."

The woman looked at her in a worried way. "You're sure?"

"I'm sure."

Billy laughed. "First I tell you I love you, then I won't tell you my real name. You must think I'm some kind of a crazy person."

"No, I don't."

"Sure, you do."

161

"People even fall in love with people they don't really trust. It happens all the time."

"I guess it does."

"Billy, I wish I were free to ..."

"Oh, for the love of Heaven," Billy said with gentle irritation, "Will you stop feeling guilty?"

Stoner blushed and grinned and felt a huge burst of warmth toward her. She scraped up the last of the wood and tossed it on the pile. "I had a lover once—the first time I met her the woman scared me to death. I reacted like a dog, hair on the back of the neck rising, found myself backing into a corner, stuff like that. Then, as I got to know her, I kind of fell in love, and I told myself not to trust that other feeling I had at first."

"So what happened?" Billy inspected the pile, made a few adjustments.

"Well, to make a long story short, I should have trusted my first impressions."

"Oh." Billy made a large skein of the rope, winding it between her elbow and hand. "This woman you have back home, is that the same kind of thing?"

"Not at all. I always trusted Gwen, even when she was straight."

The woman glanced up. "Straight?"

"Uh ... heterosexual ... married ... you know."

"Yeah." Billy grinned. " 'Straight.' That's a heck of a word. What does that make you, crooked?"

"Technically," Stoner said, "I think the opposite of straight is not-uptight."

"Uptight. Sounds like something that happens to men when their pants don't fit." She hitched her pants up and stood on tip-toes, her face screwed up in a grimace of pain. "UP TIGHT!"

Stoner giggled.

Billy tossed the rope into the wagon and bent to release the mule. "What's it like for you," she asked, patting the animal's velvet nose, "being this way? I mean, how do folks treat you?"

"Some are okay," Stoner said. She climbed up onto the wagon. "Some aren't. Sometimes you can tell who's going to treat you all right, and sometimes you can't." She shrugged. "Life's full of surprises."

"Certainly is." Billy swung up beside her. She picked up the reins.

Stoner stopped her. "Billy, I really am sorry about ....you know. I wouldn't hurt you for the world."

"I know that."

"If things were different ..."

"Well, they aren't," Billy said, and gave the mule a slap.

As they passed the house, Stoner caught motion at the edge of her vi-

162

sion and looked up.

Caroline Parnell let the curtain drop and drew back into the shadows.

"What's with her?" Stoner said. "First she comes out and yells at us, then she hides from us."

Billy stopped the mule and tossed Stoner the reins. "I think I know the problem."

She swung over the side of the wagon and went to the door and knocked. "Miz Parnell."

Silence.

Billy waited, then knocked again. "Miz Parnell!"

More silence.

Billy stepped back from the door. "Miz Parnell," she hollered through cupped hands, "your husband already paid us. So don't stop whatever you're doin' and I'm sorry if I bothered you."

The upstairs curtains opened. "That's fine, Billy," Caroline Parnell called through the glass. "I'll tell the Reverend you did a good job."

Billy touched her fingertips to her hat. "Yes, Ma'am. Thank you, Ma'am." She got back into the wagon and took the reins.

"That was a nice thing to do," Stoner said.

"Hell." Billy turned the mule toward town. "I know the Old Booger keeps her on short rations."

"How do you know that?"

"You watch next time those ladies go shopping in town. When they come out of the Emporium, she'll be the only one without a package."

Stoner touched her arm. "Well, it was a nice thing to do, anyway, considering how they treat you."

Billy shrugged. "Doesn't do much good to keep adding mean to mean, I guess. That never accomplished anything."

≈ ≈ ≈

They returned to Dot's Gulch to find Dot in a frenzy of mops and brooms and buckets. The saloon looked as if a tornado had swept through it. Tables were overturned. Chairs upended. Lolly was frantically polishing brass, while Cherry dusted liquor bottles.

"My God," Stoner said. "What happened?"

Dot wiped the perspiration from her face with her apron. "Guests."

The place smelled of kerosene. "Did someone try to burn you out?"

"What?" Dot said.

Billy giggled.

"Somebody dumped kerosene in here," Stoner said.

"Coal oil's what we use for cleaning," Billy said.

"Oh." She took a moment to allow herself to feel appropriately ignorant.

"Billy," Dot said brusquely, "stop standing around and get that fire going in the stove. We have to wash all the bed linens. And the girls' clothes."

"I knew this was going to be a terrible day," Billy muttered, and stomped off toward the kitchen.

"And your stuff, too," Dot called after her. "You have to look decent by tomorrow night."

Stoner took a cloth and set to work polishing the top of the bar. "Seems like you're going to a lot of trouble for a bunch of cowboys."

"Cowboys!" Dot's eyebrows shot up. "Great God help us, I forgot all about the cowboys!"

"Let's close the place," Lolly grunted. She spat on the cuspidor and scrubbed at it with a piece of chamois. "If I have to look at one more cowboy, I swear I'll gag."

"If it's not for the cowboys," Stoner said, scrubbing furiously at a glass ring, "what's all the fuss about? You're having company?"

"Not just company," Cherry said. "Important company. The worst kind."

"I invited them months ago," Dot said as she wrung out a cloth and began scrubbing the floor. "I'd completely forgotten about it. Didn't even know they were speaking here. 'If you're ever in Tabor,' I said. Meant what I said, but I never thought ..."

"There have been notices at the Emporium for a week," Cherry said. "It didn't occur to me they'd be staying here."

"Of course it didn't," Lolly said. "You don't expect to find ladies like that in a whore house."

"I told you," Dot said, "as long as those women are under this roof, it isn't a whore house, it's a hotel."

"Excuse me," Stoner said as she finished with the bar and started on the shelves, "I still don't know what you're talking about."

Dot put her mop down. "Colorado's going to become a state in a few years. We want her to come in with votes for women. So these ladies are going around the territory making speeches, trying to do for us what they almost managed over in Kansas."

Stoner felt a tingle of excitement in her fingertips. "Suffragists!"

Dot nodded. "Well, last summer, in a moment of enthusiasm, I invited them to stay here at the Gulch if they were ever in Tabor. 'Course, I didn't call it the Gulch, just said 'my place'."

"Wait a minute," Stoner said, bouncing on the balls of her feet. "You have Suffragists staying here?"

"That's right," Cherry said. "On their way to Denver." She began to gather up the stained and ragged tablecloths and dump them into a basket.

164

"Which Dot would have realized if she ever read the notices posted just inside the door to the Emporium, which she doesn't, choosing to remain ignorant."

Dot muttered under her breath.

Lolly rolled her eyes. "And now we have to pay for your lies."

Dot dug into her apron pocket and took out a crumpled letter and handed it to Stoner.

She smoothed it out. The letter was written in a flowing, ornate script.

Topeka, Kansas
10 October, 1871
Dear Mrs. Gillette,
On behalf of Mrs. Jenney, Mother Armstong, and myself,
I thank you for your very kind invitation. We would be
delighted to partake of your hospitality on the occasion
of our visit to Tabor.
We expect to arrive in Tabor on Saturday, November 25.
As Mrs. Stone and her husband, Dr. Blackwell, will be
accompanying us, we will require one additional bedroom,
for a total of three (Mrs. Jenney and I are accustomed to
sharing a room).
We look forward to meeting you and the citizens of your
fine town. Our cause is just. We shall prevail.

Cordially,
Clarina Nichols

Stoner looked again at the arrival date. November 25. Today must be Thanksgiving. She wondered why no one seemed to be celebrating.

"So," Cherry went on, "the first we hear about these fancy guests is when the stage arrives from Denver bringing the letter." She backed into the swinging doors to the kitchen and pushed them open. "Which went the long way around because some idiot in Topeka put it on the train instead of handing it to a west-bound stage driver with the newspapers and mail as any sensible person would have done."

The doors whooshed shut behind her.

Stoner dug into her pocket for her lucky Susan B. Anthony silver dollar.

"Look." She shoved the coin at Dot.

Dot studied it. "Susan B. Anthony?"

"That's right. You know who she is, don't you?"

"Well, of course I do," Dot said. "I'm not ignorant." She peered at it.

165

"1979? Why does it say 1979?"

"That's when it was minted. Will be minted." Here we go again. "It's commemorative."

"That certainly explains it," Dot said with a laugh, and handed it back to her. "You must be a real admirer."

"I am." She gripped the edge of the bar, hardly daring to hope. "The Mrs. Stone in the letter ... is that by any chance ..." She took a deep breath. "... Lucy B. Stone?"

"That's right," Dot said as she turned back to her mopping. "Mrs. Lucy Stone. Kept her maiden name, you know. Jesus God, this place is a mess."

"I can't believe it," Stoner said excitedly. "I'm actually going to meet Lucy B. Stone."

Dot glanced up. "You will if you don't arouse yourself into a heart attack."

"I was named for her!"

Lolly put her chamois down. "Lucy B. Stone?"

"That's right. That's my real name, Lucy B. Stoner McTavish."

"Golly, then you must know her."

"Well, not really."

"Your family knows her?"

Stoner shook her head.

"I don't get it," Lolly said. "How come you were named for someone your family doesn't know?"

"She was a great woman."

"I suppose that's true," Dot said. "But when you were born she was probably still a girl."

"When I was born, she'd been dead for years."

Dot sighed and shook her head. "Whatever you say, honey."

≈ ≈ ≈

Friday morning was clear and warm.

The back door to the Chinese laundry stood ajar, oozing steam. May tapped gently and waited. From inside she could hear the chatter of voices. She listened for a moment, enjoying the familiar rhythms, then knocked again, louder. A man's face appeared. He wore the traditional work clothes, his head covered with a tight-fitting cap. When he saw her, he registered surprise briefly, but quickly assumed the blank, non-committal look she had seen so often in her countrymen here.

"Excuse me," May said. "I'm looking for Kwan Lu."

The man turned to the room behind him and spoke quickly and in an undertone. He returned to the door and stood aside, gesturing her in.

It took a moment for her eyes to adjust to the shadows after a day in the

166

sunlight. She knew she looked terrible. Her dress and hair and suitcase were thick with dust. Her shoes were caked with mud.

"I'm sorry for my appearance," she said. "I've come a long way to see Kwan Lu."

Over the smell of soap and steam, she caught the pungent odor of cooking. An aroma from home, unlike the thick, greasy smell of the kitchens she had smelled along the way. She had to smile.

A shadow materialized into the shape of a thick-set, middle-aged woman. The woman rose from a straight-backed chair. "I am Kwan Lu."

"You sent me a letter." May dug in her purse and pulled it out. "You said you have information for me. I've come to speak with you about that."

"What information?" the man asked.

"This is woman's business," the older woman said.

The man made a gesture of disinterest and went to the store out front.

"How many times," Kwan Lu said with a laugh, "have we used the man's arrogance to our own advantage?"

May nodded, relieved to finally be in the presence of someone who spoke woman's language.

"Please sit down," said the other woman. "We will have tea, and then talk."

They sipped tea from cups so fine the light shone through, and talked of trivial things. Of life here and in San Francisco. Of how May's mother had been brought over by her father, just as Lu had been by Peter (he called himself Peter Kwan, wanting to be American). Of how their employers had tried to forbid it, but the men saved their money secretly to pay for the trip. Of how the Kwans had escaped from the railroad gang, slipping away in the night, hiding out for weeks, living on scraps of food smuggled to them by the men who stayed with the railroad. Their long migration east from Nebraska, afraid to stop until they reached the safety of remote, isolated Tabor. Of China and relatives, and possible connections.

At last Lu, nibbling on a cookie, sat back in her chair and said, "So."

"The man is here?" May asked.

"If this is the man you're looking for."

"He killed my father," May said. "The night was dark and cold. My father had been drinking ..." She didn't know why she said this. It was irrelevant, and yet she always linked her father with the smell of alcohol. "The man must have leapt on him from behind, and strangled him. He has to be avenged."

Lu nodded.

"We didn't know where to look. He could have gone anywhere. Finally I decided to speak with some of my cousins who work on the railroad.

167

They might hear a rumor. I asked them to spread the word that we were looking for this man. I knew, if he was still anywhere around, sooner or later we'd hear something."

"And so you did."

"In your letter," May said, "you say you're certain this is the man. May I ask, how are you certain?"

"Two autumns ago, when the railroad bed north of here was being built, a group of our countrymen camped near here. Naturally, we went out to see what could be done to make them comfortable. They told us of a man who had travelled with them from San Francisco to Kansas—a white man—who bragged of killing a Chinese in the way you described." Lu shook her head. "This man knew he could throw his words around that way and no one would threaten his life. It was his way of asserting his superiority. He knew he'd never be punished for killing a Chinese, but if one of our people raised a hand against him ..."

"I know," May Chang said. "But he was wrong."

Kwan Lu gave her a frightened look. "Do you really believe you can bring this man to justice?"

"I do."

"The courts will never convict a white man on the word of a Chinese woman."

"He's already been tried and convicted," May said. "In my heart."

The older woman sat silently for a moment, digesting what May had said. "I see," she said at last. "This is a very dangerous thing you're doing."

"No," said May. "What he did was a very dangerous thing. What makes you say he's here now?"

"He was pointed out to me then," Lu said. "I saw him again 18 months ago when he came to Tabor. He had changed his appearance, but it's the same man. When I heard you were looking ..."

"Thank you for your help," May said. Now that she was so close, she wanted to get it over with. She was rapidly losing her taste for violence in this violent land. She stood to go. "And for the tea. If you'll tell me how to find him, from now on we'll forget we ever had this conversation. You mustn't get in trouble over this."

Kwan Lu rose and put a hand on her shoulder. "I really have to warn you. The man has made himself a respected member of the community. The people of Tabor won't sit back and let you harm him without reprisals."

"I'll get away quickly. I can ride like the wind."

"Where is your horse?"

"I'll have to rent one."

168

"How? Will you stride into the livery stable and demand service? You're Chinese, May, and a woman. They won't let you rent even a broken down wagon and a half-dead mule. And you'll be noticed." Lu shook her head. "I don't think you can do it."

May sank back into her chair. To come all this way ... She had to finish what she came to do. It was a matter of honor. Brothers would have taken care of it, of course, but she had no brothers. But to die? Was that the price she'd have to pay?

"Perhaps," Lu said thoughtfully, sensing her despair and determination, "I know a white woman who would rent a horse for you."

May looked up. "Who?"

"Go to the saloon, to the back door, and speak to the owner, Mrs. Gillette. Mention my name. She'll help you. We've done each other favors from time to time." She smiled. "The outcasts in this place are good at helping one another."

"She'll wonder why I don't get the horse myself."

"She only has to look at you. She won't wonder. Or, if she does, she won't ask."

May straightened the folds in her skirt. "I'm grateful for your help."

Kwan Lu brushed her thanks aside. "You'll stay here until you've done what you came for, of course?"

"I can't involve you in this."

"Listen to me," Lu said. "You have to stay out of sight. This isn't San Francisco. Strangers are noticed and discussed. Where would you sleep? In the brothel? The stable? Besides, I'd welcome the sight of another Chinese woman's face."

May smiled. She understood loneliness. "For one night only. I think I should get away as soon as possible, before they begin to wonder."

"Good."

"Now, tell me how to find the man."

"It'll be easy," Lu said. "He's the town preacher."

≈ ≈ ≈

Cullum Johnson arrived in mid-afternoon the next day, just as Billy pulled the wagon to a halt in the alley beside the saloon.

Billy gave the stranger a casual glance. Then looked again, sharply. The color drained from her face.

"What is it?" Stoner asked.

Billy threw the reins into Stoner's hands, jumped down from the wagon, and ran toward the back, pulling her gun from its holster as she ran.

"Billy!"

She tied the wagon to the hitching post and started after her.

169

"Whoa, there," Dot called from the back door.

Stoner whoaed.

"I need to talk to you."

Torn, she looked after Billy. "There's something wrong," she said.

"Adolescent trouble," Dot insisted as Billy set something on a fence post at the far end of the corral. "He'll work it out getting off a few rounds." She pulled Stoner toward the kitchen. "I need to talk to you."

A Chinese woman sat by the stove, erect in a bent wood chair, hands folded primly in her lap.

"This is May Chang. From San Francisco. She needs a favor from you," Dot said.

From me? "Okay."

"Can you go down to the livery stable and rent a horse for tomorrow?"

"Sure," Stoner said. "But why me?"

"You're a stranger. Everything you do is strange. They'll gossip, but they won't ask questions."

They will if they see me ride, Stoner thought. She could hear Billy out back, firing shot after shot after ... "Do I have to ride it?"

Dot looked at her. "Is that a problem?"

"I don't ride well." The truth is, I'm terrified of horses. And the one time I did ride, had to ride, did nothing to relieve my anxiety.

"All you have to do is get it here," Dot said. "Think you can look as if you ride?"

"I guess so. What time?"

"Sunset," May said.

"Any particular type of horse?"

"A fast one."

My favorite kind. Fast and mean. Wonderful.

She wanted to ask what the woman wanted it for, but everyone was being so close-mouthed it looked like one of those the-less-you-know-the-better-off-you-are situations. "No problem. Is something wrong?"

"They won't rent to me," the woman said. "They won't do business with a person of my race."

"You know," Stoner said in frustration, "people out here have a real attitude problem. They don't like other races, they don't like certain professions, they don't like orphans and out-of-wedlock children, they don't much like women ..."

May looked up at her. "Is it different where you come from?"

"Well, not really," Stoner admitted. "But at least it isn't so overt." Or wasn't, until the past few years when Mr. Reagan rolled us back 40 years by looking the other way when hate crimes happened, by setting the classes and the races and the sexes and the sexual preferences against one another. By making bigotry fashionable once again.

Dot turned back to the woman. "Tell Lu Kwan I'll stop over one of these days soon. We haven't had a good chat in ages."

Dismissed, Stoner hurried back to find Billy.

"Think you might tell me what's up?"

Arms held straight out in front of her, Billy took careful aim at the tin can on the fence post. "Nothing." She fired the pistol and missed the target. The report was numbing.

"Don't give me that," Stoner said when she could hear again. "That man freaked you out. Scared you."

"Did not," Billy snapped, and fired again. The tin can stood untouched. She pulled the trigger frantically, again, again, again.

Stoner grabbed her arm. "Stop that and talk to me."

Billy pulled away and dug a handful of bullets from her pocket. "It's nothing," she said as she rammed the bullets into the chamber.

"Billy."

She fired six times in rapid succession. The air reeked of gunpowder. The tin can was unmoved. "Damn it!" Billy said in a frightened voice.

"Come on, tell me what's wrong."

Billy dug in her pocket for more bullets. "I know him. Never met him. Seen him around."

Stoner waited.

"He's a bounty hunter from back home."

Fear gripped her coldly. "Do you think he's ..."

"Hell, yes, I think he's ..." She looked at Stoner. The hand holding the gun slumped to her side. "What am I going to do?" Her voice was small.

Stoner felt helpless. "I don't think he recognized you."

"He will."

"How do you think he found you?" Stoner asked, stalling for time to think.

Billy's hands were trembling. Stoner took the gun and put it in its holster and wrapped her own hands around Billy's.

"If I knew that," Billy said shakily, "I'd have stayed one jump ahead of him." Her eyes got wet and glisteny with tears. "Do you think my Ma sent him after me?"

"Maybe," Stoner said gently. "Or maybe your father isn't dead after all."

"I can't go back there, Stoner."

"I know. You don't have to."

"I'd rather die."

"We'll think of something," Stoner said, trying to sound more positive than she felt. "There are other things you can do."

171

"I didn't tell you all of it," Billy said desperately. "He did stuff to me …"

Stoner shook her lightly. "I told you you wouldn't have to go back, and you don't."

"… bad stuff, stuff I don't like to talk about."

"You don't have to tell me," Stoner said, and took her in her arms protectively, not caring who saw or what they thought. "I know what you're talking about." She held her for a moment. "Look," she said at last, "I'll go inside and find out what he really knows, before we get ourselves in a state." She kissed the top of Billy's head. "Okay?"

Billy nodded.

"You can keep on practicing, but for Heaven's sake, calm down. You're wasting bullets."

≈ ≈ ≈

She was the most beautiful woman Cullum Johnson had ever seen. As beautiful as the red-haired gal, but with the added ripeness and dignity of maturity. He took his glass and went and sat at a table where he could sip his drink and look at her and try to catch his breath.

She finished drying glasses and poured herself a shot of bourbon and came to his table. "Well, sir," she said as she sat down, "What brings you to Tabor?"

He was blushing like a school kid. He hoped his skin was weathered enough so she wouldn't notice. "Business," he said gruffly.

"What kind of business are you in, Mr. … Mr.?"

"Johnson. Cullum Johnson." He took off his hat and placed it carefully on the table and combed his hands through his hair.

She held out her hand. "Dorothy Gillette. Most folks call me Dot."

His big, rough hand swallowed hers. "Pleased to make your acquaintance, Mrs. Gillette."

He waited for her to correct him, to say "Miss Gillette". She didn't. His heart cracked a little. "This your husband's place?" Might as well try and take the measure of the man before he went any farther.

She threw her head back and laughed. Sweetest sound he'd ever heard. Sweeter, even, than that travelling opera singer he'd heard some years back.

"No sir," she said. "My no-good husband would have run this place into the dust inside of two months." She shook her head. "There's no way I'd let that useless individual get his hands on what's mine and mine alone."

Hope made his heart pound. "Separated?" He realized what he'd said, and blushed again. "I don't mean to pry."

"As good as," Dot said. "Haven't seen the old coot in …" She sipped

172

her drink. "... must be five, six years now. Last I heard he was drinking himself to death somewhere over in the Texas panhandle." She took another sip. "Unless the Indians or Mexicans got him."

Cullum thought this must be one of the best days of his life. "Some folks don't know when they're well off," he said philosophically.

"That's the Heaven-sent truth. Are you planning on staying with us long, Mr. Johnson?"

"Depends. What kind of accommodations do you have in this town?"

"You're looking at it," Dot said.

He raised one eyebrow. "No hotel?"

"No need for one since the railroad bypassed us. Tabor isn't exactly the hub of civilization."

Cullum cleared his throat, feeling suddenly shy. "Well." He cleared his throat again. "Don't suppose you could put me up?"

"You can stay in the spare room for tonight," Dot said. "But we're full up for tomorrow."

"That's all right," Cullum said. "By tomorrow night, I'll either have my business done, or I'll be moving on."

He glanced up as Stoner came in through the door under the stairs. "Now, there's something you don't see every day," he said. "Woman in pants. Funny kinda shirt, too."

Dot looked over at her. "She says that's called a 'sweat shirt'. Isn't that the darnedest name you ever heard?"

Cullum grimaced. "Foreigner?"

"Far as I can tell."

"You know where from?"

"Well, she claims Boston," Dot said, and shook her head. "I don't know. Could be anywhere."

He took a swallow of his drink. "England, I'd bet. They got terrible words for things over there."

Dot smiled at him. "You seem to be a man of the world, Mr. Johnson."

Hearing his name said that way, by this absolute grand champion of a woman, almost made him wet his pants. "Oh," he mumbled, "I guess I been around."

"You never did say what your line of work is."

For the first time in a long time, he was almost ashamed to say it. "I reckon you could say I'm in the lost and found business."

The woman's eyes went flat a little, as if she didn't entirely approve. "Well, now," she said at last, looking at him hard, "I've always wondered what makes a man take up that means of making a living."

He searched his mind to try to come up with the truth. He wanted to tell this woman the truth. "Always been kind of restless. Don't like crowds,

173

though, so that let out cowboyin' and leadin' wagon trains. Gave some thought to looking for gold, but never been real lucky. And I'm good with a gun, and handy at tracking."

"Who are you tracking now?"

He rubbed his hand over his chin and wished he'd stopped for a shave before coming in here. "Young gal from back home. Gave her Pa a good knock over the head and lit out. Thought he was dead, I reckon. But he ain't dead, just mad as hell."

Dot frowned. "Doesn't seem right. She probably had good reason."

"Probably did." He was beginning to feel depressed.

"What do you figure he'll do to her if you find her?"

He hung his head. "Nothin' good, no doubt."

"No doubt," Dot said disapprovingly.

"Don't suppose you've seen her around."

"Nope, but I wouldn't tell you if I had," Dot said. "It's a reprehensible thing you're doing, Mr. Johnson."

He wondered if he should shoot himself now, or wait until sundown. "Well, I didn't really think about it that way."

Dot snorted. "That's a man for you. What were you thinking about?"

What the hell? She couldn't think any worse of him than she already did. "I was broke," he said, "and couldn't come up with any other reason for living."

"Just because you were broke?"

"Broke and a fool. Let myself get romantic over a young gal. Even asked her to marry me." He laughed harshly. "An old buzzard like me."

Dot poured him another drink. "That's how it is with young ones, Cull. Break your heart every time."

She gave his arm a sympathetic little pat and made the sun come out all over again.

They sat for a moment in silence. The foreign gal was making herself busy washing clean glasses.

"Stoner!" Dot called. "Leave that stuff alone."

She looked up. "Huh?"

"If you want to be useful, try doing something that isn't already done."

The gal gazed around. "What?"

"Did you pick up the fancy linen from Kwan's like I asked you?"

"It's in the wagon."

"Then give Cherry a hand in the kitchen."

"I don't cook very well."

"Well, God Almighty," Dot said. "You can take orders, can't you?" She made a shooing gesture.

The foreign gal sidled out of the room.

174

"Stoner?" Johnson said. "That's a different kind of name."

Dot rolled her eyes. "Want to hear something really different?"

He nodded.

"She claims she was named after someone that died before she was born."

"Nothing strange about that."

"Nothing except this person who died before she was born is coming here tomorrow."

He frowned and tried to think that one through, but it didn't make any sense. "Know what I think, Mrs. Gillette?"

"I told you," she said in a flirty kind of way, "call me Dot."

"Dot." The word was like warm muffins and strawberry jam on his tongue. "What I think, Dot, is the world's turning much too peculiar, much too fast."

"Amen to that, Cull" Dot said, and poured them each another drink.

≈ ≈ ≈

"You were right," she said to Billy.

Billy sank onto a wooden crate and let her hands dangle between her knees. "Shit."

"But you didn't kill your father."

"Double shit."

Stoner sat down beside her. "I think Dot's trying to talk him out of chasing you."

The woman looked up. "Dot knows? About me?"

"I don't think so. She disapproves on general principles."

Billy took off her hat and turned it around and around in her hands. The sun was going down, spreading liquid pewter across the prairie. A chicken set up a ruckus somewhere down the alley. That set the livery stable dog to barking. Billy looked up. "I guess I'd better hit the trail."

"Where would you go? You don't have any money, do you?"

Billy shook her head.

"You don't even have a horse."

"I can steal a horse."

"No," Stoner said. "You can't just go on piling one crime on top of another. You have to stop sometime."

Billy gave a sharp, humorless laugh. "I almost believed it," she said. "For a few minutes back there I thought I could start making plans. God, Stoner, I don't want to spend the rest of my life running."

Chapter 10

The cowboys began to drift in late Friday afternoon. By seven pm word had spread that the upstairs of the Dot's Gulch was closed to business, and things started to turn mean. By eight pm they had frightened the Reinhardt's cow so badly her milk went thin and she'd have to be freshened. Which led Gus Reinhardt to remark that he thought old Daisy Belle had just been looking for an excuse to get herself in the pasture with the Svensens' bull all along. They tried to set fire to the livery stable, and shot out the upper panes of Doc Kreuger's office windows, scaring the old man so bad he swore off the bottle for the next twelve hours.

Dot took it pretty much in stride. She'd seen plenty of mean, disappointed cowboys in her life. As long as they did their helling outside in the street, she figured it was none of her affair. She broke up a couple of fights inside the saloon, and just as it seemed things were getting out of hand, Cull showed up and appointed himself bouncer for the evening. Lolly and Cherry flirted and teased and picked up a few dollars from boys who thought they still might have a chance if they tipped big enough for their drinks.

At one point Cherry excused herself and went upstairs with a black cowboy from Alabama who'd served in the Union army—just for the unique experience of having a toss with a gentleman of her own race—and returned shortly to whisper to Lolly that black boys did seem more skillful than white boys but not by much.

Someone started the rumor that Cullum Johnson wasn't just Big Dot's bouncer, but actually the town sheriff—so tough and ornery he didn't have to wear a badge, his presence alone could quiet a mob. That put a considerable damper on things, and Dot congratulated herself for having the foresight to start that particular bit of gossip.

Around nine, Lolly, coming behind the bar to fetch a broom to clean up broken glass, remarked to Dot that "if those suffergits are as rowdy as

176

these cowboys, we won't make it through the weekend."

"Suffragists, not suffergits," Dot barked, her patience beginning to wear thin. "And I want you to treat those ladies with respect."

"Ladies," Lolly moaned, and plunged back into the fray.

≈ ≈ ≈

He'd expected to hear from the Beast before this. He'd thrown down the challenge. Surely ...

Suppose they hadn't found the knife.

He crossed his arms over his chest and stared into the twilight sky.

A few wispy clouds hovered near the horizon. A flock of geese arrowed high overhead, their honking like the distant barking of dogs.

What if he'd hidden it too well? In the excitement of the moment, he might have buried it too deep.

The Sanctified Man chewed his lip.

Careless. That's what he'd been, careless. Just like his Pa always said. Careless and good-for-nothing.

But Pa was one of Them. One of the Satan-people. Like the Stranger that followed the Beast. Not so powerful, maybe, but he'd had the ability to transform.

What if the Beast called them back, all the ones who'd been destroyed? What if the Beast could raise his Pa from the dead?

His hands were trembling. Trembling like quick sand.

The knife would protect him. The Sacred Symbols would sap the Devil's powers right through Its skin. They'd think they had found his own weapon. They'd pass it back and forth, gloating. They wouldn't know the thing They passed between Them was the instrument of Their own destruction.

But if they hadn't found it ...

He couldn't sit here wondering, thinking bad thoughts. He had to know.

He scurried to the barn, threw a saddle on his horse, and set out for the burned-out farm.

The night was cold, the stars hard and distant. Not much of a moon. But he knew the way. He'd ridden it a dozen times – to stop by for a pastorly chat, to offer comfort when the youngest child took sick and died. And last night.

He sensed as much as saw the standing chimney. Got down from his horse. He stood for a moment to take his bearings, then crouched close to the ground and put a match to his lantern. Closing the shutter almost to a sliver, he swept the light back and forth among the ashes, then searched the earth close to the fire.

He found the oil can. But not where he'd thrown it. Someone had been here, all right.

He dropped down on his hands and knees and searched for foot prints. It didn't take long to find them, the lantern light casting deep shadows with sharp edges. Two sets. And, most telling of all, one set showed a tread he'd never seen before. Deep triangular indentations scattered across the print's surface. Nobody he'd ever heard of made boots with that kind of patterned sole. Nobody in this part of the country.

It didn't take a genius to figure out whose boots had made those prints.

The Beast had the knife.

A smile broke over his face.

He could to do it now. Tonight. All he had to do was lure them into town. The Witches would come, tomorrow, not knowing. With the Beast gone, their power would be nothing. Nothing compared to his.

Already he could feel how The Power would surge through him from the very ground he stood on. Pulsating. Throbbing. He would be an unstoppable, relentless machine. A machine of Righteousness. Purity. Virtue. Justice. A machine of Vengeance.

He raised his arms toward the sky, toward the last of the fading day.

Tonight he would have the Power.

≈ ≈ ≈

The crisp, clear air carried the uproar all the way out to Blue Mary's. Gunshots, shouts, breaking glass. Stoner hadn't heard this much noise since the last time the Red Sox won the AL East Championship.

Blue Mary seemed completely unperturbed. She sat in her rocker, stripping leaves of herbs from their stems and crumbling them between her hands, placing them in labelled jars. Every now and then she glanced up to give Stoner an encouraging nod and smile.

Stoner paced the room and tried to walk the edge off her anxiety.

She wished there were something she could do. Now. Tonight. All she'd accomplished today was to deliver a horse to May Chang.

There was no way Billy could stay in Tabor. Not with the bounty hunter on her trail and closing in. If she could take the woman home with her.... But she didn't know if this trip through time was a one-person junket as Blue Mary said, or had space available for a group tour. More important, she didn't know if she'd even get back herself. It might be a one-way trip, and she'd be doomed to spend the rest of her life in Tabor trying to explain thinsulate.

Don't think like that, she told herself roughly before she could sink into depression. This whole thing is like one of those computer games. As soon as you accidentally push the right button, you'll be out of here.

Billy seemed to have lost her capacity for thought or action. She sat slumped at the table, staring down into a rapidly-cooling mug of coffee and biting her lip. "She's going to be furious with me," she said at last.

"Who?"

"Dot. She needs help tonight, and I ran out on her."

Stoner raked her hand through her hair in exasperation. "Is that what you're worried about?"

"Sure."

"For God's sake, Billy! There's a bounty hunter after you. And you're worried about your job?"

"When people are counting on you, it's not right to let them down."

Stoner went to her and took her face in her hands. "Listen to me. Dot will understand. If I know her, she's doing just fine. You're the one ..."

"You haven't seen that place with two dozen drunken cowboys in it."

"We have to figure out what to do about you," Stoner said emphatically.

Billy put her head down on the table. "I don't even want to think about that."

"You have to think about it."

"Just leave me alone, Stoner," Billy said in an exhausted voice.

"I'm sorry." She rested her hands on Billy's shoulders.

Billy slipped her hands under Stoner's, locking their fingers together. "We could go somewhere together," she mumbled.

Stoner wrapped her in her arms. "I wish we could. But I'm afraid we can't. It's ..." She glanced at Blue Mary for confirmation.

"You can't stay," the woman said firmly but gently. "And Billy can't go back with you. If she meets herself coming and going ..." She shook her head sadly. "Truly an impossible situation. We planned it badly."

"I never planned this," Stoner said.

"Yes, you did, dear. We all did. Even Billy."

"There she goes again," Billy said.

Stoner laughed without much humor. "She's hopeless. Just like Aunt Hermione." She pulled Billy tight against her, drinking in the feel of the woman's back against her breasts.

"I really love you," Billy said softly.

Stoner rested her cheek on Billy's head. "So do I. I feel as if I've known you forever."

"Me, too."

"You have," Blue Mary said.

Billy moaned.

"I'll never understand," said Blue Mary, "why people insist on making a mystery out of what is actually a very simple thing."

"It's simple for you," Stoner said. "Lots of people think it's pretty whacko."

179

Blue Mary smiled. "That's because they prefer to agonize." She finished with her stack of herbs and took another. "I just can't grasp that." She looked up thoughtfully. "I suppose, if I ever do, I'll be satisfied to move on to another Plane."

"The reason I can't believe it," Stoner said, aware that Billy could feel her heart beating against her back, "is that it's so attractive."

Blue Mary shook her head. "Bewildering. Totally bewildering."

Someone in town set off what sounded like a string of Chinese firecrackers.

"They certainly are rowdy tonight," Stoner said.

Billy ran her cheek along Stoner's arm. "Last August we had three cattle drives come through in the same week. I'll bet there wasn't a pane of glass left in town by the time they left."

"Why do they put up with it?"

"No sheriff."

"Maybe they could hire one."

"Maybe they will," Blue Mary said.

Billy laughed. "Who'd want to settle down in this place? That's why I figured I'd be safe. Nobody'd ever come here."

"Seems to me," Stoner said, "it's the height of the tourist season right now. Cowboys, suffragists, and time travellers."

She wished Billy didn't feel so good in her arms. It made her confused inside, off center, out of balance. She pulled away and slipped her hands into her pockets.

Her hand touched the strange knife. She pulled it out. "Mary, have you ever seen anything like this?"

Blue Mary took it from her and studied it. She drew in her breath in a little gasp.

"What is it?"

"Satanic symbols."

"You're kidding."

"Look." The older woman pointed to the crude carvings. "The reversed pentagram. The inverted cross. The signs of the horns ... Where did you find this?"

"Out by the Allens'."

"This isn't good."

Billy looked at her. "What do you mean?"

"What we're dealing with here is bigger than life."

"Magic?" Stoner asked.

"Perhaps. But Black Magic is unpredictable, more likely to turn on the user. No, what we're faced with is someone who believes he has the power of Magic. And that can be the most dangerous kind of person."

"I don't understand any of this," Billy said.

Blue Mary got up and went to her bedside box. She searched through the contents and brought out a handful of sparkling, polished stones. "Take these. Both of you."

Stoner shared the stones with Billy.

"Are these magic?" Billy asked.

"Maybe," Blue Mary said enigmatically. "It depends on who believes in them."

A movement at the window caught Stoner's attention. She looked out. The sky above the horizon glowed pinkish yellow. Pillars of light reached into the night, then fell back. "That's amazing," She said. "I've never seen Northern Lights like that before."

Blue Mary followed her glance. "That's the south window, dear. It can't be ..."

She ran to the window and shoved the curtains wide. "Something's wrong." She reached for her coat. "Billy, hitch up the mule. Hurry!"

Billy bolted from the cabin.

"Come on, Stoner," Blue Mary ordered, handing her her vest and Billy's jacket and hat and gun belt.

"What is it?"

"Tabor's burning."

≈ ≈ ≈

By the time they reached town, Dot's Gulch was gone. The cowboys, who had sobered up considerably in the melee, were beating at the flames with wet blankets. The towns people had formed a bucket brigade, but the long summer had left the town well low, and they couldn't pump water fast enough to keep ahead of the blaze.

People were shouting. She could see them shouting, but the roar and crash of falling timber drowned out the sound of voices. A wall collapsed. Sparks flew into the sky like swarms of fireflies. For an instant she glimpsed the gilt-edged mirror, reflecting the fire back onto itself. Then a swirl of black smoke blew in front of her eyes, and when it cleared the mirror was gone. The balcony collapsed in a cascade of embers.

Stoner jumped from the wagon and threw herself into the mob. She grabbed a passing cowboy. "Dot! Have you seen Dot?"

It seemed to take him a moment to focus. "Yeah. Yeah, she's out."

"Lolly and Cherry?"

"I dunno." He pulled away and ran back to fight the fire.

Stoner followed him, pushing at milling bodies. Ogling bystanders formed a thick wall around the scene. She hurled herself against it, shoving and elbowing until she had forced a crack. Slipping through, she was flung backward for a second by an explosion of heat that singed the hairs on her arms. Near the flames she saw Dot, pacing back and forth, her hair flying. Her face and arms were black with ash. Tears cut rivers through the soot on her cheeks.

Stoner grabbed her. "Dot!"

The woman clutched at her sleeve. "The girls," she shouted above the flames. "In the back room."

"Come on!" Stoner seized Dot's arm and pulled her toward the alley. She snatched a damp blanket from a cowboy. Sparks rose from the crashing walls and settled on Dot's dress. Stoner brushed at them frantically. She saw Joseph Hayes with a bucket of water, about to waste it in the flames. "Here!" she shouted. "Throw it here!"

He turned, saw the tiny tongues of fire that licked at Dot's dress, and tossed the water in their direction, soaking them both. The sudden chill cut deep.

The back wall of the kitchen was still standing, but the door and window panes were gone. Stoner peered through the billows of smoke. Someone was in there, moving, turning in circles, disoriented. She couldn't make out who it was.

"Stay here!" she ordered. Before Dot had a chance to argue, she pulled the water-soaked blanket over her head and hurled herself through the flames.

The sound was deafening. The light blinded her. The water in her wet clothes seemed to boil. She took a breath. Fire seared her nose and mouth and flashed in her lungs.

She had to work fast. Looking around desperately, she caught a glimpse of a human form on the floor. She bent low and ran over to it.

It was Cherry, hugging the floor boards, her body flung protectively over Lolly's.

"Cherry!"

The woman looked up.

"Cherry! Keep your head down. Crawl."

Cherry shook her head. "I'm not leaving her."

Stoner hit the ground and inched close to her. She tossed the steaming blanket over them. "You grab one arm, I'll take the other. Hurry!"

She thought she saw the outside wall begin to move, to bow inward.

"Pull!" She set her feet against the floor and hitched backward, dragging Lolly behind her.

Cherry snatched up the other arm. "What are you doing here?" she panted. "We're just a couple of whores."

"Shut up and pull."

They reached the door just as the wall swayed outward, then in, then outward ...

182

"Dot!" Stoner screamed. "Get out of the way."

... and began to fall.

She saw Dot start to run toward them.

Stoner tried to wave her off. "Get out of here!"

"You mind your own damn business!" Dot shouted. She reached them, added her strength to theirs.

The wall hung in the air for a moment, wobbled, swayed ...

Pulling, crawling, they reached the blackness behind the saddler's store.

... and fell.

The fire began to die, eating itself from the inside.

Stoner sprawled in the dust for a moment. She gulped cool air. Cherry lay beside her.

Dot knelt by Lolly and lifted her wrist, feeling for a pulse.

"What?" Stoner asked.

The woman didn't answer. Her fingers went to the artery in Lolly's neck.

Dot sat back on her heels. "Damn," she said.

Cherry crawled to her side. "She's not dead, is she, Dot?"

"I'm afraid so, honey."

Cherry lifted Lolly's limp body into her arms. "You're not dead, kid. Tell me you're not dead." She shook her. "Come on, this is me, Cherry. Don't you go teasing old Cherry at a time like this."

"I'm sorry, Cherry," Dot said.

Cherry tightened her grip on Lolly's body and stroked her face. "Damn white whore," she whispered, tears furrowing through the ash on her cheeks. "Damn old white whore." She looked up, her face twisted with loss. "I never told her I loved her."

"It's okay," Dot said.

"I really did love her, Dot. Do you think she knew?"

"Sure, she did, honey. We all knew it."

Cherry threw back her head and howled, a howl of rage and sorrow and loneliness. It rose above the sounds of burning, above the shouts of the people. It flowed out onto the prairie.

Far in the distance, a wolf answered.

Dot sat back, gasping for breath as tears streamed down her face. "She was a good kid," she said. "A damn good kid."

Stoner could feel her own heart breaking, and knew she really cared about these people. They might be from another time, another world, or even a figment of her imagination, but she cared about them.

Dot's face was badly burned. Cherry was pale beneath her dark skin. Going into shock, Stoner thought. She could do her own grieving later. She pushed herself to her feet. "You need help," she said.

183

"Don't make me leave her," Cherry said, and clenched her friend's body in a hard grip. "I don't want to leave her."

"You can't do anything for her ..." Stoner began.

Dot cut her off. "She needs a little time. It'll be all right."

"Okay. I'll get the doctor."

"He won't come."

"Of course he will. You need him."

"Stoner," Dot said firmly, "we're whores. He won't come."

"Not even for something like this?"

"Not even."

Stoner looked at Cherry. "Is that true?"

Cherry nodded.

Fury made her head ring. Without waiting for an answer, she trotted back toward the street to find Blue Mary. She'd help. She'd know what to do. Blue Mary knew more than everyone in Tabor put together.

She searched the faces in the crowd, looking for a familiar one. In the firelight they glowed red, cut with black shadows, demonic and anonymous. They stood like statues, like figures in a nightmare, and watched the dying flames. Mary had to be here. Or Billy. Where was Billy?

"Stoner."

She turned. Blue Mary pushed toward her through the crowd.

Stoner caught her hands. "We need you. Lolly's dead. Cherry and Dot ..."

"Have you seen Billy?"

"No."

"One minute she was right beside me, and when I turned around she was gone."

Stoner craned her neck and searched the crowd. "I'll look for her. Cherry and Dot ... Down the alley."

"If we get separated," Blue Mary said, "meet me at Kwan's Laundry. Back door."

The heat was fading, cold night air rushing in across the prairie. The wind fanned the glowing coals that were all that was left of the Dot's Gulch. Fire broke out again briefly, then subsided. The darkness deepened.

A hand touched her shoulder. She started.

"Your name Stoner?" a cowboy asked.

Stoner nodded.

"Preacher said to tell you Billy Devon's with him up at the church. Says he got hurt bad and you're supposed to come right away."

She turned away and started running through the darkness toward the church. Lolly dead, Cherry and Dot hurt. And now Billy. She couldn't bear it.

184

The air stung her lungs. She shouldn't run. She'd breathed hot smoke. She ought to take it easy.

She couldn't.

Not Billy. Dear God, not Billy.

She realized she was crying. Sobbing with fear and exhaustion. It made her chest hurt. Made it hard to run.

The church door stood open, darkness inside.

She hesitated, panting, then called "Billy!"

A rough hand clamped over her mouth. Startled, she tried to turn. Someone slammed her back against the wall. The man pressed his body against hers, pinning her.

"Don't move," he whispered. "I don't want to have to shoot you."

She saw the gun he held up, glowing silver in the light of the rising moon.

What the heck? It wouldn't hurt to find out what the gentleman wanted. She nodded.

He took his hand away from her mouth and stepped back a little. The gun was pointed directly at her face.

"Nice gun," she said.

"You don't recognize it?"

She didn't recognize the gun, but she recognized the man.

"It belongs to your friend," he said.

"Reverend Parnell, this is not behavior one expects from a man of the cloth." Good God, every time I get in trouble, I start quoting bad movies.

"Shut up," he said.

"I don't blame you," she said. "The things that come out of my mouth at the darnedest times ..."

"Snails. Toads. Serpents of Satan."

"Actually," she said as he shoved her toward the altar, "I was thinking mediocre dialogue."

He kicked her ankle and sent her sprawling. "I know who you are," he said. He grabbed her hair and banged her forehead against the rough wooden floor. The room turned over. She felt sick.

The man was on top of her now, sitting on her back. The gun lay near her head unattended.

She started to reach for it and realized he was holding her wrists. "If this is a rape situation," she said, "I think you should know I tested HIV positive."

"Quiet!" he shouted, and yanked her arms toward her shoulders until the joints screamed.

Oh, shit. She felt him tie her hands together with a coarse, heavy rope.

"You won't tempt me with your wiles," he hissed into her ear. "I know

185

who you are."

"I can't tell you," she said, "what a comfort that is to me."

He yanked her to her knees and slung a rope around her neck.

She began to realize, through her pain and surprise and her mind's funny way of momentarily refusing to recognize the seriousness of life-threatening situations, that she was in trouble. Big Trouble. To quote the President, Deep Doo-Doo.

≈ ≈ ≈

They had the knife.

The Beast had handled it. Perhaps had held it for a long time. Even though It had struggled and thrashed in his grip, It hadn't been able to overpower him.

The Minion was stronger, but not strong enough. It, too, must have held the knife. Otherwise their Evil strength would have been too much for him.

Now that their physical advantage had been erased, nothing could stand in his way. He had already proven he could outsmart them.

He wanted to kill this Creature now. To put the pistol to the vile Thing's temple and spatter Its brains from the altar to the steeple. But the Word said that would only abolish one of Its manifestations —that's what The Word called them "Manifestations." "The Demon and its minions appear in many Manifestations, so hideous that the mere sight of them will destroy all but those Chosen of God."

It made him a little uneasy. To be destroyed by the mere sight ... Then he laughed at himself. He had been given The Word. He had been sent here. Here, of all the places he could have gone. Here, where the Thing would finally surface. He had the Power. He was one of the Chosen.

But it had to be done right. He had to dismember the Thing, torture It until It revealed each horrible face. Then each face must be destroyed in turn. Only then, after the Showing of the Ten, and the Destruction, would the world be safe.

And there were the rituals to be done. The Sacrifice of the Animals while the Demon watched. It would try not to watch. He'd have to cut off Its eyelids. Yes, that would do it.

Then the Purification by Fire. Soaking Its clothes with coal oil. Striking the match.

The flames. God's Holy, Glorious Flames.

The Demon would twist and curl in Its agony. Would beg for mercy. Would pretend to die.

But he knew about Its tricks.

So near the end now. So close to Glory.

Tabor was nearly saved. Burning the brothel had been only the final

186

step in a process begun six months ago. First the Mexicans with their Catholic ways. The Selders with their deformed son. The ones he liked best were the innocent ones, the ones he had destroyed to disguise the pattern—the way wind blowing on sand swept away all footprints. The Godly sacrificed in His Name, to point the arrow toward the Beast they called Billy. The town was cleansed now, except for the Witch Mary, and when her sister Witches came tomorrow they'd be easy to find, their gathering place demolished. He'd pretend to be one of them, lead them here to the church with promises that they'd find their Master. Then, when they were all together ...

The Sanctified Man grinned. Burn the Church. Blame it on the Witches. He'd wait until a crowd gathered, then pretend to run back inside to save the Bible.

Their silly Bible, a child's Primer compared to The Word. But saving it would please them.

After that, the town would be his to command. The people would be his sheep, his lambs.

He'd have to change the name of the town to reflect its changed status.

Change it to Parnell, of course.

"I don't mean to be rude," Stoner said, "but if you're planning on standing around here all night, could you loosen that rope a little?"

He came to himself and gave the rope a yank. The fibers cut into her neck. "Silence, vile creature."

Stoner swallowed hard. "Hey," she croaked, "we have homophobia where I come from, too, but isn't this carrying it a bit far?"

He hit her between the shoulders, forcing her face to the floor. "Crawl!" he ordered. "Crawl like a dog."

Okay. Sure. Dogs are cool. Whatever turns you on.

She looked up at him and shrugged. "Lead the way."

The man flew into motion, striding toward the door beside the altar, dragging her behind. It wasn't easy to keep up, shuffling along on her knees like pilgrim to a Shrine of Improbable Miracles. As he threw open the door and lurched through in his scarecrow-in-the-wind way, the rope played out, jerked, threw her off balance. She fell, pulling him down beside her.

Ah, the Imp was clever. He must be more careful. He must keep it in front of him.

He jerked on the rope and ordered it to stand. It stood, a little wobbly.

He wasn't about to be fooled by that show of weakness. Chuckling over his own brilliance, he took the burlap bag down from the coat peg, and

187

crammed it over the Stranger's head.

"Now," he said with a smirk, "we'll see who's in charge."

Obviously, Stoner thought, he is.

The burlap was coarse, and smelled like old dirt-floored basements.
The kind that houses six generations of resident vermin at any one time.
The bag was probably crawling with mites and lice and mealy bugs and
grubs and maggots and ...

Not a good idea to let her imagination run free. Not under the circumstances.

Her body began to speak up, reminding her that the circumstances were
not the least bit favorable. Her skin was sensitive. Blisters were forming
where the fire had touched her. Her head ached from being pounded
against the wall. A rodent of fear chased its tail in her stomach.

She may have warped through a hundred years of time, but pain was
pain no matter what quadrant of the Cosmic Mind you were in.

Stoner felt herself pushed down some stairs, led across a small patch of
dried grass.

"Get in the wagon," Parnell ordered, and stuffed her legs in after her.

She couldn't tell where they were going, but she knew she shouldn't be
in a hurry to get there.

≈ ≈ ≈

Cullum found Dot at last, behind the Saddler's, sitting on the ground
with Cherry and what was left of Lolly. It was obvious from first glance
the little gal was dead.

He dragged his hat from his head. "Aw, gosh," he said. "I sure am sorry
about this."

Dot nodded absently.

He squatted down beside her. "We oughta get you two out of this alley.
You got anywhere to stay?"

"Could go to Mary's, I guess," Dot said in an apathetic tone. "She was
by here a minute ago. Went to get something for the burns." She held up
her hands. They were torn and cracked, ugly black gashes cutting across
her palms where charred skin had split open.

He caught his breath. "Jesus Lord, gal. You are a mess."

Dot nodded. "I'm about done in, Cull."

Slowly, carefully, watchful to be sure he wasn't stepping out of line, he
slipped an arm around her shoulders. Dot leaned against him and let herself go limp and heavy for a moment. He could feel her tears through his
shirt.

He stroked her head. "Gal, gal, life does wear a person out sometimes,
don't it?"

188

"It does indeed," Dot said. She let him hold her.

The figure in the alley shadows was Kwan Lu. "Mrs. Gillette," she said softly, "you need a place to go. Come to my rooms."

Dot shook her head firmly. "You don't need that kind of trouble. We'll make our way to Blue Mary's."

"I'm right here." Blue Mary's voice came out of the darkness. "I think we should take advantage of Mrs. Kwan's hospitality for now."

Cullum relinquished his hold on Dot. "You go along, sweet woman," he said, risking the endearment. "I'll take care of things here."

Kwan Lu helped Cherry to her feet and turned to Cullum. "Bring her to my place," she said, indicating Lolly's body. "We can take care of her there."

He touched his finger to the brim of his hat in agreement. "Ma'am."

The town was nearly deserted as they crossed the street. A few of the cowboys had stayed behind to poke through the ashes of Dot's Gulch, rooting for hot coals and souvenirs.

Dot turned her head away. Tomorrow, maybe, she could face the dead remnants of her dreams. Not tonight.

Blue Mary squeezed her arm. "If I know anything about men," she said, "they'll find a way to help you rebuild. They need you here."

"I know," Dot said. "But I sure wish they could have saved the mirror."

"How did the fire start?" Cherry asked Kwan Lu. "Did you hear?"

Kwan Lu shook her head. "Someone broke into the Emporium and stole a gallon of coal oil. They found a jug in the alley behind the saloon. But no one knows if there's a relationship."

"Of course there's a relationship," Cherry spat out. "I've never been anywhere yet that someone didn't try to run me off sooner or later."

Carrying Lolly's body, walking some distance behind them so they wouldn't have to see, Cullum Johnson wondered what to do. If he caught the runaway now, he'd have to haul her back to Tennessee. But if she wasn't here – and he'd find that out pretty soon, he reckoned – he'd have to keep moving west. Either way he'd have to leave Tabor. And leaving Tabor meant leaving Dot Gillette.

He wasn't sure he had the stomach to turn his back on that lady.

≈ ≈ ≈

Parnell slid the bar from in front of the low, narrow door, and shoved the Demon inside. He replaced the bar, took up his hammer and nails, and pounded it shut. There, he thought as he wiped his sweating hands on his pants. That would hold Them until he was ready.

He wished he could find out if they had the Jesus knife.

189

Stoner sprawled on the ground and lay still. The darkness around her was solid. She thought she was alone, but she was afraid to move. Something could be there, in the pitch-black.

The air was frigid. The ropes cut into her wrists. The earth was hard and smelled faintly of ashes. Or maybe it was her own clothes she smelled. She couldn't be certain. And there was an odor of freshly cut lumber.

She tried to breath quietly, glad for the moment of the cold which dulled the pain of her burns. But knowing, too, that the cold that soothed her now would kill her if she had to stay here long.

Well, that's life's irony for you, isn't it?

Gradually, she began to sense that there was something else in the small space.

A living thing.

The worst kind of living thing.

An Unidentified Living Thing.

She wondered what kind of unidentified living things lurked about out here. Hiding in small spaces. Breathing.

She could definitely hear light breathing.

Breathing and waiting and not moving.

No, scratch that last statement. The Something was moving. Not much. Not in any meaningful way that might give a person a clue as to what it was.

Of course not. This Something was Sneaky.

She ran through her mental file of Sneaky Somethings. Cats, mice, opossums, snakes, some dogs with personality problems, people ...

Lots of people. Sneaky People. People like ... like the Reverend Henry Parnell.

But she could be pretty certain it wasn't Mr. Reverend Parnell. Mr. Parnell was on the outside.

Wasn't he?

Of course he was. He had nailed the door shut. From the outside. She'd heard it. She still had enough sense about her to know outside hammering from inside hammering.

At least she thought she did.

God, she thought, I hate total blackness. It's so disorienting.

There were people who paid outrageous amounts of money to float around in total blackness and warm water and get completely disoriented. She wasn't sure what they called it now. When she was in college—Psych 102—they'd called it "Sensory Deprivation". It made you go crazy and hallucinate.

190

Which just goes to show, no matter what you're selling, somewhere there's some damn fool who'll buy it.

Sneaky Something was moving. Just a little, but moving.

Moving toward her in a stealthy, up to no good way.

Probably an animal. Come to think of it, the place had a slightly animal smell, under the ashes and new wood.

Okay, if it's an animal we just lie still, go limp, let it root around at you. If it thinks you're dead, it'll move along. Animals don't eat dead stuff.

Except for wolves and hyenas.

There are no hyenas around here, she told herself as it rustled around a little. And wolves don't creep and sneak. Wolves are direct, no-nonsense, upstanding, out-in-the-open creatures. If I ever have to be stuck on a desert island, wolves are what I want with me.

So this thing wasn't a wolf. This thing was a creeper. This was one of those play-dead-and-it'll-go-away creatures.

She made herself go limp. Tried to still her breathing. Wished she'd taken one of those stress-reduction workshops where they teach you to slow your heartbeat.

Something touched her.

"Erk!" she said.

"Stoner?" Whispered.

"Billy?" Her heart started pounding a whole different kind of pound.

"I thought it was you, but I wasn't sure. Are you all right?"

"I will be if you untie me," she said.

"I can't. He tied me, too."

"You touched me just now. Do it again."

Billy moved her foot. The toe of her boot nudged Stoner's shoulder. Using Billy's leg as a guide, she edged her way to the wall and struggled into a sitting position. "Do you know where we are?"

"In the Reverend's pig house."

"I thought the Reverend's pig house burned down."

"It did," Billy said. "He built a new one with the lumber we brought him yesterday."

"That was considerate of us." She moved, painfully. "Do you know what this is about?"

"No." She could feel Billy shrug in the darkness. "He was raving about God and the Devil, but preachers always rave about God and the Devil, don't they?"

"I guess so. I'm not much of a church-goer, myself."

"I used to go, with my family. But when the War came along ...well, we kind of moved around a lot. Didn't show our faces in public."

"Why? Were you spies?"

"Hiders," Billy said.

She liked the feel of Billy's warmth against her. "What are hiders?"

"People that didn't want to fight. There were a lot of them ...us....
Whole families just sort of disappearing into the woods."

"We had that in our war, too," Stoner said. "Except they went to Canada."

"Is that a fact?" Billy asked.

"Why didn't your father want to fight? Was it against his principles?"

Billy laughed sharply. "He didn't have any principles. He was just afraid to fight."

"Well," Stoner said, "from what I've seen of the way you handle yourself, I'm surprised he didn't send you in his place."

"He would have if he'd thought of it," Billy said.

This was crazy. Sitting in a freezing cold pig house, trapped by a man who was demented and clearly intended to do them harm—and they were discussing draft resistance.

"We should be trying to think of a way to get out of this," Stoner said.

"Sounds like a fine idea to me."

"Any suggestions?"

"I've been working on it the last hour or so," Billy said. "I haven't come up with anything."

"Are you okay?"

"Freezing to death and scared out of my wits. Other than that, I couldn't be better. How about you?"

"I'll live," Stoner said, and hoped it was true. "He knocked me around a little. Did he hurt you?"

"Some," Billy acknowledged wryly. "Sets a fine example for the community, doesn't he?"

The thought of the man hurting Billy, putting his filthy hands on her, enraged her. "I'd like to do something awful to him," she spat.

"Do whatever you want, long as you save a little for me."

From the distance came a strange rhythmic, rasping, wheezing noise. Stoner couldn't place it, but it seemed like a funny sound for the middle of the night.

"What's that noise?"

Billy listened for a moment. "I'm not sure."

"You didn't offend this guy or anything, did you? Inadvertently?"

"No. For Heaven's sake, Stoner, you're always accusing me of stuff."

"Sorry. Maybe he didn't like the way we stacked the lumber."

"Maybe," Billy said thoughtfully, "he didn't like the way I saw him steal Dot's wagon."

"That's a definite possibility."

192

"But I didn't think he saw me."

Her hands were beginning to go numb from the rope around her wrists. "Listen," she said, "if we scootch around back to back, do you think you can untie these ropes?"

"I can try."

Sitting, backs together, knees bent and feet against the walls, they barely fit in the tiny house. "My hands are upside down and backward," Billy said as she fumbled with the knots. "I don't know if I can..."

"You have to."

The little threads of hemp jabbed her tender skin. Stoner bit her lip and tried to concentrate on something else. But all there was to concentrate on was that far-away rasping sound.

"Is it some kind of insect?" she asked.

Billy paused and listened. "Nope. Sounds familiar, though." She went back to work. "Listen, is everyone all right? Back at Dot's?"

"I'm afraid not. Lolly's dead."

Billy paused. "Aw, shit." She tugged feebly at the rope. "Aw, shit."

"I know," Stoner said. "Billy, do you have any idea who set the fire?"

"Yep."

"Who?"

"It won't comfort you to know."

"I want to know, anyway."

Billy gave the rope a yank. "Parnell."

She wasn't surprised. "How did he get you into this?"

"I don't know if I should tell you." She loosened an end of rope and pulled it through the knot.

Stoner clenched her teeth as it scraped along her raw, burned palm. She blinked back tears. "Why not?"

"You'll think I'm a complete idiot to fall for such a stupid trick."

"I doubt that." The burning in her hand was receding. She felt Billy attack the other side of the knot. "Want to go a little easy with that?"

"Sorry. He told me you'd been hurt, and you were up at the church, and I fell for it. You ever hear of anything as stupid as that?"

"I fell for the same story."

"Is that a fact?" She chuckled. "Well, aren't we a pair?"

Billy got the other end of the rope free and pulled it through. Hard and fast.

"Jesus!" Stoner shouted as red lights flashed behind her eyes. "Take it easy!"

The rasping noise stopped, as if whoever was making it had heard, was listening.

They held their breath.

193

The sound started up again.

"I didn't mean to hurt you," Billy whispered.

"I know you didn't. My hands are kind of a mess, that's all."

"How come?"

"I went into the fire. To get Lolly and Cherry out."

"God," Billy breathed. "Why didn't you tell me?"

"The subject didn't come up until now."

She felt Billy go back to work, more gently this time. "How are Dot and Cherry?"

"Cherry's taking it pretty hard."

"I'd imagine. Those girls didn't have anybody but each other."

"Billy, why are people so intolerant?"

Billy pulled at the rope. "Aren't they where you come from?"

"Yes. But out here, where there are so few people, you'd think they'd cherish everyone."

"Back when we were hiding out in Kentucky," Billy said, "I used to watch the squirrels." She laughed a little, remembering. "There wasn't much else to do. I couldn't go to school because we were hiders. And my Ma was too busy trying to please my Pa to pay much attention to me. So I was kind of on my own in the world, you might say."

Another bit of rope came loose. Stoner felt the blood rush back into her hands.

"Anyway, one day these two old squirrels were putting away acorns against the winter. They'd go up the tree, grab a nut, run down the tree, and scoot off into opposite directions. Well, there was this one clump of nuts out at the end of a branch near the ground. First one of them would run out, and the branch'd bend down almost to the ground. But as soon as that old squirrel let go enough to reach for the nut, he'd slip right off and that branch'd go flying back up. Then, while Mr. Number One Squirrel was cussing and thinking it over, old Mr. Two would try it, and the same thing'd happen. Now, if they'd been willing to work together, one of them could have held the branch down while the other pulled off the acorns. But not those two, no sir. They couldn't put aside their differences if they starved to death." She pulled the last of the rope away. "I guess people are like that, too."

Stoner smiled. "That sounds like one of Gwen's back-home parables," she said as she stretched her aching wrists and shoulders. "Except hers are always about Georgia."

"Are you planning to untie me?" Billy asked irritably, "or just sit there enjoying your freedom?"

"I'm sorry." She turned and set to work on Billy's knots. "I might be kind of slow. My fingers are stiff."

194

There was a hardness in Billy's silence.

"Is something wrong?" Stoner asked.

Billy replied with an icy stillness.

"Billy? Look, if I upset you somehow ..."

"It seems to me," Billy muttered, "if a person takes the time and effort to tell you personal things about herself, and trusts you even though she hardly knows you and you might be dangerous, and goes out of her way to tell you stories so you won't think about how much you're hurting ... Well, it seems to me there's better ways to show your appreciation than throwing some other girl in their face every time you open your mouth."

Stoner stopped, ashamed of herself. "Oh, Billy, I'm so very sorry." She put her arm around the woman's shoulders. "I wouldn't hurt you for the world. I didn't mean to be self-centered."

Billy sighed. "Well, it's not your fault I love you."

"I love you, too, Billy. I really do. If I could stay here...."

"You don't want to stay here."

Stoner buried her face in the back of Billy's neck. "No, I don't. But not because of you. I don't belong here, Billy."

The woman's back was hot. Stoner knew she was crying. She held her tight, and felt tears burning behind her own eyes. "Oh, Billy."

"This isn't fair," Billy said.

"I know."

"You ever try to wipe your nose with your hands tied behind your back?"

Stoner squeezed her. "You don't have to make light of this."

"The hell I don't." She shifted her shoulders. "At least we finally have some privacy. Are you going to untie me, or not?"

"All right, all right." She went back to fumbling at the knots. "Aunt Hermione says," she said, "we all get together between lifetimes—those of us who have a special feeling for one another – and decide what part we'll play next time around." She got one end of the rope free. "If she's right, let's promise to arrange it better next time."

As she said it, she felt a funny tingling deep in her stomach. Just about where Aunt Hermione said psychic truth was likely to hang out. It made her go all cold inside her skin for a moment.

She shook it off and finished with Billy's rope. "There you go. Now what do we do?"

She felt Billy turn toward her in the dark, felt Billy's arms around her, felt Billy's mouth pressed against her own.

Mysterious, visceral, wonderful throbbings stirred within her, like waves felt deep on the ocean's floor. She pulled Billy tighter and returned her kiss.

195

Her hands seemed to have a mind of their own, tugging Billy's shirt out of her jeans, reaching inside to the soft, smooth skin of her back. Then working their way around her sides, feeling the fragile bones, the warm, yielding, satin pillow breasts.

She could feel the pounding of the woman's heart, the tightening of her muscles. She wanted to make love to her, to touch and move each cell and fiber of her body. To excite her, and comfort her, and melt into her ...

"Stoner," Billy whispered in the darkness.

"Yes?"

"Is this what it's like?"

It brought her to her senses. "Yes," she said. "But ..."

"You think we better stop?"

"I think ..."

"On account of Gwen."

Stoner considered that. It might not bother Gwen, but it would change her. She knew that. Even if she could believe—really believe and not just suspect it as a rationalization—that Billy would one day be Gwen, it would change her. Little by little, her body would shut down. Little by little, she'd pull into herself, closing Gwen out, closing even herself out. And it wouldn't have anything to do with Gwen. It would be because she wouldn't feel right about herself.

"I wasn't thinking,"she said. "I'm sorry."

"Stoner," Billy said softly, and took her hand, "the important thing isn't whether or not you make love to me. The important thing is that you wanted to. And I wanted to make love to you. I know what that feels like now. And that's something I'll always be grateful to you for."

Stoner reached out and touched her hair. "You're a remarkable woman, Billy. I'm awfully glad I met you."

Chapter 11

The grinding sound went on and on, chewing her nerves until she wanted to scream. "What in the world is that," she muttered.

"I almost have it," Billy said softly. "I heard something like it back home once or twice."

"Some kind of wheel?"

"I think ... uh-oh."

Stoner tried to see her through the dark. "Uh-oh what?"

"It's a grinding wheel."

"What do you do with a grinding wheel?"

Billy's voice was small. "You sharpen things."

"Things?"

"Axes. Knives."

Stoner sat very still, trying not to awaken the anxiety wasps in her stomach. It didn't work. "I don't think," she said at last, "that the Reverend Henry Parnell has taken up knife-sharpening as a hobby."

"I agree," Billy said in a frightened voice.

"In that case," Stoner said, "I have a suggestion."

"What's that?"

"That we stop sitting here like a couple of pigs in a pig house and concentrate on getting out of this mess."

"Suits me."

"Okay, first we'll try to find a weak point in these walls." She got up on her knees and pushed along the boards. They were firm as rock. She could sense Billy testing the walls on the other side. "Any luck?"

"No. It's solid. Pig houses usually are, you know. We probably can't knock it over, either."

Stoner tried to rock the little house. No luck. The corner posts had been set deep in the earth. "Nope."

"Well, it'd probably make too much noise, anyhow."

197

"Probably." Think, she told herself. There has to be a way out of here.

The grinding stopped suddenly. The silence was even more frightening than the sound had been. She could picture him, sitting back on a stool, testing the edges of the knives with his thumb, smiling ...

Someone was coming toward them across the frozen wheat stubble. Crushing the little leaves and hollow stems underfoot. Slowly. Determinedly. No question about destination.

"Billy!" She whispered, feeling around on the dirt floor for the ropes.

"What?"

"Pretend you're still tied and unconscious. He'll have to pull us both out. One of us might have a chance to jump him."

She found one rope, handed it to Billy, ran her hands frantically through the dust and ashes.

He was nearly outside the door now. She couldn't keep searching. He might hear.

Parnell paused, listening.

She could hear the night, more still than stillness. More silent than silence. An absence of sound where sound should be. Waiting silence.

Then she heard his breathing. Soft at first. Growing heavier, more rapid. Excited.

For God's sake. It's bad enough this maniac has us in this mess. Don't tell me it turns him on.

It was Time now. The ritual knives were sharp as demons' teeth, laid out on their holy cloth inside his sanctuary. The altar was cleaned and polished, the candles burning, the Word opened to the proper readings.

Time for the Holy Carnage.

He stood by the Containment House and listened.

Careful! The Demon was tricky.

He licked his lips and stuck the torch into the ground. Taking the jug of coal oil into both hands, he drenched the house and the ground around it.

Kerosene.

The smell filled her nose, cutting off her breath.

He was going to burn them.

He struck a match and held it over the glistening ground. Once he began, he would have to act fast. The fire would hold One while he dealt with the Other, but there wouldn't be time to spare. No time to play with the Beast, no time to torture it beyond the stipulated tortures. No time to be creative.

But before he began, while It was still contained ...

He blew out the match and took up the crowbar. With all his strength, he slammed it down on the roof of the pig house.

It fell with the sound of Hell's thunder. He swung again and imagined it was the Demon he struck with each blow.

Again.

And again.

He slammed the side of the house. "Filth!" he screamed.

Crablike, he scuttled around the perimeter of the tiny building.

"Filth!"

Faster and faster. Striking the wood.

Pounding.

Crash!

Crash!

Stoner felt each blow inside her head. She covered her ears with her hands, but it didn't help.

Crash!

It struck her chest like an explosion of air from a cannon.

Crash!

She wanted to scream. But she sensed it was what he wanted her to do.

Crash!

She'd be damned if she'd scream.

Crash!

Her brain felt bruised.

Crash!

Stop it, stop it, stop it.

Crash!

Oh, God, make him stop!

Then, suddenly, silence.

She reached out in the darkness and took Billy's hand. She tried to pass encouragement to her through her touch.

She was afraid all she passed was fear.

Billy squeezed her hand.

Parnell dropped the crowbar and let the night air cool his fevered skin.

He picked up his torch, struck the match, and set the oily rags to burning.

No air to cool the Demon's skin, he thought as he braced the torch in the ground. He forced the crowbar between the pig house wall and the cross-bar and yanked. The nails squealed like rats in agony.

He smiled.

Orange light from the burning torch glistened from his sweat-soaked face.

Quickly, the other side.

He rammed the crowbar home. The wood screamed. He snatched the falling 4x6 and hurled it away into darkness.

She dropped Billy's hand.

Scratched frantically through the dirt.

Her fingers found her bit of rope. She twisted it around her wrists. A feeble attempt, but if he let his guard down ...

Parnell took a deep breath, snatched up the torch, and threw open the door.

Nothing moved inside.

He leaned down cautiously and peered in, his free hand reaching for his gun.

The two bodies lay entangled in one another, like a pile of waiting snakes.

Carefully, he touched the nearest body with the toe of his boot.

It didn't move.

He put the torch aside and took out the gun and reached his free hand toward It.

Nothing.

Its foot was near the door. He grabbed It around the ankle and pulled It outside.

The Stranger lay on the ground, unconscious.

The Beast inside hadn't moved.

He bent to the Creature at his feet and poked his finger into Its carotid artery. Its heart was beating. Fast. Little quick beats that felt the way a centipede would feel, racing over your hand.

For a second he was afraid. That was no human heartbeat pulsing beneath his touch It was the heartbeat of the Thing that lay beneath, the Thing he had to uncover in his basement Sanctuary.

Quick. Before It woke.

He slammed the pig house door and said a quick prayer and touched the torch to the soaked wood.

Flames rose in a "Whump!" and ball of black smoke.

He was burning the house, and Billy was inside.

Stoner pulled herself free from the loosely-tied cord and kicked out. Her heel caught him on the shin and he went down. His gun flew from his hand, out of reach, beyond the firelight. She threw herself on top of him.

Rage stopped her voice in her throat. She wanted to strangle him, to beat his head into the ground, to squeeze his neck in the vise of her hands until his eyes popped from his head.

"Son of a bitch," she screamed at last, and smashed her fist into his mouth. "You God damn son of a bitch!"

The man spit in her face.

She wrapped her hands around his throat and pressed.

He worked his arm under hers and flung her sideways with a grunt. She landed in hard dirt.

Firelight played over his twisted features. He sucked his cut lip and wiped his mouth. The torch dangled from his hand.

Get out of there, Billy. Please get out of there.

The man's foot lashed out, catching her in the ribs. Streaks of pain shot through her body. She grabbed for him weakly and missed.

He thrust the spear of fire at her face.

She rolled to the side.

He came at her again, poking, stabbing with the torch, driving her backward along the ground.

She scuttled out of his reach.

Back....

... and back ...

Something stopped her from behind. Something large and flat.

The side of a barn.

He had It trapped.

He could kill The Creature now. Burn it. Shoot it. Get rid of it before it got its strength back.

But he wanted to cut it apart, piece by piece. He wanted to watch it suffer.

His own strength was Greater than the Creature's. It was his to torture. Better than the animals. Better than his father. It would be the Ultimate Sacrifice to the Omnipotent and Merciful God.

Reaching into the darkness, he grasped the rusting pitchfork that stood propped against the barn door.

He lifted it up, pressed the tines against the Creature's throat.

One good thrust and It would be impaled. It wouldn't die. But it would be caught there, in pain, until he could find the rope.

He pressed against the pitchfork and prepared to ram it home.

"If you're going to kill me," she said in a voice so calm it frightened her, "at least look me in the eye."

He grinned.

She felt the tines dig deep into the skin of her throat.

"Give me the knife," he rasped, and laughed.

"The knife?"

He pushed the pitchfork deeper. One of the tines punctured skin.

"The knife."

"Oh, was that your..."

Still pressing the fork against her throat, he reached out with one arm and began pawing at her pockets.

"If you'll just tell me what you want ..."

"Give me the knife."

The pitchfork dug deeper. Another tine broke through.

"Jesus!" she gasped.

It sent him into a fury. "You dare defile the Holy Name! I should kill you now!"

"Well," she said, "that does seem to be your intention."

The man grinned. "Oh, no," he said in a voice like Vaseline. "I have much more interesting plans for you."

It can't get much more interesting than this.

The pig house roof collapsed. She wondered why she hadn't heard Billy scream. Smoke inhalation, maybe. Unconscious.

Oh, God, Billy.

Not now. Think about it later. You have to save yourself.

Save yourself. With the tines of a pitchfork digging into your neck and a crazy person on the other end.

"Wouldn't you like to hear my plans?" Parnell asked.

"I suspect ..." she choked "... you'll let me in on them in time."

"First the fire. You'll enjoy that. Hearing your flesh bubble. Smelling the odor of your cooking skin." He smiled. "Human flesh smells like roasting oxen when it burns. Yours will smell like pig."

She was shaking down to the marrow of her bones.

She shot her eyes right, then left. They were alone, in the dark. Dark except for the remains of the pig house, still flaming, reminding her that Billy was still somewhere inside.

"But you will live a while. And watch me destroy your Master."

"My Master?"

The man threw back his head and shook his finger at her. "I will set you free, Oh Slave of Satan."

"Sounds like a good idea to me, setting me free."

"I will free your SOUL."

"Oh, that." She twisted a little, to test his concentration on the pitchfork.

He pressed harder into her neck. "Don't try to trick me," he growled. "It'll be worse for you."

"Hey, just checking to be sure you had the situation under control."

Parnell laughed. "I'll show you more control than even your Master."

"Listen, what's all this 'Master'' stuff?"

"The Devil," Parnell sneered. "Satan, who even now writhes in agony in the flames."

He was talking about Billy. Billy? Satan?

Billy?

But Billy was gone, somewhere beneath that pile of charring wood.

Billy was gone, and there was no one around to help her.

The crazies win again.

A flash of anger shot through her. "If you're going to kill me, get on with it. Cut the fucking around."

He stared at her for a moment. Seemed to be considering … Made up his mind.

"It's time to begin," he said smoothly.

She closed her eyes.

She felt the minute drawing-back movement of the pitchfork as he got ready to plunge.

Waited.

Nothing happened.

She forced her eyes open.

There was a sound of something cutting through air. A dull "thud". The pitchfork flew from his hands. The torch rolled off into the darkness and set fire to a few blades of stubble.

Billy stood in front of her, holding a length of lumber. She reached for Stoner's hand.

"I thought you were dead," Stoner said.

"I thought you were."

She looked at the man's body. "Think he is?"

"I doubt it," Billy said. "I couldn't manage to do in my father with a half-full whiskey jug." She hefted the length of lumber. "This thing doesn't have one quarter the weight."

Stoner checked the man's position and calculated the direction of his fall in an instant. "Not bad. The Red Sox could use a good left-handed batter."

"What's the Red Sox?"

She looked back at Billy, and wanted to go on looking at her forever. She laughed. "How did you get out of there?"

"Fire makes holes." Billy looked down at their interlaced hands. "I think you just broke my ring finger."

"God," Stoner said, and dropped her hand. "I'm really sorry."

Billy threw her arms around her. "I was only kidding. Stoner, I was so afraid for you."

203

"So was I. I thought you were dead."

"I knew you weren't. Too much talking out here for anyone to be dead." She looked down at Parnell's crumpled body. "You know what we really ought to do, don't you? To be sure we're safe?"

Stoner nodded. "Kill him."

"You want to do it?"

"Not particularly," Stoner said. "Do you?

"Not particularly." Billy glanced up at her. "I think you should."

"Why?"

"Because it's your turn. I already killed one man. Or thought I did."

"So did I."

"But I did it more recently."

"I did it more successfully."

They both contemplated the heap of black clothes. The sky to the east was beginning to muddy with dawn. The fainter stars withdrew.

Silence flowed in. Through the silence came a faint, muffled bang.

"What's that?" Billy asked.

Stoner listened, and traced the sound from inside the barn. "Someone's in there. Or something."

"Jeez. You don't think there's two of them, do you?"

"Better check it out." She looked around for a weapon, and found Billy's gun where Parnell had dropped it. She picked it up. "If he wakes up, sock him again."

Billy took a firm left-hander's grip on the lumber.

Carefully, she pulled the barn door open a crack and peered inside. It was too dark to see, but there was the thumping sound again.

Okay, what would Cagney and Lacey do in this case?

She tightened both hands around the gun, took a deep breath, kicked open the door, and aimed straight-armed into the darkness. "Police! Freeze!"

"Huh?" Billy said.

Nothing attacked her from inside. She gave her eyes a few seconds to adjust to the deeper darkness, and stepped through the door.

Caroline Parnell lay against the far wall, bound and gagged.

Stoner ran to her. "Hang on," she said as she tore at the ropes. "I'll have you out in a minute."

"God bless you," Caroline Parnell said when she could speak. "I was sure he was going to kill me."

"He probably was," Stoner said. She helped the woman to her feet. "Are you okay?"

"I'll be all right in a minute." Caroline leaned heavily on her shoulder. "Just let me catch my breath."

204

Stoner walked her around a little.

"That dreadful man," the woman said. "I can't imagine what you think of me, marrying a dreadful man like that."

"Hey, it happens."

"Blue Mary tried to warn me, but I wouldn't listen." Caroline started to sob, a little hysterically, Stoner thought. " I was never very pretty, you see. He flattered me, then he took advantage of me." She gave a great, heaving sob. "Oh, what's-your-name ..."

"Stoner," Stoner said. "Stoner McTavish."

"I'm so humiliated."

"Listen, you're not the first. You should see some of the stuff that goes on on 'Unsolved Mysteries'." She smiled at the woman until Caroline was forced to smile back. "I'll bet I could get you a gig on Giraldo."

Mrs. The Reverend Henry Parnell gawked at her, trying to make sense of what she was saying. But at least she had gotten control of herself.

"Hey, Stoner," Billy called. "The Old Booger's moving."

Stoner eased Caroline Parnell toward the door.

They looked down at the twitching body.

"Miz Parnell," Billy said, "I'm afraid we're going to have to kill your husband."

"That's all right," Caroline said distractedly. "Whatever you think best."

"It's your gun," Stoner said. "You do it."

Billy hesitated.

Stoner hesitated.

The man was beginning to get up.

"One of us better do it," Stoner said.

They looked at each other.

"Oh, for Heaven's sake," Caroline Parnell said. "I'll do it."

"You don't have to ..." Billy began.

The woman took the gun from Stoner's hand. "Oh, yes, I do." The woman's face was tight and gray with hard anger. "I owe it to the town to. He's a cruel, heartless individual."

"A little nuts, too, if you want my opinion," Stoner said.

Caroline Parnell turned to her. "My dear, you have no idea of the depths of this man's depravity. The things he planned to do to you ..." She shuddered. "I can't even say them."

"That's okay," Stoner said quickly. "I don't need to know."

The man was getting to his knees, gasping for breath, shaking his head back and forth in a confused, dog-like way.

"You'd better leave," Caroline Parnell said. "Take the wagon. It belongs to Mrs. Gillette, anyway. Tell her ... tell her I'm sorry about the saloon."

"It wasn't your fault," Billy said.

"I knew he was going to do it. I could have warned her. I hope she'll forgive me."

"I'm sure she will," Stoner said. She turned toward the wagon, then turned back. Parnell was trying to get to his feet, stumbling and falling in the dust. "He's coming around. Maybe we should stay, just in case."

Caroline Parnell waved them away. "I have a few things to say to him first. But I need privacy."

They hesitated.

"Don't worry. I won't let him get away. I've come to my senses."

"Well, okay," Stoner said. "Careful. He's tricky."

The woman smiled in a frightening way. "I know all his tricks."

Billy was trotting toward the wagon. "Come on."

Stoner followed her. "Don't you want your gun?"

"Nah. Thinking of giving up my life of crime." She hopped up into the wagon and took the reins. "Move it, mule."

Stoner swung up onto the seat beside her. "I don't know what we'll find back in Tabor. It was a mess when I left."

"Then we'd best make tracks." Billy stood up and slapped the reins. "Hee-YAH!"

The sky was fading to water color blue when they heard the shots at last, back on Parnell land.

≈ ≈ ≈

Cullum Johnson came into the parlor with his hat in his hands. "Ladies," he mumbled.

Cherry turned on him. "What do you want, white man?"

May Chang put a calming hand on Cherry's arm and turned to the bounty hunter. "She's upset," she said.

Cullum nodded. "It's all right." He looked around uncomfortably. "I wonder if I might sit in here with you ladies while ..." He gestured vaguely toward the store room. "I'd give them a hand, but it seems kind of personal."

"Of course," May said.

"No!" Cherry snapped. "You ought to be out looking for the person who did this."

Cullum shifted from one foot to the other. "Trouble is, everyone I talk to says the same thing. They think it's that boy who worked for you."

"Billy?" Cherry looked hard at him. "Billy wouldn't do a thing like that."

"I'm not saying he did, Ma'am. I'd like to hear your thoughts on the matter."

Cherry sank into a chair and put her face in her hands . "Anybody in

206

this town could have done it. They all think we're trash."

"Even so," Cullum said, "not everyone goes around setting fires. From what I've been hearing, these fires started not long after the boy arrived."

"Well, it's a pack of lies," Cherry said as May poured her a cup of tea. "And if that's what you think, you can get on that horse of yours and ride back to wherever you came from."

"Miss Calhoun," Cullum said in the softest, most respectful voice he could manage, "I don't necessarily believe those stories."

"People in this town just can't tolerate anyone who's different, is all."

"Well," he said, "that's the way of the world, I'm afraid. Trouble is, I can't seem to come up with a better explanation."

May came forward and steered him toward a chair. "Please, Mr. Johnson. We have to put everything out on the table, no matter how bad or improbable it looks. Then maybe we can reach the truth." She turned to Cherry. "Are you willing to set your anger aside long enough to do that?"

"All right," Cherry grumbled. "But I'm telling you it isn't Billy."

Johnson took the cup of tea May offered him. "Miss Calhoun, I know how you feel about the boy, but ..." He cleared his throat, trying to make time to find the right words. "Well, I've been thinking it over, and ... well, I'm not so sure he's even a boy."

Cherry stared at him, and the color rose to her cheeks. "Of course he's a boy. Just because he doesn't act like some old puffed-up, cussing, tobacco-spitting, swaggering, mangy, stinking peacock, that doesn't mean he's not a boy."

"That's true," May Chang said. "In San Francisco, where I come from, there are men who aren't like that at all."

"I agree with you ladies," Johnson said, "and I hope I don't fit Miss Calhoun's description. But ..." He paused to wipe his forehead with his handkerchief, and cursed the life that had brought him into this particular conversation. "Forgive me, but I have a hard time expressing myself."

"Perhaps," May Chang said, "if would be better if you just spoke out."

He nodded to her gratefully. "You probably know why I'm here."

Cherry gave a snort. "Bounty hunter."

"Yes, Ma'am. Not an admirable occupation, I know. But I have a certain talent for it, and not much for anything else."

"Well," Cherry said grudgingly, "I guess I have to sympathize with that."

He took a deep breath and pushed on before he lost his nerve. "I was hired to find a young woman ..."

"A woman," Cherry barked. "You'd track down a woman? Know what that makes you? The scum off a cess pool, that's what it makes you."

"Yes, Ma'am," Cullum said. "But this woman tried to kill her father.

207

Succeeded, as far as she knows."

"What's so awful about that?" Cherry demanded.

"The father doesn't quite see it that way. Anyhow, I've been following the trail for quite a few months now, and it leads here to Tabor. Now, the only person new in town ... other than that strange English woman in the funny clothes ... or whatever she is ... is your boy Billy."

"And that makes him a father-killing woman?" Cherry said derisively. "First time I ever heard of hanging a person for being new in town."

Cullum took good tight hold on his temper. "He also," he said firmly and evenly, "matches the description of the young lady in question, allowing for his clothes and short hair. Furthermore, I've watched him shoot a pistol, and from the looks of it, it doesn't come naturally to him."

"I suppose you were born with a Colt .45 in your hand," Cherry said. Her voice dripped sarcasm.

Cullum Johnson sighed heavily and got up. "All right, ladies. I can see I'm not going to get much help here, so I'll go back out on the street and see what I can pick up."

"Wait," May said. "I have another suspect for you."

They both looked at her.

"Your preacher."

Cherry burst out laughing. "The Old Booger? All that turkey knows how to do is shout Scripture and play with himself, not necessarily in that order."

"Listen to me," May insisted. "I came here looking for the man who killed my father nearly two years ago. I recently received word through relatives that the man is here, and he's the town preacher."

"That has to be a joke," Cherry said, round-eyed.

"No. He bragged about it to them himself. There's no mistake."

"Why would he brag about murder?" Cherry said with a disbelieving snort.

"He's not afraid of Chinese. He knows he's safe in the white man's world."

"Well," said Cherry, "that's true, but it doesn't count for beans in the Chinese community, I'll bet."

"Exactly," May said. "That's why I'm here."

Cherry smiled a little for the first time. "You came to kill our preacher?"

May nodded.

"I'll be damned," Cherry said. "A girl after my own heart."

Cullum Johnson shook his head. "Well, I'll be a son of a bitch."

"No doubt you are," Cherry muttered.

"I don't know that he set your fire," May went on. "Or, if he did, why he did it. But I do know the man isn't in his right mind. Don't you think it's a possibility?"

Cullum looked around the room, taking in the dimness, the heavy brocade curtains, the mingled odors of incense and laundry soap. Yeah, it was a possibility. A damn good possibility. But that still didn't solve his problem about the boy—the girl, if the boy really was the girl—and he was just about certain of it. Logic and instinct both pointed that way. If he had really found the girl, and didn't take her in, he'd be guilty of accepting money under false pretenses. Not all the money he'd been promised, of course, just the half he'd taken up front to cover his expenses. But stealing was stealing, and didn't sit well with him.

On the other hand, judging from the Calhoun woman's reaction, he had a pretty good idea, if he took this girl back to Tennessee, he'd better forget about ever seeing Dot Gillette again. And he didn't know if he could bear that.

So there you are, old man, he thought. Caught between the Devil and the Deep Blue Sea. Not that Mrs. Gillette has given you the slightest reason to believe she has any feeling for you. But she could, in time. If you treated her real nice and didn't make a nuisance of yourself. Maybe she could learn to like you just a little.

And wouldn't that make the long, cold winters feel like spring?

They were looking at him, waiting for him to speak. "Yep," he said, "it's a possibility worth considering."

The curtains into the store room parted, and Dot looked in. "Cherry," she said softly, "would you like to help dress her?"

Cherry hesitated, the skin going pale beneath her olive complexion.

"She looks fine," Dot said. "Mary says you should see. It'll help you remember the good times."

Cherry straightened her back, nodded solemnly, and left the room.

Dot watched her go. "Poor kid," she said. "Her heart's broken." She sat in a chair and accepted a cup of tea from May.

"How are you doing, Mrs. Gillette?" Cullum asked.

She brushed the tangled hair from her forehead with the back of her hand. "Not the best day I've ever known, Cull." She sipped her tea. "What are they saying on the street?"

He looked at her lovely profile against the window. Like a precious cameo, she was. If there were any fairness in the world, she'd be Queen of the Universe. "A lot of talk."

"There's always talk. Any substance?"

"Lot of folks pointing the finger at your boy."

Dot nodded wearily. "Figures. Can't be true, though. He was out at Blue Mary's, courtin' that gal from back east, when it started." She took

209

another sip. "Not that that'll mean a thing to anyone once they've got their bile up. They'd as likely hang him as listen to him. Guess it's time for him to move along."

She put her cup down and turned to him. "Cull, I want you to find the boy. Give him this." She reached into the bodice of her dress and pulled out a roll of bills.

Johnson blushed and looked at the floor.

"Well, are you going to take it, or not?"

He glanced up. "Yes, Ma'am." He wrapped his huge-feeling hand around the money. It was warm with her warmth. His fingers tingled where he accidentally touched her fingers.

"Tell him to get as far away from here as he can. Tell him our hearts go with him. Tell him he's a good kid and we love him."

He tucked the money into his shirt pocket. "We have another suspect. The preacher."

Dot's eyebrows shot up. "Is that a fact?"

"It's possible," May said.

"Well, that would improve my morning."

He was halfway to the preacher's house when he came across Billy and the stranger, driving hell-bent for leather toward town. He pulled Tobe up tight and approached them at an easy lope. Wouldn't do to spook the girl now, when he'd just about made up his mind about her.

He tipped his hat in a genial way, said "Ma'am" to Stoner and "Son" to Billy.

Billy saw him, turned pale, and started looking for something in the back of the wagon.

But not before he got a good look at her eyes.

Yep, they were deep, dark brown, with a tiny scar over the left eyebrow, just like the father had said.

Durn.

"I see you've been out toward the preacher's," he said, starting in conversationally. "How are things over that way?"

Stoner said to get his attention away from Billy, "There's been some trouble. Parnell tried to kill us. I think he started the fires. He's dead. You should probably take a look ... "

Well, this was a strange turn of affairs. The money and the questions could wait.

He tipped his hat again and rode on.

≈ ≈ ≈

Tabor was quiet this early in the morning. The odor of charred wood and damp ashes hung in the air. Footsteps were loud and sharp on wooden sidewalks.

Stoner cringed as the sound of the creaking wagon echoed through the town. Something didn't feel right. She wanted them to keep out of sight. The bounty hunter knew who Billy was. She could tell that by his studied casualness. But why had he let them go?

Maybe she shouldn't have told about Parnell. But somebody'd find out soon enough. After all, tomorrow was Sunday. The whole town would notice when he didn't show up for church services. But Billy could have been far away from here by then.

On the other hand, so could Caroline Parnell. And then Billy'd be blamed for sure. The only thing that would get them out of this would be for Caroline Parnell to tell the truth.

Billy fumbled around under the wagon seat until she found the strangely-decorated knife and tucked it into her belt. "Best keep this handy. You never know."

"Okay," Stoner said, "where do we go from here?"

"To the laundry."

"The laundry?"

"Dot's a friend of Mrs. Kwan. She'll know where they are." She pointed the mule down the alley and parked beside an entrance door.

Blue Mary peeked her head out, saw who it was, and motioned to them emphatically. "Inside. Quickly."

Billy spotted Cherry right off, and ran to embrace her. "I'm so sorry about Lolly."

"I know," Cherry said, wiping her eyes. "I just want to get the son-of-a-bitch that did it."

"It was Parnell," Stoner said. "He tried to kill us."

Cherry's mouth tightened. "Where is he?"

"Dead."

"You do it?"

"No," Stoner said. "His wife did."

"Humph," Dot grunted. "Didn't know she had it in her."

Blue Mary came in from tying the mule. "Have you seen Mr. Johnson?"

"The bounty hunter?" Billy's eyes flashed. "Yeah, we saw him."

"He was supposed to give you something from me," Dot said.

"Well, he didn't."

Dot sank slowly into a chair and said, "Damn."

"Now, Dorothy," said Blue Mary. "Let's not jump to conclusions."

"I thought he was about to say something," Stoner said. "But when we told him about Mrs. Parnell, he took off that way."

"He's looking for you," Cherry said to Billy.

Billy sighed. "I figured."

"He knows who you are."

Dot looked over at them. "Knows who you are?"

"Yes, Ma'am," Billy said. "I'm the reason he's here. You see ..." She took off her hat. "I haven't been telling you the truth, quite."

Stoner couldn't help herself. "Quite!"

Billy glared at her.

"Sorry."

"See ..." Billy turned to Dot. "I did something, back in Tennessee ..."

"You told me you were from Illinois," Dot said.

"Yes, Ma'am. That wasn't quite the truth."

Dot wiped her hand over her face. "All right, tell me the worst of it."

"I killed my father. At least, I thought I did. See, he was always beating up on my Ma and me. That and other stuff. Trying to get me in bed with him. Succeeding sometimes." She glanced quickly at Stoner.

"I know," Stoner said softly.

"And then one time I couldn't take it any more so I hit him with his whisky jug. I thought he was dead when I ran off, but I guess he wasn't because he hired Mr. Johnson to find me."

Dot wrinkled up her face and sat staring at her hands.

"I'm really sorry I lied to you," Billy said. "Lying to you was worse than anything I did back in Tennessee."

"Hush," Dot said. "I'm thinking." She was silent for a moment. Then her face lit up. "He's not after you, Billy. He's looking for a girl."

"Dot," Billy said softly. "I am a girl."

Dot stared at her. "Come over here."

Hat in hand, Billy went and stood beside her.

Dot looked hard into her eyes. She fingered her hair, then ran her fingers down the side of Billy's face. "Soft as a baby's behind," she said, and shook her head with amazement. "Kid ..."

"She's not a kid," Stoner interrupted. "She's twenty-five."

"Well, it's a good thing she is," Dot said fiercely. "Or she'd be over my knee faster than she could whistle."

Billy took Dot's hand. "Please forgive me, Dot. You were the first person who ever treated me decently, and I was afraid to ..." A tear slid down the side of her cheek.

"Oh, hush," Dot said gruffly, and pulled Billy down onto her lap. She wrapped her arms around her and rocked her gently. "I'm not mad at you, Sweetie. And as for lying to me, well, shoot, it's a woman prerogative to lie about her age, isn't it?"

The murmur of angry voices—a lot of angry voices—rose in the distance. Like a far-off flock of geese, but coming nearer.

Stoner didn't like the sound of it. She slipped into the front of the laundry and peeked through the curtain. A mob was advancing down the street, raising dust, headed their way. About fifty or so, from what she could tell. Men in the front, women to the rear.

She looked for a possible leader, and thought she found him. Walking backward, shouting to the others.

Joseph Hayes.

She couldn't hear what they were saying, but it didn't look good. It looked as if they were satisfied they'd found their culprit and were about to take matters into their own hands.

She'd never seen a real mob before. Just choreographed confrontations between anti-abortion crazies and pro-choice demonstrators. And an occasional milling, boozed-up gang of overgrown adolescents when she accidentally took the T through Kenmore Square just as a Red Sox-Yankees game was getting out.

This was different. These people didn't look self-righteous or argumentative. These people felt anonymous, safe, each no more vulnerable than an individual cell in a body. And they were angry, hatred sparking from their eyes. And, most frightening of all, they were focused. They knew where they were going, and who they wanted, and what they'd do when they got her.

She ran back to the other room. "They're coming."

"Billy!" Blue Mary said sharply. "Take the wagon, stay behind the stores until you reach the end of the alley, then drive to my house. I'll try to stall them here."

"Right," Billy said. She started for the door.

Blue Mary grabbed her shirt tail. "Take Stoner with you. When you get there, hide the wagon. Go down in the storm cellar. You know where it is. Keep out of sight."

"What about you?"

"They won't hurt me," Blue Mary said.

Stoner hoped that was true. Right now, nothing felt safe.

The older woman gave her a shove. "Don't waste time."

They raced through the back door and clambered into the wagon. Billy lifted the reins.

"Move, God damn you!"

The old animal set off at an amble.

She could hear the mob's individual voices now. "We want the bastard." "Hang him!"

"Jesus Christ," Billy muttered. She brought the reins down hard on the mule's rump.

They broke from the shelter of the alley and started across open prairie. Stoner looked back. The mob was clustered around Kwan's Laundry, milling and shouting. She strained to see, but the dust and glaring sun obscured her vision.

"I don't feel right about this," she said. "What if they need us?"

"I know," Billy said, concentrating on her driving. "But Blue Mary knows best. Besides, it's me they're after. Probably safer with me out of the way."

She supposed so. Still, she felt torn.

Billy sensed the conflict behind her silence. "Want me to go back?"

No, that wouldn't do, either. And she couldn't go and leave Billy alone. If they did come looking for her at Blue Mary's—and they were bound to sooner or later—her presence would at least double Billy's chances.

Which wasn't saying very much.

Oh, God, she thought as the wagon lurched and bounced along the dirt track. Don't tell me I came all this way to fail.

"Durn," Billy said over the rush of air and the clatter of wagon wheels, "I wish I'd held onto my gun."

"What for? Your aim's terrible."

"Yeah, but I could sure put a scare into them."

She thought she heard breaking glass in the distance, but she couldn't be sure. She looked behind, trying to penetrate the distance.

The mob seemed to have increased in size and fury.

Her stomach was tight and crawling with fear.

What do we do after we get to Blue Mary's? Hide, naturally. But for how long?

Maybe until dark. We could slip out after dark and Billy could get away.

They rolled over the top of the first hill and started on the down side. She couldn't see Tabor now. But when they came up the next ...

They were going up again. Any second now they'd see the town.

Billy should probably go toward Denver. She could get lost in the crowds there.

Or north, into the wilderness.

Either way she'll have to cross the plains, where you can be seen for miles.

Travel by night. Hide out by day. In river banks and gullies.

How will she keep warm? What will she eat?

Blue Mary says I can't go with her. I have to go back to my own time.

But how can I let her go off alone?

Stoner felt a flash of terror. Billy. Alone. In the darkness and cold. She'll never make it.

214

Tabor was visible now, but they were too far away to ...

"WHOA!" Billy yelled, and pulled on the reins. The wagon jerked to a halt, nearly tossing Stoner over the side.

"For Heaven's sake, Billy, what ...?"

She turned and looked.

There, in the middle of the road, embracing his rifle, stood The Reverend Henry Parnell.

Chapter 12

"Well, well," he said with a smooth grin. "Isn't this a surprise?" He raised his gun and aimed it at Billy. "Son, I'll thank you to return my property."

"Huh?" Billy said.

Stoner nudged her. "The knife. Give it to him."

"Will not," Billy said loudly. "Let him come and take it, the old Booger."

"For God's sake," Stoner mumbled, "keep your voice down."

Billy stood up in the wagon. "Old Booger!" She shouted. "You're nothing but an Old Booger, Parnell."

Stoner couldn't believe her ears. "You're out of your mind."

"Well, damn it," Billy said angrily. "I'm sick of people pushing me around." She faced Parnell. "GET OUT OF MY WAY, YOU UGLY OLD THING!"

"Billy," Stoner said firmly, "calm down."

Billy turned on her. "I've been ordered around by men all my life. I'll be durned if I'll be ordered around by this one."

Stoner glanced toward the Reverend Henry Parnell, who hadn't moved. "Look," she said to Billy, "it's one thing to get politicized in a nice, safe Consciousness Raising group. It's something else again when you're looking down the barrel of a gun."

Billy ignored her. "Go on and kill me, Mule Piss."

The Minion was afraid. Good.

The town was ready to spill blood. Hayes had whipped them up into a frenzy of hate and vengeance.

Poor old Joseph Hayes. He'd been easy to win over. A natural coward, bowing and scraping and drooling over anyone who came along with a few cents to spend. And a wife he couldn't control. His life had been miserable, until one day Parnell had suggested—subtly, of course—that maybe some of his troubles could be laid at the doorstep of the Suffragists. He'd jumped at the thought like a dog after a fresh bone. And when his wife became one of them ...

Yes, he could count on Hayes to do what he wanted.

They'd made a good team. Hayes worked in the background and spread gossip, while the Preacher looked as sincere and clean and gentle as a dove.

They were hungry to hang the Bastard for the burnings. All right. The Demon could be first. While their blood was running hot as molten steel.

He'd keep the Stranger for himself, for later.

But first he had to make them touch the Jesus knife.

Stoner didn't like the way his eyes glinted. A hard, cold, silvery gleam, like mirrors. Not that she was any expert on the subject, but it sure looked like Psycho time to her.

"Come on," Billy said to Parnell. "Fire the damn thing or clear the road."

Stoner wondered if it would do any good to hit Billy over the head with a blunt instrument.

Parnell lifted the gun to his shoulder and pulled back the firing pin.

"Look, Mr. Parnell," Stoner said, "I'm sure, if we all sit down and discuss this calmly ..."

He squeezed the trigger.

The explosion deafened her, freaked the mule, and gouged a hole in the side of the wagon.

It also calmed Billy down considerably. "Jeez, Stoner," she grunted as she struggled with the mule, which was dancing and rearing and pulling against its harness, "I'm sorry."

Stoner grabbed the reins from her hands. "Let it go!"

The mule took off across the prairie. Stoner gripped the wagon seat. "Hang on!"

Billy hung on.

The ground peeled away beneath them. The wagon bounced and jolted and seemed about to shatter into splinters. It made all the VistaVision, Cinerama, 3-D movie run-away wagon scenes she'd ever seen look like a quiet evening on a water bed. And this one came complete with sensory enhancement. Her heart pounded in time to the mule's hooves. Her body slammed against the wagon seat. Thrown to the right, her leg smashed against the wooden side. Every bump threatened to hurl her skyward, out of control. She gritted her teeth hard enough to crack them. She hung onto the wagon seat so hard her hands went numb. Panic turned her insides to a scream.

Maybe she was screaming.

Or Billy was screaming.

Or the mule was screaming.

Someone was screaming.

A large rock lay in their path. The mule headed straight for it. If they hit, it'd blow the wagon apart and send them to Mars.

Stoner tightened her grip.

Billy tightened hers.

They glanced at each other in a helpless and farewell kind of way.

And missed it.

And hit the one behind it, the one they hadn't seen.

Stoner felt herself jolted upward and to the side. Her hand was wrenched from the edge of the wagon seat. She flailed out at the air.

She was going over.

Billy grabbed her belt and held it.

She managed to get a hold on the wagon and hauled herself inside. Her heart threatened to thud itself right out of her chest.

But at least they'd left Parnell behind.

The mule tired at last. Slowed to a trot, then a walk, then stopped.

There was nothing around them but prairie.

"My God," Stoner said as she felt for breaks—none—and bruises—hundreds. "If this is your only means of transportation out here, no wonder everyone stays home."

"Uh, Stoner ..." Billy said in a high squeak.

She looked over.

Parnell was holding the rifle to Billy's head.

Oops.

"Hi!" Stoner said. "Been here long?"

The Reverend Henry Parnell grinned, showing rotten teeth. "Thought you could get away, didn't you? Guess you forgot I have the Power."

"I don't know about the Power," Stoner said. "But you have the gun."

He pulled back on the hammer. "I'll thank you to pick up that knife, Son," he said to Billy.

Fortunately, good sense prevailed. Billy reached for the knife and offered it to him.

Parnell shook his head. "You keep it," he said, and laughed.

"I thought you wanted it," Stoner said. "Isn't that what this is all about."

The man glared at her. "A little present. From me to your friend. Let's go back to town, now. Nice and easy. No tricks."

Billy picked up the reins and turned the mule around. "If there's one thing I can't stand," she grumbled, "it's people who go and jump in your wagon and stick a gun in your head without even waiting to be invited."

It was a silent ride.

It looked as if the townsfolk had found a focus for their excitement. From the distance they resembled a swarm of ants scurrying busily around a picnic basket.

Stoner had a sneaking suspicion she knew what the excitement was. And she'd seen enough old westerns to know what it meant when townsfolk scurried around a tall central upright and a cross-piece.

They were getting ready to hang someone.

And she had a pretty good idea who they were planning to hang.

She glanced over at Billy, who had apparently come to the same conclusion. The woman was grim and ashen.

Okay, what do we do now? Try to take him here? Or stall for time and hope for help or inspiration, whichever comes first?

She glanced back at Parnell. The point of his gun was firmly planted at the base of Billy's skull. His eyes took in the town, Stoner, and Billy in rapid and constant movements. Just like they taught you in driving school: road, rear view mirror, speedometer, road, rear view mirror, speedometer, keep sweeping.

The chances of taking him off guard looked pretty pathetic.

She caught the Old Booger staring hard at her during one of those sweeps. He had something on his mind. Maybe it was the thinsulate.

She doubted it.

She waited until he came around again, and stared back. Parnell smiled and gave her a knowing wink, as if they shared some secret knowledge.

Odd.

Caroline must be dead. He wouldn't take a chance on her getting away. And it probably wouldn't bother him greatly to kill her off.

Everything he'd done had been directed at Billy. The fires. The kidnapping. The murder attempt. And now this.

All of this to get rid of one runaway woman?

Even if he'd been Billy's father's best buddy, this was excessive. And Parnell had been in town since before that incident. Besides, Billy's father had sent the bounty hunter. Why do that if he had Parnell to take care of things?

No, what was going on here was bigger than Billy. And from the way he was staring and winking, it looked as if it involved her, too.

She wished she'd paid more attention to what he'd said last night— God, was it only last night? —instead of writing it off as maniacal raving.

She caught his eye again.

He smiled. "Did you like my fires?"

"Well," she said carefully, not wanting to provoke his trigger finger, "I'm really not sure I understand the symbolism."

"Oh, yes, you do." He grinned. "You might even say I did it all for you." He nodded toward Billy. "And him."

What? "It was thoughtful of you, but you shouldn't have gone to all that trouble." She looked down at the town. Last night she had only been aware of the saloon burning, and this morning she'd been too focused on their problems to notice. But it was more than Dot's Gulch that had been destroyed. The entire eastern side of the street, up to the alley between Dot's and the Saddler's—at least a third of Tabor—lay in ashes.

No wonder the townsfolk were annoyed.

Parnell gestured that way with his head. "Purified," he said.

"What?"

"The town is purified now. The Evil has been burned away."

Resurrect in a hundred years, Parnell, she thought. They loved that kind of we-had-to-destroy-the-village-to-save-it reasoning in Vietnam. "I think you went a little overboard."

He laughed.

Somehow she didn't think he was laughing at her conversational skills.

"What does that do to your Powers?" he asked with a sly look.

"You have a point," she said agreeably. "It does take the wind out of my sails."

The Creature was toying with him. It made him nervous and angry. He wanted to be at the end of this trip. Back in town, where they were waiting for him.

He looked up. His people were milling around the hanging tree, idle. That was bad. Inactivity was wasteful, and cooled their blood.

In one quick movement, before the Demon could react, he swung the barrel of his gun up into the air and fired.

The people turned and looked in his direction.

He rammed the shotgun back into the Bastard's neck.

Stoner felt the explosion from the top of her head to the soles of her feet. Like hot sparks racing through her nerves. She wanted to rip the gun from his hands and smash his face in.

She glanced over at Billy.

Billy was crying, done in, anger shifted to fear.

Stoner wanted to touch her.

To hold her.

She wanted this to be over.

220

He had fired two shots from the gun now. It might be empty. Or did these shotguns have magazines?

Come on, you don't even know what guns do what in your own time. Except for semiautomatics. Everyone was an authority on them in 1990 America. The news media had provided endless crash courses on Semiautomatic Weapons and the Constitution.

If the gun was empty, they could get it away from him, toss him out of the wagon, and head out of here.

Before they reached that unfriendly-looking crowd of Taborites.

If the gun wasn't empty ...

The crowd cheered.

He wanted to let out a whoop and a hollar, but it wouldn't be dignified. Not for him.

Not for one of the Chosen.

"Faster," he barked, and the Bastard slapped the reins.

Its strength was diminishing fast now. He could afford to enjoy his victory.

Henry Parnell rode into Tabor to wild acclaim, on the back of a broken-down wagon pulled by an exhausted mule. Just like Jesus on the donkey.

Men reached up to shake his hand. Women waved handkerchiefs.

Toward the back of the crowd someone started a chant.

"Hang the Bastard!"

"Hang the Murderer!"

It was glorious.

Stoner looked around wildly, searching for help.

Blue Mary was gone.

And Dot was gone.

Not a friendly face anywhere. They were on their own.

Parnell faced the crowd and raised his hands triumphantly.

The crowd cheered.

He grabbed Billy by the collar and hauled her to her feet. "Here he is," he shouted. "Your fire bug, your killer."

The fine, Church-going residents of Tabor roared for blood.

Billy's face was gray with terror.

"Wait a minute!" Stoner heard herself shout as she got to her feet. "This isn't right."

The Reverend Henry Parnell laughed in her face.

"Listen to me!"

The crowd made a roaring, jeering noise that drowned her out.

Parnell gestured to a pair of angry-looking men in ragged black pants and flour-sacking shirts. "Lock this one in the old warehouse," he ordered.

Rough hands reached up and dragged her from the wagon.

The look of panic and hopelessness on Billy's face tore her heart.

The men jerked her away from the mob, toward the abandoned building she had seen her first full day in Tabor. The one with the dirt floor and spiders and mouse droppings. Not her idea of a vacation cottage, but she had the feeling she wouldn't be there long.

They threw her inside and slammed the door and leaned against it.

It was the only door in the place.

The only window faced the street.

She had to get to Billy.

Out on the street, Parnell was holding court.

The wagon was stopped at the foot of the gallows. Townspeople swarmed and milled around it like sheep at a feeding trough.

"Behold," he was saying in his Sunday-Preacher voice. "Today I will show you things you never knew existed."

He gave Billy a shake. The knife slipped from her hand. He held the gun to her head, forced her to pick it up.

"God has tried this miserable home-burner and murderer. God has judged him guilty. Now we ..." He thrust one fist into the air. "...WE HAVE BEEN CHOSEN TO DELIVER GOD'S PUNISHMENT."

It wasn't doing either of them any good for her to stand around watching and feeling helpless. Stoner left the window and went in search of a break in the walls. She could hear Parnell droning on and on outside.

Count on the clergy to deliver a half-hour sermon before every minor event.

She hoped she could count on the clergy to ramble on and on.

"Today," Parnell brayed, "I will show you wondrous things. Things you never dreamed of."

Wished he'd show me how to get out of this mess.

She kept going around the walls, slowly, forcing herself to concentrate, knowing time was running out fast.

And there it was. In a dark corner where the sun seldom reached. A few boards, rotten and decayed where the wall touched the ground.

Someone had been there before her, in fact. Some small someone with teeth—mice or rats, maybe even a porcupine—had gnawed away a nice, fist-sized section of the wall. She pushed at the crumbling boards. Chunks of sawdust and wood particle fell into her hands.

"A thousand wonders. God's wonders."

The crowd murmured, growing restless.

They'd sit still for that stuff through a month of Sundays, but when it came to killing ...

222

A whole slab of board came away.

... don't keep 'em waiting.

She grunted and pulled. There was enough space now to slip her leg through.

Come on, Parnell, get their attention.

"Today YOU, dear friends and residents of Tabor, will see ..."

He paused for dramatic effect.

She pushed against a board. A nail squealed. She held her breath.

"... THE DEVIL HIMSELF!"

Yeah, right. They're looking at the Devil and don't even know it. Been looking at Old Nick every Sunday for the last blessed ...

The board broke away.

...ever-loving year.

She thought she could get through. She slipped her feet into the hole and worked her body toward daylight.

It occurred to her that someone could be waiting out there, just standing around whistling silently and waiting for her to get all the way through so they could put a bullet right through her head.

Well, she thought as she worked her shoulders around and made them small, you certainly do think about cheerful things at the most opportune moments.

"THE DEVIL!" Parnell shrieked.

She was out. Nobody shot her.

In fact, nobody was around.

Okay, now what?

"THE VERY PRINCE OF DARKNESS."

"That ain't no Prince of Darkness," a voice of reason shouted from amid the ashes of Dot's Gulch. "That there's Dot's boy."

A set of short boards had been nailed into the side of the building, steps leading to what looked like the opening of a hayloft. She studied them.

She knew she didn't have a chance against the mob on the ground. Not without a gun and half the U.S. Cavalry. But from an elevated position ...

They didn't exactly look safe. Sort of soft and punky, like the boards she had just torn apart with her bare hands.

Beggars can't be choosers.

She took a deep breath and swung up onto the first step.

"A boy?" Parnell was saying. "Yes, it looks like a boy."

Things improved as she went higher.

She heard a sound like ripping cloth. The crowd gasped.

"But it is also FEMALE!"

She had reached the top. The roof seemed solid enough, pine boards covered with tarpaper and bird dung.

223

For God's sake, she thought. Another of those dress code types.

"It thinks to make itself the equal of a MAN!" he shrieked.

"FEMALE! And it dares to wear the clothes of MEN!"

Now what? She didn't know what to do next. She took a deep breath and let it out slowly. She forced her attention inward and sent out psychic feelers, trying to get an impression of the man, searching for weaknesses she could use against him. What came to her was more frightening than what she had seen so far. All the impressions of a lifetime—things felt and heard and seen and sensed, things said and done—had been dropped into the box of his mind and shaken and dumped out again, and the pattern they formed was what he believed to be the Truth. Henry Parnell's mind was a computer, programmed to randomize all input.

So much for outguessing him.

"LOOK!" Parnell screeched.

Stoner eased her way to the peak of the roof and looked.

He was holding up a piece of paper, a little larger than a playing card. Painted in vivid colors.

A Tarot card.

"Look at this. I took this from the Witch myself. It is a page from the Witches' Book. This is a portrait of Satan."

Oh, for the love of Heaven. If people were willing to believe that ...

She looked at Billy. The man had torn her shirt. She was breast-naked in the cold November air.

He snatched the knife from Billy's hand. "With this knife," Parnell raved, brandishing his strange dagger. "With this very Jesus knife, this instrument of vengeance carved with the sacred symbols of God's justice, I will show you the true nature of ..." He whirled about, pointing the knife at Billy's face. "... the Beast!"

She looked around. They couldn't possibly be buying this.

The crowd's attention was riveted on Parnell.

"I will plunge this dagger of Justice deep into its flesh," he screeched. "And you'll think you've seen it die. But immediately a new manifestation will come to life, each more hideous than the last. TEN TIMES THE BEAST WILL DIE AND BE REBORN."

Spittle flew from his lips. Droplets of sweat hung like raindrops from his beard. "AND WITH THE ELEVENTH DEATH, THE REIGN OF SATAN WILL END!"

He reached for the rope. "Let the first death be by hanging!" Hayes moved up behind her and tied her hands.

He slid the noose around Billy's neck.

Okay, it's now or never.

Carefully, aware that standing on the peak of an old roof with a bloodthirsty mob below had its hazards, she stood up.

"Parnell!"

Parnell stopped dead in the middle of quoting Scripture, some good, woman-hating Gospel according to Paul.

"THIS IS WRONG!" The words tore from her throat, ripping the membranes like nails. "She didn't do anything."

She scanned the crowd pleadingly, trying to catch their attention with her eyes. "Parnell set the fires."

From the way their faces went hard, she knew it had been the wrong thing to say.

"She dares accuse your pastor," he screeched. "Shame!"

The crowd took up the chant. "Shame. Shame."

He listened for a moment, drinking in the sounds.

His people.

Echoing his words.

He threw back his head.

"Let the hanging begin!" he crowed.

The Beast thrashed against Its bonds, shouting for Its life.

Someone came forth with a gag to muffle the Demon. He motioned him away. Let them hear Its misery. It would only fuel the fires in their blood.

"You'll have to live with what you're doing," the Beast shouted. "Every day, for the rest of your miserable lives, you'll remember this. YOU KILLED AN INNOCENT WOMAN!"

Parnell laughed.

"Listen to me!" Stoner shouted. The crowd turned back to her. "That man is insane." She looked around wildly.

Two figures ran out the back door of Kwan's Laundry. Dot and May Chang.

In the distance she could see a horse and rider, heading hell-bent for Tabor. It looked like Cullum Johnson.

Okay, okay. Stall for time.

"He killed his wife!" she yelled at the top of her lungs. "Caroline Parnell is dead."

"LIAR!" He shrieked.

Ah, ha. A vulnerable point. He was afraid to let them know about that.

"I saw him do it. Look around. Is Caroline Parnell here?"

A few of the townspeople searched through the crowd and whispered among themselves.

Progress.

Parnell raised his rifle. "You get down from there now."

225

For a split second they looked at each other down the barrel. Why didn't he go ahead and shoot?

Maybe he was afraid the crowd would turn against him. Shooting an unarmed woman. Frontier chivalry... something like that.

His finger tighten on the trigger.

She was frozen.

Hands tied, noose around her neck, Billy managed to land a well-placed kick in Parnell's rear end.

He sprawled on his stomach and got up, his face scarlet with fury. He pointed toward Stoner. "Stone the Demon," he shouted.

A rock struck her shoulder. She ducked behind the roof peak.

Pebbles and stones rained around her.

It gave her an idea. Digging into her jeans pocket, she got to her knees. This was going to be tricky. If someone threw a big one and knocked her off balance ...

She reached out quickly, pretending to grab at the rocks in mid-air. "Hey, Parnell, you want to see Magic?"

She made a gesture of throwing the stones back...

... and threw down her handful of Blue Mary's crystals instead.

"Jewels!" someone shouted.

The people closest to her turned their attention to the ground. They fell on their knees in the dirt fighting over polished pebbles.

Parnell was furious. "Don't listen to her!" he screeched. "It's a trick!"

He was losing them. Fickle sheep! Stupid creatures, to fall for the Devil's trick.

He had to get their attention back. "Hang the Bastard!"

Out of the corner of his eye he saw a glint of silver.

Ignoring it he faced the crowd. "Count with me! Count down the seconds of the Bastard's life!"

They were interested again. He had them back.

"Ten. Nine. Eight...."

He felt someone staring at him. Hard.

"Seven! Six!"

A slant-eyed woman. Away from the crowd, on the other side of the wagon.

"Five!"

Her face was calm as a rock.

"Four!"

Then he saw the tiny pistol in her hand.

The bullet ripped through his chest and exploded his heart.

The world went red.

Slowly, he fell to the ground, facing his attacker.

Her face seemed to change.

His eyes widened with surprise and terror.

"Father?" the Sanctified Man said.

And died.

The crowd moved back silent, shocked.

May Chang daintily replaced the pistol in her cotton string purse. She turned her back to the wagon facing the crowd. "For my father," she said clearly, "and the honor of my family."

"She killed the Preacher," someone shouted, and the crowd surged forward.

"He killed my father." May said.

They hesitated unsure. It wouldn't take them long to find their nerve.

Stoner raced down the roof. She half-climbed, half-fell to the ground.

Her ankle twisted. Pain knifed through her.

To hell with that.

She ran down the alley behind the remains of Dot's Gulch just as Cullum Johnson reined in his horse.

"I'll explain later," she barked, and stripped the rifle from his hands.

The crowd was milling now, uncertain which way to turn.

"Get the Chink! Her gun is empty." It was Joseph Hayes. "Hang them both."

They went for May Chang.

Stoner fired into the air.

The crowd froze and let her go.

Stoner jumped up onto the wagon pulling May up behind her.

"Untie her," she snapped at Hayes.

He hesitated.

Stoner raised the gun. "Do it!"

Hayes took the rope from around Billy's neck and untied her hands then got down from the wagon.

Billy sat down in the wagon, arms wrapped around herself to hide her naked breasts.

Stoner put one hand on Billy's head. They weren't out of it yet, but she had to touch her.

"Excuse me," May Chang said. She stripped off her shawl and tossed it over Billy's shoulders.

Billy glanced up at her gratefully.

The sea of bodies was undulating, coming to life again. They were surrounded now, with people whose Preacher had just been killed.

Stoner picked up the reins in one hand. She held the rifle in the other. It was awkward. She wasn't sure she could do it.

A grumbling went through the crowd.

She tried to move the mule forward.

The crowd held them back.

It was a stalemate.

The grumbling rose to a complaint. Then a grievance.

"Stop them!" Joseph Hayes whined. "Don't let them get away."

The crowd closed in tighter.

"Now, jest a damn minute," Cullum Johnson said. He worked Toby through the mob. In one hand he held a pistol. Another pistol was strapped to his waist. A bandolier of ammunition was slung across his chest.

The crowd fell silent and looked at him curiously.

"Seems to me we're about to make a serious mistake here," Cullum said.

Joseph Hayes turned to him. "Who the hell do you think you are?"

Cullum touched the barrel of his pistol to his hat. "Johnson's the name, Cullum Johnson. From back Tennessee way."

Hayes smirked. "Well, Mr. Johnson, I think we can handle our own affairs without any help from outsiders like yourself."

Someone in the crowd seconded the motion.

"It's come to my attention," Cullum said, "that this here town is severely lacking in law and order. So I've decided to appoint myself sheriff."

Hayes chuckled. "And what makes you think we want you?"

"'Course you want me," Cullum said with an easy grin. "I got more guns than you." He turned to Stoner. "Leastways I will, when you give back that borrowed weapon."

"Gladly." She handed it to him.

Joseph Hayes found his voice at last. "Wait a minute!" he shouted into the crowd. "How do we know we can trust this man?"

The townspeople shifted uneasily. But no one made a move toward him.

On the edge of the crowd Stoner spotted Big Dot, looking about to bust a gut with pride. Dot stepped forward. "Because I say so."

"Are you willing to take the word of a whore and a bounty hunter?" Hayes said.

"You're willing enough to take my word the girls are clean, Joseph," Dot said. "Don't know why you'd doubt me now."

It was corny, but it worked. Hayes was silenced for a moment.

Leaderless, the crowd drew back uncertainly, reverting to individual and self-conscious men and women.

"Joseph Hayes!"

Across the street, riding a wave of righteous indignation, marched Arabella Hayes. Hayes' face took on the look of a dog caught trashing the neighbor's garbage.

"Just what do you think your doing, Joseph?"

He tried to put on a brave face "These people let the Chinawoman kill our Preacher, Arabella. They have to be punished."

Arabella looked at Parnell's slumped body, at the last of his blood trick:-ing into the dust. She snorted. "Good riddance, if you ask me. Nothing but a wife-abusing, woman-hating, excuse of a man. Poor Caroline probably dead at his hands too..."

"Excuse me, Ma'am," Cullum said. "She's not dead, just shot up pretty bad. I left her with that Mary Gal."

"Woman," Dot said under her breath, "Show respect."

"Woman," Johnson corrected himself.

"Well Lord," said Arabella Hayes, her voice gruff to hide her pleasure. "Man wasn't just a no-good, but incompetent on top of it." She made a shooing gesture toward the crowd. "Now you folks go on home. This isn't a social gathering. Mr. Johnson has business to take care here and we should let him do it."

The crowd shuffled and muttered.

"Good people," Cullum Johnson addressed them. "I know this presents a genuine confusing situation. But Miz Parnell told me—and you can be-lieve me or not as you see fit—but she told me the Reverend here set those fires. Bragged on it to her, only she was afraid to say, and she's mighty sorry for that." He glanced at Arabella Hayes for confirmation.

"Sounds like Caroline to me," said Arabella. "Scared and sorry. I'll wa-ger he wasn't even a real Preacher, either."

"Yes, Ma'am," Johnson said. "She mentioned that."

After the people had begun to leave, Cullum turned to May Chang. "Ma'am, from the looks of things I'm going to be settling down here, and my horse Tobe don't take kindly to town life." He swung down from the saddle. "You'd be doing me a favor if you were to take him off my hands."

"Are you sure about this?" May asked.

"Yes, Ma'am. Only I suggest you go like the wind, because these folks are going to recover from their comatosity any minute, and I really don't know what they're going to take it into their minds to do."

May nodded. "I'll take good care of him," she said, and mounted.

"You take care of this gal, now, Tobe," Cullum said, his heart breaking. He patted the animal's velvet nose. "You was the best horse I ever knew."

May bent down quickly and touched Cullum's rough cheek, then turned the horse and took off at a gallop.

Dot slipped up to the wagon. "Don't mean to give unasked-for advice,

229

but this looks like a good time to take your leave."

Stoner lifted the reins. "Thanks for everything, Dot. I hope it'll be okay."

The woman reached up and squeezed her hand. "It'll be fine, honey."

She moved the wagon forward.

"Hold it," Cullum said. He reached in his shirt pocket and brought out a roll of bills and tossed them to Billy. "There's a couple hundred in there. Some from Mrs. Gillette, and some left over from what your Pa paid me to bring you back."

"You're going to let me go?" Billy asked.

Johnson shrugged. "You might say ..." he glanced shyly at Dot, "... I lost interest in bounty hunting."

"Well, thanks ..." Billy said.

Dot took his arm. "You're one big man, Cull. I'm proud to call you my friend."

"Mrs. Gillette," Cullum said, "before the winter's out, I hope you'll call me more than friend."

"I might," Dot said, looking up into his face with a flirty smile. "I just might."

He turned back to Billy. "But you best put some distance between yourself and Tabor, sweetheart. Your Pa was one mad and determined gent last time I saw him. Only a matter of time before he sends someone else after you."

"Pa is still alive?"

"Was last time I saw him. Alive and mad as... "

Billy nodded grimly. She turned to Dot. "You were good to me, Dot. I'm sorry I brought you all this trouble."

"Trouble," Dot said gruffly. "Life's trouble. Probably what we're put here for. You ever come back this way, look me up."

"Say goodbye to Cherry for me?"

"I will, honey. She's just a little torn up right now. You understand."

"Sure." She reached down and threw her arms around Dot's neck. "I'm going to miss you."

"I'll miss you, too. If you find yourself up South Dakota way, look up Miss Mary Jane Cannary. She's an old friend of mine. Talks tough as nails, but she's got a good heart. And don't you listen to rumors about her, either." Dot gave her a quick kiss and turned away to dab at her eyes. "Get out of here before I disgrace myself."

Billy slipped down into the wagon.

Stoner jiggled the reins. "Thanks again for your help, Dot. You sure are one formidable gal."

"Your not so bad yourself," Dot said. "Oughta do something about that

230

temper, though."

Stoner laughed and clucked to the mule. The wagon moved forward, away from Tabor.

"Where will you go?" Stoner asked after a while.

Billy shrugged. "Just keep moving, I guess."

"Alone?"

"Looks like."

"I wish you could come with me."

"Wish you could stay with me."

"Maybe," Stoner said, "we'll meet again sometime."

"Maybe."

She knew neither of them believed it.

The mule, wandering without direction, had brought them close to the spot where they had first met. She recognized the hill, the long slope to the Topeka-Denver trail. The weathered sign.

Something told her this was as far as she could go.

She stopped the mule and sat looking into the distance. It felt as if her heart was being ripped from her chest. "I'll miss you."

Billy slipped her hand inside Stoner's. "I'll miss you, too." With her free hand she touched Stoner's face. "Don't forget me when you get back home."

Stoner covered Billy's hand with her own. "Oh, Billy, I'll never forget you." She reached out and ran her fingers across the woman's lips, felt the softness of her cheek. "I hope you have a good life."

Billy smiled. "Right about now, I'll settle for a long one." She contemplated the horizon. "I'm sorry you never got to meet that woman you were named for."

Stoner caught her breath. Of course!

She reached into her jeans pocket and brought out her Susan B. Anthony dollar. "Find them," she said. "Show them this."

Billy looked it over. "All right."

"Tell them it's from the future. Tell them not to give up. Tell them they'll get the vote. Maybe not in their time, but it's coming. Tell them I voted for a woman for Vice President ..."

"You never," Billy said.

"I did. Tell them some day there'll be a National Organization for Women, and demonstrations in Washington for women's rights, with hundreds of thousands of women there. Tell them there's a Women's Revolution coming and it'll change the world." She handed Billy the coin. "And tell them a hundred years from now in colleges there will be departments of Women's Studies, and people will look back at the things they did here and know this was where it all started."

She handed Billy the reins. "Join up with them, Billy. They'll take care of you." She grinned. "And I'm sure they can use a smart woman like you to take care of them."

Billy looked at her with deep, liquid eyes. "So long, Stoner," she said, and took her in her arms.

Her kiss was long and sweet and heart-breaking.

Stoner couldn't watch her leave. She slipped from the wagon and stood staring at the ground. She heard the mule's hoof beats receding into the distance, strained to catch the last faint vibrations through the earth.

Then it was silent, with only the sound of breeze playing through the dried and broken grass.

She took a deep breath and wiped her eyes and turned north toward the trail.

Blue Mary stood in front of her, holding her knapsack. "Well, dear," the woman said cheerfully, "I suppose you'll be leaving us."

"What happened to you back there? You just disappeared."

The older woman chuckled. "I did, didn't I?"

Stoner felt a prickle of annoyance. "If you could do tricks like that, maybe you could have prevented the whole thing."

"No," Blue Mary said with a sober shake of her head. "I can't interfere with what's meant to happened, only help move it along. And you didn't need me, really. As usual, you did a fine job on your own."

"I don't think I did much but get in the way. It was really Billy's story, wasn't it?"

Blue Mary smiled affectionately. "In the play we call Life," she said, "we can't always have the starring role. Sometimes we're just the supporting cast. But he would have killed us all, you know. Dorothy and the girls, Billy, even me. And your old friend Lucy Stone. We needed your help."

Stoner shrugged. "I guess ..."

"And you've had an impact on Billy's life that won't be realized for years. Everything you do, no matter how small, changes the world forever."

Right now, she didn't care about changing the world. She looked down at her hands. "I'm going to miss her, Mary. I don't think I can bear it."

Blue Mary took Stoner's face between her palms. "Stoner, Stoner, haven't you figured it out yet?"

"I know," she said. "But it's not the same."

"I suppose it's not." She gave her a little kiss on the cheek. "It's a hard thing, living on this plane. I wonder why we're always so eager to do it." With a sigh, Blue Mary handed her the knapsack and pulled her shawl tighter about her shoulders. "Well, I have to be going. Have a good trip, and I'll see you in Boston." She began to walk away over the hill toward

Tabor.

"Wait," Stoner called. She ran after her.

But when she reached the top of the hill, Blue Mary was gone.

There was a sound behind her. A low, distant rumbling sound. She turned back.

The eighteen-wheeler pulled into the center lane to bypass her car, and barrelled its way east on I-70.

Chapter 13

She didn't know why she was drawn to the hotel. Motels were more her style. Carry your own luggage, in and out with a minimum of fuss or interacting. No elevator rides with strangers, staring at the row of lighted numbers over the door and pretending to meditate on the significance—both social and cultural—of '70s protest songs played on Muzak. No wondering if your worn jeans, perfect for long drives, will be met with overt hostility in the lobby. No overpriced restaurants. No cute little handy gift stores offering the Wall Street Journal and the latest make-up-and-fashion rip-off magazines, and camera film at twice the normal price.

Bed, bath, and privacy. A near-by drive-thru restaurant. That was all she needed.

But there was something about the Whitley. It was an old hotel, on a back street in downtown Topeka. She wouldn't have even found it, except that there had been some kind of accident or power disruption or water main break—one of those mysterious events involving police cars, flashing orange lights, steam, and general unexplained confusion. Whatever it was had caused traffic to be routed past the downtown area through side streets.

So there she was, detoured onto Remington and left to find her own way back to the business district—and she wasn't sure how she'd gotten into the business district in the first place, except that she'd taken the wrong exit and overshot the motel and fast food strip. It had been dark for hours. She was tired and cranky. Apprehensive. And trapped in some kind of temporal no-woman's-land, her body in Topeka 1989 and her heart with Billy in 1871.

Even stopping at the nearest hospital Emergency room for a tetanus shot hadn't brought her to Now—though it had answered that age-old question: do wounds travel forward in time? Not even the familiar haggle over insurance, the familiar endless wait, the feeble attempt to explain the

234

puncture holes on her neck. (She'd gotten them trying to cross a barbed-wire fence, she'd said. The young intern had looked dubious. Probably thought it was from mainlining drugs. She wished she'd told him it was the bite of a Vampire.)

She'd thought about calling home from the hospital. But she knew, as soon as she heard a familiar voice—no matter how dearly she loved that voice—Billy and Big Dot and Blue Mary and Tabor would be lost to her forever.

She just couldn't let go. Not yet.

It was cold. She wondered if Billy was cold, wherever she was. Had she found the suffragists? Or was she wandering around the prairie, alone and lost and unloved?

She missed Billy. She'd probably always miss her. Even if they were lovers now, in a different incarnation—well, Billy was still Billy, and a huge hunk of her heart transcended time and longed for her.

The angry blare of a car horn yanked her back to present reality. She had missed that millisecond window of opportunity between the time the light turns green and the guy behind you blows his horn. She inched forward passive-aggressively, pretending to be looking for something along the street.

And there it was. The Whitley. Separate from the buildings on either side. Old but clean. Small. And an empty parking space out front.

In her experience, empty parking spaces were a Sign. Like shooting stars, or having a butterfly light on your shoulder. Signs that say, "Pay close attention. Something of great significance is happening."

She pulled over, got out, and locked the car. As she opened the trunk and took out her suitcase, she wondered what was happening to the parka she had left for the Arapahoe woman back in Tabor. Maybe someday she'd go back, find the remains of the old town. Maybe she'd even find a shred of thinsulate. What if archaeologists found it first? What would they make of it?

Probably call it a hoax, the way they labelled anything they couldn't fit into their narrow scheme. Between "hoax" and "mass hysteria", the scientists had managed to do away with just about anything interesting.

She'd come a long way in ridding herself of that kind of thinking, but she knew she still had a long way to go. Maybe she could start a support group—Survivors of Science.

"Boythink," Gwen called it.

She slammed the trunk lid and ran up the steps of the hotel.

The lobby was dark and Muzak-free. Oak panels covered the walls, and potted plants stood by gilt-overlaid pillars. Deep, well-used armchairs were placed for small conversational groups. The carpets had once been deep-hued Orientals, but had been worn thread-bare. The redheaded woman in her late sixties at the registration desk looked as if she had worked there most of her life.

She smiled as Stoner approached. "Something we can do for you?"

"Do you have a room for one? For tonight?"

"We almost always have room," the woman said. "We're a little hard to find."

"To be perfectly honest," Stoner said as she signed the register, "I wouldn't have known about you if it weren't for the detour."

"You know," the woman said as she slid a key across the counter, "I have to admit I like it this way. It's a lot more personal. Would you like help with your suitcase, or would you rather carry it yourself?"

"I'd rather."

"Okey-doke. Your room's on the second floor. Turn right at the elevator and go on to the end. It's a quiet room. No telephone, I'm afraid." She grinned in an embarrassed way. "We've been planning to put them in since—oh, probably about 1965. Never can seem to get around to it. There's one in the lounge, though, and if you get a call someone'll track you down. Have you had dinner?"

"Not yet."

"The dining room stays open until ten, but I'm afraid there's not much of a selection. Tonight's feature is ..." She consulted a scrap of paper that was wedged in the corner of the blotter. "Stew."

Stew? That gave her an unreal, the-past-is-just-around-the-corner kind of feeling.

"Plus the usual assortment of sandwiches," the woman added. "And save room for the homemade pie. My specialty."

"Sounds great."

"Anything you need, give me a hoot and a hollar. Name's Bea."

"Thanks."

Right now, all she wanted was a long bath. It had been either twenty-four hours or ten days since her last one.

The hot water was comforting, soothing. Gently, it peeled the sadness from her. Billy was gone, like an old friend moving to another country. No matter how much she missed her, Billy was a part of her past now. She might see her again some day, at least in a dream, certainly in memory. That would have to do. She washed and dried carefully, making a healing ritual of it. She slipped into fresh clothes. She thought she was ready.

The bartender, who looked enough like Bea to be her son and probably was, pointed her to the telephone in the corner. She placed the call to

Gwen first. She could feel her heart start beating a little faster. Her fingertips felt all tingly. A pleasant blend of excitement and a tiny bit of anxiety. It was a familiar sensation, one she always felt when she hadn't seen Gwen in a while. As if her body had forgotten that they were friends and lovers.

The phone rang. Four times. A bad sign. Gwen could reach it in two from anywhere in her apartment, which meant she would probably get the answering...

"Hi. This is Gwen Owens. I'm watching Designing Women. Why aren't you? You can reach me after the show, or leave your name and number ..."

Stoner hung up and tried Aunt Hermione.

"Hello. You've reached the answering machine of Hermione Moore and Stoner McTavish. We're meditating at the moment, but leave your name and number and we'll get back to you. Blessed be."

Marylou had to be home.

"You have reached the winter residence of Max and Edith Kesselbaum and the full-time residence of Marylou Kesselbaum. Unfortunately, we can't come to the phone. Edith decided to cook tonight instead of sending out, and it was an absolute DISASTER. We are either repairing the damage or running out to the store. However ..."

There's nothing sadder or more frustrating than going through a life-or-death situation in another century, and coming back to find nobody home to tell about it.

Might as well have a drink. Designing Women wouldn't be over for twenty minutes.

She put the receiver down with a sigh and went to the bar and climbed up on a tall stool covered with cracked green leather.

The bartender slid a paper coaster in front of her. "Get you something?"

"Double Manhattan, please."

"You got it."

She looked around the lounge. It was darkly lit by lamps with green glass shades. More old wood, dark and polished. There were booths against the opposite wall, and Monday Night Football holding forth silently on the TV at the end of the bar. Just your standard, ordinary hotel watering hole, complete with shelves of bottles under a portrait ...

She caught her breath.

The woman in the portrait looked to be in her fifties. Her hair was done in a style popular at the turn of the century. Dressed in a white silk shirt and velvet riding pants. She leaned against a white-washed fence, head turned slightly to the side. Behind her stretched endless miles of prairie grass and blue prairie sky. Her expression was self-contained, and yet she

237

looked as if she might burst into laughter at any moment.

It was Billy.

The man brought her drink.

"Excuse me," Stoner said as he turned toward the television. She indicated the portrait. "Who's that?"

He barely glanced at it. "People always want to know that. Must be something about her."

"Yes, there is. Do you know who it is?"

"Billy Whitley. Started this hotel. According to some folks, she once owned a fair amount of Topeka and most of Emporia."

She could hardly believe it. Of all the places she could have stayed... But, of course, according to Aunt Hermione, there are no accidents. All our souls just got together and decided to meet here. Kind of like a reunion. "What do you know about her?"

He shrugged. "Not much. Bea might. She's into that kind of stuff."

She grabbed her drink and headed for the lobby.

Bea marked her place in a paperback novel called *The Rich are Decadent* and put it down. "Something?" she asked pleasantly.

"That woman over the bar. Billy Whitley. Do you know anything about her?"

The woman smiled. "This was her hotel, you know."

"Yes, but anything else? I mean, where did she come from? How did she get her money? That kind of thing."

"Well," Bea said, "let me think a minute." She thought a minute. "We had some local historians here back in '76, made up a brochure about her. A lot of interest in history back then, you know. I must've memorized the durn thing myself. The way I recall it, Billy Whitley started out as some kind of outlaw or something out in the Colorado Territory, back before it became a state."

"Why was she an outlaw?"

"Nobody seems to know. Some said she'd set some fires out that way. Others claim she killed a man in Tennessee, Kentucky, one of those states. But that's just speculation. What is known is that she hooked up with a bunch of Suffragists back when Colorado was deciding what kind of state it wanted to be—you know, equality for blacks and women or not. When the Colorado legislature voted to come in without giving women the vote, she moved on to Wyoming and worked there until they came in as the Equality State, in '90." She paused to calculate. "Billy must have been about, oh, forty-four or so then."

"Do you happen to know," Stoner asked, "if she ever learned to read and write?"

Bea looked at her. "Funny question. What makes you ask about that?"

238

"Uh ..." Stoner shrugged. "I picked it up somewhere, I guess."

"Well—again, this could be just rumor, but—the story goes, she didn't know how when she first joined forces with the Suffragists. But Mrs. Stone—that's Lucy B. Stone—she was active in the early Suffrage Movement ..."

"Yes, I know."

"Mrs. Stone took her under her wing and taught her the basics. Mrs. Stone was a great one for causes. Kept her maiden name, you know."

"I know."

"It seems Billy was a bright young woman who caught on fast. So Mrs. Stone passed her along to her friend Frances Willard over at Evanston College for Ladies in Illinois."

Stoner had to laugh. Billy at a "College for Ladies" made quite a picture. She wondered how the Ladies took to Billy's gunslinging ways.

"But," Bea went on, "she didn't stay there long. Said it made her restless to be cooped up. So she went back on the politicking trail. Settled down in Wyoming, then, and took up wheat farming. When the Depression of '93-97 hit, she was one of the few well-to-do farmers who'd turned her money back into the land. So when the European wheat crops failed in '97, Billy struck it rich. Used those profits to buy up real estate in Emporia and Topeka and God knows how many other places. But this was her favorite spot. She died here in 1930, in the front room, second floor. Eighty-four years old, and she still had all her faculties."

"What did she die of?"

"Old age, I guess. Went to sleep and never woke up." She smiled. "There's some folks say her ghost still haunts that room. But you know how people are. Always looking for a way to make a good story."

Stoner swirled her ice around with her finger. "Did anyone ever say what she was like? As a person?"

"Well, folks liked her. She could be a lot of fun, was good with a bawdy story and never put on airs. Friendly to everyone. Except the clergy. For some reason, Billy never could abide the clergy."

"Did she ever marry?"

"Not that anyone knew. There were plenty of men after her. You've seen her portrait. Easy to see why. Plus being wealthy. And lucky. But she was always kind of stand-offish with men. Women, too, really. She'd laugh and carry on with whoever, but no one really got close to her feelings. Not that she seemed to be lonely. At least, if she was she never said."

Bea looked thoughtful. "There was one story about her, that she had a great love once in her life. Never could give her heart again to her dying day. A Scot. One of the ones that came out here during those days, most likely. A lot of British of one sort or another passed through this part of the country. Name of ..." She looked at Stoner with a delighted look. "McTavish! My gosh, it could even have been kin of yours."

Stoner smiled to herself. "I doubt it. My people never settled this far west."

"Yeah," Bea said. "You're probably right. I'm an incurable romantic. Story might not even have been true."

"Well," Stoner said, "it would be too bad if it were. She must have had a lot to give, if the right person had come along."

"One thing she did get fierce about was how men treated women. She got quite a reputation for it. If she saw a woman mistreated by her husband, she'd just march in and order that gal to pack and take her right out of there and into one of her hotels. Sometimes half the rooms were filled with those women. Sort of like the shelters we have nowadays. If it looked as if the man wasn't going to straighten himself out, and the woman didn't have anywhere else to go, Billy'd send her out to her ranch in Wyoming. The whole place was run by women. Man didn't dare go near it, or he'd find himself gelded."

She was here, Stoner thought. She died in this place. And some folks say ...

The thought made her sad and happy and frightened and excited, all at the same time.

"I wonder," she said to Bea, "if it would be possible to see the room where she died."

Bea hesitated. "Well, I don't know ..."

"I wouldn't touch anything. I'd just like to—well, knowing a little about her, I guess I'd just like to feel close to her."

"Oh, what the heck? You have an honest face." She reached in a drawer and pulled out an old key and handed it over. "Take your time. Just lock up when you come out."

By the time she was standing outside the door, she wasn't certain she wanted to do this. Life goes on, and there's enough to handle without blending past and present—and maybe even inviting the future to drop in for a chat.

Oh, don't be silly, she told herself firmly. It's only a room.

She turned the key and pushed open the door.

A wave of terrible sadness swept out at her. Sadness so deep she could almost touch it. Sadness that wrapped around her heart and twisted it tight as rope.

"Oh, Billy," she whispered. "I'm so sorry."

She touched the top of the bureau, running her fingers over the silver brush and comb and hand mirror. A few threads of hair were still caught in the brush bristles. Hair as soft as rabbit fur and white as snow. A small

240

porcelain dish held tiny earrings and a single strand of beads made from brightly colored, polished stones. The stones Blue Mary had given her. She wondered what Billy had done with the Susan B. Anthony dollar. Had it been found among her things? If so, what did they make of it? Or had she gotten rid of it years before her death, lost or spent it, or even given it to a special friend. Stoner hoped she'd had a special friend to give it to.

She glanced up at the age-mottled mirror that hung above the bureau. It reflected the shadows in the room, but behind those shadows were other shadows, shadows entombed in the mirror itself.

She thought she caught movement in the mirror, and whirled to look behind her. But the room was empty.

Looked empty. It didn't feel empty.

She's here, she thought.

She backed away from the bureau and sat on the edge of the bed, careful not to wrinkle the bedclothes.

The atmosphere seemed to thicken.

"I'm here, Billy," she whispered.

The air took on an odor like hay and lavender.

She could feel the room's vibrations gather at the head of the bed, and turned toward it. There was nothing visible, but she knew someone was there. She held out her hand.

She could have sworn someone touched it. Rubbed a finger across her knuckles.

A flood of pictures raced through her mind, like memories unfolding at breakneck speed. Places she'd never been, faces she'd never seen. Crowds by torchlight, seen from a platform of some kind, faces upturned, excited, hopeful. Wide expanses of prairie. Grass fires by night, a flicker of flames that circled the black horizon like a burning necklace. An invasion of grasshoppers, black clouds of them like swarming bees, chewing up everything in their path—crops, gardens, grass, even clothing and the wooden sides of barns. Trying to trample them underfoot, their bodies making popping sounds like the cracking of walnut shells. Mountains covered in snow. Years of drought and flood. Sewing quilts from clothing scraps, and clothing from grain sacks and old blankets, even Conestoga wagon canvas. Tiny rooms in rough cabins. Sheets of paper with awkward handwriting, the same letters and simple words practiced over and over. More rooms. Endless rooms, and wagons, and the insides of railroad cars. A farm of wheat, stretching as far as the eye could see, and all the farmhands women. Always women. Women laughing together, crying together, arguing, teasing, dreaming, loving. Range fires, women swiping at the racing flames with water-soaked blankets and burlap bags and even worn petticoats. Women dead, dying. Her first view of a motor car—barbaric, dog-

241

killing machine, nothing good'll come of it. First electric light, and tele-phone, and radio. Everything moving too fast, changing too much. Can't keep up. Emotions—joy and fear and tenderness and sorrow and triumph. And, running through them all, loneliness.

She closed her eyes. The track of memories slowed, and there were Big Dot, and Lolly and Cherry. Blue Mary and the Reverend Henry Parnell. Tabor and the fire. The blizzard. Billy's dugout in the creek bank. The white wolf.

And then she saw herself, the way Billy had seen her first. Standing on top of the hill, little more than a dark shadow against the mauve-gray western sky. Looking lost and bewildered.

An overwhelming feeling of love swept over her and around her, taking her breath away.

She felt the tears well up in her eyes and spill over. She put her face down on the pillow. "I love you, too, Billy," she said in her heart. "I won't forget."

Something touched her hair, something like a warm breeze, stroking.

And suddenly the air in the room grew light, buoyant. Stoner found her-self laughing, remembering Billy playing the adolescent boy, her James Dean pose, her gruffness. "Hey, Billy," she said aloud. "I never got the chance to tell you, but as a boy, you were a great woman."

She got to her feet and smoothed the bedspread. "Drop in on Gwen and me on Monday nights," she said. "You'd love Designing Women."

She locked the door behind her carefully.

"What'd you think?" Bea asked. "Is it haunted?"

"Not that I could tell." She picked up the Manhattan that was slowly turning to water where she'd left it on the counter.

"Well," said Bea, "it's a harmless enough fancy, don't you think?"

"Definitely," Stoner said. "Thanks for letting me see it."

She left Bea to The Rich are Decadent and went back to the phone. This time it was answered on the second ring.

"Hello?"

Her heart jumped. "Billy?"

"Stoner?" Gwen asked in a puzzled voice.

She shook her head. "Yeah, it's me. Were you worried?"

"Why should I be worried about you?" Gwen asked with a smile in her velvet voice. "You're an adult. Ask me if I missed you."

"Did you miss me?"

"DESPERATELY!"

Stoner found herself grinning from ear to ear. "Gwen, what day is it?"

"You don't know what day it is?"

"Well, yeah, sort of. I just wondered if it was the same there as it is here."

242

There was a brief pause. "Are you out of the country?"

Stoner laughed. "I'm in Kansas."

"Is there any reason why it would be a different day there than here?"

"Anything is possible," Stoner said wryly. "Want to just tell me the day?"

"Monday."

"Monday of this week? I mean, Monday of the week I was supposed to call you?"

"If it weren't, dearest," Gwen said, "there would be wall-to-wall F.B.I. agents out there. Do you want me to fly out?"

"What for?"

"If you don't even know what day it is, you're obviously not in your right mind, and a potential danger to yourself and others."

"I'm fine. I need to know the date."

"Hang on a minute." Rustling papers. Gwen was pawing through the pile of clutter on her desk. "Got it. The 13th."

"November?"

"Of course, November. Where are you, anyway?"

"Kansas."

"Where in Kansas?"

"In a hotel in Topeka. The Whitley. I'll be home ..." She calculated rapidly. "Late Thursday."

"You'll miss *China Beach*."

"Tape it for me, will you? We can watch it together."

"That's a great idea," Gwen said. "Dana Delaney always turns you on."

Stoner felt herself blush. "Gwen!"

"What's wrong? Is someone listening in?"

"They might be."

"You," Gwen said, "are the silliest woman on the face of the earth, and I love you tremendously."

"I love you, too." She took a sip of her drink. "Listen," she said, not wanting to go into it all but unable to hang up now that she could finally hear Gwen's voice. "Was there ever a time when they didn't celebrate Thanksgiving?"

"Not that I know of. Are we getting into patriarchal genocidal holidays now?"

"No, I just wondered ... did they change the date?"

Gwen thought for a moment. "Yes, they did. Sometime in the '40s or '50s, I think. Want me to look it up?"

"Nineteen-forties?"

"Yes."

"Well," Stoner said. "That explains it."

"Explains what?"

"Why they didn't have Thanksgiving where I was."

"Stoner," Gwen said carefully, "where were you?"

"In 1871."

"That does it. I'm coming out there."

Stoner laughed. "I know it sounds funny. I can explain it later." Can I? Can I ever really explain it? "Listen, Gwen, do you ever have the feeling we've known each other before? Like in a past life or something?"

"Of course. Don't you?"

"I think I might have met you. I mean, another you. In that other time."

"Did you like me?"

"Very much."

"Thank God."

"Well, I almost ... I mean, I ..."

"Stoner," Gwen said, "were you unfaithful to me?"

"No, but I ...well, it was you, anyway."

"If you didn't do it, and it was me, anyway, you didn't do it with, why do you sound so guilty?"

Stoner looked down at the ground. "I was tempted."

"I forgive you," Gwen said.

"Well, it might have been you, but you then isn't the same as you now. But I was the same me, even if you weren't the same you. So it doesn't really matter who it really was, you or not you, because it was completely me being tempted ..."

"People are often tempted, Stoner. It's part of life. I just hope she was nice to you."

"She was. You were. The problem is, I nearly did it."

"Well, you didn't."

"You don't understand. I might have ... I mean, there were circumstances. I was lonely and frightened, and I didn't know if I'd ever see you again. Or anyone, for that matter. But that's no excuse." She knew she was blithering, but couldn't seem to stop. "I mean, an excuse is just an excuse. No matter how cold it was. It doesn't matter that he was going to kill us." She took a deep breath. "Gwen, I wanted to make love to Billy."

"Is that the mystery woman's name? Billy?"

"Gwen, are you listening to me?"

"Look, whatever happened or didn't happen, it's all right. If you want to discuss monogamy, we'll discuss monogamy, but let's not make AT&T rich while we do it."

Stoner rubbed her hand over her face. "I feel awful about this, Gwen."

"Just tell me one thing," Gwen said. "How much of a threat is this Billy?"

"Huh?"

244

"Is she going to move to Boston and try to steal you away from me? Is she going to come slithering into our life like a snake in the grass and cast her evil spell over you while I stand helplessly by, wringing my handkerchief and sobbing?"

Stoner laughed. "Of course not. She's been dead for fifty-nine years."

"Stoner McTavish," Gwen said, "that's disgusting."

"That's not what I mean. Damn, I can't explain it."

"I think I'd better catch the next plane out there," Gwen said. "Where did you say you're staying?"

"At the Whitley. Her hotel."

"Are you trying to tell me you're staying in a hotel with a fifty-nine-year-old corpse that you're sexually attracted to?"

"She wasn't dead when I ..."

"I'll be there tomorrow noon at the latest. I'll let you know the time."

"Gwen, you don't understand."

"I understand one thing, dearest. I don't care what you've done, or who you've done it with. I love you and miss you, and I can't wait three days to see you."

Stoner felt her insides turn to mush. "I love you, too, Gwen." Something in her chest gave way. "Damn it, I've been having adventures again." She began to cry. "I think I'm too young for adventures."

"It's okay, hon," Gwen said softly. "I'll be there before you know it."

"What about your job?"

"Watertown's adolescents can wait. The day my job is more important to me than holding the woman I love, I'm being tested for testosterone poisoning."

Stoner smiled shakily. "You always know what to say."

"And I hope I always will. Now, let me go and call Marylou for tickets."

"I tried her. I got her machine."

"I'll call her beeper number."

She couldn't believe it. "Marylou has a beeper?"

"It's her new toy. The Carharts gave it to her."

"The Carharts? The Carharts aren't speaking to us."

"They are now. She went over to their house, cooked them dinner, and spent the entire evening looking at their slides. Do you realize they've gone to St. Croix every year for ten years? And every year they take at least six rolls of slides? And they never leave the grounds of the Pirate's Cove?"

She couldn't help laughing. "Serves her right, hanging around with Yuppies."

"I'm going now, Stoner. I'll call you later."

"I love you, Gwen."

"I love you, too."

"I mean it. I really love you."

"I know. I'll call you ..."

"I've never known anyone like you. Ever."

"Fine. I'll call you when ..."

"I don't ever want to lose you."

"Well, I'm not going anywhere," Gwen said. "Especially without airline tickets."

"If I ever do anything you don't like, you'll tell me, won't you?"

"Yes. Now get off the ..."

"Even if you think it'd hurt my feelings, you'd tell me?"

"Yes. Time to go now."

"Because I wouldn't want to ..."

"Stoner, do you want me to come out there?"

"Of course I do."

"THEN GET OFF THE COTTON-PICKING PHONE."

"Oh," Stoner said with a little laugh. "Yeah. Right."

"I'll see you soon."

"Okay."

"And I'll rip your clothes off, and you rip my clothes off, and we'll rub all over each other's bodies."

"For Heaven's sake, Gwen! Someone might be listening!"

"Who? Your friend Billy?"

"You never know."

As she hung up the phone she glanced at the picture over the bar. She could have sworn Billy winked at her.

photo by Helena Negrette

In addition to writing Stoner McTavish novels, Sarah Dreher is a practicing clinical psychologist and playwrite. She lives in Amherst, Massachusetts with her life partner, two dogs and associated wildlife.

Mystery/Adventure by Sarah Dreher

Stoner McTavish ($7.95) ISBN-0-934678-06-5 The original Stoner McTavish mystery introduces psychic Aunt Hermione, practical partner Marylou, and Stoner herself, in the Grand Tetons rescuing dream lover Gwen.

Gray Magic ($8.95) ISBN-0-934678-11-1 Stoner's friend Stell falls ill with a mysterious disease and Stoner finds herself an unwitting combatant in the great struggle between the Hopi Spirits of good and evil.

Something Shady ($8.95) ISBN-0-934678-07-3 Stoner travels to the coast of Maine with her lover Gwen to rescue a missing nurse and risks becoming an inmate in a suspicious rest home.

Adventure/Romance

Mari by Jeriann Hilderley ($8.95) ISBN 0-934678-23-5 Argentinian political activist Mari meets New York musician, Judith. They fall in love—and struggle with the differences between their cultures and their lives.

Dark Horse by Frances Lucas ($8.95) ISBN-0-934678-21-9 Fed up with corruption in local politics, lesbian Sidney Garrett runs for mayor and meets Joan.

As The Road Curves by Elizabeth Dean ($8.95)ISBN-0-934678-12-X Ramsey had it all; a great job at a prestigious lesbian magazine and the reputation of never having to sleep alone. Now she takes off on an adventure of a lifetime.

All Out by Judith Alguire ($8.95) ISBN-0-934678-16-2 Winning a gold medal at the Olympics is Kay Strachan's all-consuming goal—until a budding romance with a policewoman threatens her ability to go all out for the gold.

Look Under the Hawthorn by Ellen Frye ($7.95) ISBN-0-934678-20-0 Stonedyke from the mountains of Vermont, Edie Cafferty, on a search for her long lost daughter, meets unpredictable jazz pianist Anabelle, looking for her birth mother.

Runway at Eland Springs by ReBecca Béguin ($7.95)ISBN-0-934678-10-3 Bush pilot Anna in conflict over flying supplies for a game hunter, turns for love and support to Jilu, a woman running a safari camp at Eland Springs.

Promise of the Rose Stone by Claudia McKay ($7.95) ISBN-0-934678-09-X Mountain warrior Isa is banished to the women's compound in the living satellite, Olyeve, where she and her lover, Cleothe, plan an escape.

Humor

Cut Outs and Cut Ups A Fun'n Games Book for Lesbians by Elizabeth Dean, Linda Wells, and Andrea Curran ($8.95) ISBN-0-934678-20-0 Games, puzzles, astrology—an activity book for lesbians with hours of enjoyment.

Found Goddesses:Asphalta to Viscera by Morgan Grey & Julia Penelope ($7.95) ISBN-0-934678-18-9 *Found Goddesses is wonderful! All of it's funny, some inspired. I've had more fun reading it than any book in the last two years.*—Joanna Russ

Morgan Calabresé; The Movie N. Leigh Dunlap ($5.95) ISBN 0-934678-14-5 Politics, relationships, life's changes, and softball through the eyes of lesbian Morgan Calabresé.

Short Fiction/Plays

Secrets Short stories by Lesléa Newman ($8.95) ISBN 0-934678-24-3 The surfaces and secrets, the joys and sensuality and the conflicts of lesbian relationships and herstory are brought to life in these stories.

The Names of the Moons of Mars Short Fiction by Patricia Roth Schwartz ($8.95) ISBN-0-934678-19-7 In these stories the author writes humorously as well as poignantly about our lives as women and as lesbians.

Lesbian Stages Sarah Dreher($8.95) ISBN-0-934678-15-4 *Sarah Dreher's play scripts are good yarns firmly centered in a Lesbian perspective with specific, complex, often contradictory (just like real people) characters.*—Kate McDermott

Order From New Victoria Publishers P.O. Box 27, Norwich, VT. 05055